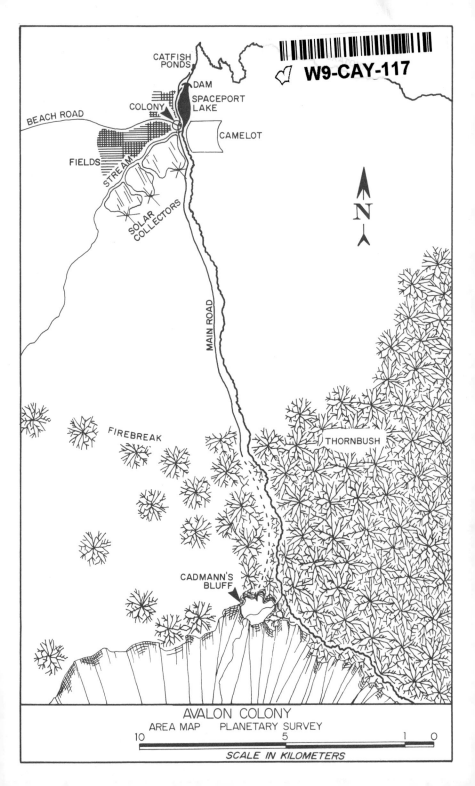

W9-CAY-117

CATFISH PONDS

DAM
SPACEPORT
LAKE

COLONY

CAMELOT

BEACH ROAD

FIELDS

STREAM

SOLAR
COLLECTORS

N

MAIN ROAD

FIREBREAK

THORNBUSH

CADMANN'S
BLUFF

AVALON COLONY
AREA MAP   PLANETARY SURVEY

10   5   1   0

SCALE IN KILOMETERS

THE LEGACY OF

Larry Niven

Jerry Pournelle

Steven Barnes

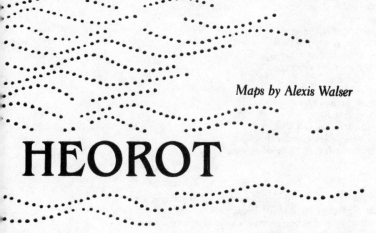

Maps by *Alexis Walser*

HEOROT

SIMON AND SCHUSTER • NEW YORK

ACKNOWLEDGMENTS

We are indebted to Meghan Lancaster for her translation of I Blas Gogerddan, *a traditional Welsh song ascribed to "Geirog."*

We are indebted to Alexis Walser for her maps of Avalon.

Song lyrics on page 270 are from "Serpents Reach" by Don Simpson, copyright © 1985 by Off-Centaur Publications (BMI). Used by permission.

Jack Cohen is one of the world's experts on fertility and reproduction. He is also a rabid science fiction fan who— inspired by his knowledge of the queerer forms of earthly life—constantly generates new concepts for aliens. He tends to give his aliens away to whatever science fiction writer is standing nearest.

He was at Larry Niven's house when he described an African frog with nasty habits.

It's been a long time, Jack. Thanks for waiting.

CONTENTS

Thou must now look to *the needs of the nation;*
Here dwell I no longer *for Destiny calleth me!*
Bid thou my warriors *after my funeral pyre*
Build me a burial-cairn *high on the sea-cliff's head;*
So that the wayfarers *Beowulf's Barrow*
Henceforth shall name it.

Thou art the last of all *the kindred of Wagmund!*
Wyrd has swept all my kin *all the brave chiefs away!*
Now I must follow them!

BEOWULF, KING OF THE GEATS

CHAPTER 1

CAMELOT

They do not preach that their god will rouse them, a little before the nuts work loose.

KIPLING, *"The Sons of Martha"*

"CADZIE! WAIT UP!"

Cadmann Weyland chuckled to himself and dug his heels into the slope, slowing his descent.

He politely busied himself, adjusting the rangefinder on his camera. After months on Avalon he still found the shadows too sharp and the sunlight too blue, subtle things, noticed only when he used familiar equipment like the camera.

The Colony sprang into high relief, and the recorder in his backpack vibrated noiselessly to make a holotape recording of the network of buildings and plowed fields and animal pens that stretched out in the valley below. The Colony was ten kilometers farther on, but the electronically enhanced lenses brought its low buildings close enough to touch.

The image jolted as Sylvia slid into him. She caught herself with a palm against his back. "Ouch. Sorry."

"Here." He handed her the camera. "See what we've built." She gratefully accepted the excuse to rest. Her short brown hair was plastered to her forehead with sweat, and her freckled cheeks were flushed.

Six miles, downhill, and Sylvia was tiring. In the last hour she'd found a dozen reasons to stop. Stones in her walking shoes. Burs inside her blouse.

Cadmann chuckled inwardly. The Colony's biologist was tough, and as stubborn about admitting fatigue as he. *She's also three months pregnant. Won't admit there are real differences between the sexes. So be it.*

Ernst loped down the slope. A brace of the large silver fishlike creatures the Colony had dubbed "samlon" slapped against his muscular back. His grin split his broad face from ear to jug ear. "Tiring out, Sylvia! You ought to work out! Exercise! I can show you."

Sylvia laughed. "Not right now, thanks, Ernst."

"Later."

Poor bastard. Ernst Cohen had been the solar system's leading authority on reproductive biology, and brighter than hell. You could watch it at cocktail parties: everyone else talking, and suddenly Ernst would say maybe two sentences, and half the room would go silent as the rest of them digested the implications. That was ten lightyears ago. Ernst had come out of frozen sleep with the mind of a child.

Sylvia scanned the valley, gave a sigh of pleasure.

"Terrific shot, isn't it?" Cadmann's voice, ordinarily a hoarse rumbling sound, was quietly thoughtful. "*National Geographic* will love it." He squatted next to her. "Are you all right?"

"Just fine," she murmured. She turned, warming him with her smile. "But I'll be happy to get back home."

She was almost twenty years younger than he. Sylvia was all quick wit and golden eyes that glowed with life above a galaxy of freckles. Her pregnancy changed nothing. It was wonderful, it was frustrating: being with her made him forget the years and the aches. *It's the eyes. She's plain except for the eyes. God help me.*

The pass they traversed was at the base of the tallest mountain on the island. The highest of its double peaks was just above thirty-two hundred meters. Both were shrouded with mist. The delicate bat shapes of the pterodons glided in and out of the cloud cover with barely a flutter of their membranous wings. Ernst stared up at them, his face a mask of puzzled concentration. *What would Dr. Ernst Cohen have made of them? They aren't really pterodons. There are other oddities. He'd have loved it here—*

"They woke him twice," Sylvia said. "Maybe if they'd just left him cold—"

"We did need him. We did," Cadmann said. But Ernst wasn't crew. He could have slept through, but they had a problem with one bank of frozen embryos and woke him, and he'd solved that, and they'd chilled him again, and then there was another problem— *And as good a man as ever lived follows me around to carry samples. Son of a bitch—*

A square kilometer of plastic-coated solar cells glittered silver on the hills above the Colony. Today's sunshine meant independence from the fission power plants of the landers. An actual fusion plant would be constructed within the next four months. Then the Colony would be fully established, and the spread of man across the face of Tau Ceti Four could really begin.

—Across Camelot, anyway. Eighty kilometers of stormy ocean separated the island from the mainland. A New Guinea-sized island was quite ambitious enough for humankind's first interstellar colony. Zack had known what he was doing. Isolate the problems. . . .

So where were the problems?

"Snow up there," Cadmann said, shading his eyes as he gazed up into the eternal clouds at the top. *Skis. We didn't bring skis. We have plastics. Carlos can make me a pair of skis.*

Sylvia handed him back his camera. Voice carefully neutral, she said, "You don't have to go to the continent, Cadmann. There's plenty for you to do around the camp."

"Nothing that any other able body couldn't do."

"You're not a geologist. You'd be doing grunt work anyway." She looked down at him, sighed in exasperation and gave him her hand for balance as he stood. "Do you just want to go hunting dinosaurs?"

"Sure! What boy doesn't want to bag a brontosaurus?" He slipped the camera back into its holster at his side. "Sometimes I wish we'd brought fetuses for a kodiak, or a few mountain lions. . . ."

He was smiling as he said it, but Sylvia wondered.

Cadmann brushed his hand through thick black hair. There was no gray in it, but his face was sun-cured leather. His body was as young as a daily hour of intensive exercise could make it. He could remember when he hadn't needed regular exercise to maintain the natural tone. Now, at the adjusted age of forty-two, he was seriously considering nudging that up to an hour and a half. *I'm slowing down,* he thought. *She's carrying another man's baby, and I'd rather be with her than . . . Mary Ann Eisenhower?* He thought of four or five women who had made their intentions clear. Phyllis McAndrews. Jean Patterson, willowy blond agronomist rumored to give the best massage on the planet. He just wasn't interested. *Time wounds all heels. The glands must be drying up.*

Sylvia grinned back. "Only real gentlemen refuse to notice when a lady is slowing them down." Ernst stood carefully out of earshot. His intelligence was gone, but not his manners. She jerked her thumb at the pair of freshly caught silver-and-black torpedo shapes hanging over Ernst's back. Fifteen and twenty pounds, at a guess. One still gaped; the gills still fluttered, too far back on its body . . . they didn't look that much like earthly salmon, but no other creature of Earth fit either. . . . "Tell you what. I'll fix dinner tonight. Everybody to the beach for a samlon roast."

She linked her arm with Cadmann's as they marched down the side of the hill. He grinned maliciously. "Are you sure Terry won't mind that?"

"Oh, come now. I'm just a poor pregnant lady biologist who appreciates the presence of a strong man—and Terry's known you for years."

"I may not be as safe as you think."

She snorted. "Fat chance. When I'm sure you want my body and not my mind, I'll faint."

He looked at her appraisingly. "Which way will you fall?"

"Hush."

They laughed. The sun shone more brightly than usual.

"Golden fields. Silver rivers."

Cadmann laughed. "I suppose. I see a year-round water supply and fertile croplands."

"You would."

Somebody'd better.

The stream flowed past the camp and over the bluff above Miskatonic River, the greatest body of running water on the island. Eight kilometers to the south the grasslands ended in a burnt, blackened semicircle of firebreak and beyond that the crest of giant brambles began. The colonists had chosen a beautiful place to start a new world, lovely enough to make him feel . . . almost at peace. Times like this confused him. It was a fight not to shut down his thoughts and find some project totally involving, and preferably a little risky.

Slender fingers dug into his arm. "Hey, big guy. Don't go brooding on me. This was supposed to be our walk day. Stay with me for a while, hmm?" He was still quiet. "Tau Ceti Four. Avalon." She rolled the words over her tongue.

"It's a good name."

"But?"

"Don't know."

"Not poetic enough?"

He helped her over a rock. It took effort to focus on the game she was inviting him to play. "I've read poetry—"

"Kipling." She laughed. "It's all right. I know you're better read than me. And I'll keep your secret. I don't know, Avalon's all right. But there are others. Beautiful, exciting places from history, or legend. Shangri-la, Babylon . . ."

"Xanadu?"

"Sure. Pellinore."

He shook his head. "You must mean Pellucidar. Pellinore was a king. One of Arthur's Knights of the Round Table."

"Well . . . maybe so. But I don't mean Pellucidar, either. There aren't really any predators on the island. Except for the turkeys and other critters we've seeded, there just isn't a damn thing bigger than an insect. Even the plant life. Low grass and thorn trees. It's like a blank slate. Or a park. Cadmann—"

He asked, "Does that bother you?"

"Well, the worst we can do is mess up one island. It isn't like we'd turned all those Earth creatures loose on the mainland."

"I meant too perfect. Why do you care?"

"Well—"

Ernst ran up, pointing. "Birds. Big Birds." Two of the fan-winged shapes swooped past. Cadmann watched as they circled out over the plain, then vanished in the mist that reached halfway down the face of Mucking Great Mountain. "Nest there?" Ernst asked. "Why there?" He frowned again.

"See? We do have company."

"The pterodons? They're way more frightened of us than we are of them. And the biggest of them is hardly strong enough to carry off a good-sized samlon, let alone a sheep."

"How about a baby?" he asked.

She took it seriously. "I don't think so. To tell you the truth, I haven't seen anything much bigger than a sea gull, and that bothers me. The ecology is just too damned simple. Take out the pterodons and all you've got is small insects and these big local fish."

"The samlon."

"Of course they aren't really fish. What with the trout and the catfish and the turkeys, we've added more animals than we found. Spooky." Sylvia turned thoughtful as they picked their way down a steep slope. "You know, there's something funny about the pterodons."

"What's that?"

"Well, remember the one we saw hunting samlon in the pool?"

"Sure. Reminded me of albatross in the South Pacific." *Sailing aboard* Ariadne *with a fair wind north, a million years—no, not a million years, but a lot more than a million miles ago. With luck we'll build schooners here before I'm dead.*

"Didn't that look funny to you? I can't quite put my finger on it, but it reminded me of an old Walt Disney nature film, with the action run in reverse, to be comical."

"Reverse?"

"A bird hits the water hard and fast, makes its grab, then takes off at its leisure. *That* bird hit the water slow and took off fast, almost as if . . ." She frowned, shaking her head like someone trying to rattle cobwebs off a thought. "Never mind, I'm trying to force something."

"Or see something that isn't there. You'd love to put some mystery into this system."

"How'd you get to know me so well?"

"I always understand other men's women."

"Ah."

Without warning Cadmann began to run, pulling Sylvia down the last twenty meters of slope. She skidded on her heels to slow herself, nonplused but exhilarated by his sudden burst of energy.

He glanced back and realized that Ernst was running too. Ernst looked frightened. "Hold up," Cadmann said. He called, "Ernst! It's okay, Ernst. We're just running for fun. Want to race?"

Ernst's brow cleared; his run slowed. "Race. Sure, Cadmann. Start even?"

They lined up, gave Sylvia a hundred meters of head start, and ran.

Even this far out from the camp, there was a blackened strip of road for them to follow. It was brittle and glassy.

"Your road," Ernst shouted. "Yours."

"Sure." It was. *The last time they really needed me.* Ernst led with the weed burner, a converted military flame thrower. Cadmann had driven the bulldozer, wishing all along that there had been enough fuel to use a landing craft. *That would have made a road! Hover across the ground on the Minerva, fuse the rock forever—* Even so, he felt pride when he scanned the kilometers of dark ribbon he had created with his own sweat and skill. He bent to look closer at the surface of the road. A few tiny bluish sprigs were nosing their way out of the ground.

Sylvia came up puffing. "Maybe we should sow the ground with salt before you make your next pass."

"I'm not even sure it matters. Not much of the heavy machinery comes out this far."

Thin clouds of dust raised by the tractors puffed like tiny fires in the distant fields. The crops had been established. Now they must be expanded. Prepare the ground for new crop tests, lay away grain and seeds against the possibility of a bad year.

The Colony was a success. Zack Moscowitz—administrator, all-around good guy, everybody loves Zack—Zack had done it. The Colony was a success, and nothing short of disaster could stop its expansion across the island and eventually over all of Tau Ceti Four.

Agriculture. Food, vitamins, some comforts. We have those, and now comes prospecting. Iron ore had been discovered on the island itself, and the orbiting laboratory had found what looked very much like a deposit of pitchblende. It was deep in the interior of the continent, across thousands of kilometers of ocean and through badlands—but it was there.

Iron and uranium. The foundations of empire. "The sons of Martha."

"Eh?" Sylvia giggled.

"Kipling. Sorry. Politicians are the sons of Mary. Then there are the others, the ones who keep civilization going. 'They do not preach that their God will rouse them a little before the nuts work loose—' Oh, never mind."

Today seemed more tolerable, more like the First Days, when Cadmann and Sylvia and the other First Ones thundered down from the heavens in their winged landing craft. *All the gliding characteristics of a brick. We left a line of fire and thunder that circled the sky. A hundred and fifty colonists waited in orbit, cold as corpses and no more active, while we scanned a strange planet from end to end, and chose the place to set our city, and set our feet in the rock of this world.*

The National Geographic Society's probes told a lot. Tau Ceti Four had oxygen and water and nitrogen. The planet was cooler than Earth, so the temperate zones were smaller, but a lot of the planet was livable. They'd known there would be plants, and guessed at animals. Humans could live there—or could they? Probably, but the only certainty would come when people tried it.

Civilization on Earth was rich, comfortable, satisfying; and crowded, and dull. Forty million university graduates had volunteered for the expedition. The first winnowing had eliminated compulsive volunteers, flakes whose horoscopes had told them to find a different sky, candidates with allergies or other handicaps, geniuses who couldn't tolerate cramped conditions or human company or people who gave orders. . . . Perhaps a hundred thousand had been seriously considered; and two hundred had set forth to conquer Tau Ceti Four. Eight had died along the way.

No world would ever be tamed by robots. It took men, crossing space, some awake, some chilled, a hundred years across space— The early days were good days. We were comrades in an untamed land.

Then we found Paradise, and they don't need me at all. They need Sylvia. They need the engineers, and the tractor drivers, and, God help us, the administrators and bean counters, but never a soldier.

Sheep and calves roamed the pastures now. Colts grazed. Soon the camp would be full of children, alive with their happy wet smells and sounds; and what need had those for Colonel Cadmann Weyland, United Nations Peacekeeping Force (Ret.)?

Animals . . . a distant lowing snapped Cadmann out of his reverie. They were nearing the rows of moist, furrowed earth. Other crews had burnt the ground, spitting jellied fuel from backpack flame throwers to clear the soil of underbrush without glazing it into slag. The charred dirt had long since been plowed under to prepare for seeding. The ground was very fertile, needing only minor nitrate supplementation to provide a healthy medium for their crops.

In the distance one of the farmers slowed his tractor to wave to them, and Ernst lifted two samlon in triumphant greeting. Further ahead Cadmann knew that there were colts and calves, still far too young to manage the plows that would be fashioned for them. It was an unusual combination—a meld of high technology and muscle-intensive agriculture. In an emergency, the Colony could fall back on the most ancient and reliable means of production.

There were rows of wheat and spinach and soybeans, and in the mist-filtered glare of Tau Ceti their leaves and stalks glistened healthily. At the base of the rows ran the irrigation ditches, fed by the stream that passed under the low bridge just ahead, flowing past the camp and over the edge of the bluff to join the Miskatonic River.

The sounds of the main camp drifted to them. The hum of light machinery, the crackle of laughter and the whining burr of saws and lathes working wood and metal.

The animal pens were on the outskirts of the main camp. Dogs and pigs had their own pens, the horses a well-fenced running space. The chickens were cooped near the machine shop, closer in to the main compound.

Cadmann stopped to examine the wire surrounding the pens. His face tautened into a frown. Their "hot wire" wasn't even warm; the power had been switched off months before. The barbed wire beyond that was down in three places that he could see. He scraped at a brownish patch of rust with his thumbnail.

"Let it go," Sylvia chided.

"Look at this." His voice was flat with disgust. "The strands are slack, and the power line is broken. Doesn't anybody give a damn anymore? We haven't been here long enough to get this lazy."

"Cad—" Sylvia's pale slender fingers covered his, prying them away from the strand. She gripped his hand tightly.

"Look, I know I keep getting outvoted, and I can live with that." He was mortified to hear the petulance creeping into his voice, to see the maternal concern softening her eyes. "Listen. You keep telling me that there are things about this island that bother you. We've only got one shot at this. Nobody's going home, and no one's sending any reinforcements. It only makes sense to be a little paranoid. That's why we picked an island, isn't it? To localize the dangers?"

She squeezed his arm. "I can't change your mind, so I'll try not to want to. Listen. Why make a big thing about it? Why not just fix the fence yourself?"

"Sounds good."

"Good. I'll send for you when we're ready for the barbecue."

Just before they took the last turn into town, Cadmann looked back at the farmers and felt a brief pang of jealousy. They, in wresting victory from the soil, were the true hunters, the true warriors. Ultimately their efforts would determine the future of the fledgling community.

The sun was warm, but far warmer was Sylvia's hand against his arm.

THE COMMUNITY had grown in a strangely organic manner; the first crew members to build their individual prefab huts had built them close together within the defensive perimeter.

Perimeters. Three rings. Electric fence, mine field, barbed wire. It made sense at the time.

Cadmann's folly.

And one of these days they'll make me go dig up the mines. No enemies. No dangers. Nothing. And all that fucking work to build fences.

Most of the colonists had only been awake for eight months, and already they were beginning to get sloppy.

As they had been awakened and shuttled down, the camp expanded, filling the defensive compound, then spreading outside it. From above, the Colony looked like a spiral nebula or a conch shell sliced sideways. Cadmann's home was at the center.

The colonists outside the fence had more room, larger lots—but their location showed their status. Colonists. They were not among the First Ones. Everyone on Avalon was equal, but some were more equal than others. The First Ones had landed four months earlier and had social status—at least those who hadn't wasted time and effort building needless fences and mine fields had status.

The muffled whirr of a power saw grew louder, and the dry smell of sawdust more distinct, as Cadmann wove his way through the narrow streets that divided off the flat-roofed houses and foam-sprayed prestructured domes. Some of the domes had been left in their original tan. Others were painted, some with a kaleidoscope of colors. Here and there were strikingly realistic murals. *We have a lot of talent here. All kinds. Speaking of which—* The saw changed pitch as Carlos Martinez spotted Cadmann and lifted a hand in greeting.

Carlos's dark, lean body glistened with perspiration as he glided the saw over the planks. The thorn trees at the perimeter of the clearing provided a generous supply of wood, but it was knotty and coarsely grained. Only a master craftsman like Carlos could have made anything but firewood of it, and the carpenter was deliciously aware of his valued position.

Half the Colony's dwellings had a table or bed frame by Carlos. It was doubtful that he would ever have to take his rotation in the field to earn his share of the crop.

"Cadmann! *Mi amigo.*" Carlos wiped his brow and extended a sweaty palm that Cadmann shook firmly. Carlos was a true mongrel, and gloried in it. Originally from Argentina, his bloodline was predominately black, his cultural leanings anyone's guess. His Spanish was atrocious, but he interjected it into his conversation regardless. "I heard that you had gone off with the lovely Señorita Faulkner."

"Señora," Cadmann corrected. He moved in for a closer look at the woodwork on the bench. It was the beginnings of a headboard for

Carlos's bed, and already penciled on it were mermaids cavorting in improbable couplings with virile mermen and grinning sailors. He sighed.

"Señora." Carlos smiled mischievously. "It is true that sometimes I forget."

"It'll get easier to remember." He patted his stomach. "She's got a passenger on board now."

Carlos raised his eyebrows in lecherous speculation. "She is taking on good flesh, no? My people, we appreciate a—" he screwed up his mouth in a dramatic search for the right word—"a substantial woman."

"Substantial."

"*Sí!* A helpmate in the fields, a comfort by the fireside. Ah, the days of old . . ."

"Cut the crap," Cadmann said without heat. "Your family never got closer to the fields than the handle of a whip. They've had silk on their backs and diplomas in their pockets for six generations. At least." He turned and worked the latch of his own foam-frame igloo.

Behind him Carlos sighed. "With men like you, who can wonder that romance is dying in the world?" The rest of his monologue was drowned out as the saw revved up again.

Cadmann groped out to find the curtain cord and drew it to let in a spray of sunshine. It might be a month before Tau Ceti Four saw such a bright day again, and he was loath to waste it. The sun was already low in the sky. Preparations for the barbecue would begin when twilight fell. The colonists who were working the day shift would put aside their farming and building and repair work and gather on the beach for good food and good fellowship.

He wanted to grab his toolbox and go out to the fence, but his solitary bed, nestled beneath a sheltering bough of drip-dried underwear, called to him in a voice that his suddenly heavy muscles couldn't ignore.

I'll just sit for a moment, he told himself. The water mattress sloshed pleasantly under his buttocks as he settled his weight into it. He rarely noticed until he was tired, but Avalon's gravity put an extra ten pounds on him every second of his life.

The waning sunlight cast deep shadows in the room, here and there glinting on the shelves and boxes that held the last remnants of another life. Everything he had been was in this room. The hundred and sixty people who made up the crew and passengers of the *Geographic* were his only family and friends.

It wasn't much, but it was enough. Enough, because the behaviorists and sociologists and colony planners said it was enough. Because they, in their infinite wisdom, had calculated exactly how many pressed flower petals and class-album videodisks were required to stave off depression: just enough to stimulate the fond memories, not enough to create an incurable homesickness.

His world. The silver-gilt college trophies, reminders of victories in Debate and Track and Wrestling, were holograms. Hologram images of smiling women whose warm lips and smooth bodies left frustratingly little impression on his memory. How long had they been dead? Thirty years? Forty?

They'd been planning another colony even before *Geographic* launched. A statuesque New Yorker named Heidi had talked about riding the next starship to build a colony at Epsilon Eridani. Maybe she had. It would have launched twenty years after *Geographic*. She might even now be wondering which of her old beaus was still alive.

There were disks of favorite movies—his personal collection, though in principle they were part of the camp library. There, a shifting hologram of his command post in Central Africa. A peacekeeping force, nothing more, until the revolutions. *"Sergeant Major Mvubi! We're moving out!"*

"Sir!"

We were needed. Then.

His clothing was all nonsynthetics that might take a generation to replace. How long would it be until they thawed out the silkworms and the mulberry bushes for them to feed on? Not exactly a high priority item . . .

He didn't remember closing his eyes, but when he opened them he was lying down, and the sun had set. Cadmann grabbed his toolbox and a folding stool and hustled from the room. Getting old is one thing, dammit! Senility will just have to wait.

CHAPTER 2

ON THE BEACH

> *Glory to Man in the Highest! For Man is the master of things.*
>
> ALGERNON CHARLES SWINBURNE
> *"Hymn to Man"*

A JEEP roared by, full of colonists who were full of beer. "Grab some wheels and we'll race you to the beach!" Cadmann waved and pointed to his toolbox. They razzed him and careened out of the compound, singing.

Electric lights were wavering to life around the camp as workers changed shifts. The party atmosphere was infectious. Avalon's inadequate twin moons would smile on a beachful of frolicking spacefarers.

The folding stool's seat was several centimeters too small, but as he bent to the task of repairing and refastening the wire, he forgot the discomfort.

Avalon's moons cast double, divergent shadows with their bluish glow, and the stars were brilliantly sharp and clear. *No crickets. And along about evening the nightbirds aren't beginning to call because the things they use for birds here don't sing. And maybe we'll fix that, with bluebirds and mockingbirds if the goddam ecology people want them. I wonder if they brought crickets?*

Cadmann unwound two meters of wire and scraped at the clotted dust surrounding the loose connection, then clipped the old wire free and attached the new. He fired the soldering torch.

Do they still stand retreat at the Academy? Cadets in archaic uniforms standing in rigid rows, plebes telling jokes in hopes of making upperclassmen laugh and be seen by the officers . . . sunset guns, bands, the Anthem, the flag lowered slowly to the beat of drums. . . . He attached the leads from the voltmeter. The needle jumped into the red. Done.

Mist had rolled in from the sea. The stars were gone; the moons were wavery blobs. Cadmann felt pinpricks of moisture on his face.

A calf on the far side of the wire grunted longingly and shuffled over, looking at him with huge, liquid eyes. Cadmann reached through and petted it, and it licked his hand.

"No mother, eh, girl? Must be tough not to have a mommy cow to love you." Its tongue was rough and warm, and it moved more urgently now as it tried to suckle at his hand.

Cadmann laughed and pulled his fingers away. The calf shivered. "Aw, come now, you can't suckle my fingers. . . ." Then he saw fear in the calf's eyes. Its head jerked to and fro, then stopped abruptly as it stared toward the stream.

The other animals moved toward him. They stood together in clumps. A filly whinnied with fear, and Cadmann came to his feet.

"What's bothering you, girl?"

The feeding stalls were enclosed by the electric fences and narrow walkways. Cadmann carefully stowed the tools and went into the compound. *What's bothering them?* The filly was to his right. Instead of trotting over to him she bucked. Cadmann opened the gate to her pen. "Heidi. Here, girl." She moved warily. "Here." He ruffled her mane. "Shhh. Heidi, Heidi," he crooned. "Quiet, girl."

Night came suddenly. Both moons were at half stage: bright enough, but they left pools of dark shadows through the barnyard, some of them back by the dog pen. There were ten young German shepherds in the pen, and their ears were flattened against their heads. They growled deep in their throats, teeth bared in the moonlight.

"Hello?" There was no answer. "Who the hell is out there?" There was nothing, in the pens or beyond in the deep shadows leading to the bluff. The sound of the panicked animals was a rattling cacophony. Cadmann stood still and listened. Nothing. Carefully he took out the Walther Model Seven pistol and checked the loads. *Silly. Nothing here.*

If Moscowitz sees me with this he'll take my pistol away. He slipped off the safety, then put it in his pocket and left his hand there.

What in the hell was going on? He looked back at the animal pens. The German shepherds, dogs bred for their loyalty and intelligence, were going berserk. The wildest of them was also the eldest, a nearly full-sized bitch who was actually biting at the electrified fence, touching it and recoiling, returning again and again.

Cadmann ran to the pen's gate and gave a low whistle. "Sheena. Come, girl. What's out there? What is it?" She came to him slowly, and stood trembling, panting, eyes fixed and staring out into the darkness. He opened the gate, careful of the other dogs. "Back. Come, Sheena."

He left the gate open long enough for Sheena to get out, then grabbed the fur at the scruff of her neck when she tried to run ahead. *These dogs need training. It's time.* She growled low in her throat. The others barked furiously. Sheena strained ahead.

All the animals were yowling now. Darkened windows behind him filled with light.

"What son of a bitch is screwing with those dogs?"

"Zee virgin, she is mine!"

Another light blinked on. A male voice bellowed, "Hey, you! I just got to sleep. *Will you for Christ's—?* Oh. Cadmann. Cadmann, a lot of us are on the night shift. Can you wrap that up fast?"

"Sure, Neal. Sorry."

The window slammed. The dog strained at his hold on her mane. "Easy, girl—" Cadmann dug in his heels. *Never go out at dusk without a flashlight. Rule One. And I forgot.*

"Cadmann!"

Cadmann jumped. Sheena strained just at that moment, and his grip slipped. The shepherd sped baying into the dark.

"Good going, Weyland."

Bloody idiot. Cadmann recognized the angry whine, had trouble matching the thin, almost effeminate frame of its owner with the label *Terry Faulkner: Sylvia's husband.* "She'll be back as soon as she's hungry."

"Eh?"

"Sheena."

"Oh. The dog. Yeah, I hope so. Listen, Sylvia sent me to get you. If you want to come to the beach party, get moving. We've got the last jeep and we're leaving *now.*"

"Yeah, well . . ." There was nothing out there now, no sound but rushing water. *Screw the picnic. I need a flashlight.*

"Are you coming?"

Damn you! "Sheena! Come, Sheena."

"I'm leaving." Terry's thin lips twitched with a nervous tick that made it hard for Cadmann to look him directly in the face. His small fists balled up and set on his hips. "Sylvia said you should come."

Did you ever recover from puberty? What if I throw you in the creek? The dogs were quiet now. Heidi nickered and came to the edge of the pen seeking sugar. "All right."

THE JEEP slewed around in a tight circle, so quickly that only the ballast of several enthusiastically inebriated colonials kept it from tipping over on two wheels. Zack Moscowitz leaned out of the driver's seat. He was wearing driving goggles above a shaggy black mustache. "All aboard! Will each passenger kindly check his or her own tokens?"

Cadmann grinned in amusement. *His or her. Like a book from the twenty-first century.* "H'lo, Boss."

Moscowitz wiped at his goggle lenses but only succeeded in smearing the dirt more evenly. "Good to see you, Cadmann. How'd the outing go?"

"Great." Cadmann stood unmoving. Terry had already claimed the seat in front next to Zack's wife, Rachel. There was no other place to sit.

"Here we go, Cad." George Merriot squeezed over to make room. It took some squeezing—George could use a few extra sit-ups.

"Thanks, Major."

"Not any more, Cad."

"Right." Weyland climbed over Barney Carr and Carolyn, one of the McAndrews twins. He wiggled his way into the middle.

"Seat belts, right? Everybody, right?"

There was a chorus of bored assents. Zack gunned the jeep and roared out of camp. The road out to the beach was smoother than that leading to the mountains, and more frequently traveled. It served the orbital shuttle, which made water landings.

"No problems, Cadmann?" the Administrator shouted.

"Ah—nothing, Zack." Cadmann was momentarily distracted by a whiff of perfume. Carolyn had taken advantage of a bump in the road to lean closer to him. Now if it had been Phyllis . . . but Phyllis and Hendrick Sills were a pair, and the twins were not identical. Carolyn was sallow in both complexion and personality. He smiled at her anyway.

"What about the fence?"

"Nothing serious. Break. I fixed it."

George Merriot laughed. "Hey, Zack, for a bare instant there, I thought you weren't playing company director this evening."

Moscowitz wove deftly around a pothole. "Never happened. Check that fence in daylight tomorrow, would you, Cad?"

"*Enough!*" Rachel Moscowitz shouted. "No business tonight. The night shift's on duty. Remember?"

"There was something," Cadmann said.

Moscowitz slowed, his eyes still on the road. "Yes?"

"Bit of disturbance with the animals. They were acting like rush hour at the stockyard. Scared. Crazy." The jeep lurched, and Cadmann gently removed someone's elbow from the back of his neck. "Might not be anything, but you never know. I took out one of the dogs. Sheena. She got away."

"Aw, not Sheena. Where's she go?"

"Who cares?" George demanded. "They all got out last week. She'll come back."

Zack kept the jeep burning along the track at a racing pace, and as they bumped over a rise near the ring of thorn bushes, Cadmann could see taillights in front of them. *We're in the last jeep? Christ, he drives fast.* Cadmann asked, "Something special about Sheena?"

Zack said, "Naw, I've been slipping her a few scraps, that's all."

"He wants her in our home," Rachel said. "And we don't have enough room."

"Wouldn't be fair anyway." When Zachariah Moscowitz laughed, his heavy arching eyebrows and thick mustache simply cried for a thick cigar and a round of "Lydia the Tattooed Lady." "Ten dogs, and a hundred sixty colonists. Doesn't make a whole lot of sense to get proprietary, does it?"

"No. Zack, stop. I'll go back and find her."

"Come on." Moscowitz flipped up the filthy goggles. "Gives me a whole new outlook on life. George, give the Colonel a drink, will you? Cad, we're not on duty tonight. Smell the sea and drink the beer and the hell with it."

Cadmann didn't laugh. The salt breezes tickled his nose now, and it cleaned away some of his worry. But he'd lost Zack's dog!

Zack was still talking. "I don't suppose that this really impacts on you, Cad, but I've been a paper pusher most of my life. Administration type."

"You're still the only man I know with pencil calluses behind his ear."

"Ah, but things aren't the same anymore. I still ride a keyboard, but I ride it lightyears from home, on a planet still two twitches this side of the Jurassic."

"And so?" Cadmann could hear the breakers now, rolling in steady rhythm against the shore.

"And so on Earth I made decisions and was responsible for maybe one five-billionth of what happened on the planet. Here, I'm one one hundred and sixtieth of this planet's history. I'll have cities, states named after me. We'll be in the history books, Cadmann, and schoolchildren will know our names."

They always did name cities after their founders. They used to name them after warriors, too, but what's to fight here?

The jeep slowed to a crawl as the road ended at the edge of the beach. Bonfires had already been lit and tended down to a low roar, and the other colonists waved in greeting.

Minerva One was ass-on to the beach. A team had anchored a winch in the rock so that the shuttle could be pulled up after landing. *Nice design there. Land on water, take off on water, never worry about finding an airport.* Its desalinization plant was a box floating alongside, with membranes inside to filter the sea water. The shuttle would be flying up to the mother ship tomorrow, one of Sylvia's monthly jaunts. She wouldn't be able to take it next month. Regardless of her protests, no one was going to allow an obviously pregnant biologist to undergo unnecessary g-stresses.

As soon as the jeep slewed to a halt, Cadmann and the others piled out. A cooler lay open on the beach. Cadmann fished out a pouch of cold beer. "Zack! I knew you were the right man to head up this trip."

"Damn straight. You have no idea how hard I fought for that beer." He dipped into the cooler and extracted a pouch. "We'll have *our* brewery next year."

"Thirty months?" Hendrick Sills shouted, his arm tight around Phyllis's admirably trim waist.

"Earth year," Zack answered. The Avalon year was two point six times as long as Earth's.

Cadmann was crowded away from the cooler by three enthusiastic partygoers. Cadmann grabbed a spare pouch, then took one of the young women by the shoulder. "Mary Ann. Juniper berries."

"Eh?" Mary Ann Eisenhower looked wary. Her blond hair was plastered down with ocean spray. "What?"

"Juniper berries. You're in agriculture. Did we bring the seeds?"

Mary Ann wrapped her towel around her shoulders more tightly, brushed a few grains of sand away from her cleavage. "Cadmann, I don't know! Why?"

"I want to make the first drinkable martini on Tau Ceti Four. *That* will earn me a statue."

She frowned, then grinned widely. "You're on. I'll look!" She reached toward him shyly. "Uh, want to swim?" Like many of the others, she had stripped down to shorts.

"Cold, isn't it?"

"Sure! But it's nice when you get out." She reached toward him.

"Mary Ann! Come *on!*" Joe Sikes called. Cadmann didn't like him. His wife had had a baby only a week before, and he was already running after other women.

Mary Ann turned, mouth set in a line. "If you're in such a hurry, why don't you just go find Evvie?"

Joe glowered, unable to think of an answer, and slunk back toward the ocean.

"Cad?"

It was Sylvia. Cadmann turned. "Speaking." The corner of his eye caught Mary Ann disappearing toward the water. Where Sikes was waiting. It irritated him, and he wondered why he gave a damn.

Sylvia was over by the fire. She wore a two-piece swimsuit, something from an Earth designer who had understood what to conceal and what to reveal.

Cadmann started toward her, then stopped as Terry came into the circle of firelight. Terry kissed her cheek, then took the roasted samlon steak from her stick and handed her a much bigger one. Terry chewed contentedly.

"Ah—Cad, did you fix the fence?" Sylvia asked.

A voice too close behind Cadmann laughed. "I am not the only admirer of Señorita Faulkner, *sí?*"

"*Señora.* Go jump in a thorn bush. Here." He tossed his spare beer pouch over his shoulder. "Think fast! Good catch."

A guitar twanged nonsensically, then produced a tune Cadmann had not heard since his youth. Marnie McInnes played while Barney Carr and her husband, Jerry, sang with good-natured tonelessness. Two much better voices dominated the choruses from somewhere on the far side of the fire: Ernst and La Donna Stewart.

Phyllis danced for her own pleasure, for the colonists, and most especially for Hendrick, who watched her with pride and hunger.

Carolyn watched for a few seconds, then *humphed* and stamped off.

Carlos watched Phyllis for a dozen bars, examining her movement with the eye of a master sculptor inspecting a block of marble. "She is good, that one," he said offhandedly. "She must learn the real flamenco technique."

"And you'll be glad to teach her."

"But of course."

"Go for it. Talk to Hendrick though. She may need a teacher, but he definitely needs a sparring partner."

"Sparring partner? *No comprendo.*"

"Hendrick Sills was Golden Gloves middleweight champ about six years before we left Earth. Bet he'd love to discuss it with you."

"On the other hand . . ."

Cadmann ambled over to the roasting pit.

Spicy meat smells rose from the grill. Much of the food was reconstituted, pouched and freeze-dried and soaked in water or wine—but there were two chickens and a turkey. Cadmann imagined he had known from the smell—

Morale must be worse than I thought if Zack authorized this burnt offering. Lost crops and too much work.

Thornwood logs made excellent coals when hot enough. The oily wood smoldered with a tantalizing hickory scent that blended nicely with the moist breeze from the ocean. Twin moonglades danced in the surf.

Sylvia poked in the grill with a long metal skewer. She glanced to her left where Terry was eating. He wasn't half finished. "Almost done, Cad." She turned the samlon steak. Even this cross section of the creature was queer, unearthly. The meat was pink like salmon, but two big arteries showed alongside its heavy spine—for heavier gravity—and the shape showed its flattened belly and strong bones.

"Big enough for two, Cad. Another minute."

"Sure." He sat beside her. "Hi."

"Hi yourself. I thought you might not come."

"So you sent Terry to fetch me."

"Sure." She speared a samlon. "Just right. Share?"

"Love to."

She hoisted it up and nibbled at it, and sputtered as she burned her mouth. Cadmann couldn't help laughing at the face she made. She looked serious, pointed toward the stars, and when he looked up, stuffed one of the hottest portions into his mouth. "Laugh at me, will you?"

"Molten metal, molten metal—you do know the punishment for witches, Esmeralda."

"Sure, they hanged her goat. But Charles Laughton will give me sanctuary. Have some more."

He held up his hands in protest. "No, thanks. My tongue would never forgive me." But the first fragment had cooled, and it tasted fine. Taste of salmon, texture of . . . what? It wasn't flaky like fish. Beef heart? Striated, no fat . . .

She jabbed the second portion at him again, and he splashed some sand at it. "Get that poor dead thing away from me before I spank you."

Her eyes sparkled. "You . . ." Terry was close behind her, close enough that she fell silent, smiled and went back to tending the sizzling barbecue. Terry watched her go, then sat next to her with his cooling plate of canned vegetables. He stared across the sea.

Ernst and La Donna stood up from where they'd been eating, hurled turkey bones into the dark and walked after them. Ernst waved cheerfully as they passed. Cadmann smiled but didn't wave; he could see La Donna's sudden embarrassment.

Good. Salvage those good genes, La Donna! With luck the kids would look like Ernst, too. La Donna was nice, but plain.

Cadmann moved to the edge of the magic circle of light, away from the others. The waves seemed vast inky shapes, rolling up and thrashing themselves into foam on the sand. There were shrieks of pleasure from the colonists playing in the water. A pleasantly rounded shape ran from the darkness to the light.

"We have them."

"Have—?"

"Juniper berries, silly. I remembered." Mary Ann shook water onto him and handed him a towel. "Dry me?"

He smiled good-naturedly and buffed her. Her hair was ash-blond, it glowed in the double moonlight, and her skin was baby smooth and clear. Her body was toned and well-rounded. Rubens would have lusted to paint her—or something. Avalon's increased gravity had added six pounds to her weight when she set foot on the ground. All of the colonists showed better muscle tone, and so did Mary Ann.

She giggled and leaned back into him in a clear invitation. Methodically he scrubbed out the wet tips of her hair and worked his way quickly down her body.

She sighed and shuddered slightly. "You have talents I didn't know 'bout, Cad."

"Part of the service. Where's Joe?" He moved his hands under the towel.

Her eyelids fluttered with brief, suppressed pain. "We don't keep track of each other." Her expression tightened. "Ah. I owe you a rub now."

Her skin beneath his hands was cool but growing warm. *She's willing, she's nice . . . nicely shaped . . . isn't she smart enough? Isn't she Sylvia?* He said, "We'll take a rain check on that."

"Coward." Mary Ann brought her pug nose close to his. "I'll never live to see the day."

He winked at her. "I may surprise you yet."

"Hah!" she said, and jiggled off to another bonfire. The men there shouted as she approached.

Cadmann looked determinedly at the twin moons. *We can't keep calling them "Big" and "Little." "Cadmus"? That's a good name for a moon—oh, hell, here comes Terry.*

Terry Faulkner said, "She's a dish."

"Yes, I've always liked Sylvia."

Terry's nose wrinkled. "Mary Ann. She likes you. She's told me."

Cadmann said nothing. Terry said, "I've noticed that you don't keep company with any of the ladies."

"That's not what I'm here for, Terry."

"True . . . ." Terry's gaze panned from Mary Ann to Sylvia. "But there is one lady you've been spending a lot of time around, you know."

"Come off it. Sylvia and I are just friends."

"I know." There was a cutting edge to Terry's voice. "You were pretty friendly the first three months you were down, while the rest of us were asleep up in the ship." He made harsh squiggling patterns in the sand with his toe.

"What's your point?"

"I'd just feel a lot better about it if you had a nice healthy interest in one of the other ladies, that's all."

Carlos was loitering nearby, his ear innocently turned in their direction. Cadmann cleared his throat loudly. "Now hear this. Boy, would I like a beer right now."

"*Con gusto, amigo.*" Carlos walked away whistling.

"Terry, you must know there is nothing between me and your wife. We talk—"

"A damned lot."

Cadmann pointedly eyed the beer in Terry's hand. "Yes. We talk. And if you talked to Sylvia more, she wouldn't need a friend so badly."

Terry froze. "My relationship with Sylvia is none of your damned business."

"You brought it up. Which makes it my business. We talk, and if you're worried that she looks for more than talk, maybe there's something else you don't give her enough of."

Terry turned away, walked two steps and turned back. "You really are an asshole, Weyland." He turned away.

"Terry."

Faulkner stopped. "What?"

"Did you think that getting Sylvia knocked up as soon as they thawed you out would hang a big 'hands off' sign on her?"

There was a sudden lull in the air around them. Every face near them was carefully, deliberately turned away from the exchange. Cadmann's face heated, suddenly flushed with blood. Terry's hands hooked into claws, and his mouth worked silently.

Too loud! Aw, shit.

The thin man kicked at the fire, sending a burst of sparks into the air. "You know, Weyland, I don't really care what went on before I woke up. Because you're not the big man anymore. You're not a farmer, you're not a builder. You're not even an engineer. You're just an assistant navigator, and an extremely expendable security arm." He leaned closer to Cadmann, who lowered his eyelids slightly. "I hear that you want to be part of the mainland expedition I'm putting together. Just watch your step. Be very careful that you don't suddenly become obsolete. I'd hate to see Colonel Weyland pulling weeds or mucking out the stables to earn his bread."

He turned and stalked away.

Wordlessly, Carlos tossed Cadmann a pouch of beer.

Cadmann bit it open and took a mouthful of brew, feeling some of the foam running down his chin. Terry grabbed Sylvia by the arm and pulled her aside for a talk. His gestures were violent and jerky, like a puppet with tangled strings. Sylvia's face was impassive, her answers calm, and finally he quieted.

The entire beach seemed to heave a sigh of relief, and slowly the music and laughter rose up from a soft burr and swallowed the silence.

Carlos poked his arm. "He's wrong about you, isn't he, *amigo?* You've never made a move on the lovely lady."

"Not yet."

"Meaning?" Carlos' dark face was split in a suggestive grin.

"Meaning that I'm going for a walk."

"Have a good walk, *amigo!* I think I'm going to investigate Carolyn."

"She's a tease."

"She's also depressed. I have just the thing for her."

"Your generosity never ceases to amaze me. *Bon appétit.*" Cadmann moved off down the beach, toward and past the huge beached shuttle. He didn't stop until he was lost in the shadows. When Marnie's guitar was no more than broken rhythm against the surf he turned to look at the wavering lights and listen to the sounds downbeach. The night wind brought a whiff of seaweed and salt and roast samlon, and the sound of merriment.

A finger stroked lightly along his spine, and he turned, startled. Mary Ann smiled at him. She was breathing heavily, wet sand splashed along her calves from a jog in the surf. Her eyes were wide and luminously dark. "You're a strange one," she said. "You know how I can always find you?"

"How?" He reached out, lacing his fingers behind her neck. Impossibly, her skin seemed cool and hot at the same time. *I don't want you,* he said silently, *but I need . . .*

"I just look for where people are having fun, they're getting together. Enjoying themselves. There you are. Cadmann Weyland, off to the side, watching."

Go away. Just go away, he thought, drawing her closer. "Watching," he said. She shivered as he traced a circle under her ear. "I don't always just watch." Suddenly, he wanted very, very much to put the lie to her words.

Her eyes reflected the glowing surf. When she spoke again, her voice was husky. "Well, I tell you what. Why don't you show me what you do when you're not just watching?" She linked her arms around his neck.

He didn't know whom he needed to convince more, himself or Mary Ann. But there are times when twin aims share a single purpose, like twin moons casting a single shadow.

She took his hand and led him away from the campfires, toward warmth.

* * *

SOMETHING was ahead of her. Sheena strained to reach it. A shadow bigger than herself, it seemed to move in jumps, waiting until she was almost on top of it, then streaking away into the dark, cutting behind the animal cages, across the stream, into the cultivated ground.

Sheena yipped in confusion, disbelieving what she had seen. Machines moved that quickly, but not animals. She sniffed the ground. The new smell was already faint, so fast had it moved, but there was no mistaking it. Wet and warm, and unlike men or calves or chickens or anything in the compound: the stink of it was a mortal insult! She streaked after it, splashing through the icy water, shaking her fur before continuing on into the dark.

She was beyond the plowed area, into the zone filled with burnt crumbled tree stumps and sprigs of tough grass just now puffing up through the blackened crust of the earth. Where was it? Clouds were moving across the smaller moon, and Sheena sniffed the ground again, purring low in her throat.

The cloud cover parted for a moment.

There on the hillock, black with lunar highlights, sat something inexplicable. A thousand generations of instincts couldn't identify it. Big. Not man. No ancestor had hunted this thing, none had fled and lived to remember. Her cortex knew what it was not, but could not say what it was.

Unknown. A threat. It might harm man or man's children. Kill!

The thing cocked its head sideways and cooed.

The sounds were disturbing. What had ever sounded like that? Where were the men? Sheena's ears flattened back against her head. This was not a dog's job. There were no men here. Sheena leaped to do battle.

One moment it was there, and Sheena's teeth were snapping at its neck. Her teeth closed on nothing. It receded like a cloud-shadow beneath the moon, and returned as fast, and now it was on Sheena's back. Its cold, broad feet clamped around her middle with sudden, terrifying strength. Sheena's ribs sagged inward. She snarled her agony and rolled to mash the thing from her back.

It walked off her while she was rolling and was several feet away. Fast, unfairly fast! Thick fleshy lips pulled back from daggerlike teeth in a grimace of pleasure. Lovingly it cooed to Sheena.

Sheena was terrified now, but she leaped.

She was in the air when the creature rolled. Its jaws flashed up and locked on her throat, reducing her death scream to no more than a terrified hiss. It drew back into the shadows before she hit the ground.

She lay on her side, struggling weakly to breathe, bubbles of air shining blackly in the moonlight as they pulsed from her throat.

She watched her killer draw close, stared into its eyes, its huge, soft, silver eyes. She whimpered.

It cooed at her, and when Sheena's flanks ceased trembling, came closer and gently licked at the blood oozing from her throat. The creature was hot, like a stove. It turned its back. Sheena felt blades entering her, and then nothing.

CHAPTER 3

FROZEN SLEEP

The broken soldier, kindly bade to stay,
Sat by the fire, and talked the night away
Wept o'er his wounds, or tales of sorrow done
Shouldered his crutch, and show'd how fights were won.

OLIVER GOLDSMITH, *"The Deserted Village"*

GEOGRAPHIC was one of the largest mobile objects ever created by human engineering. Seen from below as the shuttle rose to meet her, the ship looked like a gigantic flashlight with a silver doorknob attached to the end. The aft end was a ring of laser fusion reactors, a flaring section twice the diameter of the trunk. The trunk, over a hundred and fifty meters in length, was the cylinder that housed the life-support systems and cryogenic suspension facilities. Minerva Two was approaching the fore end: the laboratories and the crew quarters, where Cadmann had spent five waking years of his life. The dock was a conical cagework at the end of a protruding arm, barely visible even this close.

Minerva Two slowed as she rounded the fuel balloon. Bobbi Kanagawa was a cautious pilot. Cadmann's fingers itched and twitched. His touch would have been surer, his approach would have been faster.

But he *wasn't* flying Minerva Two.

Geographic's fuel balloon was shrunken, spent, and half its original size. Only a breath of gas remained of a half-kilometer sphere of deuterium ice. The Colony could not produce deuterium, not yet. *We were Homo interstellar*, Cadmann thought. *We will be again.*

Some of the external paneling had been stripped away from *Geographic* and shuttled down to Tau Ceti Four for building material. The shuttle maneuvered past a drifting mass. The tightly wrapped cylinder, scores of kilometers of superconducting wire, waited to be loaded in Minerva Two's bay by robot limpet motors. These would become part of the fusion plant. Its completion meant limitless power.

Eventually the Orion craft would be a skeleton, just an orbiting splinter of light in the sky. Perhaps she might survive in smaller form, with most of the life-support cylinder removed: an interplanetary vehicle, a gift of space to grandchildren yet unborn.

Bobbi Kanagawa counted softly to herself as *Geographic* loomed on the screen, the onboard computer continually checking her approach pattern. "Almost home," she said without looking back at her passengers.

Sylvia reached over and pinched Cadmann's arm. "Are you all right?"

"I've never liked dockings," Cadmann muttered. *Geographic* was half the sky now; more, as the silver wall of the fuel balloon slid past and the conical cagework opened like a mouth. "And if you're a Freudian, I don't want to hear it."

The shuttle's nose grated along the cagework and nuzzled into the lock at its base: *click-thump.* Cadmann sighed in relief and released his shoulder straps. Bobbi made her last-minute checks, then swung out of her seat with practiced ease. "All right, folks, this is a two-hour turnaround. Hope you don't need more time." Some of her straight black hair had escaped its binding, and drifted out at disconcerting angles when she moved.

"Two should do it." Sylvia strapped on her backpack.

The door at the rear of the shuttle hissed open, and Stu Ellington's voice chuckled at them from the control module. "It's about time. Swear to God that's just like a woman. Two-tenths of a second late again."

Bobbi glared at the speaker, drumming her fingernails against the console. "Just keep talking, Stu," she said sweetly. "You need all the friends you can get—the last vote was dead even for leaving your worthless carcass up here another month."

"*Oops.* Tell you what. Drop your friends in the lab, come on up to Command, and we'll discuss my carcass for an hour or so."

Bobbi's pale cheeks reddened. She ran her hand over her hair, discovering the flyaway strands. "I . . . uh, well—" she looked at Sylvia, who winked sagely. "I'll see you in a month, huh?" She scurried to be the first through the hatch.

She disappeared down a narrow connective hallway as Sylvia led Cadmann to the central corridor and back to the biolab section. Cadmann clucked in puritan disgust. "Sex. I remember sex. Highly overrated."

"Great attitude for a biologist."

"Just a Bachelor's, and it was marine biology," he sniffed. "Fish are damned civilized about it. She lays 'em, and he swims over 'em."

"You're a romantic, that's what you are." Sylvia worked her way along the handrails gingerly and seemed ill at ease. "All this time," she said, so softly that he wondered if she had intended for him to hear.

"What?"

"After all this time, I still get a little claustrophobic in here." She laughed uneasily.

"You're not the only one." He slammed the flat of his palm against one of the steel-and-plastic panels that lined *Geographic*. The vibration thrummed along the hexagonal corridor, damping out before it reached the first corner. "This place was home and prison to all of us for a long time. Some of the colonists won't come back up at all."

"It doesn't make sense, really. Just forget it."

He leaned up behind her and whispered in her ear. "It's return-to-the-tomb syndrome." A Karloffian leer lurked just behind his solemn expression. "All of us spent at least a hundred and five years asleep in a little coffin-shaped box, awakened from the dead by a trickle of electricity through our brains."

"Lovely. We'll put you in charge of bedtime stories. I'll manage the sedative concession."

The door to the biolab was sealed to protect both the life within and the crew without. Some of the substances and microscopic life forms were extremely vulnerable, and others extremely dangerous. Sylvia punched in her four-digit personal code, and the door opened inward. In case of a loss of atmosphere in the main section of the ship, air pressure alone would keep the door sealed. "We'll have this reprogrammed to admit you."

The lights came up automatically as the door closed behind them. The room was the second-largest on *Geographic*. Its floor space was crowded with medical and analytical equipment, its walls completely lined with cryogenic vaults. There were hundreds of the dark plastic rectangles, and they held the future of Tau Ceti Four.

Sylvia sighed, shucked her backpack onto a wall hanger and pulled herself over to a rack of Velcro slippers. She handed him a pair. "One size fits all."

"I was hoping for something in a wing tip."

She led him to the nearest bank of cases. "Look," she said contentedly, triggering one of the dark panels into translucence. Within, barely discernible as canine, were dozens of dog embryos. Their dark eyes were filmed with transparent lids, tiny naked paws drawn up to their gauzy bodies in peaceful cryosleep. Each hung in its individual sack, connected by its umbilical to an artificial placenta.

"So." She studied the temperature and pressure gauges on the door of a sealed cabinet, nodded and opened it. "Alfalfa seeds. Check. Swiss chard. Check. Tomatoes. Check." She closed the cabinet. "Now for the embryos. The carriers are in that case over there. Inflate three for me, will you?"

"Sure."

She busied herself at the cryosleep carrier console.

"You don't trust the computer?" Cadmann asked.

"Not anymore. Not since Ernst. Not since eight of us never woke up. Barney says it's fine, but I'm a woman of little faith these days."

"Good thinking."

She typed in the last commands. "There. So we lost one of the dogs. We've got over a hundred more."

"And thousands of chickens, I suppose?" His voice was too flat, too distanced from his feelings.

"Look, Cad—I don't care what anyone says, it's not your fault. Sheena got loose a week ago. So—she came back last night and broke into one of the chicken cages. Fine. We'll either catch her or kill her. Nothing to worry about."

He heard her words, but his mind was still on the chicken cage as they had found it that morning, its wire mesh ripped out and mangled, the wooden frame shattered, blood and feathers and little clotted chunks of raw chicken littering the ground like the aftermath of a ghoulish picnic.

"That is what you're worried about, isn't it?"

Annoyed with himself, Cadmann derailed the morbid train of thought. "Sure. That's it."

Although he had worked the biolab before, she gave him the grand tour. There was a complete assortment of dairy and work animals, as well as millions of earthworms, ladybugs and "friendly" insect eggs. "We have to have quadruplication of any needed form. There are going to be failures," Sylvia said bluntly. "The alfalfa crop, for instance. We don't know why yet." Her eyes glittered, and the sudden determination in her face cubed her attractiveness. Cadmann's chest tightened.

"But I guarantee you we'll know. And soon. We're going to lose more animals, and we've got to be ready for that, too. That's where you'll come in. Routine checks, Cad—any emergencies, and we'll hustle up Marnie or her husband, Jerry. We've got to be ready for anything."

She darkened the panels and took his hand, leading him to the other side of the room. The vaults were identical to those opposite, but he could feel her increased excitement. "Look," she whispered, and illumined the panels. "Our children."

They hung in rows, lost in endless dream. (Cadmann was startled at the thought. Were there dreams in cryosleep? The neurologists said no, but his memory said yes. Perhaps it was only that before the drugs took hold and the blood chilled there was one final thought that remained locked in a frozen brain, a thought that unthawed along with the body. Just a wisp of dream at the beginning of sleep and one at the end, linked by decades of silence and darkness.)

One of Sylvia's hands strayed unconsciously to her own belly, its roundness barely noticeable beneath her jumpsuit.

There were hundreds of the embryos, frozen at ten weeks of age. They were thumb-sized and milky pale, heads as large as their bodies, with their fluid-filled amniotic sacs billowing about them.

Cadmann came up close to the glass, counting the tiny fingers and toes, gazing at the gently lowered eyelids, the amber umbilicals attached to artificial placentas.

"They're all perfect," Sylvia said. "Every one of them certified perfect, genetically and structurally."

His breath had fogged the glass. He patted her stomach. "Not like Jumbo here, who has to take his chances."

Sylvia drew away from him, face troubled. She shut off the light in the embryo bank. "Cad . . . if you'd try to be a little nicer to Jumbo's father, things would be easier for all of us."

There was nothing in her face he could feel angry with. His hand still tingled from the contact. "I knew it. A nice trip for old Weyland. Find him a useful job. Then try to civilize him a little, before he gets sent to the outback where he belongs. Cadmann Weyland. First of the Great White Abos."

She shook her head and gave him a hug. "We know things aren't easy for you—but at least you know why you've got problems. Terry just knows that when he thawed out he wasn't quite the same anymore. Terry and Ernst . . . Carolyn . . . Alicia . . . Mary Ann . . ."

"What? Mary Ann Eisenhower?"

"Well, she's not one of the bad ones."

"She seems—"

"Sure, she's normal. Cad, she lost some brain cells in frozen sleep. She isn't stupid, but she used to be brilliant, and she remembers, Cad. She and Hendrick Sills were the top bridge players, and they shared a bed too, before we put the colonists to sleep. Tom Eisenhower woke up dead, and Hendrick gets very uncomfortable if he's in the same room with her. He remembers. So Hendrick is with Phyllis now, and Mary Ann cries on Rachel's couch."

Cadmann touched her hand.

"But she's a normal, healthy, sexy woman if you didn't know her before. These changes can be very subtle, Cad. Carolyn McAndrews was second in command to Zack. Nobody wants to work with her now. She didn't turn stupid, but she goes into hysterics."

"And maybe there's a dead place in old Cadmann's brain too."

"Not that we can tell—like I said, you've got reasons to feel out of place. The others just know that the cryogenics weren't perfect. That the nightmares are a little darker. Maybe it isn't quite as easy to remember a favorite poem, or extract a cube root, or run the Twelve-Fourteen Convention in bridge." She paused, and her voice dropped. "Or make love. We don't know what it is yet. It'll be twenty years before we get any answers from Earth. In the meantime, there are mood stabilizers, and make-work projects. And there's hope. Most of us are fine. Our genes are good. We'll do everything humanly possible to keep you on the team. Can you blame us?"

He took her shoulders, gazing down into her eyes. The air was tart with disinfectant and dehumidifier; her perfume was a wisp of citrus and crushed rose petal, the only thing in the ship that smelled alive. "What 'us'? What about—?"

The intercom crackled, and Stu Ellington said, "We've got a message for you, Weyland. Development landside. Something about some chickens."

Sylvia disengaged herself from him gently, triggering the nearest intercom phone with an unsteady finger. Her eyes were still locked to Cadmann's. "D-don't worry. We'll be bringing down more embryos."

"It's not that." It was Bobbi who spoke this time, and her voice was excited. "Mits Kokubun found some tracks." She paused. "They might be tracks, anyway."

"Paw prints?" Sylvia frowned.

"Don't know. Zack said that they just didn't look like anything he'd seen. Wants Cadmann to take a look at them. Soonest."

"Pipe it in."

"They didn't send pictures."

"Think you two can cut your snuggle session down so Stu can give us a ride home?"

Stu groaned massively. "Oh, if I must—" and dropped off the line.

Cadmann cleared his throat, backing up a half step. "Was there anything else you wanted to show me?"

She retrieved her backpack, fumbled out a handful of dark plastic cartridges and held them before her like a shield. "You've used the computer. You'll be running some programs for me, and I . . ." Her eyes dropped. "Oh, hell, Cad. I don't know what I wanted. We . . . I just want everything to work out for you. We don't want you closing up, Cad. I don't want to lose you." Suddenly she seemed very small and awkward. "I love you. You're my friend."

The moment that followed was uncomfortably long and painfully silent. Then Cadmann's lips curled in a smile. "Tell you what. Let's go roust Stu's ass and get a lift home. How's that?"

"Perfect."

THE CHICKEN COOPS were nestled next to the single-story sheet-metal structure of the machine shop, and the ground around them was well trodden. It had never been plowed, and was the same burnt, packed earth that lay beneath most of the Colony.

When Cadmann got there, a fifteen-by-thirty-meter block of ground had been marked off with rope to protect the footprints. A score of colonists were still huddled around the periphery. Joe Sikes's wife, Evvie, held her baby tightly against her breast, the child's reddish scalp shining through thin, limp blond hair. The baby gurgled, unconcerned, but the woman looked stricken. Their baby was the colony's second. The first, April Clifton, was still in intensive care.

Carlos stood with Mitsuo Kokubun and Harry Siep, and they were grinning. Harry preened his heavy growth of beard, hiding his mouth behind his fingers as he whispered something to Mits. All three choked on repressed laughter.

Zack ran his fingers through black hair that had been noticeably thicker only months before. When Cadmann broke through the ring of spectators and squatted to take a close look at the tracks, Zack punched him lightly on the shoulder, relief and gratitude tattooed across his face in bold strokes.

"Glad you're here," Zack said. "What do you make of this?"

Cadmann hitched his trousers and bent, peering closely at the depressed ridges of the footprint. It was just broader than his hand, with four distinct, roughly triangular toes. He ran his finger along it lightly.

He asked, "Have we taken a cast of this?"

"Marnie did. We're reinforcing the fences, and we can put the power back through them if we have to."

There were eight of the prints, some faint, some clear and sharp. One in front of the chicken coop was smeared. He stood and looked back along the path the tracks had taken—they led in the direction of the mountains, but disappeared long before they reached the plowed ground. Suspicion niggled at the back of his mind.

"You know," Cadmann said finally, "I could have sworn there weren't any tracks here when I left this morning."

Zack shook his head. "Beats me. There was someone here all the time, Cad. The overcast was pretty bad. Maybe the sun had to be just so high before we could spot them."

The crowd had thinned a bit.

"*Hola, amigo.* Any ideas?"

Cadmann studied the ground, then Carlos's overeager smile. Little Rick Erin, standing next to Carlos, was having trouble managing his face.

Cadmann walked slowly up to the historian-carpenter. "Yes. I do have an idea. I think it was made by something that was highly skilled, bipedal, not overly intelligent, and weighed about—" he looked Carlos over carefully. "About seventy kilos, I'd guess. We'll call it *illegitimus estúpido* for the time being. I'm mixing languages there, but I think you get my drift."

He turned on his heel.

"Cadmann—"

"Yeah?"

"Nothing."

As he walked away Cadmann heard sniggers and the sound of back-slapping. *Idiots.* He doused the flare of anger as he came back to the ruined coop.

"What do you think, Cad?" Zack looked puzzled.

"This was a hoax. *This* was." Cadmann's face was still burning. "I like the idea of checking the fences. Get them ready." He looked out over the flat ground, past the fluffy cultivated rows, past the ring of thorn trees to the mountains and jungle beyond. "Listen, Zack, maybe the footprints were a hoax, but these chickens are still *dead*. I don't think we've got anyone dumb enough to murder a bunch of our chickens for a joke. I don't much care who laughs at me—let's be ridiculously cautious for a while, eh?"

Cadmann stepped on the nearest print. If he had strapped, say, a rubber cutout to the bottom of his shoe, he could walk carefully back and forth, making those goddamn prints right in front of everyone's nose, and then stand back and watch the fun. . . .

Behind him someone made a doglike yipping sound. He didn't turn to look.

CHAPTER 4

RAINY NIGHT

> *Cruelty has a human heart,*
> *And Jealousy a human face;*
> *Terror the human form divine,*
> *And Secrecy the human dress.*

> WILLIAM BLAKE, *Appendix to the "Songs of Innocence and*
> *Experience: A Divine Image"*

SIX WEEKS after the incident at the coops, a mild eruption on the northwest side of the island shook the ground. Three days later threadlike wisps of ash still drifted from the air. The mists that enshrouded the mountain peaks had dropped in a gray blanket, diffusing the light of Tau Ceti.

Streamers of light flashed within the cloud banks, and thunder echoed distantly onto the plain. Cadmann slipped his tractor into neutral and watched the clouds cautiously. The engine's hum strummed his spine.

"Don't worry," Mary Ann called to him. "That's just a little mountain storm. It doesn't care about us." She moved between knee-high rows of plants, checking the slender soil-meter rods for moisture and pH.

The alfalfa replanting was being cautiously hailed as a success. Failure of the first crop was attributed to the thorn trees which had once dominated the plain. When the trees were burned away their taproots remained alive underground, leaching moisture from the soil. Alfalfa, with a potential yield of ten tons per acre, requires tremendous amounts of water. Omar Isfahan and Jon van Don, two of the Colony's engineers, had planned and installed a more extensive irrigation system.

"We could use the water, either way. But if it's going to rain, I'm wasting my time up here."

"Practice. Practice. We all take rotation in the fields." Mary Ann's smile was as brilliant as her hair, and it warmed him. They had grown closer in the weeks since his talk with Sylvia aboard *Geographic*.

Hibernation Instability. He saw her differently now. She wasn't bright . . . and yet she had been. Wounded in the war to capture Avalon; wounded in *his* war.

The electrified fences had been expanded and strengthened. When there was no additional trouble, the animals were turned out into the northern pasture. Some of the older lambs and calves were already grazing contentedly.

No additional trouble . . .

Cadmann liked the sound of that, even if there was a part of him that didn't quite believe it. (Didn't want to believe it?)

He had returned twice to *Geographic*. He liked that. Checking the embryos was sheer routine; but one side of the crew lounge was a wide window. Cadmann could sit and look up at Avalon, and feel peace.

So beautiful. Spirals of white storm, blazing white of polar caps, the spine of jagged white-capped mountain range along the single continent . . . white against the rich blue of a water-and-oxygen atmosphere, a world that men could take and tame.

Zack had been right. Their grandchildren would conquer this world, and the first hundred and sixty colonists would be remembered for all time.

Immortality.

At what price? A century of sleep? Brain damage for a few; Ernst and Mary Ann and Carolyn and, yes, Terry, were paying the price for all. But for the rest: bruises and sprains, and maybe a few bad dreams? He had to laugh. The pilgrims who had founded the American continent had paid far more dearly to accomplish less.

Tau Ceti Four's colonials had it easy.

The air was suddenly cold. Raindrops spattered against his hands and the hood of the tractor.

"Shit-oh-dear," Mary Ann said, gazing up at the clouds. They coiled angrily in the sky like a vast heap of coals: black around the edges, fire flickering in the core. The lightning flashes were brighter and closer, and the thunder was no longer a distant rolling explosion.

"So much for the weather report, Mary Ann." The wind was whipping the rain into sheets, and he turned up his collar. "Come on, hop aboard—I'll give you a ride back to the shed."

She clipped a handful of green sprouts and stuffed them into her blouse pocket. She hunched her shoulders and clopped through the broken ground, climbed up behind him on the tractor and wrapped her arms around him. He felt her shiver as her breasts pressed into his back.

He said, "We'll just have to have Town Meeting early. Good. I want that damned current turned back on. I'm sick of hearing about how I'm overreacting." He lifted the digging tool from the ground and headed back toward Civic Center.

She squeezed him tight, in a special rolling way that she had. It took the edge off his ire, but he grumbled on. "Well, it sure as hell isn't the power. We've got all the power we need, rain or shine."

"Everybody says it's a lot of trouble just to stop a dog."

"Right. A dog." He sighed. "All right. They're entitled to their opinion. I'm entitled to mine."

Her voice was muffled against his back. "You're not alone. You have me, too. But we're just two."

The rain was still fairly light as he drove the tractor into the shed. The other farming equipment was being brought in, and the colonists were beginning to gather, heading for the meeting hall. Cadmann shut down the tractor and squeezed water from his hair.

"I'll be in in a minute," she called, hopping down from the back of the tractor. She paused at the doorway to turn up her collar, then ran out in the direction of the corral.

Maybe Mary Ann was right. His was a minority opinion. Madman Weyland sees bogeymen in every corner—while crops grow, animals thrive and tame earthworms enrich the soil with their bodies and their wastes.

When he thought of these things, he should have thought of life, instead of a dog that had never come back, and a mangled chicken cage. . . .

IT LOVED a rainy night.

It could always move about on land, slowly, lazily, and tolerate the heat for hours at a time; but movement at hunting speed required a quick kill, then a frantic race to the river to shed the terrible heat within. Night and rain extended its time on dry land.

It had changed when it became an adult. Its mind and senses adapted for life out of water; but from birth it had been intensely curious. Frustratingly, there had been nothing for its curiosity to chew on. Birds and swimmers were its world, a prison for its starved senses, until the intruders introduced it to the world beyond the rock wall.

They were so strange! They built angular nests. They tottered on their hind legs or attached themselves to creatures with hard, weirdly scented, tasteless shells. Sometimes they would let themselves be swallowed up by them, much like swimmers would. They lived with creatures even stranger than themselves.

On the first night it had killed a four-legged thing. The dog had run after it rather than fleeing. It had played with the dog, dancing around it and watching its antics. When the game grew tiresome, it tore out the animal's throat. The blood was thick and hot and delicious.

Afterward it had felt overheated. It had hooked its tail spines into the dog's throat and dragged the corpse back toward the river, where it could cool itself and eat at leisure.

Sport! Swimmers were never such fun. The flying things that sometimes fed on them were too much of a challenge. It thought about that night, and pleasure rippled through its body.

There had been another night when it broke through prickly barriers, following a tantalizing scent.

The nest of wood and thin tough vine had resisted only for a moment, and then it was among them, one thick paw and its wedgelike head squeezed into the box. What noise they had made! They had tried to fly, but badly. None were fast, none could fight. It was not even sport. It was only feeding . . . but feeding was its own reward, and anything that didn't taste like a swimmer was food for thought.

That was days past. Now it watched something that looked to be good sport.

A single invader was walking out by the rows of thorned vines that protected a group of four-legged grass-eaters. The invader looked frequently up at the clouds, no doubt enjoying the fall of rain, and shook water out of the dark fur on its head.

The invader never looked behind the tarpaulin-sheltered jeep parked to the side of the grazing land. The man walked to within ten feet of it, leaned against the fence with one arm outstretched and spoke to one of the grass-eaters.

The grass-eater walked clumsily to the fence and licked something out of the man's hand. The man turned and took a step toward the jeep.

The creature's limbs trembled, tingled, its blood singing with anticipation. *Come. Just another step . . .*

Disappointment washed through its mind as the man turned at the call of another of its kind and ran torpidly back toward the lights.

Ah, well. There was still the grass-eater.

It was near the thorned vines, chewing at something on the ground. It was plump—more than twice as large as the dog, almost as large as the creature itself—but that was no worry. It could feel that the grass-eater was no fighter.

The creature crawled forward until its flat, roughly triangular head peeped from behind the jeep. A raindrop spattered directly into its eye, and its ocular covering thickened momentarily.

THE CALF chewed the handful of alfalfa sprouts Mary Ann had brought it. The rain was just beginning to chill its skin, and soon it would head for the metal-roofed shelter in the corner of the pasture to huddle for warmth with its brothers and sisters.

There came a rippling cooing sound from beyond the fence, and the calf pressed against the wire until it felt the first touch of pain. It lowed plaintively. It shuffled at the fence, afraid to press forward, reluctant to retreat.

The shape was a massed shadow flowing around the curve of the jeep. A squat, flattened shadow with disklike, unblinking eyes and a dolphin's smile.

The creature burbled happily.

The calf backed away. Sudden, uncomprehending fear pumped adrenaline into its system, sent it stumbling backward toward the shelter. The creature waddled with almost comic clumsiness up to the fence, sniffed at the wire, bit at it experimentally, drew back.

The other calves had picked up the scent of fear, and two of them poked their heads from the shelter, looking out through the rain, making deep braying sounds. Calling for the protection of the herd, for the adults, for the bull! But there were only calves.

The rain had grown into a downpour now, and Tau Ceti, already low on the horizon, had disappeared behind massive, inky clouds. The wind whipped the droplets almost sideways. The young grass was pelted down and mired itself in the mud. Back in the camp, one of the lights flickered, dimmed, then strengthened again.

Lightning arced jaggedly in the sky, and the calf saw, without comprehending, that the wire was broken, curled back inward, shivering in the wind.

A thick shadow squatted in the grass a few feet ahead of the break. It had eyes that glistened, hypnotically vast.

It crept slowly forward, even as the calf loped toward the shelter. There were eight of them beneath the sheet metal, packed against each other now, the shared heat of their bodies no match for the wind or the rain or the sudden, crippling fear.

The shadow was closer now, very close, immediately in front of the shelter. Great webbed claws landed pad first, then hook-nailed toes gripped the ground to pull it along the grass on its belly. Rain pelted against its skin and unblinking eyes as it seemed to evaluate them, choosing.

They crawled over each other, bleating their terror to the wind and the night. Two of them began chewing at the wire at the back of the enclosure, ignoring the pain in their lips and gums, thinking only of the thing that crept in the darkness, eyes wide, unceasing grin opening to reveal rows of chisel teeth.

Cooing to them, it sprang.

It landed among them, lashing out with claws and teeth. The screams, the smell of alien blood, the terrified eyes that rolled, flashing white in the darkness: it would remember all of these things, and study its memories later, analyze the prey's habits and its own mistakes. Its ancestors had needed such caution. The prey they had evolved to hunt were more devious, more dangerous than any calf.

It snapped and tore at them in the confines of the shelter. Despite their weight it smashed them out of the way, flicking its tail with stunning force, ripping wet strips of flesh from the bone. Finally it fastened its teeth deeply in one warm neck, worrying until the skin and cartilage parted and blood spurted warmly into its mouth. The calf trembled. Its last sound was a strangled bleat of despair.

The others fled the shelter, escaping through the break in the wire, running out in all directions.

The calf's chest heaved as it lay on its side, heart struggling to beat, to stave off the shock of pain and massive blood loss. Its killer folded its legs and lay down next to it, peering into its eyes as it died, watching them film, the lids falling for the last time.

It barbed the grass-eater by the neck and dragged it out of the fenced enclosure. Exertion caused heat to build up in its body. Without the cooling rain it would have had to run for the river.

The rain quenched the inner fire and the calf's flesh, warm and rubbery-slick in the darkness, eased the fatigue.

THE AROMA of roast turkey mingled with fresh green vegetables, home-grown onions and spices that had traveled ten lightyears to give up their pungency.

The walls of the communal dining hall were alight with color: news-reels, technical briefs and documentary, personal messages and listings of the material to be found in condensed form, whenever the colonists had the time or interest to decode their messages from Earth. Despite the riot of shape and shade, almost no one was watching: dinner had stolen the show.

For the first time in years (or decades!) the majority of the food was not freeze-dried or powdered or syruped. Mary Ann bit into a forkful of fresh green salad and savored the explosion of mingled flavors. The let-tuce, tomatoes and mushrooms were all fresh and crisp. Tau Ceti Four bugs seemed uninterested in Earth vegetables; no pesticide had been used.

The milk, the salad dressing, the cheese cubes and the bacon bits had been reconstituted. But soon . . .

Beside Mary Ann, Cadmann poured gravy over sliced turkey and stuffing. Across from them, Ernst had done serious damage to an entire turkey drumstick, handling it one-handed. All around them were the sights and sounds of a healthy community, and she leaned her head against Cadmann's shoulder and felt totally satisfied.

Out of the corner of her eye she caught his expression, an absent, crooked smile. The tastes and scents and fellowship had driven his con-cerns into a corner for the time being.

There was a ringing thump in the front of the room, and Zack stood, his cheeks stuffed with mashed potatoes.

"My fellow citi—" He got that far before the words were muffled on his food, and his wife Rachel whacked him heartily on his back. He pinched her cheek firmly. "Take two! We have almost everybody here at the same place and the same time, and although the rain rules out a lot of the work—"

Mary Ann leaned over and pouted. "Can't go out checking the fences tonight, mister man. You're all mine."

Cadmann smiled absently. Often he would do that, or not respond at all. She knew better than to let it bother her . . . intellectually.

"—it doesn't rule out all of it. So the group will be splitting up as soon as the meal is over. This is a good time for a general progress report."

Rachel handed him up a clipboard, and Zack flipped through it, hawing to himself. "All right. As most of you know, the Cliftons' baby, April, came out of intensive care, and is doing fine in the nursery—"

"Wrong again, Zack!" Gregory Clifton nudged his wife, Alicia, and she stood, Avalon's first baby asleep in her arms. The colonists applauded roundly. April woke, looked puzzled.

Mary Ann watched mother and baby covetously. The child seemed so peaceful, the mother so happy. There was jealousy and happiness mingled there, because Alicia was one of the nightmare cases. Sleep trauma and some loss of memory had made her one of the colony's liabilities. Thank God she was a healthy mother. The genes were good, and the child would be smarter than her mother.

Without conscious design, she found herself leaning closer to Cadmann, brushing his skin.

Zack continued. "We're expecting three more babies next month, so let's everyone pitch in and give those ladies a hand. We haven't had a single miscarriage or accident, and we want to keep that record clean.

"Agriculture . . . Mary Ann? Do you have anything to say?"

She wiped her mouth hurriedly and stood. "We've having no more trouble with the, um, alfalfa. The soybeans and the rice are both doing fine. The bees are happy. We'll wait for a young queen before we try them on any of the native plants. And let's have a hand for the hydroponics team—it's their tomatoes we're eating tonight, not mine!" There was more applause, and Mary Ann started to sit down, then said "oh!" and popped up again. "The fish are doing fine, both in the breeder ponds and in the rivers—the catfish are doing a little better than the trout, but that's to be expected. The big news is that turkeys have been spotted as far as a hundred kilometers away!"

Zack grinned. "It looks to me like we can forget that seeding expedition. Let's have a vote on that—all in favor of dropping the idea?"

He did a quick scan of the forest of hands that sprouted. "That ain't no majority. I think you're just giving Agriculture a picnic day, but I guess they deserve it. Now—before we get on with the newest broadcasts, is there any more business?"

There was. There were complaints about living space, work duty for postnatal mothers and completion schedules for the fusion plant. Then Cadmann stood, and there was an undercurrent of groans in the room.

He waited it out. Mary Ann saw the pain in his face, saw him decide to laugh it off as best he could.

"Listen—I know that I keep getting outvoted about security, so I'd like to try something different. I know that everyone is up to their ears in work, but a few volunteers, working in shifts, could really beef up security."

Terry Faulkner stood, and Mary Ann watched Sylvia's face closely. Sylvia was a nice lady—bright, hard-working, friendly—but Sylvia and Cadmann shared something that made her feel shut out. Not sex; she was sure of that. But she knew that Cadmann had secrets with Sylvia, secrets he wouldn't share with anyone else, not even his lover.

"Listen, Cadmann," Terry said. He must be in a good mood, Mary Ann thought wryly. Usually he just said Weyland and left it at that. "We've been going around and around on this for more than a month now. I think you should let it rest." There was vocal agreement, and Cadmann gritted his teeth.

Mary Ann leaned across to put a hand on Ernst's wrist. Ernst was trying to decide whether to stand up and wring Terry's neck; he looked up now, and Mary Ann shook her head. He thought it over; nodded.

"I don't want blood, toil and tears," Cadmann said. "I just want a little more security, and one man can't handle it alone—"

"But wouldn't you really like to? Isn't that what you want? An opportunity to play hero?"

Mary Ann saw the anger sizzling in Cadmann's eyes; his fingers gripped the table. He looked down, trying to control his voice. "Terry, that's not what I'm after. There's something going on around here, and I think—"

"I think the chickens are going to be fine—"

Carolyn McAndrews shouted, too loudly, "Oh, shut up, Terry!"

Zack raised his hand. "That's enough, both of you. I think that Cadmann's concern is unfounded but heartfelt. It deserves your respect, if not agreement. If anyone wants to donate time to an informal militia, please see Cadmann after the meeting." He slapped his palm down on the table. "And now, if there is no more business, let's get the lights down and start the tapes."

Cadmann sat down, looking at his hands as the mess hall began to reorganize, the chairs turned around to the wall. Mary Ann shook his shoulder gently. "Cadmann?"

He muttered something that she couldn't hear, but it sounded like "Idiots."

The lights dimmed, and as they did there was a general movement in the room—some leaving, off to bed or indoor jobs, and as they left, the rain was a drumming rhythm that washed in through the door.

Mary Ann moved her chair up behind him, stroking the back of his neck, trying to be as close to him as he would let her. He reached up and grasped her hand, holding it too tightly. His fingers were cold.

The wall went blank for a moment. Then the MGM lion roared, and a video copy of the two-hundred-year-old *Wizard of Oz* began to play, to the cheers of the colonists.

Cadmann squeezed her hand and stood.

"Where're you going?" Mary Ann whispered. "Can I—?"

He shook his head, and in the dark it seemed that he smiled.

Ernst was on his feet. Cadmann pushed him down into his chair (even he wasn't strong enough to do that to Ernst against resistance) and whispered in his ear. Then he was gone into the milling press at the back of the dining hall. Mary Ann heard the door open and shut, but wasn't sure whether or not he'd left.

She cursed herself. You could have said or done something. He's just not a farmer, and he feels like the third glove in a pair. . . .

And that thought was depressing. If she hadn't been able to make him feel needed in the six weeks they had been sleeping together, she wasn't sure what she was going to do.

DOROTHY and her friends were crossing the poppy field in a flood of yellow Earthly sunlight. There was sudden, inappropriate laughter from the back of the mess hall, and Marnie McInnes said, "How did she get out?"

"Flying monkeys!" a joyful cry from Alicia Clifton. Ernst's teeth gleamed in the flickerlight. Both had returned to a world in which it was all right to be a child.

"Damn!" The veterinarian's curse cut through the laughter. Someone triggered a handlamp, and there was a scream, and a cry of "Turn on the damned lights, somebody. We've got a problem!"

Mary Ann was out of her chair before the lights came up. She worked her way to the back of the hall. A circle of people had formed around one of the calves, and as the light strengthened, she could see that the poor thing was wobbling, barely able to stand.

Blood drained down its legs, and skin hung from its ribs in a fold, exposing the bone. It looked at her and staggered, almost collapsing into her arms, smearing her with water and blood.

A scream split the driving sound of the rain: "The fence is down!" and lights all over the camp blinked to life. Coats were grabbed, and rain hats.

Mary Ann ran out into the mud and the bleeding sky, pulling on her coat as she went. They moved across the compound in a broken wave, running north to the grazing grounds. She splashed through puddles, slipped in mud, blinded by the rain. There was a scream to the left: "I found another one." She saw Jean Patterson struggling with a weak, terrified calf, wrestling it to the ground.

Mary Ann wiped the rain out of her face, tilted her head against the wind and, panting, headed for the swarm of handlamps buzzing around the fence. The wire was broken. It was ripped away from the posts, almost as if a jeep had been driven through it. The corrugated metal shelter was a shambles, and the corral was empty.

Desperately, in confusion, she began looking for tracks, spoor, anything. She recognized the wild laugh that came to her lips for the hysteria it was. In this rain, a herd of mastodons could have tromped through, and there simply wouldn't be any trace.

Cadmann was already at the shelter and stirring at the ground. A flash of lightning revealed a mass of blood and tissue working between his fingers. He grimaced in disgust. "No dog did this."

There were more yells, as more of the calves were found staggering in the darkness, braying into the wind. Zack puffed hard as he ran up. "What happened here, Weyland?"

"Hell if I know, and I don't think we're going to find out until morning, either."

"Take the calves over to the horse corral. They'll keep." Zack bent, looked at the metal. The sheeting looked as if it had been ripped with a power tool. "Jesus Christ. What could do something like this?"

Cadmann shook his head, but when he looked up at Mary Ann, there was both concern and vindication in his frown, a mixture that made her feel uneasy.

"What happened here?" Zack whispered again.

"I can tell you what happened," Terry said. Mary Ann whipped her head around at the ugly tone of his voice.

"What happened is that someone's been predicting trouble, and now we've got it. Happy, Weyland?"

Mary Ann wanted to spit in his face, ashamed that someone had spoken aloud the words she was whispering to herself. Instead, she balled up her hands and shouted, "Just go to hell, Terry!"

"To hear your boyfriend tell it, we already have."

Then he turned, walking away into the rain. Mary Ann knelt beside Cadmann, putting her arm around his shoulders.

He was shaking.

CHAPTER 5

AUTOPSY I

THE SKEETER autogyro hummed up from the bank of the Miskatonic, crested the gorge and pivoted slowly, hovering. Its shielded tail rotors beat a curtain of dust from the ground.

Tau Ceti crawled towards the western mountains, a tiny glare-point momentarily eclipsed by the tarpaulined shape swinging from the belly of the gyro. Zack Moscowitz shielded his eyes against the glare with one hand, with the other held the veterinary clinic's door open. Sylvia Faulkner and Jerry Bryce emerged running. The doctor kept ahead of the dust cloud. He waved the Skeeter along the approach corridor between the animal pens and the shops.

Jerry must have come straight from his bed. His eyes were puffy; his unruly brown hair looked like the brambles that circled the plain. Sylvia wondered if he would be able to handle tonight's work.

"Where'd they find Ginger?" Zack coughed dust, hawked and spat.

Sylvia flinched. That kind of rudeness was totally out of character for Zack. "Half a kilometer upriver. Barney spotted it on his third flyby."

The Skeeter's engine whined, laboring as it hovered. Surely an illusion: the two-man craft could handle a ton of cargo. The calf's remains shuddered on the nylon palate as it spooled down, until palate and corpse flattened against an aluminum gurney.

Sylvia and Jerry wheeled the gurney into the clinic. The bulge beneath the tarp was not the shape of a calf. This wasn't going to be fun.

Stamping feet thundered in the horse pens as the colts and fillies backed as far away as they could. They tossed their manes, snorting, nostrils flaring. Zack sympathized totally. "No, it doesn't smell pretty, does it?" He stood back as the cart was wheeled up the ramp into the clinic. Sylvia guided, Jerry pushed. "I still can't believe this is happening." He eased the door shut behind them.

Jerry took the cart the rest of the way in. Sylvia watched as the Skeeter dipped toward the western wall of brambles. "We haven't found *anything* on the infrared?"

"Nothing but turkeys and pterodons," Zack said quietly. "I've been checking every half hour. Nothing on visual, nothing on audio, nothing on infrared or radar. For a hundred square kilometers." He wagged his head in disgust. "I don't know what to think. If there's something out there, it means trouble. But if there *isn't* anything out there . . . did you say who found this?"

"Carr."

"Yes, right. May I?" She handed Zack the clipboard and he jotted a note to himself. His handwriting, neurotically neat at the best of times, looked machine-printed.

Sylvia took his arm affectionately. "Zack—don't try to be everywhere at once. We'll take care of this." He started to protest, and she turned his chin, examining his bloodshot eyes. "You get any sleep?"

"Usually I count sheep. You wouldn't *believe* what was vaulting the fence last night—"

Jerry peeled back the outer tarp.

"Sheez!" Sylvia moved back from the sudden stench of unrefrigerated flesh. It smelled wet and suncooked and corrupt: the kind of odor that conjures an image of hungry flies and heavy spices; the smell that permeates a back-street butcher shop on a warm summer afternoon.

Zack was trying to back out of the room, but the sight and moist sound as the tarp was peeled away held him transfixed. As the last layer of cloth left the corpse, he grunted in disgust and turned his head.

One of the calf's legs was gone. Another was broken, chewed almost completely through, hanging at an angle. A hideously raw wound gaped in the center of the body. Skin and muscle had been ripped away, ribs snipped cleanly or shattered, jagged edges jutting through the flesh. The bones were grooved and splintered as if something had tried to push Ginger sideways through a wheat thresher.

Marnie hooked a gauze mask around her ears. "All right, Jerry, start the camera." Her voice had a lisp that turned "Jerry" to 'Sherry," although she pronounced each word with extreme care.

Jerry looked up at the ceiling. "Cassandra. Program. Autopsy assistant. Run."

A glowing crystal at the end of a gooseneck extension snaked down from the ceiling. The video camera paused patiently as Jerry adjusted a collar at the top of its neck. Its red eye winked on. "Okay. Program is running. Recorders on. Go, Marnie."

Marnie wheeled over the tray of instruments and pulled on rubber gloves. The stomach wound swallowed her arms to the elbow.

"I note puncture marks around the throat without further damage inflicted there. Buttocks and abdominal muscle removed. I suggest that death was caused by severing of the jugular and carotids, but that the attacker dragged his prey to safety, and there consumed the, ah, missing tissue and internal organs." Her delivery was precise enough to compensate for much of the mushiness of her lisp. Years from now this would be seen all over the Earth.

"The bones are neatly sheared—almost too neatly, I would think. Jerry, take a look at this."

Her husband came to her side and pulled on a pair of plastic gloves. "Sylvia," he said quickly. "Get on the console and follow us with the camera." The glowing crystal wound its way to Marnie's shoulder and perched there, peering. "What have you got?"

"Just a moment." Sylvia fiddled with the controls: suddenly the abdominal wound was floating in front of her, in living color. Her own stomach rolled, and she leached some of the color from the video stage. Little of this would be seen by Earth's billions. Too much blood. Maybe there was an underground market?

Jerry's hand walked into the image, pointing at a rib that hadn't been ripped away. His scarecrow body moved smoothly now, in familiar habit patterns. "We have bite marks here—" His fingers traced several notches. "I want a projection based on bite radius, jaw pressure and overall strength. Whatever killed Ginger had *power*. It had to move her fast."

"I'm not doing anything useful," Zack said. "I'm going over to

Control to check the infrared returns." No one answered. "I just hope to hell something has come up."

As soon as he was out of the room, Marnie looked up. "Nothing yet? Not a flicker?"

Sylvia shook her head. "Nothing. Not one of the Skeeters has picked up anything larger than a turkey."

"And Cadmann's still out there looking?"

"First out, last back. You know Madman Weyland." The torn flesh disappeared from the video stage, replaced by a two-dimensional column of numbers. Sylvia turned to the computer monitor. "Cassandra. Imaging." As she talked her words and numbers were transformed into lines of color. She manipulated them with an optical pencil until they became teeth and a crude mandible.

Marnie exchanged terse words with her husband. They looked at the wounds and the luminous outline hovering in the air in front of the pregnant biologist, and tried to shut down their imaginations. They were not entirely successful.

GINGER had yielded up the last of her secrets, and lay quiet now, refolded within her shroud of waterproofed canvas.

The operating room reeked of disinfectant and strong coffee. They sipped coffee while they examined the video image. A disembodied brace of teeth without muscle or flesh floated in the air, grinning, mocking their confusion.

"I come up with something like a hyena's jaw, more teeth, broader bones." Sylvia's finger traced the jawline.

"Not strong enough," Jerry sighed. "Remember the way the ribs were sheared. Cleanly. I can't think of anything strong enough—"

"—to cut those bones?" Marnie shook her head. "We're not talking strength here. There are plenty of animals who have the strength. It's the *pressure* I can't believe." The camera hummed. "So much force concentrated in such a small area. You're talking about a carnivore built like a stegosaurus—leviathan body, peanut head." She drained her cup, clattering it down on the counter. "And I don't believe that, either."

"Don't believe what?" Sylvia was staring at those jaws. The teeth would be like shears, and unbelievably powerful. She shuddered.

"I don't believe a carnivore the size of a rhino with the speed of a leopard." Marnie threw her hands into the air. "I'm sorry! There's just nothing that size on the island."

"Maybe it swam over," Sylvia said in a small voice.

"But there's nothing here now."

"Maybe it swam *back.*"

Jerry stared at the image for a long moment, then shook his head uneasily. "We'd better hope to hell that that's just exactly what it did."

THE PTERODON beat its leathery brown wings in slow motion, craning its claw-hammer head to skaw displeasure at the humming, hovering intruder in its domain. Frightened at first, it had lost some of its natural caution, spiraling closer and closer to the thing, trying to decide if it posed a threat. Suddenly the bulbous head of the intruder erupted in light, turning dusk into midday, burning brighter than Tau Ceti at its height. Blinded, the pterodon cawed and reversed its arc, heading for the safety of its nest, high in the crags of Mucking Great Mountain.

Cadmann chuckled and wiggled the searchlight toggle, playing the Skeeter's beams around the pond at the base of the mountain. It scanned clear, except for a few samlon near the surface. Nothing large had been near it recently: the infrared would pick up a man-sized heat trace half an hour old.

Fed by trickles of snow melt and a tributary from the southern highlands, the pond was the largest body of still water for fifty square kilometers. If there was a large carnivore in the vicinity, surely it knew of this watering hole. Perhaps it even fished for samlon here. . . .

The pond stared up at him, a blind eye around the edges, dead black in the center. The water shivered as he brought the Skeeter down for a closer look. "How deep are you, fella—?"

Before the thought could congeal, his earphones buzzed. Cadmann cleared his throat into the microphone. "Weyland here. Found anything?"

It was Zack on the other end. "Not a thing, Cad. You?"

"Not yet, but—"

"We need to have Town meeting tonight. Head on in."

"I've still got a quadrant to sweep."

Cadmann could almost hear Zack counting under his breath. "Cadmann—you've already swept your entire area twice. Everyone else is in. We've been at this all day. We need to talk, and nobody wants to wait any longer."

"But—"

"I'm too tired to play martinet, Cad. Do me a favor and just come back in."

The pond stared at him. Something about it made his stomach itch with tension. He wheeled the Skeeter around for a long look at the plateau. The brambles were struggling for a foothold on the square kilometer of naked rock, and Cadmann saw that yes, a trap could . . .

Suddenly he was smiling as he climbed, spun the Skeeter around and dived toward the lights of the Colony.

THERE WERE no colorful newsreels or densely worded technical briefs displayed on the walls of the communal meal hall. There were no sharp, tangy vegetable smells, and no warm buzz of camaraderie.

A low mutter of disgust tinged with fear wound its way through the group as they faced the floating image of the dead calf, its wounds marked with flashing green labels.

Mary Ann gripped Cadmann's hand: her nails bit into his palm every time the camera zoomed in on a wound, until he carefully disengaged her hand and put it firmly in her lap.

At the head table, Zack paused in his comments to take a drink. It seemed to brace him. Cadmann wondered what exactly was in that pitcher.

"This is our best reconstruction," he concluded, rather apologetically. "Sylvia extrapolated this from the spread and depth of the bite marks. We have an eighteen-centimeter jaw base, and a roughly wedge-shaped head. It looks like something sired upon a rattlesnake by a bear." Nobody laughed. "Um . . . massively strong jawbones and corresponding muscles.

"We can't be sure how much such an animal would weigh. Certainly enough to destroy any credibility the tracks by the chicken cages might have had." He peered out into the audience. "I'm afraid that that incident was a particularly unfunny prank."

Gregory Clifton handed a drowsy April to his wife, Alicia, and stood. "Zack, let's cut the crap. I worked on the computer map. Half the Colony saw the information as it was coming in. There isn't an adult here who can't interpret the technical data for himself. How about opening up the floor?"

The applause shook the room.

Zack shrugged, spreading his hands. "All right, Gregory—what's your idea?"

"We know about the pterodons. None of them get too large. But maybe there's another species of flying carnivore. Something the size of —oh, crap, let's say a California condor . . ."

There was a quick spate of derisive laughter. Jon Van Don yelled, "What the hell, why not a roc, Greg?"

Barney Carr brayed with laughter. "Watch out for flying elephants!"

"Wing span-to-weight ratio, Greg," Stu called. "It would have to be *huge* to lift a calf. Much larger than a ground carnivore capable of bringing down the same size prey. And how would it evade the Skeeters?"

Greg held up his hand. "Hear me out. It wouldn't need to fly away with the calf. It could fly in, and then drag a heavy victim to a safe place. And maybe it nests up in Mucking Great Mountain—"

There was a shout from the back of the auditorium, and Andy Washington, the big black man from the engineering crew, stood. He was fighting a losing battle with an evil grin. "I say our mistake is thinking it had to be big. Maybe it's not an *it*. Maybe it's a *them*, like a herd of *Marabunta* army mice—"

"Something like a glassfish," Jean Patterson added. "A super-chameleon—"

"It has to be coldblooded, to evade the infrared—"

"The hell it does! There're hot springs everywhere you look!" The opinions were flying too thick to stop now, and Zack sat back, pleased and relieved by the healthy creative energy being released.

La Donna Stewart stood, tiny fists poised lightly on her hips. "Has anybody considered a borer?"

"I think we're listening to one—Ow!" There was the sound of an affectionately brisk slap as she whacked her fiancé, Elliot, and the room quieted for a moment.

"I mean like a mole, or like ants or termites. This entire area could be riddled with tunnels and we'd never know it. It could operate like a trapdoor spider. Engineering should put together a seismic detector, Zack. . . ."

Andy whipped out a pad of paper and started making notes to himself.

Zack Moscowitz took the opportunity to grasp control again. "A good suggestion, La Donna. All good suggestions . . ." He glared at the engineer. "Except maybe the *Marabunta* mice, Andy."

He touched a switch, and the grotesque skull disappeared from the wall. He chuckled darkly. "I know that some of you don't even *believe* in this thing. There is . . . one possibility that Rachel suggested to me. As camp psychologist she felt it was time we discussed it openly."

He took another sip from the thermos, then plunged ahead, dead serious now. "We all know about Hibernation Instability. It's no joke to any of us. Personally, I've noticed that I don't parse as well as I once did. That I need a calculator for operations that I used to do in my head. And I wonder: is that just age? Or could it be those little ice crystals that weren't supposed to form?

"We've had major memory losses, impairment of motor skills, mood swings and clinical personality disorders—all of which we've been able to handle by juggling work duty and schedules. A few cases have required chemical stabilization."

The muttering in the room had quieted. They were ahead of him, and heads nodded in anticipatory agreement.

"Maybe things have been too placid here. The crops are thriving, we've had no deaths—hell, no real *injuries*—"

Cadmann looked around him in the dark. *A little white lie there, Zack. Ernst walked right of the cliff and broke his ankle his first week down.*

"Just maybe there are those among us who feel that it's been *too* easy, and perhaps for our own good want to—" His fingers fluttered as he fought for the right words—"want to keep our guard up, our spines stiff, by creating a bogyman. A harmless joke, perhaps, except that the loss of the dog, the chickens and now the calves suggests a rather disturbing trend.

"I won't suggest that this is what *has* happened. But I would be remiss to exclude the possibility from this discussion. So . . . if anyone has anything to talk about, please . . ."

He looked out over the audience, which was dead silent. Zack gripped the edge of the table, his knuckles pale. He moistened his lips nervously. Alicia's baby started to cry, and she blithely offered it a nipple.

Zack cleared his throat uncomfortably. "No one has anything to say? Carlos?"

Their carpenter/historian shook his head. He peered at his fingernails, inspecting them in the dark. "Not me, *amigo*. I uh . . . I heard that the tracks by the chicken cage might have been a prank. We all heard Cadmann say that, and I guess that's possible."

There was silence for another long moment, then Cadmann stood. His big hands were splayed out on the table in front of him, and his face was grim—not a shred of regret or admission or apology there. "I know what I think. I think that we're wasting our time here, talking about Hibernation Instability. That's *bullshit.* I have a good idea of what we're up against here: something that is fast and strong and smarter than a wolf. Smart enough to use the rivers and streams to foil other predators, maybe. At any rate, *that's* how it dumps the heat, and why we don't pick it up on the scans."

There was a murmur of approval, and Cadmann continued. "This thing is checking out our territory one bite at a time. I'm not trying to alarm anyone, but it's pretty obvious that our present defensive plans are insufficient."

Terry stood up, brows furrowed petulantly. "We're using standard procedures, Weyland. In fact, our patrols are heavier than the situation really warrants. We're taking people away from other projects."

"I agree, Terry. So let's not take them away for an indefinite period. I say an aggressive defense could handle this situation in a week."

"Aggressive defense?" Terry asked, arched eyebrow and tightly pressed lips punctuating the words with sarcasm.

"We don't wait around for this thing to find a hole in our defenses. We set traps. We hunt it down. This is *our* world. We're masters of this island, damn it, and I for one don't have much stomach for just hiding behind a fence."

"And we can guess who'd like to play Great White Hunter." Terry turned to look at Zack, but he was still talking to Cadmann. His voice was calm and measured, as if speaking to a child. "There's no call to jump the gun. We need to evaluate the situation carefully. See how it responds to standard procedures. Then, if necessary, we can make a coordinated sweep of the island. There's no need to turn this into a safari. Especially since, as Rachel has suggested—there may not *be* an exterior threat to this colony."

He turned back to Cadmann. "Before you get your back up, no, I'm not accusing you or your friends." He flickered an eye at Ernst. "But it wouldn't shock me if you wish I had. There are some people who need a fight to feel alive. Who feel old and useless without one."

He sat down, leaving Cadmann the only man standing in the room. There was a disgusted ripple of whispers, and Carlos's barely audible voice stage-whispering, "What a crock."

Cadmann closed his eyes and told his bunched stomach muscles to relax. "Listen to us. The only thing we can agree on is that *something* is happening here. I say that until proven otherwise, we make the simplest assumption—that there is an unknown life form, and that we have invaded its territory. Now if you put me in charge of a small group of hunters, I can—"

Zack shook his head. "This has all happened too quickly, Cadmann. Until we evaluate the information further, we simply can't judge the relative merits of our defensive options."

"Spoken like an accountant," Carolyn McAndrews said stridently.

Cadmann glared at her. "This is between me and Zack, lady. Button it."

Zack blew air. "This is uncalled for. Both of you, cool down. For the time being, I think we should sit tight, on our home ground. After all —" Zack smiled—"this camp is *our* territory. Let's make it come to *us*, all right?"

"Damn it!" Cadmann was yelling now, and frustrated with himself for doing it. "I demand the establishment of a militia, and I'm going to organize it. I'm better suited than anyone else here for that position—"

"Cadmann, I think we should wait—"

"Wait? All right. You hurry up and wait. None of you understand—" Cadmann bit his lip, sealing off the torrent of words. He turned and stalked out of the hall.

Behind him, Ernst stood. Silent, impassive as a golem carved from ice. He studied their faces as if memorizing, judging, weighing options somewhere in the crannies of his damaged mind. Then he said, "You shouldn't treat Cadmann like that. He knows. He's smart. You should listen to Cadmann." He followed Cadmann out.

When the doors had swung shut behind them, Terry said softly, "I think maybe someone should keep an eye on him. On both of them."

Mary Ann stood, shaking the hair out of her face. Her face was filled with anger, but her voice was little-girl vulnerable. "He just wants to *help.*" Her voice broke on the last word and she averted her eyes, then ran from the room.

CADMANN wasn't answering his door.

She was no stranger here. She had actually left some toiletries on his dresser, and a few items of clothing in his closet. Still she waited for permission before intruding.

"Cadmann?" She hugged her arms to her sides. "It's cold out here. Can't I come in?"

His words were leaden with disgust. "Mary Ann, what do you want?"

That was probably as much of an invitation as she was going to get. She opened the door.

The only light was a pale halo surrounding a holographic Earth

globe, a half-meter sphere of sparkling blue ocean and drifting clouds
that revolved above Cadmann's bed. He was lying on his side, fingers
playing with the video control box, bringing silvery dawn or cloaking
darkness to the continents. Cadmann stared at the globe moodily. A
flicker of his thumb and the western coast of Europe was alight. Another
and the globe misted, cleared on a satellite panorama of the United
Kingdom. The island swelled to fill the video field. A hooked nugget of
land near the foot of the island flashed green, and again the globe
misted, and the mountains of Wales floated in the air. As if he had done
it a thousand times, Cadmann guided the camera in on a southeastern
corner, to a valley rampant with golden-green trees and rolling hills, a
vast quilt of farmland stretching away into the distance.

He laughed flatly, self-consciously. "A sovereign remedy for homesickness, they say."

She sat next to him and reached for his hand. He lay back, kicking
his feet up onto the blankets, not bothering to take off his shoes. His
shirt was open halfway down the great corded barrel of his chest; wisps
of silver hair reflected the spreading light. Her urge was to bury herself
against him.

There was a movement in the corner of the room, and she saw
Ernst's enormous bulk perched on an incongruously tiny stool. He
watched her expressionlessly, and seemed to her like an engine idling in
neutral, waiting for Cadmann to throw him into gear. A less flattering
metaphor, one having to do with tame dogs, came to mind. She repressed it and smiled at him, still unnerved by his lack of response.

"My grandfather came from Wye Valley," Cadmann said quietly.
"It doesn't look like this anymore." There was resignation in his voice,
and he hit a button on his control. Once again the Earth globe spun
slowly above his bed, segueing from day to night to day in steady
rhythm.

"Well," Cadmann said finally. "Nobody can say I didn't try it their
way."

Mary Ann reached out to touch him again, gratified when he took
her hand. His fingers were cool and stiff, and she had the distinct impression that the contact was more for her benefit than his.

"What do you mean by that?"

The barest trace of a smile flickered on Cadmann's lips and then
died. "Just . . . what I said. That's all. Really."

"Cadmann—we've scanned the island from one side to the other."

A line of shadow fell on Cadmann's face as the holo globe revolved, and night fell on the Americas.

"Cadmann?" There was no answer.

She rose from the bed unsteadily and crossed to Ernst. He looked at her incuriously. The angle of his head only changed as she knelt beside him and took one of his huge callused hands in hers.

"Ernst," she whispered to him. "Please—leave us alone for a while?"

"Oh . . ." He grinned childishly. "You want make rub with Cadmann? That fun." His ice-blue eyes clouded for a moment as if searching lost memories. "You make rub with Ernst once. I remember! On ship. Maybe sometime—"

He blinked, as if something sad had suddenly occurred to him, some flash of understanding that was intensely, profoundly depressing, and the great craggy expanse of his face went slack. "No. I forget sometime. Good-night, Cadmann." He resurrected a smile for Mary Ann. "Goodnight, May-ree."

Mary Ann followed him to the door, and latched it behind him. She turned quietly, watching Cadmann's motionless figure on the waterbed. She sat on the bed and took off his shoes.

Dawn broke over a miniature Asia: the Himalayas glittered, flamed white. The China Sea was a riot of warm blue diamonds.

SHE WAS riding his hips. She saw the sudden delighted surprise in his face, and he said, "Earth mother."

She didn't know what he meant, or care. Only afterward did she guess how she must have looked, her face and shoulders glowing within the globe of the Earth.

Like all of the times and all of the ways that she had made love to Cadmann, this time was utterly precious to her. If there was a barrier between them, it wasn't the disdain that she felt from Marty, who laughed to his friends as he knocked on her door. Or Joe Sikes. Good old available Joe, who knew her weaknesses so well. Who rapped on her window when his pregnant wife was asleep.

It was different because she knew there would come a moment when he would smile as she kissed him, and then they would laugh together. The barrier would crumble for a while, a fragile crystalline moment, and Cadmann would really be with her, caring for her and letting her fill his needs. And when that time came she turned her face away, unwilling for him to see the dampness on her cheeks.

Later, long enough later for any tears to have dried and any tremors to have ceased, he held her softly, as if afraid that she might shatter. Gazing at her, he ran his thick blunt fingers over and around the curves and shadows, touching, soothing. Finally he sighed, laid his head gently between her breasts and fell into a deep, soundless sleep.

CHAPTER 6

AT THE WIRE

What the hammer? What the chains?
In what furnace was thy brain?
Where the anvil? What dread grasp
Dare its deadly terrors clasp?

WILLIAM BLAKE, *"The Tyger"*

IT DIDN'T MATTER a damn that the stars above Carlos's head, twinkling in Avalon's eternal mist, were not those of Earth. It didn't matter that the wind carried the ticklish scent of alien blossoms, or that the plants beneath his feet were mingled Terran and Avalonian grasses. Beneath the smiling face of a con man, the quick and nimble fingers of a carpenter and the mind of a superb historian, there lurked the soul of a farmer. Like it or not, Carlos felt absurdly at peace.

He ran his gloved fingers above the electrified wire—without touching. The wire was connected to power leads and pressure sensors. Any attempt to climb over, push under or break through it would trigger a shock: the more pressure exerted, the greater the voltage would grow, terminating in enough electricity to barbecue anything on the short side of a rhino. Huckleberry, the year old gray-brown German shepherd on the end of Carlos's leash, had learned to be quietly respectful of the wire. He could stand within two feet of it without flinching but would venture no closer.

The wire extended around three sides of the camp, starting north of the living quarters, running west near the main road, curving south past the animal hospital, the machine shop and the air pad. There it met the cliff again, stopping shy of the fields.

There were more calf pens across the main road, these fenced separately, each enclosed in another "graduated" electric fence.

Huckleberry sniffed the cages as they turned west towards the cliff edge, the fifty-meter drop behind the camp that led to the sluggish waters of the Miskatonic.

"Hey!" He threw an arm over his face as a wandering searchlight temporarily blinded him. *"Cuál es su problema, eh?"*

With an apologetic bobble, the searchlight glided on its way. Lamps and video cameras had been mounted on the communal dining hall, the roof of the machine shop and a corner of the animal pens. There was barely a centimeter of the camp that their glaring ovals did not flare into momentary day. Saucers of light skimmed along the road, circling, dipping, interweaving.

Carlos watched those circles and pulled his jacket tighter. Suddenly he felt a chill, and the heat-reflective windbreaker didn't help at all. This cold blossomed within him.

Silhouettes dimmed the window of the yellow Quonset hut next to the air pad. He watched enviously. In the communications shack there would be coffee and companionship and hot crullers, things he couldn't expect for another forty minutes.

Huck whined as footsteps approached, and Carlos's attack of hunger died instantly. He squared his shoulders and put a little more pep in his step. *At least I can look like a sentry!*

"Terry." He smiled. The dark softened a malicious grin. Terry looked fatigued and disgusted. His face, never plump, was drawn even thinner, and he looked as if he thought Cadmann was boffing Sylvia while he walked patrol.

Terry fished a pack of cigarettes out of his vest and offered one to Carlos. "Just the thing, *amigo.*" They stood for a time, savoring Earth-grown tobacco.

"Might as well enjoy 'em." Terry exhaled a long white stream of smoke in the darkness. The mist and the night formed a wall that obliterated everything more than a kilometer from the camp. Their entire universe consisted of a few buildings and pens and fields and the pale, silent glow of the moons above them. "It'll be a long time before anyone gets around to planting tobacco."

"You may have discovered the real reason I came," Carlos said contentedly, smoke trickling from his nose. "The only way I could ever quit these damned things is to get ten trillion miles away from the nearest convenience store."

"Yeah." Terry's smile was tentative.

"You know, *amigo*, you look about ten years younger when you let yourself go."

Terry was grinning now, but covered it with his hand as he took another drag on his cigarette. "Think we're wasting our time out here?"

A shrug. "Maybe. A couple of nights should tell the tale. Your wife is going to have her babies here. Wouldn't you rather be sure? I mean *really* sure?"

Terry inhaled deeply. "On a night like this it's nice to have an excuse to be outside." The grin was open now, and infectious. "You're right. Thanks, Carlos." He adjusted the rifle on his shoulder. "Got to keep moving. Another butt?"

The searchlight cruised back through the fields. As it passed the pens, the colts and fillies froze their nervous motions, moist eyes glistening like frozen flames. Huckleberry growled, then subsided.

"We'll have the infrared up tomorrow night," Carlos said quietly. "Got a jiggle along the southern fence. Not enough to trigger the electricity, though. May not have been anything at all, but . . ."

"Could have been a turkey," Terry said hopefully.

"*Si* . . . except Bobbi told me that she's seen damned few turkeys in the last week. Maybe they ran into something poisonous." He considered that for a moment. "Or maybe it's Thanksgiving on Avalon—"

The yowl of a bobcat caught in the gears of a clock could have been no more sudden or piercing. The fence alarm hammered at the night, at their ears, stripping the haze from their speculations in an instant. Another sound was mixed into it: an animal sound, something wet and angry.

Carlos's arm wrenched at the shoulder socket as Huckleberry spun on the end of the leash, running north for the Armory.

"Jesus Christ!" Terry screamed, lowering his rifle to port arms, and running behind them. The searchlights swept along the fence, which was vibrating wildly. A ragged chorus of howls split the air as the other dogs converged on the wire.

Carlos was gasping, the sudden exertion burning his lungs, a silent litany of Dios mío, *let it be a turkey*. Por favor, *let it be a turkey*—He stumbled, lost his grip on Huckleberry. Before he could catch the leash, the animal was bounding toward the fence.

Carlos charged after him.

There was nothing to be seen, nothing heard except the dreadful screeching. Huckleberry was charging full tilt, snarling his challenge as if he could see something, smell something that Carlos could not. Charging directly at the fence—and with dreadful certainty Carlos knew the dog would not stop in time. "Cut the powerrr!" he screamed, but there was no time, and in the darkness, in the frenzy, Huckleberry leaped directly into the triple strands of the fence. His fur shot up away from his body like needles in a spray of cactus. His startled, agonized yelp was cut short by the hideous sound and smell of meat singeing in the fire. Sparks sizzled whitely from the relays as the section shorted. Huckleberry's body twitched and leaped like a frog on a griddle.

Carlos turned away, choking as his dinner jolted sourly from his stomach. He swallowed hard, forcing it back down, gagging. No hurry now. After a few moments his vision cleared.

Huckleberry's body, wreathed in strands of wire, sagged motionlessly now. Jon van Don cut the power. Elliot Falkland pried the blackened, smoking corpse loose with a shovel. The surviving dogs were howling, sniffing, frightened. The stench of death was gut-wrenchingly strong, and a couple of the other colonists had turned away, covering their faces. Lights were coming up all over the camp, and everything was confusion and the patter of feet.

Zack was there, skidding on his heels, and then covering his nose. "What happened here? Carlos?"

"Alarm. Huckleberry went nuts. I think that he smelled something. He tore his way—hell, I let him go. He ran right into the fence. God, I'm sorry, Zack."

"No time for that. *Did you see anything?*"

There was another sound now, the sound of a motor coughing to life, then purring smoothly. Rotors engaging. A dust cloud swirled up behind the animal hospital as a Skeeter rose from the air pad, orange landing lamps blazing.

One of the searchlights spun to follow. Light sheathed the craft in silver.

The Skeeter wobbled, off balance. There was a weight beneath its belly: a calf dangling in a sling at the end of a four-meter line. The animal wiggled feebly. Its legs and head hung with woeful vulnerability as the Skeeter corrected itself and buzzed off to the north.

"Shit *fire*," Zack moaned.

"—and save the ammunition," Carlos muttered, shielding his eyes as they tracked the Skeeter. "I wonder who that is?"

Terry was right behind them, hands gripping the rifle. "I'll give you two guesses. Weyland and his tame ape, that's who."

"What is going on here!?" Zack yelled, running for the communications shack. "Will someone tell me what is happening?"

"I'm sure someone can," Terry said in disgust. Carlos had the distinct impression that Terry wanted nothing so much as to sight his rifle on the flying machine that was even now vanishing into the wall of mist. "I'm damned sure that somebody knows *exactly* what is going on."

THE CREATURE was curious and hungry, but mostly curious. There was often enough to eat, but never enough to learn, since the invaders came. Their mobile nests with the hard shells, the odd animals that shared their domain . . .

Its short lifetime had offered too little to stimulate its senses. Strangeness exerted a fascination. In the murky racial past there had been challenges, lethal unless understood. The threats were long gone, but the curiosity remained.

The invaders seemed to have captured tiny pieces of the sun and moons, and could make them shine where they wished.

It could not grasp how this could be so, could not even form the proper questions, and so the wondering died before it was truly born. Only a trace remained, in healthy caution and a driving urge to learn more.

Caution was virtually no inhibition at all. It could see their weakness: they were slow, they moved in herds like other beasts. They were merely interesting meat.

Still, there was something. . . .

It crawled around the edge of the encampment, rounding the hill to the southwest, a hill that glittered with shiny squares. It bit one of them experimentally. The square was hard and tasteless and moist with dew.

The creature headed west around the fields, past the blowing wheat and corn, past a smaller field planted with soybeans, around to the edge of the calf pen.

It had been here once before, during the rain, and had been well rewarded for its efforts.

It was about to taste the fence when one of the circles of light glided its way. It scampered to the side, almost directly into a second glaring oval, and scampered backward for a few steps, staying in the darkness, playing hide-and-seek with it, while speed began to fizz in its veins. There was always a corridor of darkness to squeeze through, and the game was irresistible. It wiggled across the road toward the main camp, staying in darkness, always in darkness, until it was across the fence from the horse pen.

It watched them, paying little attention to the lights now, the patterns of movement absorbed so that it automatically moved enough to stay out of them. That game was too simple now. There was another, better game at hand.

The horses paced nervously now, staring out into the darkness as their noses scented what their eyes could not see.

It prowled around to the side, watching the horses. They moved quickly. Their skin was glossy and rich. The way their hair tossed with their fear was almost unendurably appetizing. It whined, its hunger assuming the proportions of lust, and sniffed at the fence. There was something wrong here, it could tell. Its nostrils burned a little to sniff it. Something wrong, but the danger meant less with every passing moment. It wanted one of the horses, wanted to bring one down, to outrun it, to leap upon it and break its neck, to rip open the flank and taste it, to gaze into its eyes in the moment of death. . . .

Its teeth met the wire. Every muscle in its body locked in unyielding contraction as electricity ripped through the line. It bit down so hard that the wire snapped. It jerked free, screaming its fear into the night.

The captured sun surged after it. It ran, terrified of the vine that bit back, of the light, of things that it did not, could not understand. And a *thing* inside its body flared to life.

From a sack behind the peculiarly flattened lungs, a complex chemical pumped into its system. Its blood vessels swelled. *Speed* surged through its body. Its movements, already quick, accelerated as if a supercharger had been triggered. Its stubby legs churned at blur-speed as its heartbeat tripled.

The searchlights that swiveled frantically after it never had a chance.

It was overheating, burning as it ran, and as it plunged into the waters of the Miskatonic its skin nearly sizzled. It lay there, marinating in mud, extending its snorkle to the surface. Its heartbeat slowed, steadied, calmed. The chemical fire in its body faded slowly to ashes.

The fear and pain gradually faded, leaving a core of rage. Anger at the invaders who hadn't the good grace to be either prey or direct competitor. The invaders were *rivals*, and they were cheats! They were something that it did not understand at all, something that could hurt it in a way that it had never experienced pain, inspire a fear that was quite new to it.

One of their flying things came humming overhead, lights stabbing out and dissolving the swirling gray mist. The creature watched through the muddy water, blinking hatefully, fearfully.

It worked its way back upriver; its thick, reptilian body rippled slowly behind. Blood was in its mouth, and murder on its mind. Murder, not killing. Killing was for food or fun. This was an urge to hurt for the sake of hurting. Not to reduce their numbers, but to make them *afraid*, as it had been afraid. To repay the invaders for their gift of pain.

How, though? How to get in? It had looked everywhere, and everywhere that it looked were the hard, tasteless firevines which bit back. Everywhere except . . .

Above the river, up along the lip of the cliff, above the straight seventy-degree rise that the colonists had considered a natural barrier, there was no fence. Its eyes narrowed as it considered.

This was it, then. It would crawl up the cliff and give them fear, and death. It would teach them. . . .

Stubby legs lifted it from the river muck, and it began crawling up the cliff. The first few meters were easy, but the farther it climbed, the steeper the wall became, until its feet lost purchase, and it slid back down into the water.

It lay there, disgusted, and then trotted a few meters to the right and tried again.

Stealthily now. Eyes narrowed, one foot carefully finding support, and then another. The purchase was a little better here: sedimentary rock, crumbling in layers, offering shelves for toeholds. The creature's heart beat faster as it considered the havoc it would wreak. It climbed higher this time, and when it started to slide, it fell a clean eight feet before its claws found purchase. It reached the water in a shower of rocks.

It seethed with rage now. Muscles flamed, eyesight blurred with red. Again its body began to boil. Its breath seemed to sear its throat. All thought, all considerations vanished in a burst of chemical speed.

It erupted out of the water, heart thundering in its chest, legs paddling crazily. There was brush, then naked shattered rock, then a flat rock face. Its momentum was so great that when the footing was gone it *skimmed* up the cliff face, momentum carrying it over places where there were no footholds at all.

Its speed carried it up over the edge. Feet scrabbled for support that wasn't there. In a moment of utter panic it realized that it was marooned in the air, sailing beyond the lip of the gorge in a great arc, spread-eagled for the captured suns.

No sun swung its way. The slanted roof of a hut rose up to meet it: its thick, scaled body slammed down, bumped over the rows of ceramic tiles to the edge and thumped ignominiously to the ground.

For a second it lay there, dazed and confused. Then as its wits returned it ran for the nearest shadows and crouched, breath whistling in its throat.

After a few minutes, the panic and surprise subsided. It was *inside*, and could do what it wanted.

From the shadows it watched the invaders scurrying about carrying shiny sticks in their forelegs, scuttling this way and that in slow, comical confusion. It was quite funny, and in the shadows, the creature's thick lips curled in a dolphin smile.

The glaring circle of the searchlight cruised past it several times. Once, reflected from a metal tower, the light slid directly over it. But there was no one to see.

Mine, it gurgled happily. *All mine . . .*

It listened carefully, heard nothing approaching in the darkness, and crept out, peering both ways.

It passed the nearest hut. The door cracked open and it scampered back to a shadow and watched as two invaders scrambled clumsily past, reminding the creature of swimmers in their mindless haste.

When they were gone it crept out again, racing from shadow to shadow.

The cliff ascent had made it hot and hungry. The Miskatonic could cool it, but there were matters to settle before it took the plunge.

It paused in a shadow. Across the way was a patch of light, and it could see into the interior of one of the buildings. There was nothing of interest until a door opened and an invader came in, carrying something small and pinkish in its forelegs.

With obvious tenderness the yellow-topped invader laid its tiny burden into a nest made of rigid twigs, and bent to lick the tiny thing's face, very gently. The invader's foreleg brushed the wall, and the mock sun went out. The invader left the room.

The creature waited another minute, then crept up to the open space, planning to crawl through and take the tender, wiggling morsel.

To its surprise the clear space was blocked. It tried again, gently, and—

Still it couldn't get through, but now it was close enough to see that what blocked its path was somewhat like the cold, hard water that sometimes slid down the mountain into its pool. The clear barrier even gave slightly under its weight, and the creature could hear sounds through it.

"—duty again, Alicia? Well, at least April is asleep."

Uncomprehending, it shook its head and tested the barrier again. There were more sounds, sounds of objects falling, creaking, and it watched the small invader in the nest wiggle, its tiny hindlegs thrusting at the covering.

The creature nosed against the barrier again, then reared back and smashed into it. The barrier splintered, sharp fragments slicing into its nose and above one eye.

It scrambled through the window and took one step toward the small nest when the larger invader threw the door open and screamed piercingly.

Their eyes met, and the creature thought that it had never seen anything more appetizing. With regret it conceded that this was not the time for the large one. A shrug of its hindquarters brought its great spiked tail back and around to smash into the invader's midsection. The invader curled in on itself; its noise stopped.

The creature shrugged its tail again. The invader flew away and smashed into the wall. Her forelegs pawed at her torso, trying to staunch the flow of crimsons. She slid to the ground.

No time now. Only moments had passed, but it could feel the danger. With a twist of its thick, powerful body it was back to the nest of straight twigs, and the small invader even now squalling its fear. The creature reached in and picked it up.

It was so small, so helpless. So like a swimmer.

Invaders killed swimmers.

CHAPTER 7

THE BLIND

Ere the moon has climbed the mountain, ere the rocks are ribbed with light,
When the downward-dipping tails are dank and drear,
Comes a breathing hard behind thee, snuffle-snuffle through the night
It is Fear, O Little Hunter, it is Fear!

KIPLING, "The Song of the Little Hunter"

THE JAGGED SHAPE of Mucking Great Mountain rose like a primordial cairn, a titanic mass of unweathered rock stacked as if by Neolithic ritual, towering, raw-edged, lost in the clouds that shrouded the plateau.

There was almost no vegetation on the mountain, nothing but moss and a little scrub brush that withered out and died within a hundred meters of its base. Pterodons lived up there somewhere, but on this night they slipped invisibly through the mist or huddled in their nests, rough gray wings enfolding the leathery eggs of their young.

The plateau itself was only a few hundred meters wide, fuzzed with brush, and walled at the northern end by thorn-tree brambles. A failed stand of larger trees formed a rough deadfall at the far southern end: the soil had never been rich, and the trees—gnarled, spiky growths full of knotted fiber—had died before their maturity, too weak to resist the first onslaught of natural parasites. Now the ubiquitous thorn brush fed on the tangled debris. A few tough, rubbery plants surrounded the artesian spring at the base of the mountain, but there was insufficient moss or lichen to break down the rock, and most of the plateau was barren.

Barren, and deserted—except for two men and a single frightened calf.

Cadmann Weyland adjusted a bowline knot around the smooth white curve of its neck, then tugged on the line to check the anchoring: it was securely spiked into the rock. The calf licked his hand, tried to run a warm pink tongue wetly over his face. Cadmann pulled away guiltily. The calf dropped its head and lowed in misery.

"Sorry about this, Joshua." He scratched it behind one speckled ear. In its eyes shone the pitiful gratitude of a retarded child given a rubber bonbon. Cadmann felt dirty.

He pulled his jacket tighter and peered up into the mist. It was deeper than even two hours before, masking the starlight, blanketing the twin moons.

Thirty meters distant, on the eastern side of the plateau, was the half-completed blind he and Ernst had constructed. The big German had worked tirelessly for three hours, driving stakes into the rock with sharp powerful hammer blows, cutting and dragging sections of thorn bush, binding them into place and meticulously adjusting the spiny walls into camouflage position.

Thorns gouged needle points through Cadmann's glove as he helped Ernst haul one last gnarled section into place. "Ouch!"

The big German turned, grinned lopsidedly. "Thorns sharp, hey? I bring lots of band-aids."

"Sylvia swears these things are harmless." He grunted, pulling off his glove. The tip of the thorn had broken off under the skin, and would take tweezers to work free. No time now.

The calf brayed miserably. Ernst clucked sympathetically. "Poor Joshua scared. We shoot, you shoot good and straight. Kill wolf. We take calf home."

"So it can grow up to be a cheeseburger. Some consolation."

"Cad–man?"

"Oh, nothing. On Earth I'd stake that calf out for a mountain lion without a second thought. Here—God, I don't know. In comparison with whatever's been pruning our flock, that calf's my second cousin. It just doesn't feel quite right."

Cadmann scanned their blind, the wall of thorn that hemmed them in on three sides. The Skeeter was hidden in the rock niche behind them, invisible from above or the sides. The blind wasn't perfect, but it would have to do.

The wire grid rectangle of their heater sputtered with flame as Cadmann squatted in front of it. The night was colder than he had realized: the waves of heat eased the tension in his back and shoulders.

He unsnapped his rifle case and lifted free his most prized possession.

It was a Webley semiautomatic express rifle. Its high-energy, mushrooming .44 slugs delivered a staggering load of hydrostatic shock. The Webley had been thoroughly checked out back at the camp, but he reexamined it now. Cadmann had a simple credo that had served him well over the years: when the game is charging full blast, with tusks lowered and turf flying, there is no time to pick grit out of the trigger housing.

He adjusted his infrared goggles and switched them on, peering at Ernst. The big German was a blotch of orangish light in the middle of a blue field. When Ernst moved, the warm air trailing him left an ocher trace image.

Cadmann reassembled his rifle and checked Ernst's, while his friend tied the last thorn section onto hinges of looped cord and tested its mobility. Satisfied, he lashed it into place.

Ernst folded his legs and sat, long face quiet.

"And we are just about ready," Cadmann said brusquely. "Here." He handed the second rifle to Ernst. Something happened to Ernst's face when the rifle touched his hands. It was as if a little light went on, as though the touch of the wood-grain stock or the smooth metal of the barrel stimulated neural connections that had been unaffected by the cryosleep.

Muscle memory. Tactile as opposed to visual or auditory cues. He works well with his hands. He remembers. Surely Rachel can work out some kind of occupational therapy for Ernst based on manual skills. . . .

Their heater died. Ernst leaned his rifle against the thorn barrier and reached around into his backpack for a new tubular cartridge of jellied fuel. He slid it into the heater, and tiny blue flames sprang to life. The flare of light from the goggles was a shade too bright. Cadmann adjusted the light level and again examined the plateau. There was very little to see: only the ghostly outlines of the rock, and the glowing red silhouette of the calf. It gazed forlornly at the barrier, then turned to sip nervously at the waterhole. It stopped, pawing at the ground, gazing into its depths. It moaned.

There was nothing left to do but wait.

CADMANN was humming contentedly to himself, and then the humming turned into words that he was startled to remember:

> *I Blas Gogerddan heb dy dad*
> *Fy mab erglyw fy llef*
> *Dos yn dy ol i faes y gad*
> *Ac ymladd gydag ef.*
> *Dy fam wyf fi a gwell gan fam*
> *It golli'th waed fel dwfr*
> *Neu agor drws i gorff y dewr*
> *Na derbyn bachgen llwfr . . .*

He sang in a soft, unmelodic tone. As he continued, the rust flaked off his vocal chords, and he began to find notes with something other than shotgun precision.

"Cad–man. What you sing? Don't know those words."

"Oh, oh—damn, I'm sorry. The song's in Old Welsh, Ernst. My grandfather taught it to me when I was a pup. Guess I've never quite forgotten it. A man named Geiriog scribbled it down, and Granddad liked it." Cadmann closed his eyes and chuckled. "He would. 'Blood and honor, Cad, That's what life is about. What a man is made of' . . ." Ernst nodded silently, and Cadmann was embarrassed to find himself wondering if the big German could understand. "The song is called 'I Blas Gogerddan,' or 'Gogerddan Hall.' "

He leaned back against his bedroll and closed his eyes. "It takes place during a great battle, when one of the warriors bolts and tries to hide behind his mother's skirts. She's not exactly a peacemonger. The best I ever translated the song went:

> *Into the hall alone, my son?*
> *Now hear your mother's prayer.*
> *Go back onto the battlefield*
> *And aid your father there.*
> *I'd far prefer your blood be spilled*
> *Like water on the ground*
> *Or have you in your shroud arrayed*
> *Than as a coward found.*

Go thou into the hall and see
The portraits of your sires.
The eyes of each and every one
Alight with raging fires.
Not mine the son who would disgrace
His family's name and home.
"Kiss me, my mother dear," he said,
She did, and he was gone.

He has come back unto the door,
No longer does he live.
His mother cries, "My son, my son!
Oh God, can you forgive?"
Then comes an answer from the wall,
"While rivers run through Wales
Far better is the hero's death
Than life when courage fails. . . ."

The silence following the song was total, and it took a few moments for Cadmann to realize how deeply into the song he had wandered. The words still resonated in his mind, now carried by the rough, untutored tones of his grandfather.

That's what a man is made of . . .

"Do you like that?" he asked, almost shyly.

"I like, Cad. I like song. You teach it to Ernst. Soon."

An unstrained chuckle bubbled up through the embarrassment, as Cadmann realized that he felt more comfortable than he had in a hundred and twenty years. At least. "You know, there's something I've always wondered." He paused, his thoughts interrupted by the soft plaintive moans of the calf. "How many of those songs do they sing as entertainment, and how many are behavioral mod? I mean—my grandfather would never have *said* that he'd rather have a dead grandson than a live coward, but the message was pretty clear." He shook his head irritably. There was a tension headache in there somewhere, but it hadn't wormed to the surface yet. "It sure as hell was. And the worst part of it is that I don't even know what I think of that."

He stared into the heater. It was a poor substitute for a campfire, and he felt vaguely discontented. He made a fist, examining it in the dim light. His skin was the same tough, weathered hide it had been since his late twenties. A faint smile: *Let's have a big hand for the oldest, strongest fingers on Avalon.*

Absently he caressed the stock of the rifle, running his thumbnail into the engraved hardwood. With sudden, disturbing clarity he realized that he had never touched Mary Ann more lovingly. He grimaced. "Maybe I do know what I think about that. Sometimes you just have to be satisfied with what you are."

Ernst reached out with one large hand and gripped Cadmann's arm warmly.

Together they waited.

RELATIONSHIPS.

There is a relationship between hunters, between hunter and prey, between a hunter and his own body, his aches and pains and fears. Between a hunter and time itself.

They mingle, this complex set of interrelationships which varies in every case, and within a single hunt varies from instant to instant.

But whatever the variables, there is one thing that remains constant:

There comes a moment in which time ceases to have meaning, when aches and pains and fears dissolve into insignificance. When friendship or antagonism, hesitation or eagerness all meld together to create an instant of pure feeling, clear intention, when the observed and the observer are one. At this moment the mixture of awareness and involvement is like a supersaturated solution: one vibration, one degree's variance of temperature triggers irrevocable change, a shockingly abrupt crystallization of potentials.

Cadmann and Ernst, cradling their rifles, gazing out into the darkness, existed in that state. The night sounds, the constant shuffling of the calf, its occasional whines all absorbed into the gestalt of the experience.

Waiting without wanting. Preparedness without hope. Empty vessels, delicate balances awaiting a trigger.

Joshua the calf strained at his tether, pulling toward the northern edge of the plateau. He was staring out into the darkness to the south, eyes huge and shiny, all sound stuck in his throat like a chunk of frozen grass. He reminded Cadmann of nothing so much as a deer transfixed by the headlights of an oncoming jeep.

For just one moment the tableau was stable.

Then the calf tried to bolt. It strained at the tether, pulled until the plastic line was as taut as a bowstring: vibrating, singing against the spike in the ground.

"Don't see anything . . ." Cadmann whispered. "Where—?"

Ernst nudged his elbow, and pointed south. Cadmann's goggles whirred noiselessly as they adjusted for range. Gradually it came into focus: a faint blotch of orange beyond the jumble of dead trees and thorn brush.

It slowly changed from an indistinct blob to a real shape: oblong, rear portion low to the ground, upper body more erect. "Komodo dragon," Cadmann said into the tiny tape recorder in his pocket. "Komodo dragon, but the tail's thicker. Head's rounder. It can walk bipedal but doesn't much. Uses the short front legs to get over the brush.

"Jesus Christ. The bastard must weigh two hundred kilos, easy."

The calf strained against the noose until he was gagging. His swollen tongue bulged from his mouth. The legs were as rigid as iron pipes, and the eyes protruded whitely, rimmed with red.

The thing stalked out of the south. It waddled toward them, toward the trembling calf, moving with confident slowness, stopping for a moment to survey the plateau, even pausing to stare at the blind.

"It knows we're here," Cadmann dictated. "Knows and doesn't give a damn. Christ, it's like it *smiled* at us." *You're next, it thinks. Well, maybe not.*

"Well insulated. Not giving off much heat. Hard to get details." Cadmann cursed and turned his goggles up another notch. The creature paused for another leisurely look at the blind, then turned away to move toward the calf again. Its infrared glow was like a will-o'-the-wisp gliding across the land.

Cadmann grinned. *Gotcha. I don't know what you are, but we're sure as shit going to find out.* "Don't shoot until I do," he whispered.

"Aye aye, Colonel."

Was Ernst remembering? No time to think of that. *Wait. Come on, baby, come on, further from the edge, out onto the plateau. I don't know what you're made of, but ten rounds of this ought to finish you.*

"Parasites," Ernst whispered. "Careful. And maybe it has young—"

"Good thinking." *Parasites. Like fleas on a dying rabbit. They can be dangerous once we've killed it. He is remembering. Adrenaline?* The creature had moved closer. *Come on, come on . . .*

The creature was within fifteen meters of the calf. It continued slowly, paused often to sweep its head around. "I think it can see in the IR," Cadmann dictated. "Probably sees us better than we see it."

The calf was bleeding from the neck as the nylon braids rubbed and cut, but adrenaline drove him on. *Just an instant now—*

The thing moved like a boneless crocodile, each step, though apparently clumsy, rippling back through its body like rhythm through the legs of a millipede. It was hypnotic to watch, and now that he could see it more clearly, he could see and sense the raw animal power of the thing. "It's smart. As smart as a dolphin, maybe. Give it enough time, it might evolve intelligence." He felt a fleeting moment of sadness.

Then the tether snapped, and Joshua bolted. The creature rippled after it.

Ernst fired first. Cadmann let the rifle swing easily to follow the creature and squeezed off a round. As he did, the creature moved again. Cadmann's shot went wide of the mark. "Jesus, it moves fast," Cadmann shouted. Ernst fired again. The creature's body was slammed by the first shell, and suddenly it was *moving.* It whirled and dashed toward the blind, moving at an impossible speed across the rocky plateau.

Shock piled upon shock. The infrared goggles flared as if a thermite bomb had ignited in the creature's bowels. The rangefinders couldn't adjust fast enough as the creature dashed toward them. Its image remained out of focus but flared until he saw nothing but a bright glare. Ernst fired three times more. It was impossible to tell whether he had hit the creature. It screamed, in pain or defiance or challenge, or all three, and it hissed like a steam engine. Suddenly it was upon them.

Ernst stood. He had removed his goggles and was firing blind into the blood-tinged darkness. The dragon hit the thorn barrier. Branches bent, split, splintered. Thorns and bark exploded into the interior as the monster slid sideways into them. It thrashed its tail and a section of the wall fractured and slammed into Cadmann. He fell. Spikes pierced his face and hands and legs. A flying broken branch struck the left side of his head and knocked the goggles askew. Cadmann tried to stand, but one knee didn't want to work properly. A thorn branch hung from his left hand. He had to set the rifle down to tear it free. Blood followed the thorns.

Less than five seconds had passed since the first shot.

The creature screamed again. The thorn branches flew again as it lashed its tail. Cadmann tore away the useless goggles. There was blood in his eyes, and he fumbled for his rifle. Everything seemed to happen at once. To his right Ernst was firing wildly at something that tore through the thorn barrier as if it were not there. Nylon line snapped. More thorn branches flew as deadly missiles.

Cadmann's left hand didn't want to work. Blood streamed from the palm, and lifting his rifle was agony.

Ernst fired once more. The creature screamed, whether in agony or rage Cadmann couldn't tell. It seemed to take forever to bring the big rifle around, and then Ernst was in the way. More blood flowed into Cadmann's eyes from the scalp wound.

"Get *back!*" Cadmann screamed. "Back!"

Everything was moving in slow motion—everything except the monster. Its speed was impossible, and Cadmann's mind, in a vain attempt to grasp the thing's rhythm, had slowed reality down until he seemed to be swimming in clear syrup. His thoughts slugged along like a holo played at one tenth speed. Too many impressions per second, too many feelings, too much surprise. Too much of anything and everything, until his entire nervous system was in overload, and for an instant nothing registered but shock.

The monster had torn the fence to shreds. The great tail lashed back and forth. Each time it struck branches and splinters flew at them. *It knows,* Cadmann thought. *My God, it knows!* The barrier fence crumbled to nothing.

The world was a blur. There just wasn't enough light. His left eye was blood-blinded, useless, and his right wasn't in much better shape.

Exactly eight seconds after the first shot was fired, the thorn barrier was a mass of splintered ruin. Faster than a cheetah ever ran, than a cobra ever struck, something that was all dark mouth and glistening teeth wiggled through the opening, and Ernst *screamed.*

It was a sound that Cadmann knew he would never, could never, forget—all of a man's hope vanishing in one overwhelming moment of agony.

The monster's head jutted through the jagged opening. The jaws clamped savagely into Ernst's thigh. Arterial blood spurted. Ernst thrashed and flailed. His arms flopped like a rag doll's. He struck at the creature's head with the rifle, then with great mallet fists that made no more impression than snowflakes on an anvil.

The jaws snapped again, clamping more deeply. The scream arced higher, wavered, began to fade. The monster backed out of the hole, dragging Ernst with it.

Cadmann was watching himself watch, the distance between thought and action expanding until he felt like a man falling down a well, sky and sun and rationality impossibly far above him, growing further with every hundredth of a second. With immense effort he fought his way past the paralysis and forced himself to act.

Outside now, Ernst was still whimpering as the thing crawled up his body, looking into his eyes. Its paws were locked onto his front shoulders, huge face so close that it looked as if it might kiss him. Ernst's own blood drizzled out of its mouth and onto his cheek.

Ernst turned to Cadmann, something beyond fear or pain in his face, only a pleading silence that was shattered by a single urgent word: "Please . . ."

Cadmann shouldered his rifle and fired: at the creature, at Ernst, at the night, as logic dissolved and terror coursed through his body like electrical sparks arcing from pole to pole.

And Ernst exploded.

The gas cartridges!

A bright nimbus of flame played around the bodies, and Cadmann shielded his eyes.

The creature howled its wrath and pain as a fireball of jellied fuel engulfed the rough wet leather of its squatly amphibian body. It reared back, shrieking, turned and ran.

To Cadmann it seemed to fly downhill like a meteor or a rocket missile: one long stream of fire ending at the pool. It skimmed across the surface of the pool, then sank almost in the center. Its agonized howl ended suddenly. The flame went out. The pool smoked and steamed like a caldron of soup. A trail of fiery webbed footprints, improbably far apart, sputtered for a few moments and died.

Cadmann pushed his foot at the thorn barrier. An entire section of it simply fell to the ground. His rifle drooped in his arms.

Cadmann doffed his jacket and flailed at Ernst's flaming, smoking corpse. The heavy nylon was melting, burning his hands, but he continued beating at the corpse mechanically, ignoring the pain that was beginning to surface, until the last flickering tongue had died.

Ernst's body was charred and broken and chewed, barely recognizable as anything that had ever been human.

Cadmann knelt by it, breathing deeply to stave off shock. His entire left side felt like raw meat.

Ernst stared at him, through him. Cadmann reached out trembling fingers to close the eyes, but there were no eyelids, nothing but singed, smoking, crinkled black flesh, flesh dark as any African's, flesh black as coal with pinkish-red pulp showing through a few cracks.

Cadmann turned to the side and was suddenly, violently ill.

CHAPTER 8

GRENDEL'S ARM

What of the hunting, hunter bold?
Brother, the watch was long and cold.
What of the quarry ye went to kill?
Brother, he crops in the jungle still.
Where is the power that made your pride?
Brother, it ebbs from my flank and side.
Where is the haste that ye hurry by?
Brother, I go to my lair—to die.

KIPLING, *"Tiger Tiger"*

"SKEETER THREE, this is home base. Do you copy?" Zack listened to the answering crackle of static, and cursed under his breath.

Standing close behind him, Sylvia Faulkner held her sides gingerly. Sudden stress had drained her, made her legs unsteady, her belly feel swollen and tender.

The entire colony was in a barely contained state of panic. There would be little sleep tonight, and a heavy demand for stimulants and mood stabilizers before morning.

Zack was holding up well, but his eyes were frightened.

Sylvia's body cried out for somewhere dark and warm to curl up and sleep, just dream the nightmare away. But she had done it: she had held herself under control while she examined Alicia's corpse and identified the bloodstains left smeared in an empty, broken cradle.

The aborted rescue party had only worsened the situation. Too many of the men had families now, wives and children that they were reluctant to leave. There seemed little reason to march out into the fog, searching for what no one really wanted to find.

Gregory Clifton's haggard face still floated in her memory. The sound of his voice as he begged desperately. *Please—I need your help. Help me find my baby. Please . . . I . . .* His words had trailed away as the sedative took hold.

"Skeeter Three, this is home base. Do you copy? We have you on radar now. Just come on in, Cadmann." Zack rubbed his hands on his pants. His voice was cracking. "Is Ernst with you? Do you have the calf?" Another pause.

Sylvia folded her hands, staring down at them disconsolately. "Maybe the radio is broken."

"I hope so," Zack said miserably. "God, I hope so. I don't want to go looking for him in the morning. For them. How in the hell did this happen?"

The door clattered open, and the air took a chill as Terry entered the communications shack. His hands clutched at the edges of his windbreaker. "Greg is out now," he said sharply. "It's not exactly what you'd call sleep, but it's an improvement. We don't want him up and around when Weyland comes back." He paused thoughtfully. "He *is* coming back, isn't he?"

Sylvia glared at him.

"All right, all right—I don't want a lynching party. Nobody's calling Weyland a baby-killer. I just want the truth. About now I don't know *what* to think."

The fog outside was still a hovering, isolating curtain. In only two hours Tau Ceti would rise and burn much of the mist away. Until then it stifled sound as well as sight and aggravated their sense of dread.

Zack rubbed his eyes. "That idiot. He had to go out and get the job done himself."

"He's an idiot all right," Terry said. Then, exhaling harshly, he added, "But goddammit, just this once, I hope he was a successful idiot. Christ, poor Alicia."

Sylvia reached out to her husband, gripped Terry's fingers tightly and pulled him close. Two deaths. Two deaths in a population of less than two hundred.

One percent of their microcosm dead in one swoop, without any explanation, any answers. Perhaps just a series of warnings that they had all been too rational to heed.

Everyone except . . .

"Cadmann. Can you hear me?" Zack adjusted the microphone's sensitivity. "Come in, please."

There was a commotion outside, yelling, and through the fog she could hear the beat of the Skeeter's rotors as they whipped the air.

"Thank God," Zack said fervently. "Weyland."

Leaning on Terry, Sylvia levered herself up out of her seat. "I want to go out," she said.

She expected opposition from Terry, but he just nodded. "Let's go," he said. "I guess everyone should be there."

The airpad was directly behind the com shack, an asphalt-paved square with a target circle painted in white and a ring of landing lights implanted around the edge.

Those lights splashed whitely against the belly of the Skeeter, beamed grainily up at the insect shape that hovered as if suspended by the fog. Its cargo hoist was empty. Its silver belly pivoted slowly on the axis of its top rotor. A ghost ship bobbing on a sea of air.

Rick Erin and Omar Isfahan were trying to wave Cadmann down, motioning with flashlights, talking worriedly into the flat rectangular comcards clipped to their shirt collars.

She could hear Zack's voice over the nearest one, could hear it grow more tense as the hovering Skeeter's transmitter remained mute.

Most of the colony was out now—a forest of frightened, weary faces graven with unanswered questions.

"Cadmann—can you hear me? Come on down. Come on and land, Cadmann. You must be running on fumes anyway. . . . Come on, Cad. We just want to talk to you. We've had some trouble down here, and maybe you can help us understand it. Come on down, Cad. . . ."

There was a long pause, and then Sylvia heard Cadmann's voice. A small, weak, plaintive voice.

"I'm sorry," it said. The Skeeter wobbled as if Cadmann was having trouble flying and talking at the same time. "I didn't mean for anything to go wrong. You've got to understand. There wasn't any way that I could have known how fast that thing is. There w–wasn't any w–way I could have known."

Terry's eyes narrowed as a low mutter swept the crowd. "What the hell happened to him?"

A million possibilities shouted against each other in Sylvia's mind. She remained silent, afraid that anything she said would make the situation worse. Somehow.

"Come on down, Cad. We'll talk about it."

"I . . . I'm coming." The Skeeter floated down, spinning on the axis of the cockpit, settling to ground like a pale blue feather.

At first there was no movement from the Skeeter, just the motionless silhouette in the pilot's seat. Then the door opened, and Cadmann fell out.

Sylvia's scalp crawled. He was burned, scratched and bloodied. His face was chalk, his movements teetering jerkily on the edge of shock.

Carlos hurried to his side, tried to help him, but Cadmann waved him away and levered himself up using the Webley like a crutch.

"No," he gasped. "Get . . . Ernst. You've *got* to believe now."

The other side of the Skeeter was already being opened. Someone gasped, someone cursed; several colonists broke for the open air. The stench of burnt flesh hit Sylvia, triggering a fresh wave of nausea.

"Let me take that," Zack said, forcing nonchalance into his voice. He reached for the rifle.

Cadmann snatched it away, screaming "No! Nobody's taking this from me." He held it white-knuckle tight against his chest. "You're scared, aren't you? Well, it's about time! Maybe some of you will stay alive." He patted the Webley. "Anyone who's smart will get one of these for himself." Cadmann laughed bitterly. "I'm not even sure we can stop it."

Another hand touched him from behind, and Cadmann wheeled, the butt of his rifle raised to strike.

"*Get a—*"

Mary Ann's eyes flew wide as the butt stopped inches from her chest. "Cadmann . . . ?"

He wiped his hand across his forehead. She reached out a hand, and when he didn't take it, she grabbed him, ignoring his feeble attempts to push her away.

"Cadmann, please . . . give me the rifle."

"No."

The pitiful bundle from the passenger seat was unwrapped. Jean Patterson turned away and bent over, gagging hollowly. Hendrick tried to comfort her and she heaved again, staining his pants.

Cadmann took a few steps, stumbled, caught himself. He reached out for Mary Ann this time. She sagged under his weight, then pushed with her strong runner's legs until he was braced against the infirmary wall. "It was . . . it was the monster. It's big. Bigger than a komodo. Fast, like a racing motorcycle! Turns better."

Sylvia knelt to look at the corpse. Terry was behind her, peering over her shoulder, and hissing in disgust. "Komodo, Weyland?" he said incredulously. "Shit. It was sure as hell a dragon, anyway."

She had never seen a human body damaged so badly.

Cadmann's eyes met hers, and there was a naked plea in them. *Please. You believe now, don't you? Don't you?*

"You're hurt. You've lost a lot of blood," she whispered. "We've got to treat those burns."

"Not yet. No sedatives until you believe me." He waved one blackened hand weakly. "Go ahead. There's a tarp on the floor of the Skeeter. In it you'll find a chunk of that goddamned thing. If you can't believe me, you can believe *that.*" He waved them away. "Go ahead—get it. Take it into the lab and for God's sake analyze it."

Two of the lab techs unloaded the chopper. The package was bulky and clumsily wrapped and weighed about two kilos. Sylvia didn't want to unwrap it.

"All right, Cad," she said. "Let's go in and take a look—but you come in and sit down. We can't afford to lose you."

Zack was watching Cadmann's eyes carefully, chewing at the corner of his mustache. Carlos pushed his way through to stand next to Sylvia.

"Carlos," Cadmann said weakly, trying to smile. He moved his mouth as if his lips were half frozen.

"Amigo." There was confusion and mistrust mingled in Carlos's face, and his dark eyes kept straying to Cadmann's makeshift crutch. "We've had a lot of trouble here."

Cadmann was having trouble keeping his eyelids high. "Yeah. Tell me something I don't know."

Several of the colonists had edged almost imperceptibly nearer, and the tension left a metallic taste in Sylvia's mouth. Something ugly was going to happen.

She broke the spell by clearing her throat. "I'm taking this into the lab. I'd like you, Zack, and Terry, and Mary Ann and Carlos. Except for lab personnel, I'd like the rest of you to wait, or go back to bed. There's nothing more to be done tonight, and we're going to need clear, rested minds in the morning."

Without another word she turned and entered the lab. She didn't look behind her, didn't want to, because she didn't want Cadmann to see her confusion. No matter what happened here, and what she found out, they had to get the rifle away from him.

He was mumbling as Carlos and Mary Ann helped him through the door. "Absolutely. Blew off of it when Ernst's fuel pack exploded. Shrapnel must have . . ." He shook his head woozily. Hysterical laughter was bubbling up through the fatigue. "It got a mouthful all right, a real mouthful, and I wish that I'd blown its fucking head clean off—"

"Cad—"

"Stay back." There was still iron in his voice.

"Cadmann," Zack said quietly, watching with eyes that missed nothing, "Alicia is dead. Her baby is gone."

Cadmann said nothing, swallowing hard. "How . . . no . . . *when?"*

"Right after you left. Something got through all of our defenses. Broke through her window. We need your help. But the first thing you've got to do is to put that rifle down."

Sylvia forced her mind to the table in front of her. There was a raging headache coming on, and it was splitting her attention when she needed it most. The only thing she could do for Cadmann now was prove the truth of his claims. The truth, or—

She cut that thought off before it had a chance to take root. He *was* telling the truth. There simply wasn't any other answer.

Not even Terry had accused Cadmann of killing Alicia and her baby. There is a big difference between a calf and a human being—

She sneaked a peek over her shoulder at Cadmann. He was staring at her, eyes dark-rimmed with exhaustion, and she was suddenly afraid.

"I'm cold," Cadmann giggled almost to himself. "A floating anvil. That's a nice image."

"Cadmann—" Sylvia and Mary Ann exchanged looks. "You need rest."

"Not until you look at that sample, damn it. But . . . I'll go into the veterinary room. I'll sit down."

Mary Ann, yellow curls flattening against Cadmann's shirt, his blood staining her nightgown, motioned to Carlos. Together, they helped him into the veterinary clinic and to an examination table. He sat, clutching the rifle.

Sylvia turned from the magnascope screen. "You need plasma, Cadmann. I'm not going on with this until you let us start working on you. You don't want a sedative or anesthetic, fine—macho it out. But I'm damned if you're going to die on me."

"All right, all right."

Jerry grunted relief and prepared a plasma bottle. Carlos peeled Cadmann's blackened shirt away from his right arm.

Cadmann winced, clutching the rifle more tightly. "You should have seen it," he muttered. "If you could see it, you'd understand. It's fast. God, it's fast. I swear it's faster than any animal on Earth. Nothing can move that fast, but it did. Be damned if it didn't."

"Come on, Cad," Mary Ann wheedled. "Put the rifle down for a minute, so that we can get—"

"The hell with that!" he screamed weakly. "I'm not letting this out of my hands until that thing is *dead,* do you hear me? Dead."

Zack whispered to Jerry just before the veterinarian slipped the needle into Cadmann's arm, and set the control on the rectangular box of the plasma pump. It hummed gently, sending healing fluid into Cadmann's veins.

"Don't look at me that way—" Cadmann's voice was pleading, slurred and drunken. He tried to raise his head but it seemed monstrously heavy. It thumped back to the table. The rifle slipped in his grasp a little, and he groaned, tightening his grip.

"Ernst had a bullet hole in him, Cad. We were hoping you could help us with that."

Cadmann, slipping further toward unconsciousness, didn't really hear the irony in Zack's voice. "The monster. It was eating him." He yawned deeply. "Must have hit Ernst. Maybe even tried to. He *screamed,* Zack. Screamed like a woman. He wanted to die—"

Zack made his move, snatching at the rifle. Cadmann twisted the stock and with a short, choppy movement drove the butt into Zack's stomach. Zack staggered back, grunting, face whey-colored.

Cadmann tried to roll from the table and stand, but fell heavily, ripping the I.V. from his arm. Dark fluid drained from the needle and dribbled onto the white tile of the clinic floor. He struggled to gain his feet, make it to his knees before Carlos landed on his shoulders, pinning him down. Zack stumbled back in, wresting the rifle away as Cadmann sobbed and collapsed to the floor.

"Please. Don't . . . just trying . . ." His head sank back to the ground, and he was unconscious.

"Jesus Christ," Carlos whispered, for once his accent forgotten. "What kind of man is he? How much somazine did you pump into that plasma, Jerry?"

"I didn't want to overdo it. Come on. Help me get him on the table."

Sylvia watched Carlos and Terry tie him down. Terry tightened the shackle loop until Cadmann's skin creased.

"Why so tight, Terry?"

"You haven't told us yet," he said nastily. "Is that a piece of Ernst or isn't it?"

"No." Sylvia shook her head, more from fatigue than relief. "I've tried human antigens. It's not calf meat, it's not dog. It reacts to all of them. It's not turkey or chicken, and it's not catfish. So it's alien."

"So he killed a pterodon. So what?"

"I'm tired, Terry. Back off." Her voice was numb. "Jerry—get the liquid nitrogen, would you?"

She tweezed a piece of the meat to a dissection tray, and sliced a quarter-inch piece away. Jerry carried over a ceramic thermos and tipped the lid. The liquid nitrogen, boiling at the touch of room-temperature air, foamed white vapor. Sylvia slipped the sample into the pot.

"We're going to do this right. Cassandra has a complete analysis of every life form we've found on this planet. I'm going to run a gene analysis. It will take about ninety minutes, and we'll have our answer. Is that all right with you, Terry?"

"Don't make me out for a villain," Terry said flatly. "Something terrible just happened here, and I want the truth."

Sylvia removed the frozen section of flesh, and Jerry started up the automated apparatus. A conveyer belt hummed, trundling into a rectangular box of chrome and white enamel. She placed the smoking sample gingerly on its tray, and it disappeared inside. There was a tiny, high-pitched hum as the laser saw sliced the meat into specimens only a few cells thick.

Cassandra would build a holographic model and then compare it in depth with the others in her memory banks. Then they would know. Sylvia wasn't sure that she wanted to.

She turned back to the magnascope, to the tissue sample displayed in a quilt of reds and pale browns. She looked disgusted, tired, heartbroken. "It could be anything. Pterodon. Samlon. Or something we never even dreamed of." It may have only been the terrible fatigue, but a tear welled at the bottom of her eye, and she wiped it away harshly.

"What are we doing here?" She snatched the sample tray from under the scope and hurled it across the room. It broke with a tinkle of crystal, and a spatter of clear fluid against the yellow plaster. "Just why the hell did we come?"

"We're all tired," Zack said. "It's going to be a couple of hours before we have answers?"

"Close enough," Jerry agreed.

"Then let's get some rest. Before this is over, we'll need every bit of it we can get. All right?"

Carlos looked at the wall, at the still form of his friend, strapped now to the table. "What about Cadmann?"

"I honestly don't know," Zack said wearily. "But I know that I'm too tired and sore to think. I need some rest. He'll keep."

"Everyone but Jerry out of here," Sylvia said.

"I want to stay." Mary Ann stood against the wall, her arms folded, eyes fixed on Cadmann.

Zack was still massaging his stomach, feeling for bruised ribs. Every few seconds he wheezed in pain. He said, "Carlos, take care of Mary Ann. We need to clear out so that Syl and Jerry can work."

"No, I'm not—"

Sylvia closed her mind to the sound until she heard the door close behind them.

Then she and Jerry methodically stripped Cadmann, sprayed his burns and minor wounds and covered them with gel. When they were done with the hemostats and the dissolving thread and the unguents, they slipped him into a clean smock and refastened the straps. Then they turned out the lights and left.

She shivered in the fog. Jerry turned to her. "What do you think happened out there? You don't really think Cadmann did that damage to *himself?*"

"I don't know. I don't know anything right now. We'll know in a little over an hour. Just let me close my eyes for a few minutes."

Jerry nodded and started back to his cottage, to the dubious, transitory comfort of a warm bed, when Sylvia's voice stopped him.

"I can tell you one thing, Jerry. No matter what we find out, we're not going to like it. I promise you that there aren't going to be any comforting answers."

"Yeah." Jerry hunched his shoulders against the chill. He turned to speak again, but Sylvia had already disappeared around a corner, or into the fog, and he was alone.

CHAPTER 9

CONTACT

A man that studieth revenge keeps his own wounds green.

FRANCIS BACON

IN THE SHADOWS beyond the fence, something watched. Something alive, silent, almost motionless save for the rise and fall of its torn and bleeding flanks.

The creature was badly hurt. It had passed the horizon of pain into territory that was strange indeed. Irreversible changes had taken place in its body. In a distant way, it even understood that it was dying. But first there was an obligation.

It hid in the shadowed fields beyond the reach of the searchlights. When it concentrated it could smell *the man*, the one who had hurt it. This one, whom it had badly underestimated, was the real threat. And every instinct screamed for it to get to him, to find and kill him.

It began to wiggle forward. It lay between rows of corn, just a few dozen meters southwest of the colony. The searchlights still swept across the ground, and the men still walked the edge of the camp.

How to get past the firevines? It moaned hungrily.

In the next instant the solution presented itself. One of the men ran his forepaw along a section of vine. He touched it—leaned on it. It recognized the section. This was the same stretch of firevine that had bitten it before. It seemed safe now. Perhaps firevines could only bite once. . . .

The man was alone and not even looking in its direction. Now. Now, as the searchlights crisscrossed, there was a moment in which darkness was almost total, when shadow licked the fence, the man, and a stretch leading almost to the fields.

It moved.

It moved as fast as a Skeeter skimming at low altitude, moved so fast that the man at the fence hardly had time to look up, had no time to scream before it hit the fence with such momentum that the aluminum fencepost buckled and the lines snapped, that its impact slammed him back into the wall of the veterinary clinic.

His head dimpled the sheet metal and rebounded directly into the creature's flailing spiked tail. It shook the man's head free of the spikes, let the corpse slide to the ground.

It flowed onward, a quarter ton of rippling muscle and bone, black as a shadow, as dark and fluid as the river flowing behind and beneath the bluff, as much a part of the night as the stars or the twin moons.

The creature nudged the door open. It sniffed tentatively at first, then entered.

There was little light inside, but it needed less than it found. Animals were caged along the walls. Curiosity was almost as intense as the pain and resolve, and it stopped for a moment to peer up into one of the cages. A small white shape curled up in the corner, hidden in a mass of wood shavings. The tiny alien stirred slowly, then jerked to wakefulness, staring, blinking its tiny red eyes.

The creature had seen that look before, many times before. Total submission. A trembling readiness, the prey's acknowledgement that it was ready to be food. No running. No fighting, its heart ready to burst before it was ever touched.

Not now. The creature could smell *the man,* and it turned toward the smell.

The man lay on a table. He moaned softly, and moved limbs that seemed tangled in short vines. That was just as well. It had no urge to play with this one.

It braced its paws on the table, stretching, feeling the hurts in its body, the pain along its sides where it was burned and torn. The long wound in its flank opened again, trickling fluid. It braced itself and tried to jump up onto the table. The table was not a boulder. It tilted. The safety blocks on the wheels popped free, and the table skidded across the room, tubes ripping free of *the man's* forelimb, dark fluid spraying as they crashed into the wall and the table flipped onto its side.

As the table thudded to the floor, *the man's* eyes fluttered open.

Their eyes met.

Here it was. Here was the moment it craved. Here was the moment when the hunger and the pain and the anger vanished, and it saw into those eyes as down a deep, chill waterhole, a bottomless grotto. *The man's* eyes grew wide, wide enough to sink in, to swim in. The creature drew closer.

This was the deadly one. His skin was so soft, so fragile. It pawed experimentally, raking away flesh. Blood streamed from pinkish pulp beneath. The man grimaced, showed his teeth. Small teeth, flat and harmless.

The man was so weak! and yet he had hurt it as nothing else in its short life. *The man* was at the moment of death, his limbs bound, drawing back as far as he could, shrinking against the table, but his eyes held nothing of submission. His sluggish muscles struggled in the bonds.

So much had changed so quickly in its life. And this one Man had been at the center of so much of it. End it now.

But his eyes. They met its own so steadily. Helpless, bound, about to die—and yet . . .

And yet . . .

There was a scream from outside, and a sound of pounding feet. Its attention was split by confusion and uncertainty. It turned back to *the man* and saw triumph in his eyes, and it knew that somehow he had won, they would win, and that its life was over.

Pain bit into the back of its head, and it spun as a second bullet missed it by inches. It charged directly at the man holding a long stick which spat fire.

It felt another, awful pain, and then it was on him, his head in its mouth. There was a moment of bony resistance to its jaw muscles, then splintering collapse and softness. It spat him out and rushed for the door.

If it could reach the river . . .

But the doorway was crowded with men and their firesticks. It howled its agony, reversed directions, flailing its tail at them, feeling the pain bite deep until the thing in its body triggered, and the entire world seemed made of blood.

It exploded in the other direction. There were more of the vinelike things, and small metal objects. Strange smells filled the room as liquids spilled. The walls of this cave were thin, and bulged when the tail struck them. Instantly it wheeled. The head smashed at the thin walls. Something ripped open. An entire corner fell away. Outside was night, and the chance to find the river, to shed the heat that was cooking it from inside.

One man blocked its way, and it slammed its tail into him, the spikes piercing his leg.

It couldn't shake him loose! He screamed and screamed, confusing and slowing it, even with *speed* raging in its body and fire raging in its mind.

Another flick of the tail smashed him against the corner of a building. It pulled its spikes free, leaving him leaking and moaning on the ground.

But the men were everywhere now, and it ran this way and that, plowing into them, its body spasming, out of control now, blind with the blood in its eyes.

CHAPTER 10

NIGHTMARE

I fled, and cried out, Death;
Hell trembled at the hideous noise, and sighed
From all her caves, and back resounded, Death.

JOHN MILTON, *Paradise Lost: Book II*

SOUNDS . . .

Someone screaming. A shot?

Sylvia groped her way up from a dream that clung like a moist membrane. The bubble of groggy sleep thinned as she wavered near wakefulness.

Tactile: Terry next to her, behind her. She felt the soft swell of his stomach against her backbone as they nestled like spoons.

Visual: Darkness. Outside, filtered by the drapes, a dim light glowed. Searchlight's glow. All was well.

Auditory: The heavy, liquid sound of Terry's snoring. Nothing new or unusual there.

Sleep yawned, beckoned.

No. Wrong thought, wrong time. Her eyes fought to focus in the dark, to find the clock. How long had she slept? Was it time to get up again—?

Another sharp *crack* of sound, unmistakably a shot. A searchlight briefly lit the drapes. From all around the camp came shouted inquiries, groggy at first, then alarmed.

She lurched up in bed, throat scratchy with sleep, groping out for the reassuring warmth and protection of her clothing. "Terry. Terry—"

"Mmmph. Fug." Terry rolled onto his stomach, surprised when her body wasn't there to support him. His arm flopped out. "Huh? Sylvie?"

She was already pulling on her pants. Terry's fingers stretched out grazingly, and brushed one of her nipples. A wave of desire warmed her, startled her with its strength.

Terry, you pick the damnedest times.

She shut that part of her mind down and focused on the window, on the wildly swinging lights that filtered in through the drapes.

Terry came fully awake as Sylvia slipped on her shoes.

"What fool's raising the roof now?"

"I don't know. It's by the animal pens, and—"

And the veterinary clinic.

"Cadmann," she whispered.

A volley of shots. Terry virtually levitated from the bed.

"What in the hell—?"

There was screaming now. "Hurry up." She paused just long enough to be sure that he was rolling out of bed, then ran for the courtyard.

The huts were generally divided into two sections, sleeping and living. Although the communal dining halls were used by all, many— *most* of the colonists had their own private cooking facilities and a place to entertain friends. The space that she shared with Terry was small and might have been considered cozy, a place of warmth and—

She crossed the courtyard and stopped in horror. Figures backed out of the clinic. They were shrouded in darkness and fog that swirled like milk in thin tea. Four stylized shadows, posed—four generic riflemen. They fired into the doorway. Something within was screaming and shaking the building like a rat caught in a milk carton, screaming with such energized venom that for a moment she was frozen in her tracks.

She made herself move. A row of garden tools leaned neatly against one of the huts and Sylvia snatched one in a two-handed death grip. She circled the bungalow, seeking a glimpse within.

No room in the doorway. Thank God! But she had to get closer. She recognized one of the riflemen. "Carolyn! What is it?"

There was no answer. Carolyn McAndrews and her companions

fired wildly, fired without targets. *They're crazy!* Rifle bullets tore through the metal walls of the veterinary clinic. There were sounds of shattering glass from three buildings away. "For God's sake, what's happening?"

Colonists poured into the main boulevard outside the clinic. Robes and pajama bottoms still being pulled on, bare chests and legs or fully armed and dressed perimeter guards, they sprouted out of the darkness. Steps pounded behind her. Terry grabbed her arm. "What—?"

The metal wall of the veterinary shack cracked wide. Something screamed. The sound locked every muscle in her body. *They're not crazy at all,* she thought, and, *It's come.* The crowd scattered as the metal sheeting peeled back farther, distended, and something black smashed through the opening.

Terry's grip was like a vise. "Oh migod. He was right—!"

"Cadmann!" Sylvia tore free from her husband. He caught her again and pulled her back as the creature bounded into the crowd. Death was alive in the night, no longer something which haunted their dreams, no longer a specter to be buried with Alicia and the bloodied scraps of swaddling. It was alive, and glistening, and it moved among them like a demon of muscle and scale and teeth.

It moved too quickly for Sylvia to get a distinct picture. Dark! Too damned dark! And the searchlights swiveling to cover it were woefully inadequate, jerking spastically around the yard.

For a moment the monster was halted by a ring of colonists with sticks and guns. It stood at bay against the shattered remains of the veterinary-clinic wall. Handlamps, then the searchlight from the watchtower swung toward it. Sylvia saw eyes the size of oranges with huge black pupils. In the same moment those pupils closed to pinpoints. It hissed. Blood sprayed from a dozen wounds that ranged from neat punctures to raw craters, a red brighter than arterial blood. The massive tail smashed at the sheet metal. The screams smashed at the ears.

For just that instant it was contained, and then—

The pupils opened slightly. The creature shook the blood from its eyes and moved. Sylvia gasped. A good racing car might have accelerated that fast. Terry pulled hard on her arm and they were both falling backward as the monster smashed through the line. Two good men flew away like dry leaves in an autumn whirlwind, and one kicked Terry across the forehead as he flew over, all before Sylvia hit the ground.

She crawled behind a huge reel of insulated wire.

The great tail swung. There were spikes on the end—and Barney

Carr flopped helplessly along the ground, spiked through the leg, as the monster whipped this way and that. Barney's head cracked into the corner of a building; his face disappeared in a smear of blood. The creature shook him loose and he lay still, only his hands clenching and unclenching spastically. Zack Moscowitz appeared from the shadows to stand over Barney. Tears streamed from his eyes. "Damn you!" he screamed. The creature turned.

Terry staggered up, muttered, "It's *killing* them!" He looked about wildly, then jerked an iron rod from a stack of fence stakes leaning against a shed. He glanced back at Sylvia, just one frightened flicker of his eyes.

"Terry—"

He turned away, turned to stand between hell and his wife and unborn daughter.

"Terry!"

He was already part of the melee.

The creature was *big*, larger than a large crocodile, and built like a tank: compact, invulnerable. It shouldn't have been fast—but, wounded and bleeding, it moved faster than anything ever bred on Earth. It leaped from the circle. Armed colonists ran to surround it. Others fired when they could see nobody behind it. Even as they ran it moved again, and again, so that they couldn't surround it.

Sylvia had never seen, never heard of anything that could move like that: streaking across the dirt, losing its balance and skidding to a stop; waiting, then blurring aside from a scattered volley of bullets. Move, stop, warily scan its enemies, see their intentions and move again— Thank God that it seemed more interested in escape than destruction, but even as it thrashed blindly it left death behind.

Red silk kimono and pale blond hair flagging behind her, Jean Patterson ran for her life. Before she could reach the safety of her hut she met the flailing spikes of the monster's tail. Her truncated scream was a barking sound in the night, and she skidded and flopped along the ground to crumple close by Sylvia's concealing coil of wire.

"Jean!"

She stared up blindly, her head twisted far around. Too far. The spine was crushed. Dr. Patterson thrashed without feeling.

Jon van Don ran to intercept the monster and haplessly blocked its way as it fled toward the road. Instantly the monster was on him. It crushed him to the ground and left him behind, but its claws had pierced and dug, ripped through jacket and pajamas and skin, snapped bone and drove jagged ribs into lungs. The searchlight slid over him to show pink bloody froth at his mouth and nose. His screams never stopped.

Sylvia clapped her hands over her ears and squeezed her eyes shut. It wasn't enough. She couldn't shut out the sounds and flashes of light: the shots, the screams, the slap of feet, and finally, the wave of heat that tore her from her cocoon. She couldn't help it, she peered through her fingers—

Greg. Somehow he had roused himself from drug-induced slumber. He staggered, legs mere rubber, but his face was a mask of rage as he advanced on the creature. On his back, slung skewed with only one of its shoulder straps buckled down, was one of the flame throwers that had been used to burn the bramble bushes from the plain. Its nozzle spewed a twenty-foot stream of liquid hell. Flame licked at the monster's bloody hide, and it reared in shock.

He was shouting something. She couldn't really hear his words over the roar of the flames, the human sounds of anguish and terror, the bellow of the creature. But she knew: Greg was screaming obscenities, the things she would be saying if her own wife and child—

Husband?

"Terry?" She couldn't see him, but there were bodies everywhere, people crawling and sobbing, and the B-movie monster skittering around the quad trying to find a way back to the darkness—the river?—its tail to the power shed now. It hissed as Greg advanced.

It sat there for a moment, and then with the speed of a flea jumping from a complete standstill, it leaped at Greg.

Greg didn't even flinch, too far gone with grief and rage to care. A tongue of flame lanced out and met the thing in midair with a horrific *whoosh!* that stole the dark and chill from the night. It hit the thing squarely, in one eye-searing moment converting it into a thrashing blur of fire.

But that wasn't what saved Greg. Sylvia had seen the creature's bullet-torn hind leg collapse as it leaped. It was sideways to Greg as the flame caught it, and it dropped in front of him, burning, motionless.

It was dead. It *had* to be dead—nothing could possibly survive the bullets, the fire—and Greg sent a steady tongue of flame licking into it. Flame rolled up from its body and exploded against the shack behind it, jellied gasoline spattering everywhere.

Then it moved. Without any warning sign at all the damned corpse was moving again. George Merriot leaped away, too slowly; the creature brushed him and he was aflame.

The burning man thrashed on the ground, arms flopping, trying to put out the jellied gasoline sticking to his jacket and pants. Rachel Moscowitz was battering at him with a blanket. Bobby Erin whipped off his robe and slapped it onto George, totally unconcerned by his own resulting nudity. All eyes were on the monster.

The monster had gained twenty meters toward the river cliff in the blink of an eye, and once again was motionless.

The smell of fuel and burnt flesh boiled up from it in nauseatingly dense clouds of oily smoke.

It moved. Its tail was a sudden blur, and then an impossible living fireball streaked for the river, fifteen good meters this time. Through the smoke and flame she could see its head wagging slowly, agonizingly, as if trying to orient itself. Its tail lashed mindlessly.

Greg followed, firing the flame thrower not in bursts but in a single continuous stream. He laughed and cried hysterically, unmindful of the havoc he was wrecking. "You—stay still—Alicia—you—" Firing the flame thrower at the tail had the same effect as firing it at a spinning propeller: a blur, a thin, curdled mist of flame.

Buildings were afire all around them. Stu Ellington, his moon face ruddy with fear and adrenaline exhaustion, cried, "God's sake, Greg, put it out! Put the damned thing out! The animal's dead!"

Stu shouldered a rifle, aiming not at the dying thing wrapped in a web of flame, but at Greg.

"Greg—" Greg didn't, couldn't hear the order, but the flame-thrower tanks spat out their last breath of fire and were empty. Trembling, Stu lowered the barrel to the ground.

"You, die, die, damn you, die—" Sylvia was startled to hear her own voice, hear herself chanting, not knowing when she had started it, knowing only an intensely morbid fascination with the thing that—

It moved, and this last leap took it over the edge of the bluff. It didn't even scream as it fell.

"Get it!" Zack bawled instantly. "Don't let it get away." Colonists ran toward fires and the injured. Zack grabbed randomly. "Jill. Harry. Ricky—no, Jesus, get some drawers on. Mits. Get a steel net on that thing's body. It's almost dead, but don't take any chances *and don't let the body wash away.*"

Sylvia pulled herself erect. Something had bruised her ankle. She pulled the robe about her swollen stomach. *I should do something—* Smoke and blood and the stench of cooking monster flesh filled the air.

A dozen bodies lay scattered and bleeding. Jean Patterson broken and twisted and still at last. Jon van Don, Sylvia's next-door neighbor, his face a mask of blood, fumbled with numbing fingers to stanch wounds across his midsection. Scenes from newsreels, from long-past wars on Earth. Sylvia wandered blindly through hell. "Terry!"

He must be all right. He must be helping to put out the fires—

Flames grew everywhere. Tanks spat white foam into the wreckage.

A thin current of wailing was an incessant background to her every thought. Broken glass and wood and plastic crunched under her every step, and Sylvia was losing it, tottering on the brink of overload. *We had time. We should have been ready. We should have known. Cadmann warned—*

Cadmann. Cadmann's still in the clinic!

She was running before she knew it. One slipper flew off, and the bare pad of her foot skinned along the ground. There was no one at the door of the infirmary, and at first she thought that it was empty. Then she saw Mary Ann and Carlos hunched over Cadmann.

Cadmann wasn't moving. Blood oozed from a dozen wounds.

She fought to get in next to him. Mary Ann turned and glared at her. "We can take care of this," she said, and her voice was frigid. "He warned you, damn you. God damn you to hell. He *trusted* you. And you tried to kill him. Go on. I'm sure that your husband needs you somewhere."

Carlos's dark face was sliced along the chin, a wound that oozed blood onto his green sleeveless shirt. She reached out to touch him. He spoke without turning. "No. It's all right. Why don't you get a first-aid kit and see who needs help?" He didn't try to smile, but there was no hostility in his face. "Go on, Señora Faulkner."

Unconscious, Cadmann groaned as Mary Ann's fingers tenderly probed his wounds.

Sylvia backed out of the room, grabbing the first-aid kit as she went, mumbling, "I'm sorry. I'm so sorry. I tried—" But no one was listening to her anymore.

THERE WAS so much damage—everywhere. Her emotions were in such a snarl that it was impossible to find a loose end, somewhere she could begin to unravel.

She counted the blanket-draped figures that she could see. At least four corpses. Three times that many wounded, and some would be dead by morning. She walked stiff-legged and numb, desperate to find a way to make herself useful.

Terry. She heard his voice to the left, barking orders. He was working with three other men to quell a blaze roaring in one of the storage sheds. Her mind wasn't working. She wasn't thinking clearly, and she wanted to, badly. What did they store in that shed? What . . . ?

The sudden realization hit her, and she screamed. "Terry!"

He turned. "Sylvia! Get back!" The sheer ferocity and alarm in his voice took her by such surprise that she did back up, and then she was off her feet, feeling the wall of air before she saw the light or heard the sound.

The shed behind Terry mushroomed into a fireball, and the men with him screamed, twitching like moths caught in a Bunsen burner. The edge of the fireball lifted Terry and flipped him into a stack of tools where he lay, clothes smoldering, as the camp burned. . . .

IMPRESSIONS:

Blackened faces, bandages. Wisps of smoke rising from twisted alloy support struts. A sky gray with ash, a dawn welcomed with low, despairing moans.

Wars must look like this, Sylvia thought. Cadmann would know—

The communal dining hall was smoke-damaged but otherwise unharmed. Now it held most of the Colony, excluding those too badly wounded to be moved.

There was little sound in the room save the few mingled, stifled sobs. She felt what nobody spoke of: the sense of relief from those who had come through the ordeal with hides and families intact. *The unwounded. There aren't any unwounded. We've all been hurt.* Sylvia thought. A fragment of song came to her. *Sometimes I feel like a motherless child. A long way from home.*

"Mary Ann—"

Mary Ann paused in her endless rounds among the wounded.

"Is Cadmann—?"

"He's alive."

"Don't go! Terry. Where is Terry?"

Mary Ann's mouth was a grim line. "He'll live. I think."

"Live—"

"Maybe. I have to go. You're not hurt. You're all right. So is your baby."

Sylvia let that thought sink in. The baby is all right. . . . Another shadow fell across her. Zack wandered aimlessly through the room with a bullhorn, counting the wounded, trying to get a feel for the extent of the damage. His eyes were red and puffy. Carolyn McAndrews followed him, a sallow wraith at Zack's heels.

Zack climbed onto a dining table and raised his bullhorn. "I don't know what to say." He paused. There was silence. "We . . . we have more than enough medicine and bandages." The bullhorn bellowed his voice: gravelly, ruined by an endless night of screaming. "If there are any bite victims that I am presently unaware of, please . . ." He wavered, losing focus, and Rachel steadied him.

Sylvia felt herself coughing, watched herself raise an unsteady hand. "Zack—what do we do now? What do we do about the defenses?"

"Full alert, of course, we activate the mine field. The electric fences. But— Goddamn it, Sylvia, you know that thing was impossible! Impossible! We couldn't have expected *that*. It's a fluke. Nothing that large can live on this island, the ecology can't support it. There's no food chain. You said that yourself! It swam over from the mainland, it must have, and how could I have known it could do that?" He wiped his forehead with a grimy hand. His voice cracked. "There just isn't enough food to support it."

"It got here, didn't it?" Ida van Don screamed. Her face was chalk, except for the smear of blood on the left side of her face. "It got—" She couldn't get the rest out, and buckled over with sobs. Phyllis draped a blanket over her shoulders.

"Not enough food," Sylvia said. She tried unsuccessfully to hold back her own tears. "Yes, I said that. All right, Zack, it wasn't your fault! Is that what you want on your tombstone? It wasn't your fault? Zack, it couldn't be, it shouldn't be, but it's *here*, and you can't *know* there aren't more, and what in the hell do we do about it?"

"Mary Ann would have a suggestion." Carlos's voice was dry and carefully controlled.

Zack's lips drew taut. His hands shook. Rachel took the microphone. Her voice was as raw as her husband's. "Is that a suggestion or a demand, Carlos?"

"Neither. Not yet, anyway."

"Then we needn't worry about it yet. Sylvia, all serious suggestions are welcome. We *know* we need more security. Please, all of you, be assured that until the entire situation has stabilized, no aspect of security will be neglected. But we have to start somewhere—right now, we have to make sure that a total inventory of the damage and losses is made, and that all of the wounds are dealt with. Yes—Andy?"

The engineer stood. His right arm was strapped to his chest. "This wasn't supposed to happen. Nothing like this was supposed to happen. I was . . . We can't go home!"

Jill Ralston, the slender redhead from agriculture, stood. Both of her hands were wrapped in burn gauze. "Dammit, I saw that freaking animal take over a hundred rounds, and half a tank of jellied fuel. It was in the water, and the water *smoked.* We got a net around it, and its tail was still twitching! It had to be dead, just spasms—but I'm telling you that it almost killed the three of us. If there had been five of them, they could have killed everyone in the camp."

"Five—hell if it would have needed five!" Ricky shouted.

Rachel tried to speak, but despite the microphone she was drowned out in the babble.

"One. One more would finish us!"

"Cadmann was right all the time, damn, why didn't we listen to the colonel?—"

"Ten lightyears, ten years away—"

"Power plant's finished—"

"Vet shed—"

"The biology lab's wrecked—"

Zack took the microphone and waved his hand. "Enough! Listen, damn it!" The babble died away. "Look, we're not going to get productive work done until we rebuild the camp, and we can't do that until our minds are at rest."

"Yeah, sure, relax," La Donna called. "Good old Zack. No-o-o problems."

"Cut the crap. It doesn't help the situation if everyone talks at once. Look, chances are we *won't* find another one of these—things. No sense in taking chances, we'll take precautions, but damn it, science is science. There's nothing for it to live on here. There won't be more of them—"

"How the hell can you *know* that?"

"There couldn't have been *that* one—"

"Stop! You're scientists and engineers, and the best people that could be chosen from a half billion applicants, and God damn it, *act like it!*

"All right. Now, just to be sure, we'll put a study team on the problem. Immediately. What do we have that will kill these . . . monsters . . . and do it efficiently? We'll find out!"

"I think we need atomic bombs," Andy said. Two people laughed. Andy sat down again.

Zack spoke through pain, pushing his voice when it should have been allowed to rest. "We weren't prepared. Whether we ever run into another of those or not, we'll soon know what will kill it. One person by himself should be able to do it. We'll find out. I swear. This is *our island*, and I'm not turning it over to any goddamned monster. *Ours*, do you understand?"

"Right." Carolyn McAndrews stood and applauded. After several seconds others joined wearily. Sylvia rose and left the room.

She walked out through the door, out into the camp, where smoke still rose from the twisted struts. Three buildings had been totally destroyed. The power plant looked bad. People dug in the ruins, trying to find valuables or irreplaceables.

Here was the hospital. Its normal five beds had been expanded to twenty. Most of the wounds would heal, thank God, but a few, just a few . . .

Terry for instance.

Terry lay torpid in a bath of saline solution. Jerry was checking Terry's wounds as Sylvia came through the door, and his face was grim. "We may have to amputate the right leg. The bones are shattered."

She nodded numbly and sat down in a folding chair next to him. Terry was still unconscious, filled with painkillers. His skin was reddish and peeling, as if he had been staked out in the Mojave for days.

"He's lucky to be alive," Jerry said.

"We're all lucky," Sylvia said soberly. "Somehow, that doesn't make things any easier."

There was one figure conspicuously absent from the expanded hospital, one figure that she wanted desperately to see. Jerry caught the look in her eye. "We moved Cadmann back to his hut. He damned well insisted. He's taking food there. I don't know. He's very weak, but there are others who need help more. He'll heal—"

Sylvia half stood, but Jerry's hand tugged at her. "Name of God, Sylvia. You're not the only one who's sorry. We screwed up, and we're paying for it. But you can't do any good. How do you think Terry's going to feel if he wakes up and you're not here? Let it be."

She twisted her arm in his hand, and then finally sat back again. Drained. "There isn't anything to be done."

"Nothing. We've got the body out of the river, and as soon as the wounded are stabilized, we'll be able to spare you. Until then . . . you're a doctor, not a lovesick schoolgirl. This is your husband. For God's sake act like it."

A slap across the face couldn't have shocked her more, and she nodded. "I . . . I'm sorry, Jerry."

"Being sorry doesn't count for shit. Broken bones don't care how you feel. They just need to be set."

What time was it? How long had Jerry been working while she luxuriated in her grief? It had been twenty hours since the attack. It had probably been two days since Jerry had slept, and he was still going. Shame swept through the depths of her. But in its wake was resolve, and a kind of nervous energy. She stood. "Jerry, thank you. There's a time for self-pity, and this isn't it. How long has it been since you slept?"

Jerry smiled raggedly, running his hand through a thatch of hair that looked as limp and tired as the rest of him. "Sleep. Sounds familiar. It sounds like something I read about once."

"Get out of here, and don't come back for at least six hours. Doctor's orders."

"Are you all right?"

"Now I am. I have to pass the favor on. Scoot."

Jerry took a last look around the infirmary and shuffled off, grabbing his coat on the way out.

Sylvia rolled up her sleeves, and touched her stomach gingerly. The baby was fine, she could feel that. If anything had happened . . .

But now there was work to be done.

A war zone. That was what it looked like in here. A goddamned war zone.

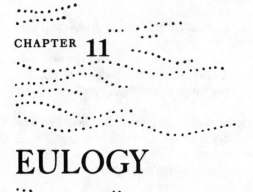

CHAPTER 11

EULOGY

He is gone from the mountain,
He is lost to the forest,
Like a summer-dried fountain
When our need was the sorest.

SIR WALTER SCOTT, *The Lady of the Lake*

FOR SYLVIA, the next three days were a stabilizing time, a time of learning who was going to die, and who would live. They lost three more during that time, raising the death toll to twelve.

It seemed that none but the dead slept during those days. There just wasn't enough painkiller or somazine to keep the wounded asleep.

If only . . .

That game was too easy, and too painful to play. "If onlys" turned wishes into guilty visions, turned thoughts of mine fields and guards and infrared scans into haunted caves, vast cobwebbed torture chambers where her sleep-starved mind whipped and racked her without mercy.

She was pregnant, and she couldn't deny it or hide it, and so every night when others went back to the hospital after dinner she was driven into bed, and given orders not to show her face until morning.

But the guilt and the pain and the sheer stark *need* drove her on. She saw Zack. He was going harder than she. Perhaps harder than anyone. And if she knew that her dreams were pits of despair and self-recrimination, his were beyond her imagining.

Her life during those vital hours was consumed with the wounded —the burns, the bites and punctures, the broken bones and ruptured internal organs, the cuts, nervous exhaustion, fatigue, shell shock and even a bullet wound.

But Zack had to pore over Andy's reports as the engineer corps examined the damage. The biology lab was almost totally destroyed. The power plant looked wounded, but was in fact dead. The plasma toroid was punctured; the only replacements within ten lightyears were in the motors of the Minerva vehicles.

And in three days, after the worst had passed—after all the fences were mended, the first tentative inventory taken and all the medical cases stabilized—it was Zack who performed the service at the mass burial.

No preachers. We didn't want any. No preachers, no rabbi, no priests. We are the scientists, rational, thoughtful—was that wise?

"They died that we might live," Zack began.

She thought of the last funeral she'd attended, the last time when she had felt grief gnawing at her like a living thing—the day they buried her father, only six months after her mother was laid to rest. The day she had turned from the rolling green expanse, the endless rows of white markers at Arlington National Cemetery and flown home without a word to anyone. And upon returning home made her final decision to accept the offered berth aboard *Geographic*. That day, and its decision, and the accompanying grief were like a wood-grain finish buried under layers of cheap, cloudy shellac. It only came to mind when she thought of how very much her mother would have wanted to touch her stomach, to hold her and cry happily with her as women cry, rejoicing in the torch of life being passed from one generation to the next.

No, today was worse. One hundred and seventy-four survivors were here for the ceremony, all those who could be moved from their beds.

Sylvia held Terry's hand as he sat in his wheelchair. The word wasn't final on his spinal damage yet, but the irony was crushing.

We've got good news and bad news.

The good news is that we won't have to amputate his left leg!

The bad news is that his spinal cord was severed, and he'll never walk again anyway.

There were twelve graves and a thirteenth marker. April, Alicia's baby, the first child born on this new world, had never been found.

Greg stood near them, and there was a quality in his face that she had associated with Ernst since the Hibernation Instability. His face was empty.

It fit. Everything fit together, a mosaic that began with the endless expanse of dappled gray clouds and the thin stream of smoke rising from the smoldering tip of a volcano just the far side of the horizon.

Perhaps most of all, what fit was Cadmann. She saw him out of the corner of her left eye, standing alone, with Mary Ann. Strange how that phrasing came to her. Mary Ann stood near him, almost touching him, but they might have been strangers in a subway: intimate through proximity, yet each sealed in his own world.

Cadmann's head turned, and he looked at Sylvia, through her, and she longed to cry out to him, realized through his inaccessibility how very much she cared.

But Terry's hand gripped hers, and Zack's voice called her from her reverie.

". . . that we might live. All of us knew the risks, but these—these few paid the price for our mistake. With time, all of us will lie beneath this soil. Let these . . . thirteen . . . be the last to die by violence. Let our loss merely strengthen our resolve, deepen our commitment."

He cleared his throat. Usually he reminded Sylvia of Groucho Marx. There was no hint of comedy now. He looked old and tired and frightened. "Does anyone want to speak?"

There was a moment's silence, then Greg spoke in a voice that was pure venom. "Why didn't we listen? Why couldn't we have listened? Did Cadmann ask for so much?"

"Greg . . ." Zack's voice was soft. "This isn't the time."

"Piss on you!" Spittle flew from the corner of his mouth. "We combed this goddamned island from one end to the other, and we didn't find a fucking thing. *Now* we can't find anything, and people are already starting to say that that must have been the only monster. That it swam over from the mainland. That's *bullshit* . . ."

"Greg—"

"*Fuck* you, Zack. I trusted you. We all trusted you. You were supposed to be the one with the big view. *Alicia trusted you.* And now she's . . . she . . ."

Tears streamed from his eyes and he collapsed to his knees at Alicia's grave, his fingers clawing at the earth, all the pent-up emotion exploding out of him at once. It was a trigger. Others were crying now, quietly or with great wracking sobs.

From the corner of her eye, Sylvia saw Cadmann turn on his crutches and hobble away. Silent, solitary again, vindicated by death, dishonored by the only family he would ever have.

IN TIME Sylvia lost herself in the work, and in greater time the flow of the work itself began to slow. Nobody was unaffected by the grief, and in a way it turned into a bond stronger than the original heigh-ho *Manifest Destiny* enthusiasm that had built an interstellar expedition.

Repairs were underway around the clock. In the middle of the mistiest night, the sparkle of laser and plasma torches lit the gloom like dazzling fireflies.

Within another week, what had happened had become a symbol almost as much as a reality. The electric wire around the periphery of the camp had been reinforced, reestablishment of full power given the highest priority. Guard shifts were doubled. Every night, several times a night, Sylvia awoke from troubled slumber, to be lulled back to sleep by the silent bob and swivel of the searchlights.

The mine field had been reactivated, providing the first dark moment of humor since the tragedy.

At just after three in the morning, a hollow explosion had shaken the camp. Frightened, hastily dressed colonists had joined guards outside the gates to find a storm of feathers still drifting down: a prodigal turkey had returned.

Grim jokes about turkey *bombe* and *flambé* had circulated for the next two days, and had helped the healing begin.

SYLVIA ceased her efforts to write a new voice-recognition program into Cassandra as a familiar, disturbing figure limped past her window.

Cadmann. A crutch under his right arm, side bandaged, a ragged, badly healed scar creasing his cheek in a false smile. A silent giant with dark, accusing eyes.

He spoke to no one, taking his meals and medication in his hut. No one challenged him. No one dared to tell him that he should not hate them for what had been done. In her mind Sylvia could see that *thing* squatting atop Cadmann, grinning down at him, slowly raking the flesh from his body.

For a warrior of Cadmann's nature to have been disarmed, doped, tied and then *abandoned* to be monster bait was an insult so deep that there was nothing that could be said. And so, to their communal shame, nothing was.

* * *

TWO WEEKS later, the door to her lab opened without warning. Zack Moscowitz came in.

"Well, he's gone."

"Hi, Zack."

"That Skeeter you heard. Cadmann stole it."

"Stole—"

"Or borrowed. He didn't say. We tried the radio. He isn't answering, and he's disconnected the tracer. We don't know where he's going, or why."

"You know why," Sylvia said. "He's telling us all to go to hell. And maybe we deserve it."

"Yeah." Moscowitz sighed heavily. "Yeah, I know. Some idiot suggested we go after him and get the Skeeter back. I didn't bother to ask for volunteers."

"So he's gone."

"Him, and he damn near dismantled his hut. He's also got two dogs, a rifle, ammunition and a case of liquor."

"It's his rifle. He'll have tools, too," Sylvia said thoughtfully. "And if you add it all up, it won't come to more than his share."

"The Skeeter's a lot more than his share."

"He'll bring it back."

"Did he tell you that?"

Sylvia laughed. "Don't I wish. No, but he will. He hasn't any use for a Skeeter, Zack. He isn't out to hurt the Colony. He just wants— anyway, you watch, he won't take more than his share."

"Yeah. I guess I always knew that. Goddamn him!" Zack exploded. "Hell, Sylvia, it isn't the stuff he took! It's him. We need the son of a bitch."

"And if you'd—"

"And if I'd said it loud enough and early enough he'd still be here. Yeah. Thanks for reminding me."

THE SKEETER returned eight hours later. It landed two kilometers from the camp. Everyone came outside, but no one wanted to go closer. After a moment Cadmann creakily levered himself out of the cockpit. One of the dogs leaped out of the cabin after him. It bounded around his feet, as if unable to understand why his new master moved so slowly when there was so much to do, so much to see. Together they walked north.

The last Sylvia saw of him was a tiny, lonely figure climbing into the pass, disappearing into the distance and the mist.

CHAPTER 12

DINOSAUR KILLER

He that goeth about to persuade a multitude, that they are not so well governed as they ought to be, shall never want attentive and favorable hearers.

RICHARD HOOKER, *Ecclesiastical Polity*

"*SAVE IT!*" Sylvia screamed as lights flickered throughout the camp. Jerry's hands flew over the keyboard. Cassandra's memory banks had just begun saving when the entire camp plunged into darkness. Shadows flashed back as the sizzling flare of arc welders beyond the communal dining hall created brief lightning storms in the Avalonian midnight.

Jerry shouted out the window to the welders. "Goddamn it, you could warn us!" There was no answer. He sighed. "What did we lose this time?"

"Maybe nothing." Sylvia glanced at her watch. "Know in a minute. I'll be glad when they get the power plant rebuilt."

"Yeah." He tapped idly at the keyboard. "They say you can get used to hanging if you hang long enough, but I'll *never* get used to the power going out." A brief flare of light, and Jerry's face was outlined in the darkness as he lit a cigarette. "Have one?"

"You know better than that."

He shrugged. "Good time to start." He put the stiff foil package away.

This was a bad time, miserable in almost every way that Sylvia could think of. If Cassandra hadn't been damaged by the monster, her automatic power backups would have allowed them to continue the process of collating the satellite data. If she hadn't been damaged, all data would have been automatically backed up. If the power plant hadn't been damaged, there'd be no need to run cables from one of the two Minerva shuttles. There would have been a smooth, uninterrupted flow of electricity to the camp.

They were lucky to have power at all. The solar collectors uphill didn't collect enough power, and the storage capacity was tiny. And they had dynamite. How do you get power out of two hundred kilos of dynamite? They'd found an answer: they'd dynamited a cliff to dam the river. Now the river featured a long, narrow lake downstream from the camp, a landing field for the Minerva, and now the Minerva's motor could be brought within reach of cables from the half rebuilt power plant.

"There she goes," Jerry said as the lights winked back on.

"I don't know how much more of this I can handle," Sylvia said, wiping moist fingers on her pants.

"All that it takes," Jerry answered bluntly.

Cassandra booted back up almost at once, and they breathed a paired sigh of relief: none of the data had been lost. Sylvia spoke softly. "Cassandra. Correlate and evaluate: optical-infrared scan, North Sea."

"*Acknowledged.*" The computer continued its cross-referencing of the data it received from the geosynchronous satellite above the campsite and the transient data gathered by the lower, faster-moving *Geographic*.

"Northland is heavily populated." Jerry's voice held irritation now. The two were like an emotional seesaw. "Conclusive signs of aquatic life. How in the hell are we going to zero in on something like our monster coming over?"

"Data, Jerry. There's an answer for everything that happened, but right now we just have to correlate data. We can't even say exactly what we're up against. If the protein spectrophotometer can be repaired, we'll get a look at the thing's DNA. Until then, we're doing autopsies on a corpse made of charcoal."

"There must be a pattern. This island is underpopulated. We *know* that. Not enough differentiation. Samlon, plants, and those damn pterodons high up in the mountains, and they all look alike. It's—"

"And insects—"

"Okay, insects. All tiny. All flying things, no crawlers, and all these empty ecological pockets. It's like . . . maybe . . . Sylvia? It's like the Earth must have been after the Dinosaur Killer. Nothing big. Most of the species wiped out. O—kay. Let's start looking for iridium in the soil, shall we? A layer of vaporized asteroid, buried, but not deep. And maybe the satellites can find us a fresh crater."

"Dinosaur Killer—Jerry, could that be it? A big asteroid strike, long winter, planetary die-off—when? A thousand years ago? Five thousand? The plants have all come back, but not the animals?"

"Even half a million wouldn't be too long." He frowned. "There are other answers, though. Something regular, something that breaks the reproduction cycle. Something subtle . . . maybe it doesn't even show up for two or three generations. . . ."

She felt momentary fear. Then she patted her bulging abdomen and laughed. "Ugly thought, but no. We've had three generations of chickens, and four generations of mice. Go for the Dinosaur Killer."

Her fingers flew over the keyboard, bringing to the screen the endless biological sets they had worked out: animal to vegetable kilotonnage, animal populations in the various temperature gradients. In the varying altitudes. In the dry climes. The wet. And on. And on, as they had for four days now. She remembered sleeping until she was entirely slept out, one Saturday following three college exams. She remembered this as she had once remembered hot fudge sundaes while dieting.

The answers were always the same. No hostile life on the island. There couldn't be. Nothing for it to live on. A simple, near-pastoral ecology. *We're missing something obvious. Something I ought to remember. Is this what the—others—Mary Ann and Ernst and the others felt like? Something I ought to know, and I don't.* She laughed suddenly.

"What?" Jerry asked.

"Nothing. Jerry, I *like* your Dinosaur Killer. I think you've got it."

Jerry carefully blew his smoke in the other direction. "Do you think that an expedition will really go out now?"

"No. Zack won't approve it."

"He'll be lucky if anyone listens a damn to what he has to say after this mess."

"Greg spoke for everyone? You included?"

"Not you?"

She paused. "I think Zack made an honest mistake, one that any of us might have made, and most of us did! Zack's a scapegoat. The fact that Cadmann was right doesn't necessarily mean that he was right for the right reasons. He'd been looking for something to go wrong right from the beginning—"

"I would have expected a comment like that out of Terry."

"No—this isn't a putdown. As far as Cad is concerned, *somebody* has to play Devil's Advocate."

The program purred on quietly and efficiently by itself. "Cadmann. What are we going to do about him?" The room lights dimmed again. "Shit! Cassandra *Save!*"

THE POWER didn't come back for fifteen minutes. *Enough,* Sylvia thought. "I quit, Jerry. You should too. 'Bye." She didn't wait for his answer.

Early dawn, but the camp was a hive of activity. The wreckage had been cleared away. New buildings sprouted, bare skeletons rising into the chill morning air. Three work crews in overlapping ten-hour shifts kept the jobs humming along smoothly. Everyone got just enough time to sleep, but not enough to grouse.

One monster did this. How many are there?

Dinosaur Killer. It just could be. The idea was exciting. She was already too tired to relax. She chose to walk the long way home. A chill breeze came from Spaceport Lake, and she wrapped her coat more tightly as she neared the power plant.

The engineers were rebuilding without tearing down the original structure. At this stage it had no shape or symmetry, only a chaos of crumbled walls and hastily erected scaffolding.

The power plant was one of the first buildings on Avalon. *About half a year ago,* she thought idly, and nodded to herself in satisfaction because she'd thought of it as half a year, not just over one Earth Standard. Avalon was home whether they liked it or not. Better learn to think so.

The power plant had flown down on a solidly packed one-shot cargo vehicle. A small solid-fuel rocket had dropped it from orbit to glide down on triangular wings. The engine was Minerva-compatible; in fact the whole package had looked a lot like one of the shuttles, with a Minerva's wing and belly. Motor, wings, hull, all were spare parts for the shuttles. *And damned near all we have, too. What's left?*

A Skeeter hovered over the power plant. A thin girder dangled from its underbelly. Omar Isfahan waved a handlamp, guiding the pilot, until the girder clicked down, was fitted and epoxied into place. Omar, tallest man in camp by three inches, looked tired. His fleshy cheeks drooped, his tight khaki shirt was dappled with sweat. Elsewhere in the structure men were soldering electric cables. When the Skeeter lifted away again someone yelled "Now!" and the lights flared back to life all over the camp. The glare stole the faint stars from their twinkling positions in the morning mist, but one of the twin moons still glimmered, a tiny dim crescent above the horizon.

She felt suddenly, unaccountably lonely. She wanted to go back to her hut and curl up next to her husband. Knowing that Terry would respond, would hold her with what strength he had. Knowing that if she began to cry he would say what comforting things he could.

If only . . . if only his new depth of understanding weren't accompanied by a complete failure of his lower body.

But she was pregnant, and he was sick, crippled, and her need for lovemaking seemed both selfish and unworthy. It didn't help that she still thought of Cadmann—not his face, and nothing so crude as a sexual image, only a memory of the breadth of his shoulders. The curve of his upper arm, where the muscle showed most clearly, the unmistakably male smell of his body and breath . . .

She held herself, watching the construction on the power plant, barely noticing when Zack emerged from the shadows.

"Sylvia."

He seemed about ten years older, but there was strength in that maturity. In the faces and manners of so many of them, now. "How are you?"

"Tired, but making progress, I think."

He nodded without speaking. He was staring out toward Mucking Great Mountain, and she didn't need to ask what he was thinking. If a camp vote had been taken the day after the disaster, Zack would have been ousted and Cadmann elected to the post in a moment. Take the vote soon enough after the disaster, and Zack himself might have led the electoral parade. Not now. Now he'd fight.

"We're surviving," he said. "We're going to keep surviving. We paid our price for this goddamned planet. It's all we're going to pay."

"I hope you're right, but how can you say that? Anyway, we all made our decision when we left Earth. We knew the risk—"

"What happened just shouldn't have happened." There was absolutely nothing of the old Zack in his tone. She wanted to back away from him. The flash of the arcs and welding lasers cast hard shadows on his face. His eyes were bright.

"We don't know if there are any more of those things on the island," she said, as gently as she could. "It's going to take time."

"We have time. Those *things* don't have any time." He turned the
collar of his coat up. "You're going to hear talk, Sylvia. Maybe you've
heard it already." His breath came in short white puffs when he spoke.
"They say that I'm too soft. That this wouldn't have happened if . . .
someone else was in charge. Had been in charge. I can't say about that.
Whatever's fair is fair. I can tell you this, though. It isn't happening
again. Whether I'm in charge or not."

Sylvia remembered the image of shadow whipping through the
courtyard to leave unbelievable carnage and stinking blood slicks on the
tarmac. The Avalonian equivalent of tiny, flying insects still hovered in
the courtyard, picking sustenance out of the cracks although they hosed
it clean again and again.

"Keep looking," he said. "Harry Siep's calibrating *Geographic*'s
telescope. Coordinating the satellites. All three will be monitoring the
island and the strait. We're going to train a second team to do the
evaluations you and Jerry have been running, so that we'll have continuous coverage until Cassandra is up to full strength again. I'm working out
a new security program. Every foot of this island is going to be re-
photographed—" He looked at her suddenly. "Have you seen the latest
pictures?"

"No. You've found something!"

"Not what you're thinking, not more of the damn monsters. We
found Cadmann."

A great sigh ran through her, as if she had been waiting to hear that
for a week, unable to admit how important it was. "Thank God.
Where?"

"Halfway up MGM. Mesa. Campfire traces three days running. He
won't answer any radio signals, but it's him all right."

She paused, waiting for him to go on. When he didn't, she said it.
"Are we going after him?"

"Why? He obviously doesn't want anything to do with us. He
didn't take anything that wasn't his—regardless of what a couple of
assholes said."

There was real confusion in Zack's voice. Muddied, mixed emotions. *Sure. He knows what he owes Cad. He also knows that right now
Cadmann could snatch the Colony from him.*

"What do you want to do?"

Zack thrust his hands deeply into his pockets. "I don't feel that an official delegation would be welcome. A few of his friends, on the other hand—people who cared about him and just wanted to make sure that he was all right—that might be appropriate. Can you think of anyone who might fit that description?"

She nodded silently.

"Good. I was hoping. Well. I've got things to do. Good night, Sylvia."

Zack walked off the way she had come, toward the rebuilt veterinary clinic.

There aren't any heroes here, she reminded herself. *Just survivors. The heroes died two weeks ago. Or were crippled. Or broken.*

Except for one man who we've shamed and betrayed. We owe him something.

TERRY was awake when she came to bed. What medical skill could do had been done. There was no need for him to be in the infirmary—the hut was like a personal hospital room, and since the accident, he seemed to need her more than ever before.

If only . . .

"Sylvia," he said sleepily, throwing a warm arm over her as she slipped between the covers.

She helped him roll over: he hadn't quite gotten the knack of doing it with just his arms. He was working out in the communal gym to improve the strength of his upper body. Already she could feel the renewed tautness in his shoulders. In short months he might double his strength. From the waist up, he would be more muscular than he had ever been in his life. A fine figure of a man, those rippling corded arms pushing his balloon-tired wheelchair around the camp.

She squeezed her eyes tightly, trying not to cry. He would taste the tears.

He pulled her close to him, and as he did now, kissed her closed eyes, his slender fingers kneading her back. "How did work go?"

"We've actually classified four different life forms on the main continent. Two are just *huge*, the size of brontosaurs. The others travel in packs. Fast. In sprints. Our monster might have been a stray from a pack like that."

"What about the expedition?"

"No word. You might still lead it, you know."

Except that we don't have any sophisticated prosthetics. So you could stay in the Minerva we send over, and watch while other men and women do the exploring. Maybe Cadmann would like to lead it now? How would you like that, Terry? Maybe we'll wait until I've had the baby, and I have my figure back. Then Cadmann and I can go over there together. What would you think of that, Terry?

Not too fucking much.

"Just problems. Manpower. We only have one totally free Minerva. If we need both Minervas somewhere else, the camp is without power. There just isn't going to be any exploration if the satellites and the telescope aboard *Geographic* can do the job," Sylvia continued.

"I suppose that makes sense."

Sylvia tried to identify her husband's voice in that comment. Like everything else in the camp, he had changed.

For a time she just listened to his breathing in the dark. Then she leaned forward to kiss her husband, kiss the father of her unborn child. His mouth tasted of sleep, but not unpleasantly. He pulled away from her embrace a few inches. "Sylvia—what news is there of Cadmann?"

"Mucking Great Mountain, halfway up."

She felt him nod in the dark. "Go up there," he said finally. "Talk to him. He's got to come back."

He strained with his arms to bring his hips closer to her, and even in the darkness she could see that tears glistened on his cheeks.

"Terry . . . why?"

He ran his hands down her body to the gentle swell of her stomach. "Because of this. We're going to have a child soon, and this planet will be hers."

"Hers," Sylvia whispered.

"I can't protect her. Cadmann can help make this island safe. I helped drive him away. I think you can bring him back."

She didn't say anything, just kissed him again, remembering a line from somewhere, *That which does not kill us makes us stronger.*

Who had said that? Kipling? Nietzsche? She decided Kipling and resolved to look it up in the morning.

"One thing, Sylvia." His voice took on a wholly different quality. "I've talked to Jerry. There are going to be . . . things that I'll never be able to do again. You . . . you might not have any more children by me unless we AI."

She cradled his head, afraid that she already knew what he was about to say. "Shhh."

"No," he whispered. "Let me finish. I don't want you creeping out behind my back, feeling guilty. Sooner or later you're going to do it. The instincts run too damned strong here. We came to make the children that will rule this world." There was a definite catch in his voice. "All right. Do what you have to. And know that I understand. Just—not with Cadmann, please. I know that it's ridiculous. I just ask you that much. Please."

She held him tightly, as if afraid that with those words he might have said all that he needed to say, done all that he needed to do, and that life might slip away from him there in the darkness.

And as they held each other, for the first time since they had landed she realized how very much she loved him, and how much he loved her.

SYLVIA's stomach jolted as the Skeeter hit an air pocket. She lurched to the side—the seat belt she shared with Mary Ann squashed them together. The Skeeters were built for two, but would seat three if the three were friendly enough.

Mary Ann stared straight ahead, as if a studied stare would part the clouds that shrouded the plateau. The tension between them was so thick you could cut shingles out of it, and on a very deep level Sylvia wished that she or Mary Ann had stayed behind.

But it was inarguable that Mary Ann and pilot Carlos were two of the closest friends that Cadmann had. Carlos was also a fine pilot, if a little nervous on landings. Lord knows Bobbi Kanagawa had spent enough time coaching him. At least Sylvia assumed that was what they were doing together. . . .

Carlos brought the Skeeter around in a circle, following the satellite-relayed coordinates. A pterodon cruised by, not so scared by the Skeeters as the beasts had been a year ago.

You get used to anything, Sylvia thought. Carlos's brow was creased with concentration. He grinned crookedly. "Well, señoritas, *el muchacho* was not looking for a meal, eh?"

The creature fluttered around them again, peering, poking, but staying carefully clear of the rotors.

"Eh!" Carlos yelled, dark face angry. *"Apátese un poco, queso de bola!"*

Sylvia grinned at him. "You must have practiced that. That's the most Spanish I've ever heard out of you at one gulp."

"One gasp. Gulps go in. Gasps come out. When a gulp comes out, it's time for the mop. What I said in my musical native tongue was an important, sensitive, poetic statement."

Mary Ann spoke for the first time since the Skeeter had taken off.

"I don't speak much Spanish," she said meekly. "But didn't you say something about moving a fat behind?"

"Ah, señorita—it is not what you say, it's how you say it."

"There it is," Mary Ann said suddenly.

The fog had thinned, and they were coming in on a mesa about half a mile across. There was tough avalonia grass up here, and Sylvia was surprised at the thickness of the underbrush. Thorn plants, of course, but other varieties too. Shrubs and flowering plants abounded. A squarish tent had been erected, and next to it a husky German shepherd leaped and barked.

Cadmann emerged from the tent. He was still a tiny, indistinct figure, but even from this distance Sylvia could see that he was walking unsteadily.

Carlos brought the Skeeter down.

They were forty meters from Cadmann's camp, and Sylvia had to admire his choice of locales. The mist was thinner up here, and there was much more vegetation than on the lowlands. Nearby was a tumbling stream of snow melt. It was clear that Cadmann was well provided for.

He could build here. Happily. There's water and food, and there may be game too. He wouldn't overlook that. If there's game anywhere, Cadmann would find it.

"Well," Carlos said, breathing a sigh of relief. "At least he left his rifle in the tent."

"Note the puppy, please."

Mary Ann didn't say anything. Her breathing had turned ragged.

"This is Carlos to Civic Center. We've reached the encampment. Cadmann appears unhurt, and any further reports will follow shortly." Carlos grinned at them. "Let's go." He unbuckled and hopped out.

Cadmann watched them for a long moment, then sat down in front of his campfire. He stirred at a pot and ignored them. A week's worth of beard shaded his face. He moved stiffly—the cracked ribs, Sylvia reminded herself. She wondered if he would let her inspect the damage or take a blood test to check infection, or even take his temperature.

There was something in his expression—something wild and uncomfortably strong, and her stomach went sweet-and-sour.

"Cadmann," Carlos said, his dark hand outstretched.

Cadmann looked at the hand and removed a flask from his pocket, taking a deep pull.

Carlos's hand hung there in the air like half of a suspension bridge awaiting completion. Finally he *humphed* and put his hand back in his pocket.

"What the hell do you want?" Cadmann said at last. The entire campsite was unkempt. The Cadmann she had come to know would never have been so sloppy.

"Just wanted to make sure that you were all right, *amigo,*" Carlos said uncomfortably. "You were hurt pretty bad."

Cadmann glared at them, took another pull and then dropped the flask to the side.

The eyes, the unsteadiness. He was drunk, roaring drunk, and had probably been drunk since he came here. "Yeah. Hurt bad. I guess you must care about that. Your conscience acting up? Hell with it."

"Cadmann . . ." Mary Ann began, moving forward. One flash from those bloodshot eyes, and she stopped.

"Keep away from me," he growled. "All of you. Not one of you came up and put your ass on the line when it would have made a difference. Stew in it."

"You can say that to me," Sylvia said. "But not to Mary Ann. She stuck up for you every time."

"Then where was she?" He screamed it. "Every night, every god-damned night I've had nightmares, waking up with that fucking monster blowing Ernst's blood in my face. I don't know why the hell it didn't just bite my head off. I don't know. . . ."

The shepherd pup sensed fear and anger, and stood next to Cadmann with bared teeth, growling low in its throat. "She cares," Cadmann muttered. He took a piece of meat from the pot and threw it to the dog. "It's all right, Tweedledee. They're friends." His laugh dwindled to a chuckle.

"That looks . . . fresh," Sylvia said cautiously. *Turkey? Samlon? Where's the other dog?*

He said, "There's a . . . critter living up in the rocks. Like a marmot. The dogs sniff 'em out just fine." He paused. "It would be polite to invite you to supper, but I'm not feeling terribly polite right now. Why don't you just say your piece and leave?"

"I miss you . . ." Mary Ann began. Cadmann glared balefully at her, opened his mouth and for just a moment Sylvia was sure that he was going to say something to send her fleeing back to camp in tears. Instead, he just closed his mouth and seemed to chew on the thoughts.

"Yeah. That's great. I can do a whole lot with that."

There was a chorus of cheerful barks from the rocks at the northern periphery of the mesa, and another shepherd came bounding out, radiating good, healthy-puppy energy.

It ran up to Carlos and, wagging its tail, sniffed his crotch heartily, immediately gave the same treatment to Mary Ann and then to Sylvia. Satisfied, it trotted over to Cadmann, who ignored him, and then over to his littermate. They sniffed at each other's hindquarters and bit playfully.

"Crotch sniffers of the world, unite!" Cadmann called.

"Cadmann," Sylvia said finally. "I'm not going to lie to you. We need you. We lost a lot of good people last week. We're trying to put the Colony back together again. You wouldn't have any opposition to the kind of programs that you were talking about."

"I don't care now." He shrugged. "Maybe in a couple more weeks I'll give a shit, but probably not. Don't tell me about your goddamned problems. I like it up here just fine. Dogs have their instincts, you know? They don't cripple themselves up with what they want to believe, and I like that just fine. Why don't you just get your asses back down the mountain and leave me alone?"

"Cadmann . . ."

"Get the fuck out of here!"

Carlos touched Sylvia's arm and pulled her back. "Ah, . . . *amigo* . . . is your radio working? If there's any kind of problem, anything we can do . . ."

Cadmann nodded wearily. "Yeah. You'll be the first to know. Don't hold your collective breath."

Sylvia turned, trying to hold the tears back. "Sylvia!" Cadmann called.

"Yes?"

"You take care of yourself." Mary Ann was still staring at him, and for a moment something passed between them: regret or loneliness or resentment. Something, but it was a message shared just by the two of them, and not for anyone else.

"Go on," he repeated. He stooped to pick up the flask. He shook it disgustedly, then tossed it aside again. "Me, I'm going to stay very very drunk until there's nothing left to drink."

The three of them returned to the Skeeter, but Mary Ann turned and faced them defiantly. "I'm not going back. He can't say it, but he wants me to stay."

"Mary Ann—"

"Can't you see him? He's killing himself up here. He really wants you, Sylvia—"

Carlos wisely made no comment at all. Sylvia opened her mouth in protest, but Mary Ann cut her off.

"Don't say it, Sylvia. Don't lie. He wants what he can't have." She stood up straight, a short, strong, pretty blond girl on the ripe edge of plumpness. A woman whose hibernation instability was far more subtle than Ernst's had been. But she was intelligent enough to know what was gone, and perceptive enough to know what was true between Sylvia and Cadmann.

"He can't say that he wants me to stay, but what is he going to do? Throw me out? I can't climb down by myself and he knows it. Leave me here. I'll be all right."

"I can't do that."

"Because you don't know what kind of man he is. Not really. I do. I know just what kind of man he is. You don't know him like I do."

For a long, hard moment they faced each other, then Carlos said. "All right. I expect to hear some kind of message from you or Cadmann about this over the radio in the next twenty-four hours. Otherwise I'm coming back."

"Fine."

Carlos entered his side of the Skeeter. Sylvia looked at Mary Ann carefully. There was something in her, some strength that had not been there since the Landing.

"It's changed all of us," Sylvia said quietly. "Maybe you're right. Maybe you're the only one who knows him now."

She hugged Mary Ann, kissed her on one warm cheek. "For God's sake take care of him, Mary Ann. He needs someone."

Mary Ann clung for a moment, then stepped back. "I will. I'll try. Now, go on."

They climbed into the Skeeter. The rotors whipped to life and Carlos levitated them, higher and higher and then to the east, until Mary Ann's figure was a tiny, vulnerable speck, walking slowly and uncertainly toward Cadmann's camp.

CHAPTER 13

HOMESTEAD

The dwarf sees further than the giant when he has the giant's shoulder to mount on.

SAMUEL TAYLOR COLERIDGE, *"The Friend"*

POWDERED EGGS and powdered milk and freeze-dried bacon didn't seem to be a promising start for breakfast. But in combination with Mary Ann's skill and the last of the samlon meat, they produced a savory fragrance that drifted up from the pan in thin wisps.

Tweedledee and Tweedledum, the twin shepherds, padded quietly around the camp, tongues lolling pinkly, looking hopefully at the fire. They sniffed at the smoke but kept their distance. If they were very polite Cadmann would let them lick the plates.

A whiff of ocean salt stirred the leaves and dried grass on the mesa. Avalon's eternal mist was blown away for minutes at a time. From the edge of the mesa she could look down onto the flatland, where the Colony was distantly visible: a flash of solar cell banks, the dim, interlocking rectangles of the tilled and irrigated land. The far-off hum of a Skeeter tickled the air.

A protracted groan issued from the tent behind her, and she turned to watch Cadmann elbow himself clumsily out past the flaps.

He glared at her, rubbing granular sleep from the corners of his eyes, and grunted, "What the hell are you doing here?"

She didn't let him see her flinch. "Cooking breakfast." She stirred the eggs and crumbled in another pinch of dried bacon crisps. Tweedledum, the male, crept up within a meter of the fire, drooling. Cadmann shooshed him away and crawled up closer, shouldering Mary Ann gently aside. His bloodshot eyes narrowed with interest. He started to say something, then caught her smiling at him and turned it into a yawn, scratching himself crudely. Mary Ann caught an awesome whiff of morning breath.

Both of Cadmann's big hands went to his head. "God, that hurt."

"You earned it. You finished off the vodka last night."

"No," he croaked, genuine distress in his voice. His voice sounded as if something small and struggling were trapped in his larynx. Cadmann backed into his tent, and emerged holding his canteen. He waggled it in one hand, grinning through a week's worth of beard at the answering swish. "Hair of the dog."

He tossed it back, guzzling with short, choppy movements of his Adam's apple. *Why do you do this to yourself? Doesn't matter. You'll have to stop now.*

He tossed the canteen to the side to clank noisily against a pile of rocks. The dogs attacked him simultaneously from either side, yipping at him to play with them or feed them or any one of a hundred other doggy concerns.

Cadmann wrestled with them for a tolerant moment, then shoved both away and glared at them nastily. "If you don't shut the hell up, I am going to shoot you both. I am going to line you up and shoot you both with the same goddamn bullet. Do you understand me?"

They arfed and snapped playfully at each other's tails and ears.

Cadmann stretched, naked but for a baggy pair of shorts. His muscular arms were only fractionally better tanned than his chest. *He's lost weight. The wounds, and then the drinking—*

Mary Ann stopped stirring the eggs as the first curl of smoke wafted up from the pan.

"What in the hell is that mess?"

"Call it an Avalon omelet. It's our breakfast," she said.

He thrust a fork into the pan, probing, and snapped at her, "How much of it is poison?"

She took the fork and shoveled a bite into her own mouth, glaring right back.

"Half, eh? Well, I'm tough. I can handle that." He tried to sit in a gracefully cross-legged position, but finally just sort of collapsed into a heap. "My head."

"Your breath. Here. Eat."

Cadmann took the fork back and scraped half the contents of the pan onto a plate. The suspicion in his eyes faded after the first bite. "Damn, this isn't half—"

At the first sign of her smile he shut up and hunched over the pan, sulking as he ate.

Mary Ann poured reconstituted nonfat milk and sipped contentedly. It was startlingly clean, and aerated, filled with tiny, needlelike ice crystals from the snow-melt stream that ran near Cadmann's campsite. *Drunk. Hurt. Mad. And he's still picked a better place than Zack ever did. . . .*

She squinted across the fire at Cadmann. *Time? Yes, while the hangover lasts.* "You can forget about me going back to the Colony. I'm staying. You can carry me down, but I'll just climb back. If you want to break both of my legs, that might stop me, but I wouldn't bet on it."

"You *are* going," he said. He ate the last forkful of the eggs, squinted at her and belched with satisfaction. "Right after lunch."

"KEEP the head *down*." One of Cadmann's broad hands clamped onto the back of her neck as they crouched behind an outcropping of rock near the eastern edge of the mesa. "Damn hangfires—"

Brapp!! The sound was not as loud as Mary Ann expected, but she heard it as much with her body as her ears. The shaped engineering charge rent the mountainside. Rock chips and clots of dirt flew in all directions. A gout of dust and powdered earth mushroomed into the sky. Crouching next to her, Cadmann grinned. "Fun, eh?"

She bobbed her head nervously. "Finest kind."

His hands were gentle as he helped her to her feet. Shielding his eyes against the dust, he surveyed his handiwork.

The third detonation of the day completed a hole in the granite face twenty meters above the mesa. It looked very like the opening excavation of a mine. Shelflike slabs of rock jutted out from the earth, their ends shattered by the concussion.

"I'm not sure I understand why you don't just build on the flat."

"Weren't you in the camp?" She heard the sarcasm change to something else. He stared at her. "Mary Ann—" His voice softened. "Yeah. Well, there are monsters here."

"I know that."

"So we—I—don't want to be on the flat. Also, I want the flatland for farming—if I decide to stay, all of the farmland will be worth its acreage in gold foil. Second, drainage—if I build underground on the hillside, rain and snow melt will run right off, if I build my roof right. Third, view. From where we'll . . . I'll be, I'll have the best damn view that ever was. Right down on their heads. And fourth, I want us to be unreachable. One path, and it twists, and I'll guard it. I won't be on some tabletop watching one of *those* come at me at ninety miles an hour."

She saw it now, and her ears burned. *My God, of course not! Why didn't I see . . . the way he looked at me? Oh.* "It was a stupid question, wasn't it?"

"Uh—"

"Cadmann, I *know*. I can accept it. But—well, sometimes it hurts."

His hand moved to touch hers, then drew back. She held her breath. He turned away to survey his work, then turned back, a deeply satisfied smile creasing his face. "There are more reasons, but those will do for the moment." He looked at her sharply. "Nobody's asking you to live in it. Or to stay here."

"I'm staying." She stood on her tiptoes and locked her arms around his neck. "I love you, Cadmann. I lost too much coming to Avalon. I'm not losing you, too."

He reached back to unfasten her fingers from the back of his neck, but she clung too tightly, and finally he just met her eyes squarely.

"You do things my way," he said. "If you don't like it, go home. Down there, things can be whatever way people decide by vote that they should be. *This* is not a democracy. Up here I'm the bottom line."

"Male chauvinist," she said, kissing him lightly.

"I'm a me chauvinist. I'd probably be the same way if I was a woman. I just want to get this straight before we . . . start anything."

"I love you," she repeated. The rock dust at the corner of her eyes was slightly muddied. "Love, honor and obey. Isn't that what women used to promise? I will, you know."

He gave her a hard, brief hug. "Then let's get started."

"Aye, aye, sir. What first?"

"Defenses. Notice anything about the—*our*—house site?"

"Many things."

"Boulder. That one."

"Big."

"And it will roll, once I dig it out. So I dig. Put chocks under it first. Levers on the chocks. Anyone wants to come up the path without permission—"

"Any *one?*"

"Or any *thing.* If it comes up and we don't like it, we roll the boulder down."

"I'm for that. What next?"

"Terrace down the hill. Vegetable garden. Divert some water from the Amazon to keep the vegetables happy, and us too. Then finish the house. I have to finish the excavation by hand to make sure that I have the dimensions that I want. Then I level the floor and set the corner posts. That will take about three weeks."

She smiled uneasily. "Three weeks. Cadmann, how long are you planning to stay up here?"

It was the wrong thing to say, and she knew it instantly. "Until I'm finished. Until I feel like going the hell back down. And the instant you don't like it up here, go."

Cadmann tore her hands loose from around his neck and without another word opened the box of tools and building supplies that he had skeetered up from the camp.

He was still limping.

A TIRELESS machine, made of polished hickory and leather. That's what Cadmann seemed to her. For all his injuries and his age, he worked on and on when she was exhausted, when the youngest, strongest men in the Colony would have collapsed and begged for rest.

He worked eight hours a day, digging, shoring, piling . . . building ridges of earth that would later become garden or upper patio. No effort was lost. He never hauled any dirt or stone uphill. He built on the hill and he planned carefully, and every wheelbarrow of earth and rock moved downhill to the growing garden structure.

In some ways the excavation was beginning to look like a smallish swimming pool, with the deep end—nine feet deep—at the lowest part, and the shallow higher. He cut deep "steps" into the hill above the excavation, so that the entire cavity measured five meters along the bottom edge and twelve meters along each side.

When he was through with the morning's work, Cadmann stretched and took off with Tweedledee to check the traps. (Mary Ann had found another difference between the twins. Tweedledee's right ear was a bit—or, more precisely, a bite—short, a souvenir of a kennel brawl that had become serious.)

And here she was able to accompany him, learning to set the wire spring traps that Cadmann set for the slow, almost friendly mammaloids that Cadmann called "Dopey Joes." He said it was a literary reference.

At first she was able to do little but help him haul dirt, and cook the meals and clean the camp. But it was too easy for her to remember a time when she had been one of the most competent women on the expedition, and there was no way that she could remain satisfied with this new role.

She learned to set snares. Nets in the stream that ran past the site of the house from the heights of Mucking Great Mountain, a tiny ice-melt stream Cadmann had named the Amazon. With a large-mouthed basket in one hand and Tweedledee's leash in the other, she explored the mountain, learning the paths and the patches of sliding rock. And it was among them that she found Missy.

The snares were set near any of the half dozen or so bushes and plants that showed the characteristic gnawed parallel toothmarks. One patch of plants interested her. They were green and broad-leaved, with thick yellow veins branching from a central stem. The flowers were delicate pink with tiny red berries clustered in the center. None of its flowers were chewed or gnawed, but the roots and leaves were the favorite food of some local creature. When she took a closer look at the flowers, she noted a dusting of dried insect segments, and more dead, delicately winged husks on the ground beneath the blossoms. The word "poison" flashed through her mind, and she was pleased with herself for making the connection.

Something was rustling behind the bush, and she carefully pulled the branches aside.

There, its neck caught in a chewproof nylon spring loop, was eighteen inches of furred frustration. The Joe had huge orange eyes almost too large for its face. The eyes were imploring, terrified, confused. They reminded her of . . . what was it?

What . . .?

She stomped her foot in frustration and forgot about it. The creature was in one of the snares, bleeding from the throat, twisting and spitting at her. Tweedledee barked, and the little Joe almost broke its own neck trying to escape.

She poked it into the basket and then cut it lose from the snare. It chattered at her. "Well, Missy," Mary Ann said. "Can't blame you for being upset."

Tarsier. That was the word she had searched for. An equatorial primate, the owner of the largest eyes of any mammal. Found in the forests of Malaysia and the Philippines.

She laughed in relief. It was still there. Some of the information was still in her mind, she just couldn't call it up on command as once she had. Maybe she could restructure the way she thought . . .

She shook the cage and held it up close to her face. "Are you a good-luck charm, Missy?"

Missy spat at her and tried to hide in a corner of the basket. She was more slender than a tarsier, almost like a thick, furred lizard. She lay on her back, claws out and scrabbling blindly.

On their way back down, Tweedledee suddenly strained at the leash, tugging so hard that Mary almost dropped the basket. Tweedledee yipped hysterically, struggling to climb up into the rocks. Missy went absolutely apeshit, squealing and clawing in the wire cage.

" 'Dee Dee, get back here!" Mary Ann yelled, suddenly suspicious. Reluctantly, the shepherd came back down, tail folded contritely between her legs. Mary Ann wound the leash tightly around a rock, then climbed up and took a closer look, Missy chattering more loudly.

Her ears were rewarded before her eyes. She heard a thin, mewling sound that reminded her of nothing so much as the cry of kittens starving for milk. There were six of them, curled up around each other like a tangle of hairy rope. They were just babies, barely able to wiggle. One lay still; it seemed dead. The others looked up at her with curiosity untainted by fear.

Mary Ann glanced from the wire cage to the babies, and sudden inspiration struck.

Missy was climbing up the sides of the basket, and Mary Ann thumped her back down, throwing handfuls of avalonia grass and leaves into the cage until the bottom was completely matted.

Then she carried the basket up the defile to the rocks. Missy chattered even more frantically now. Down below her, Tweedledee leaped and danced, yipping enthusiastically.

Mary Ann braced herself between the rocks, thankful now for hours of jogging, because her calves were starting to burn from all the climbing. She reached down into the crevice and gently drew up one of the Joe kittens. It struggled and bit her hand—a scratch, hardly enough to break the skin. Mary Ann set the fur ball back down and pulled her jacket sleeve down over her hand in a makeshift glove. This time she couldn't feel the teeth at all when she transferred the second Joe into the basket.

Mary Ann had to knock Missy down from the side of the cage again, and then a third time when she tried to bite through the jacket. When the first baby was deposited in the cage, Missy scampered around and around in a furry flash before finally slowing down. She sniffed at her child, then licked, and finally wound herself around the kitten, enveloping it.

One at a time, Mary Ann transplanted the Joes to the cage. Then she trundled it back down to Tweedledee.

The mother chattered up at her vilely, then continued to tie her children into a ball for maximum warmth and protection. Mary Ann looked at the last small, sad body down in the crevice, and shook her head.

"Time to head back to camp, Dee," she said, unleashing the dog. She stood with small fists on hips, looking around the area. What did these things eat? The adults, anyway? The Joes looked close enough to mammalian; there would be some sort of milk gland for the young.

There were several types of plants: a kind of lichen or moss seemed to be breaking down some of the rocks, and a viny thing that resembled a colony of long-legged spiders. It grew out of the rocks in symbiotic relationship with the moss. There were shrubs up here, and flowering plants, which she had noticed from the helicopter.

Which would the Joe family prefer? She took a chance: the broad-leafed plant that had concealed the snare. She tore loose a cluster of red berries and dropped them into the cage.

Nothing. Momma Joe ignored them.

Still following the hunch, she tore loose a clutch of leaves, sorted through them for the tenderest, and dropped them in.

Missy sprang on them. After careful sniffing, she began to chew.

Well, that answered that.

Feeling absurdly proud of herself, Mary Ann carried the cage back down to the camp.

The sun was unusually warm, and the air sweet, and her mind was already buzzing with ideas for cages.

There was something . . . something bothering her about the enclave she had found. What was it? It was beautiful. More beautiful, more *lush*, than anything she had seen down on the flatlands.

Down on the flatlands there was little in the way of tender shrubs. Only the gnarled thorn bushes seemed to thrive down there.

More variation of plant life at a higher altitude? And come to think of it, animal life, too. That implied something, but what? What? Her mind wasn't quite clear enough, and she cursed softly.

Damn it. Why wouldn't it come into focus? Suddenly all the pleasure she had felt disappeared in a welter of frustration. Why wouldn't her mind work for her?

Hibernation Instability. There. Say it. Accept it. Don't try to pretend that it didn't affect you, as some of the others do. Don't try to pretend you still have capacities that have fled. That kind of egotistical nonsense gets you laughed at or killed. Work within your limits, and learn the steps you always pitied 'tweens for having to take.

Where a Bright can lead, a 'Tween can follow. There used to be such smugness in that saying. A genius can take huge leaps, wearing intuitive seven-league boots. Then a corps of engineers and technicians can turn the theories into inventions and principles. A competently trained repairman can fix something that it took a genius to devise in the first place.

I lost my seven-league boots. But the germ plasm is still mine! We can make good kids. . . .

All right. There was something wrong here. But if she had the time and the patience, she could reconstruct the thought processes that once came to her so easily. And it was important for her to reconstruct these. Very important.

With the basket in hand, she traveled back down the hill.

MARY ANN found it amazing.

In three weeks, using a constant, unvarying work schedule, Cadmann had carved the patio and shoring, tamped down the floor of his new house and covered it with layers of polyethylene sheeting. He had set the corner posts using the lightweight foam-steel braces ferried down from the zerograv smelting facility aboard *Geographic*, and lined the walls with more of the polyethylene.

The roof girders and additional support beams were finally in place. Cadmann disassembled their tent and laid it across the top in a makeshift roof, and they spent their first night in the new home. The northern wall was earth, but the southern, uphill side was open to the broad, high steps that Cadmann had cut into the mountainside.

Their stove warmed the makeshift dwelling beautifully, and there was plenty of headroom and walking space, more than in some of the 1800s pioneer cabins she had visited in Kentucky museums.

They sat cross-legged in the shelter. The stove and the body heat of the two dogs were quite enough to keep her warm as she wrote. Two sheets of paper were spread out, and on one she was listing every plant Missy had accepted as food. So far, there were six varieties.

The other sheet was blank. *I ought to be recording something, but I don't know what it is. Damn. But—I am useful. Cadmann built it, but it's our house.*

The earth that surrounded them on three sides was terrific insulation, and there was something womblike about it. *So I'm missing some brain cells. I had billions to spare.*

She heard Missy's angry chattering in the distance. Four of the youngsters had survived with her and were old enough to run around the cage. If they could be bred . . .

"A garden there," Cadmann said with vast contentment, pointing back at the series of deep, rising steps cut into the mountain behind the house. "Hanging garden . . . climbing . . . I forget what you call it. Walk path cut in the middle. We'll be able to mount mirrors at the top. We already get full sunlight as it crosses east to west—we can do even better. Roof next, and we'll top it with soil." He laughed lazily. "We could plant on our roof if we wanted to."

"It would be nice to have a little more natural light." Mary Ann folded the sheet of paper and tucked it in with her backpack.

He sipped at his coffee, then put an arm around her. It still sent a shiver of pleasure through her to feel it.

They hadn't slept together for the first week, and when he had finally taken her into his bedroll and made love to her it had been an angry, demanding, selfish kind of love—and she had not demanded in return. She was happy to be able to give. But now, as his house was taking form, as the Joes and turkeys filled their cages and makeshift pens, as the plot of worked land doubled and trebled, and the mesa became Cadmann's Bluff, his personality and signature scrawled more boldly upon it hour by hour . . .

He was softer with her at the end of the day, and spoke of "us" and "we." And she was happy, despite her frequently aching muscles.

In the weeks since the attack on the camp, Cadmann seemed to have purged his anger. It had taken useful work, done his way, in his time, to his ends. And the fruits of that labor were his. She moved closer to him, and kissed his shoulder gently.

"I'll dig the channel tomorrow," he said. "I need the channel before I can blast. Mary Ann, I think I can run the channel *through* the house, through the living room."

"For what? Oh, the Amazon," she remembered. He wanted to divert water for the vegetable garden. Something ticked at her memory . . .

"F–F–Falling Water."

"What?"

"I remembered! Falling Water, a house by F–F–Frank Lloyd Wright, and the water ran right through the living room!"

"That's what I was trying to remember. You're amazing!"

I've never felt like this, she thought to herself. And I've been married, and in love before, and have had . . . enough lovers to know the difference.

There was something about the darkness and the warmth. About being next to a man who had built his dwelling by the strength of his back and his wits. Something about watching Cadmann rediscovering himself, and her, that made her feel warm and small and protected.

Protected . . . A competent, civilized human being didn't need a protector. Mary Ann Eisenhower, Ph.D. in Agricultural Sciences, had been quite capable of taking care of herself, thank you. She remembered the doctor . . . she remembered. Now she was the dependent of a brawny, self-sufficient warrior.

And yet there was no cruelty in this man, no demand for her subservience or helplessness: she was sure that he had accepted her because she *could* do certain things, she *could* take care of herself. She could go when she wished, and he made that clear. Yet he had accepted with pleasure her suggestions about breeding the Joes. She wanted to do anything for him, be everything to him—but if he ever abused her, that urge would vanish.

How strange, and how wonderful. How natural to be here, in the earth, huddled with the man she loved, who she hoped would one day love her in return.

So there, Sylvia. She grinned fiercely, briefly, and kissed his shoulder, her lips parting slightly, tongue flickering out to taste the salt dried on his skin.

He pulled her to him, and there, in their home, made love to her on the packed earth of the floor. And they rejoiced together until both were exhausted, until sleep stole the thoughts from her mind as she curled against his side. The two of them, surrounded by their home, their dogs, the whispering wind and the small night sounds. Together.

CADMANN had finished digging the French drain—the rock-filled slit, a foot wide, five feet long and three deep, at the uphill mouth of their home. It would trap rain or snow melt before it could flood their home, and was just another of the little things, the thousand little things that Cadmann had done to their home—

Their home!

—to make it safe, and warm, and ideal for her. For them.

Their home was roofed now, and planted with grass seed. Rows of strawberries and lettuce and carrots and corn stretched across the mesa wherever there was enough soil to give anything a chance. Much of it would be lost. She expected the strawberries and the hybrid melon-cactus to do the best. Two pens of captured turkeys and their cage of Joes were thriving, and as she fed the Joes their morning leaves, they were actually happy to see her. The kittens had sprouted into twelve-inch furred lovelies, only slightly less beautiful, and better-tempered, than young foxes. The furs would be useful, and the flesh . . .

A sudden cramping wave of nausea fanned through her, and she doubled, gasping, choking back the sour fluid in her throat. This was the third morning that . . .

Morning . . . ?

She grinned, looking up at Cadmann toiling at the drainage slit.

Mary Ann threw the rest of the leaves into the cage and dusted off her hands.

"Well, Missy, I think that I have some news for Madman Weyland." The Joe looked up at Mary Ann and chattered friskily. "Guess who's coming to dinner?"

CALL her Mama.

The taste of the river changed with the seasons. For a time the water would run sluggish and cold. Then the taste of life was scarce; the flying things were scarce; the swimming things were dead.

Later the water would race, carrying the taste of past times. Mama had seen scores of cycles of seasons. She was wise enough to ignore the ancient tastes: bodies or blood or feces of life her kind had long since exterminated, long buried in mountain ice, released as the ice melted.

In the hot season the water would be bland again, carrying only spoor of flyers and swimmers and another of her own race.

Mama's taste was discriminating. One of her kind lived upstream. Another lived even farther upstream, and that one was a weakling. It lived where game was so scarce that Mama could taste starvation in its spoor. Not worth killing, that one, or her nearer rival would have taken her domain.

In winter there was something strange in the water, something she couldn't identify. Not life; not interesting.

The world began to warm again . . . and something new was on the island. Something she had never tasted, something weirdly different, was leaving spoor in the water. It was as yet too faint to identify. Mama began to think about moving.

If she followed that spoor she would have to fight, and that was no step to be taken lightly.

By summer she could taste several varieties of prey! The things weren't merely leaving feces in the water; she tasted strange blood too. Her rival was eating well. Was it time?

Her rival was youthful (Mama could taste that) but large. The faintness of her scent placed her many days' journey upstream. She would be rested and fed when Mama arrived . . . and Mama settled back into her pool. She had not lived two scores of cycles by being reckless.

If her rival sickened, she would taste it.

Days flickered past. The time of cold had come. Ordinarily Mama scarcely noticed passing time, for the taste of swimmer meat was always the same. Nothing attacked. Her curiosity lay dormant . . . but it was active now, for living things were leaving spoor even in dead of winter, and blood ran down the river now and again.

Oh, the variety! Here was blood from something vaguely like a flyer. This one must have been big, a plant-eater; she had to dig far into her memory to find anything similar. That horrible chemical stench was entirely mysterious: hot metal and belly acid and thoroughly rotted grass. This unfamiliar scent, judging by its components, would be the urine of a meat-eater not of her own kind. Hunger and curiosity warred with discretion, for Mama had never tasted anything like that, nor seen one either.

Once there was a living thing in the water. She snapped it up and chewed contemplatively, trying to learn of it. A swimming thing, primitive, built a little like a swimmer . . .

The world was warming when the river gifted her with two larger members of the same species. Bottom feeders tasting of mud, they must be breeding despite the presence of her rival upstream.

And *that*, one bright hungry morning, was the burnt blood of her own kind!

Taste of fear and *speed* and killing rage, taste of chemicals, taste of burning. If lightning or a forest fire had killed her rival, then an empty territory lay waiting for her upstream. If another rival, then Mama would face a formidable foe.

The swimmers were startled when Mama came forth in an eating frenzy. Swimmers were nothing; the taste did not engage her curiosity at all. But Mama's rival would be fat now, and hyperkinetic from impact of sensory stimuli, and Mama dared not come upon her as a desperate starveling. She had not fought a serious rival in many years.

CHAPTER 14

REUNION

Alas how easily things go wrong!
A sigh too much, or a kiss too long,
And there follows a mist and a weeping rain,
And life is never the same again.

GEORGE MACDONALD, *"Phantasies"*

THEY SANG as they strode downhill.

Tweedledee bounded around Cadmann's feet. She was leaner, stronger now than she had been only eight weeks before. She was acclimated to the heights and rigors of Mucking Great Mountain, but still seemed happy to be coming back to the Colony.

Even here, only a few meters past the firebreak, the distant grind of machinery assaulted Cadmann's ears.

That sound, a constant background hum down on the flatlands, never reached his home in the mountains. A thin line of dust marked the bass rumble of a tractor tilling the fields.

Mary Ann walked next to him, her blond hair barely rising to his shoulder. Her presence was a comfort in ways that would have been difficult to imagine just a few short weeks before.

How long ago had he walked this path with Ernst and Sylvia? Back before any of the grief. Back when he could reasonably expect a quiet slide into old age amidst herds of children. And he'd wished for kodiak bears.

The view had changed. The fields had expanded; there were more buildings. The wreckage left by the monster's assault was not visible from here. With twelve adult casualties out of a hundred and ninety-two, the Colony felt pressure to work. There was healing to be done.

Now Cadmann had his home, and something new . . . something very new with the only person in the camp who had believed in him. He put his arm around her waist and pulled Mary Ann in closer to him. She had lost some weight, much like Tweedledee, but her curves were still rounded, and now . . .

Now . . .

His arm wound all the way around her shoulder, down to her belly, which was firmer than it had been—the work and the life up on MGM was not conducive to softening. Soon her figure would be filling out. And out! And then . . . He looked at her almost surreptitiously. The nine-mile walk hadn't tired her. All downhill, half a mile altitude change—the walk had strained his own healing wounds, and if someone offered them a ride back he'd take it.

He smiled, utterly content.

The machine stutter was more distinct now, and when Cadmann looked up, the tractor was rumbling up the glazed earth road toward them, and someone atop it waving his hands semaphore style.

Cadmann cupped his hands to his mouth. "Yo!" Tweedledee galloped off down the road, kicking her hindquarters up into the air with every lope.

In his backpack he carried skins and dried meat and samples of all of the plants near their camp, carefully bundled and labeled. Cadmann Weyland, first of the mountain men! Much better than Great White Abo.

The tractor was close enough to make out the driver. It was Stu Ellington taking his rotation in the fields. "Hey, hey! If you'd waited another two days, I would have won the pool."

Cadmann laughed, yelling back, "If you'll split it with me I'll vanish for another forty-eight hours. Who wins?"

Stu stopped the tractor in front of them and put the engine into neutral. Hot air curled from the engine in waves.

"One of the twins. Phyllis, I think. Not sure. Hell with it. It's great to see you, Cad. Mary Ann. Back to stay?"

" 'Fraid not. Opening negotiations. Somebody had to break away from the Colony first."

Stu looked down at them from his seat, his grin cutting through the dust and sweat, and shook his head. "Just glad you're both back, man." His expression grew somber. "I'm so sorry for what happened."

"Yeah." Cadmann looked decidedly uncomfortable; then Mary Ann hugged him and patted her stomach.

"Stu! Think I've got a piglet in the pen!"

"Oh! Whoa! Well, this is an occasion. M'lady!" Stu swung down from the tractor and offered a hand to Mary Ann. She looked back at Cadmann, who just picked her up by the armpits and hoisted her aboard the tractor.

"You know how to drive one of these things, I believe?"

"Betcha," she said happily, and swung up into the seat. She gunned the engine. The tractor made a great, lazy circle. The two men followed it at a short distance.

For a while there was companionable silence, and then Stu broke it. "We've done a lot of rebuilding since you've been gone. Not just buildings, Cad. We've got the defenses up, and stronger. Stupidity. Just stupidity." He seemed to need to hear something in return. "We got blindsided once, but it's not going to happen again, I can guarantee it."

"Good to know that."

Stu was almost as tall as Cadmann, but somehow at the moment he seemed much smaller. "Do they know that you're coming back? Did you radio?"

"No, I sent a homing pigeon."

Stu looked stricken, and Cadmann felt a little disgusted with himself. "Look, Stu—if you did what you really felt was right, then fine. I have no interest in seeing or hearing anyone crawl. What's got me twitchy—skip it." *They have defenses. Great, but where do I come in? Can they make me inspect them? Damn.*

There was a general shout of greeting ahead of them as Mary Ann and the tractor passed the first of the outer pens. Within moments Cadmann was the center of attention.

I've only been gone for five weeks. . . .

But any momentary discomfort was quickly drowned in a sea of reaching hands.

"Cad! Welcome back!"

"—to see you—"

"—things haven't been the—"

And other fragments piled one atop another, overlapping, irritating and at the same time deeply soothing.

Mary Ann stopped the tractor by the machine shops and dismounted with Cadmann's assistance. She melted into his hands with a calculatedly sensuous grace that put him on guard.

What was she projecting? She was using that "forced float" that insecure women use when . . .

When presenting themselves before a rival.

Sylvia.

She wore her lab smock, which was freshly pressed and looked like nothing so much as a maternity gown. And a maternity gown that she wouldn't be wearing much longer. She waddled a bit when she walked, and was carrying the baby low in her belly.

She smiled at him, at them both, and there was something very like a wall of glass between her emotions and the smile.

Her pageboy haircut was a little longer than the last time he had seen her, and needed a trim around the edges. She held out her hands to him, then, not quite smoothly, shifted positions to offer them to Mary Ann first. "Mary Ann. You look wonderful."

"So do you. I'm hoping to get some of that glow pretty soon now."

"You mean . . . ?"

"Yep."

Sylvia hugged Mary Ann hard, then held her hands out to Cadmann. He took them, fighting to follow her lead, to maintain the distance between them. Some sense of proportion was called for here, but the instant he touched her skin, something inside him melted. He ached for her.

"Cadmann." Her mouth tweaked in an attempt at a casual smile. "Is Mary Ann right? You haven't been shooting blanks?"

"Nope, someone slipped a live round in there. At least, that's what we're hoping. At least, that's what we came down to find out." He hesitated. "Would you take care of my lady for me?"

"You know it." There were tiny moist jewels forming at the corners of her eyes, and she squeezed his hand. "Hey, big man—are we going to be seeing more of you? I'm going to be losing a passenger in a month."

It had to be his imagination, but her hands suddenly flushed with warmth. He released them, embarrassed by the strength of his reaction. "I wouldn't miss it. As soon as you're in labor, I'll head back down. Promise. Aside from that . . . I've got livestock now, and crops. I just don't know."

She nodded, unwilling to pressure him. "Listen . . . I'll take Mary Ann for a full checkup. Stay for dinner?"

"Count on it."

Mary Ann hugged Cadmann and planted a long, proprietary kiss on his mouth, pressing herself against him, to the appreciative guffaws of the crowd.

Then she and Sylvia linked arms and marched off together.

Cadmann shifted his pack around until the pain in his ribs eased (and a fresh ache started in the bone of his right hip). He continued on into the camp. A zigzag walkway through the mine field was painted bright green, and he followed it, noting the guns placed to cover that path. He nodded approval.

None of the children were walking yet. *We'll have to fence off the mine field when they get older. And— No! Not my department!*

He grinned when a small pink face passed him carried in a papooseka backpack.

What the hell. He didn't have to live here to love those little faces. It wasn't the children's fault that their parents were idiots. Dammit, these were his children too.

The veterinary lab had been repaired. Its side was a mass of patches welded in great discolored blotches at the corners. The structural damage to the quad had been repaired. Nothing could hide the scorch marks, but there were strings of colored ribbon wired up around the edges, and the beginning of a banner painted in bright orange and green.

In the center of the quad was something new that glistened in the morning light. Cadmann bent to read it. Set into the concrete was a metal tablet, tinted to look like brass, that said simply:

"Day 295, Year One. REMEMBER." Following those words in a silent tribute were etched thirteen names. He traced them with his fingers. Alicia: gone. Barney, Jon, Evvie Sikes: gone.

Jesus.

"I didn't know what else to do," Zack said behind him, and Cad turned to greet him, clasped his hands strongly.

Zack didn't look tired—he looked hard and wiry and serious. He had trimmed his mustache short, and there was a partially healed burn scar along the inside of his forearm. "We were wrong—you were right. I'm sorrier than I can say."

"Don't bother being sorry. Just don't let it happen again."

Zack took Cadmann by the arm. "Come on. Let me show you Monster Watch."

"The mine field—"

"We turn it on at night."

"And new fences along the gorge. I like it."

"You'll like it better."

Zack held the door of the com shack open as Cadmann shucked his backpack. Pain eased in ribs and hip.

Two extra screens had been mounted in the room, and there was a cot in the corner that looked recently used. Andy, the big man from Engineering, sat in a swivel chair, his dark face speckled with crawling dots of reflected light. He distractedly waved a hand in greeting.

One of the six flat video screens was dark, but three others viewed the Colony from varying local angles, and two scanned their island from the geosynchronous satellites.

"We've got the ocean-observation program going—this is the long view. We're also analyzing weather patterns to attempt to build up a model. But we've got optical and infrared sensors working. We should be able to track anything man-size moving close to the surface. If the computer scans an object moving in our direction, it'll call our attention to it."

The picture abruptly changed to a high-altitude view of the ocean itself. Endless gentle white waves rolled in from the west. The ocean seemed deeply and peacefully azure. The illusion was one of guileless transparency. Of an ocean without secrets, welcoming their inspection, soothing away their fears.

"The ocean lies," Cadmann muttered.

"What?"

"I was just wondering if anything has surfaced yet."

"Nothing notable. Not so far." The screen flickered again, and a roughly fish-shaped outline flashed darkly across the display. A wave of liquid crystals, and the silhouette became an animation. A statistical table ran its estimate column along the edge.

Andy watched the figures hawkishly, then relaxed. "Twenty meters along the side, surfacing fifty kilometers east of Landing Beach. Totally aquatic, Zack—I've seen these before. They don't pose a threat to anything on the land."

Zack traced a finger across the image. "Keep me posted. We can't have damage to one of the Minervas." To Cadmann: "We can get a lot more precise than that."

"I was just about to ask—but you've made a good start."

"We need more, a lot more. All the intelligence that we can

gather." He paused a careful moment, then asked, "What can you report from the highlands?"

"That's what I was hoping to talk to you about. Mary Ann and I have kept journals. I have skins from six different small animals, and botanical samples. I want to trade my knowledge of the island for other services. I'll map the interior, let you know anything that I find. In exchange, I want medicine and more vitamins. Mary Ann said Avalonian soil doesn't have the right mineral balance."

The computer zoned up on another large, shadowy form. This one was smaller than the first, but was tracked moving in toward the island. It broke the surface of the water for a moment, cresting, then dived deeply. The video image was lost.

"We need you, Cad. We have to assume that the thing we killed was one of a set. If there's more than one, then there's *lots*. We're not slowing down expansion. We can't. I swear that this colony is going to be a city one day. But we have to be more cautious. You're best qualified to check our defense plans and suggest alternatives. If you don't want to stay here, I won't try to change your mind. We need a test outbacker. Someone to give us an idea of how an individual family would fare in the south country beyond Mucking Great. Someone is going to do it eventually, and no one is better suited than you. What do you say—be our guinea pig?"

"I already am that. But outback guinea pig sounds better than hermit."

"Same situation, different definition."

Cadmann's face split in a grin. "Bureaucrats. Damned if you can't take misanthropy and turn it into a virtue."

"Damned straight." A huge weight seemed to have been lifted from Zack. The creases in his forehead vanished, and he sighed deeply. "Oh. Cad, will you take back some tools to take rock cores? We're hoping we'll find an iridium layer."

"Iridium?"

"Maybe not iridium, but something widespread, with the makeup of an asteroid. Evidence of a Dinosaur Killer. Something that simplified the ecology."

"Huh. Maybe. What about the monster itself? That thing sure didn't act like a carrion eater, and what else would have survived an asteroid strike? Have you finished the analysis of the corpse?"

"Oh, sure, *corpse*. Well, we lost a lot of equipment in the fire. Some we repaired, some we worked around, but . . . anyway, Greg cremated too much of the monster. You can hardly blame him, but we've been analyzing charcoal! What we get is a picture of something that has a cell structure similar to the samlon or pterodons. Closer to the samlon; pterodons have a lot more quick-twitch muscle fiber. We'll be interested in looking at your samples. Half a dozen? Damn. You've found more in seven weeks than we did in the year we've been down. You probably want to talk to Sylvia about that."

Cadmann just watched the screen for a while longer, and then nodded. He turned and left the room. Zack followed him out.

The sun was high, and Cadmann shielded his eyes with one hand. Workers bustled around the quad. They were setting tables and stringing an orange-and-green banner along the west edge of the courtyard—

"Celebration?"

"Sure—anniversary of Waking Day. Don't you remember?"

"I guess that I reckon time in terms of Landing Day."

"Most of them weren't even awake when we were down here. They outnumber us, Cadmann."

"I guess they do at that." He stretched and picked up his backpack from the com-shack stoop. "Where's Sylvia? I guess we should talk."

THE CREATURE hovered in the air above the holo stage, only a fourth its actual size, but still too vivid for Cadmann's taste. He could almost smell its wet lizard stench, feel its heat, see Ernst's blood drizzling out of its mouth.

Marnie said, "The creature is amphibian, and the major speculation is that it swam over from the mainland or that it was carried by driftwood."

Cadmann repressed a shudder and forced his mind back into the discussion. "Fifty miles! That's a long swim. Why are you so sure it's not native to the island?"

"Not enough food. Not enough variety of food for a sound ecological base. Not enough of *them*, either. A stable population needs numbers. Any pair of anything produces one pair that survives to breed, on average." Sylvia shut down the projector, but the thing still hovered before his mind's eye.

Marnie was examining a Joe carcass. It lay in the middle of a dissection tray, its fur lusterless and limp. She flipped it over on its back, and pressured the paws, hawing as the dark little claws slid out. "You say that you're domesticating these?" Marnie's lisp was still a bit jarring to Cadmann, but she was so totally unself-conscious of it that he felt momentary shame.

"Raising them, at least. It's Mary Ann's project. You'd need a lot of furs to make a bed cover. They're not all that sweet-tempered. Something like a mink. Anyway, it's something else that's bothering Mary Ann."

"She told me."

With the gleaming tip of a scalpel, Marnie drew a line down the middle of the dead Joe's pink, furred belly, then gingerly peeled away a layer of skin to inspect a fatty layer beneath.

Sylvia sat on a stool with her knees pulled up flush with her swollen stomach. She looked like a pregnant elf perched on a mushroom.

"In general," Marnie continued, pinning the flap of skin back, "we don't know a hell of a lot more now than we . . . should have known before. Built for speed. Incredibly strong. The thickness of the bones gives it enormous leverage. The skin is like armor plating. My point is that as underprepared as we were, we were very lucky." Some silent message passed between Marnie and Sylvia, and Marnie slid the dissection tray into a refrigerator.

"I told Jerry I'd meet him at the breeding pond," she said, smiling shyly. "I'll see you both later." She slipped quietly from the room, leaving Cadmann and Sylvia alone.

They stared carefully at the empty stage, and silence hung in the room.

"Cad . . ." she began.

He leaned back against the wall, crossing his arms, eyes thoughtfully half-lidded. "You know, it gets so damned quiet up there in the mountain. Sometimes, when the air is really still, and the dogs are asleep by what's left of the fire, I look down from the mountain, and I can just hear sounds from the Colony. Machinery. Maybe singing. Maybe the mill. Maybe animal sounds. It sounds warm, and so damned far away." He looked at her. She was close enough to touch, but he didn't. "It feels like everything is getting farther all the time."

"I miss you, Cadmann. I didn't know how much I would."

"Yeah. How is Mary Ann?"

"Knocked righteously up. You did a good job there. Three weeks pregnant, and she's healthy as a horse, and I'll bet it's a boy."

"What do you mean, 'you bet'? Isn't there a test or something?"

"Spoilsport. Half the fun is the speculation. She almost glows. She's so in love with you, Cadmann. So . . ."

Cadmann watched the slow rise and fall of Sylvia's belly. "Do you suppose that she'll be as beautiful as you are?"

"All pregnant women are beautiful. And think that they're ugly. Didn't you know that?"

Cadmann turned, staring out into the wall as though there were answers scrawled on the far side. "I'm changing, Sylvia. I can feel it. It's this planet. There are so few of us, and we know nothing about this place. When Mary Ann said that she was pregnant, I was happy . . . but it was different. I have a daughter—you didn't know that, did you?"

Sylvia looked at him, startled. "No—it isn't on any of the records."

He grinned. "You've been spying on me."

She reached out and took his hand. Her thumb rubbed the soft webbing between his knuckles. "I missed you too, big man."

"I was only about eighteen. Elva was twenty-four, and wanted the kid. Wanted to have it by herself. Picked me. Said that she thought I would probably make pretty good basic daddy material."

"I'd say she was right."

"I only know she had it, Sylvia. And on the little girl's third birthday, Elva sent me a holo. That was it—she didn't want to be bothered with a husband."

"Would you have married her?"

"I suppose so. And resented the hell out of her."

"There you go."

"But still, to know. To know that you have a child somewhere. Learning to walk and talk and swim and read, and everything else, and you're not there. It's a little crazy-making. Anyway, that's just background."

"What's the payoff?" Her hand closed gently on his. So warm.

"That I was shocked at how hard it hit me. The thought that Mary Ann is the mother of my child. It doesn't matter how much or how little I love her. What matters is that she's going to be the mother of my child."

"I see." Sylvia released his hand and stood up. "Well, that's what she's going to be, all right, and if preliminary workup indicates anything, she's going to be a damned healthy one. Take care of her, Cadmann. She really cares for you."

"I know." Sylvia moved a step back, just out of touching range. "I love you," he said quietly. "I wish that it meant something."

"Shh," she whispered. "We don't just belong to ourselves, Cadmann. This isn't an ordinary situation, and we're not ordinary people.

It's wonderful, and it's terrible, and it makes me feel old sometimes. But it's what I chose when I came here, and I can't back out now."

"And if it was different?"

"Then . . . it would be different. Lay off."

"All right." The moment was past, and he let the atmosphere lighten again.

"Waking Day is day after tomorrow. Won't you stay?"

"So that's why Zack loaned me a Skeeter. It's a conspiracy. We'll be back. Right now, I think that I need to be alone. With Mary Ann."

"I understand." She held out her hands to him, and he took them. She was so close, and so achingly far away.

"Goodbye, Sylvia."

"Goodbye, Cad."

He bent and touched her lips with his, barely repressing an urge to taste more deeply, knowing that here, in the shadowed clinic, she would have resisted for only a moment, and then held him, even with the swell of another man's child between their bodies.

We're not ordinary people. . . .

Cadmann turned and left.

MARY ANN was outside, waiting for him, and he was suddenly very happy that he hadn't given in to that impulse. He was able to meet her eyes squarely and to hold her.

Please. Let me learn to love her. God knows I need to.

But for now, the light in her eyes was enough love for the both of them, and together they headed for the Skeeter pad.

MAMA had never toured the island. The others of her kind did not like visitors. The map in Mama's mind was not made up of distances, but of the changing taste of the river.

The pond reeked of samlon blood when Mama departed. She staggered with the fullness of her belly. Three days later she was hungry but hopeful. Four mud-sucking alien fish had fallen foul of her. There would be more.

The water ran clean again. Mama understood *that* lesson. She had tasted the burnt meat of her daughter in the water; but the decaying corpse was gone almost immediately. Whatever killed her daughter had eaten the corpse.

Once she was able to streak off the edge of a low bluff and catch a flyer rising from below. She caught another hovering just above the water. The flyers weren't timid enough here between territories. She fed when she could. If her enemy were to find her half starved, her body might betray her, holding her slow while her enemy boiled with *speed*. If she did not find enough food she would turn back.

She moved cautiously, in fear of ambush. For long stretches she paralleled the river, moving among rocks or trees or other cover where she could find it, returning to the river only when she must.

None of this was carefully thought out. Mama was not sapient. Emotions ran through her blood like vectors, and she followed the vector sum. Anger against the creature who killed her daughter. Hunger: the richly, interestingly populated territory upstream. Curiosity: the urge to learn and explore. Lust: the urge to mate with a gene pattern other than her own. And fear, always fear.

She moved slowly enough to learn the terrain as she traveled. Rocks, plains, grassland; a waterfall to be circled. She found fish of interesting flavor before she would have had to turn back.

Farther upstream, things began to turn weird. There were intermittent droning sounds. Chemical tastes in the water and smells on the wind: tar and hot metal and burning, unfamiliar plants, pulverized wood. Her progress slowed even farther. She kept to rocky terrain or crawled along the bottom where the river ran deep and fast. Sounds of an alien environment might cover her enemy's approach. Her enemy must come. She would find Mama; she could be watching her now; she would come like a meteor across terrain she knew like the inside of her mouth. Mama's life would depend on also knowing the terrain.

There was a cliff of hard rock, and softer rock below, and caverns the river had chewed below the waterline. One of the caverns became her base. Life was plentiful, foraging was easy; she might wait here for the enemy, for a time.

She found things pecking on dry ground. They tried to run (badly), they tried to fly (badly). She ate them all. There were bones all through the meat, and half of it was indigestible feathery stuff.

On another day she saw something far bigger flying too far away to smell. It veered away before she could study it. If she could catch something like that, the meat would surely sustain her until her quarry *must* come to deal with an invader.

The next day something came at her across the water.

CHAPTER 15

YEAR DAY

The hour when you go to learn that all is vain
And this Hope sows when Love shall never reap.

DANTE GABRIEL ROSSETTI, "The House of Life"

BY TEN in the morning, the small white disk of Tau Ceti had burned the eternal mist into fluffy white clouds that drifted across the startlingly blue sky like flocks of sheep.

It was appropriate, almost as though their sun were cooperating with the festivities, had offered them the first vivid day of the year.

In the ribboned and bannered quad beneath that hard, clear sky, a dozen food and drink booths had been erected, and from them curled the sweet aromas of half a dozen international cuisines. The stands were all but deserted now, most of the colonists drawn by the sound and movement within the dining hall.

Spring had come to Avalon.

"Allemande left to your corner gal—"

Zack wore a blindingly bright pair of red suspenders over hand-stitched overalls. A fiddle was tucked tightly under his chin, and Cadmann was damned if he didn't actually coax music from it. Zack was playing the hayseed image to the hilt as he stomped and sang on the low stage, guiding the flux and flow of the square dancers with a theatrically midwestern twang in his voice. His voice was flat but lively: the colonists followed his lead in an explosion of joyous energy.

The music itself was an odd mixture of synthesizer keyboard, traditional woodwind and string. Some of the instruments had been shipped aboard *Geographic*, justified as vital cultural treasures. Some had been cobbled together after landing.

> *And now all promenade,*
> *A-with that sweet corner maid,*
> *Singing "Oh Johnny, Oh Johnny Oh . . .*

Cadmann leaned against the wall, halfway through his third mug of beer. The last cold knot of tension in his stomach was coming unsnarled; his head began to buzz politely. He hated lines. He had waited until the music blared from the hall and the dancers returned to their marks before tapping the cold kegs of beer.

On the far side of the crowd Mary Ann danced, swirling her bangled green skirt, throwing her head back to laugh deeply. The smooth white expanse of her throat flashed above a red kerchief. She caught Cadmann's eye and crooked a challenging finger, blowing him a kiss, silently mouthing *Come on* before Elliot Falkland caught her hands and swung her around to the opposite corner of her square.

Cadmann stretched. Tight spots, wounds not quite healed? Yeah, he could find the pain in chest and left arm and hip and knee, if he needed an excuse not to dance. It was more fun to watch.

Carlos bowed out of the dance, pecking Ida van Don on the cheek as he released her hands. She looked around uncertainly, with almost a touch of panic, then spotted Omar's huge frame and pulled him from his seat, tugging him into the patterned chaos, whooping with glee. The glee was not entirely spontaneous. Her smile seemed too rigid. Cadmann wondered if her dreams still rang with Jon's dying screams.

Carlos mopped sweat from his dark brow, fanned the dark circles staining the armpits of his red flannel shirt. "Ah, *amigo*. I am getting old. The señoritas are too much for me."

"Then don't get married."

"Vertical and horizontal dancing are much different." He smiled evilly. "Bobbi lets me lead." He took a sip of Cadmann's beer, smacked approvingly and drew himself a glass. He downed a third of the mug before coming up for air. He followed Cadmann's gaze to Mary Ann.

"Your señorita—she also likes the dance, yes?" He paused, considering.
"I think one can tell much from the way a woman moves to music. The
hips, the hands, the way she holds—"

"Don't you think about anything but sex?"

"Life is short. One must find one's great gift, and practice it—how
do you say?—assiduously."

Cadmann sputtered out a noseful of suds.

Together they strolled around the outside to the quad, where Bobbi
Kanagawa worked at a food booth. Her long black hair twisted and
pinned beneath a white paper cap, Bobbi was oblivious to the music
piped out from the hall and didn't notice her fiancé's approach.

With a long, thin knife, she carefully pared strips from one of three
samlon on her cutting board. Movements almost mechanically precise,
she sliced those strips into thinner pieces, then positioned them atop
formed and pressed blocks of rice.

Although not in full production yet, the rice fields were healthy
enough for Zack to authorize the release of some of the grain stored
aboard *Geographic.*

Carlos leaned across the counter and kissed her wetly. Startled at
first, she smooched back, then rubbed noses with him. "Leave me alone
for fifteen minutes, then do with me what you will."

"I'll hold you to that, chiquita."

"You had better." She squeezed his hands, and there was enough
heat in her emerald eyes to scorch stone. *That's what it would take to
nail Carlos.* . . . "I'm taking you down the rapids, mister."

Carlos grabbed a strip of samlon before she could protest and
popped it into his mouth. Bobbi waved her knife at him as he skated
away, chortling over his mouthful.

"What a woman. Don't you think we'll make beautiful babies?"

Cadmann reflected for a moment. "The loveliest woman I ever
knew was half Japanese and half Jamaican. Assuming the kids take after
their mother, they've got a chance."

The square dance ended with cheers and a thunderous round of
applause, and the hall emptied into the quad.

Mary Ann worked her way to him through the press, holding a
foaming mug. She panted, face glowing and sticky with perspiration.
"Cad, you're such a stick. Why won't you dance?"

"War wound. Both legs blown off. Medics screwed up, sewed two
left feet on."

She stuck her tongue out.

"Look on the bright side: somewhere out there is a guy with two right feet, killing 'em at the Waldorf."

"You're just ashamed of me. You don't want anyone to see us together."

Carlos nodded sagely. "It is true. Many times he has told of how he likes to hide you away in the dark, covering you with his own body if need be—"

"Carlos—"

Martinez took the hint. "I've got to get ready for the Rapids."

"Turning into a tradition, isn't it?"

"Around here, anything that happens twice is a tradition."

Carlos disappeared into the crowd.

The day just felt so damn good.

Contests and exhibitions had been running since breakfast. Cadmann had watched the archery and wrestling, cheering but not competing. Soon would begin the three-day boat race between the honeymooning couples. That he would enjoy! Then the dance contest . . . silliness, that was really all it was, but he had to admit that he was catching the bug.

True, he was pleasantly drunk. (Who had brewed the beer? If he could work out a private deal with that worthy—say, fresh melon cactus every month in exchange for a keg?) He felt more comfortable around the camp than he had in months. But something was pulling him back from wholehearted participation. A voice that was weakening by the minute. Or the mug. Whatever.

He politely squelched a burp.

Watching Mary Ann dance was good for him. He hadn't had a chance to really compare her with the other women.

There was no question that they were a couple: she had fixed the judges, bribed his cornermen and K.O.'d him before he even knew the fight was on. But it warmed him to feel a healthy physical tug when a twirl or gust of wind raised her skirts. Her hard work up at Cadmann's Bluff had trimmed away fat and added healthy muscle. The pregnancy didn't show yet, but there was something special about her. She did glow. . . .

She squashed her lips against his in a beery kiss. "Cad—when are you going to—" her face changed in the middle of the question, became more mischievous—"dance with me?"

Shoot the rapids with me?

The real question was behind the smile, behind the laugh. It lived in the way she leaned against him, letting him feel the muted fire in her belly.

What the hell. It's just a formalization. Why not? But not now. Not on Holotape, for God and the whole world to see.

"Later," he promised. "You'll see."

The stands on the north edge of the quad displayed a mosaic of the Colony's artistic craftsmanship. Cadmann was startled and gratified by the breadth and reach of the work on display. These people had not been chosen for artistic talent. They had hidden depths.

Here was a kinetic sculpture, a globe filled with clear fluid, holding iron flakes spiraling in a slow nebula of magnetic flux.

There, a painting of Avalon's twin moons setting over the bramble bushes. The artist had precisely captured the mauve sunset.

Mounted on a linen-covered table was a sculpture of woven, wired and glued bones. Hundreds of samlon and pterodon bones, sliver thin, formed and painted into a golden bull. As a sumi painting suggests flight or motion with the barest strokes, somehow the bull was challenging and frightened, bursting with animal power and aching vulnerability. The artist's signature was simply "Sylvia."

Cadmann glanced over his shoulder, suddenly wondering if anyone was watching him study the incredible piece, then forced himself to move on.

Next to it was a cameo of native obsidian, and several of Carlos's scandalous thornwood carvings. They would have been right at home on the wall of a Nepalese temple, and Cadmann was suddenly glad that none of the children were old enough to point and ask embarrassing questions.

The crowd was flowing into the meeting hall. Food must be ready to serve. Cadmann followed the flow. He claimed two empty seats next to Terry's wheelchair.

Mary Ann brought two plates piled with Bobbi's samlon sushi, with a dab of the precious powdered wasabi horseradish shipped from Earth; fresh spinach pasta, fresh tomato marinara, whole-grain wheat bread. Most of the food was from the fields and the nets. Avalon was yielding up her harvest, making what reparations she could for the damage done to her newest, strangest children.

Terry ate quietly, slowly chewing each mouthful into liquid. Always thin, he seemed to have gained a few pounds since his injury, and it made his face less pinched and severe. "I approve," he said neutrally.

It took a beat for Cadmann to realize Terry was talking to him. "Food's pretty good," he agreed.

"No. You and Mary Ann. Good match." Terry took another careful mouthful. Cadmann noticed the streaks of gray hair coursing through the curly brown. "How are things up there on the mesa?"

"Nice. Quiet." Cadmann glanced at Mary Ann. "Wait until Sylvia has the baby. Come on up for dinner."

"I'd like that, if we can get this damned chair into a Skeeter."

"Sure, we can do that. Or have Carlos make you a folding model."

The projection equipment was wheeled out to the center of the floor. An enlarged holo field shimmered like a heat mirage: the faces and figures against the far wall were pale, wavering ghosts.

The lights dimmed. The holo image hardened, and the speakers piped in sound.

A motorboat was being lowered down the ravine and into the river below the dam. The boat was a ten-foot black oval, tough synthetic elasticized skin stretched over a metal frame, two low seats and crescent steering wheel mounted in the front. The Skeeter-type engine aft looked too big for the boat. The plastic-sealed knob of a holotape recorder showed above the central mast.

It had reached the water. A second, identical boat dropped to join it.

Sylvia came to sit between Cadmann and Terry, and she smiled shyly as she lowered herself uncomfortably to her seat.

"You look ready," Mary Ann said.

"You know it. Now Marnie's saying next week! Cadmann, don't ever get pregnant." Her complexion was a little blotchy. She wheezed with relief as she settled herself, balancing a plate heaped with food in her hands.

"I'll remember that," he said. "Last time Mary Ann gets on top."

"Hush."

Someone yelled, "Ta-ta-ta-*daah!*" as Elliot Falkland and his fiancée, La Donna, dashed to the center of the floor amid a rowdy chorus of cheers. "Chunky!" Falkland was all grin and jug ears and peeling tan, with a body almost twice the size of La Donna's. But the little woman was known as an indefatigable construction worker. Behind Cadmann, Andy guffawed something about La Donna "sweating that blubber off Elliot before they reach the ocean."

Cadmann raised a cheer as Carlos and Bobbi joined the first couple.

Carlos swept off a broad-brimmed hat in a low, gallant bow. Somehow, even dressed in denims, Bobbi managed a shy curtsey.

Carlos rushed over to Cadmann and Mary Ann. He wore a yellow safety vest, and skintight rubber pants. He carried a bedroll in his left hand. He and Bobbi would take the boat all the way to the ocean, camping along the way. Three days later they would be picked up by Skeeter, officially married.

Cadmann chortled to himself, guessing that Carlos would triple-check that the recording equipment was off before turning in for the evenings. . . .

"Wish me luck, *amigo*. Falkland has more water experience than we do."

"More than anyone but the samlon. He's got flippers for feet." Elliot Falkland and Jerry minded the catfish ponds downriver. Falkland also coordinated the underwater repair operations and had overseen the construction of the dam. That was where he had come to know La Donna. "Anyway, it's not when you get there, it's how."

"Loser paints the winner's house."

"I see your point. Kill him."

"Señor Falkland sleeps with the fishes."

"Good luck," Terry and Sylvia chimed.

Carlos shook hands with the men, kissed the women, then hustled out to supervise the lowering of his boat.

Sudden envy stirred in Cadmann. A three-day trip down the river would be a nice honeymoon. *But we had ours while we built the camp, and it was fine!*

The holo field flickered to a different vantage point. An aerial view of the Skeeter pad swiftly expanded to take in the entire camp. Cadmann's stomach lurched—the reaction he always had when in the air under another's control.

The Skeeter zoomed and veered explosively, rose straight up, then dive-bombed Civic Center. There was clapping, cheering and groaning. The holo field was expanded to fill the room, the magnification bleaching a little of the color from the image.

The three-dimensional aerial panorama was stunning, especially when it veered east, across the Miskatonic. There, Camelot, their new community, was already blocked out.

Camelot wasn't the cramped curlicue of the first year's temporary dwellings. It would be Avalon's first permanent city, and was designed as such. Now that the crops were established, there was time to work on a more leisurely layout. Camelot covered a square kilometer of homes, boulevards, parks and meditation groves, recreation centers. . . .

Each plot of land was huge, larger than any of them could have afforded on Earth. Unbelievable wealth by any standard that they had left behind. And room for almost infinite expansion, as their worms and insects and terraforming lichens churned Avalon's soil into something that the less hardy plants and animals could use. Mineral supplementation and acid balancing created an ideal medium for their crops. Huge homes, ranch houses. Mansions that would one day overlook gracious estates.

Room for a man to grow!

The boat engines were no longer ear-jarring burrs, and the Skeeter zipped off to follow the race. The camp cheered, bets flying and changing: Who would be the first through the rapids? They were twenty kilometers from the northern mountains, and it would be a while before the real action began, a few minutes before the boats worked their way through the dam locks.

In the meantime, the band had apparently rested long enough. Zack mopped his forehead with a bandanna and yelled, "All right— we've got enough time for a couple more turns around the floor. Let's get it moving!"

He shouldered his fiddle. His fingers danced across the strings, producing sounds of surprising sweetness.

> Hey there ladies, grab your man
> Hold that lad as tight as you can—

Sylvia's hand sneaked around behind Cadmann and tapped Mary Ann twice, sharply, and they exchanged a silent message.

It's a conspiracy. I'm doomed. . . .

Mary Ann stood, politely but firmly pulled his plate from his hand. Setting her heels into the composition floor, she dragged him to his feet.

Sylvia and Terry and the surrounding crowd howled at his obvious discomfort, and Cadmann let that bolster him.

"It's been a long time," he whispered, "and I am sore wounded," relieved that others were moving out on the floor. They formed a square with Hendrick and Phyllis.

In a few moments there were squares all over the hall, and Zack was calling and fiddling, the band was playing, and Cadmann's considerations were lost in the urge to keep the rhythm and watch his feet.

Mary Ann was an excellent square dancer, and she pulled him along with her into the mood. Soon Cadmann was part of an interweaving pattern of human rectangles, do-si-do-ing and skip-stepping as their square broke and re-formed, changed places and swiveled joyously around the floor. Sharp reminders from half-healed wounds eased as he warmed up. The seated observers whistled and clapped and stomped their feet.

Before he realized it, Cadmann was grinning and sweating and thoroughly convinced that he was keeping better time than anyone out there.

At the end of an hour the dance broke up with a spontaneous cheer and hugs all around, and Cadmann's drunken whoop was as loud as any. What the hell—this is your family. You need them—at least Mary Ann does. And don't be surprised that square dancing makes you feel like part of the community. Earth magic, that's what it is. What it's always been.

The holofield projector was wheeled back to the center of the quad. Once again the air shimmered, causing squeals of delight—Carlos's boat had breached the rapids, and it was deliciously easy for Cadmann to lose himself in the illusion.

He was aboard their boat, hovering directly above Carlos's shoulders as he spun the wheel, guiding the boat through the rushing water. The water was beginning to churn white, and there an outcropping of glistening wet rock scraped the side of the inflatable. The boat jumped, and beside him Bobbi screamed delightedly.

Elliot's boat was right behind him, and with a jolt the holofield changed its perspective. La Donna was at the wheel, and the couple were whooping it up more than competing. As the boat hit each spill, they grabbed each other in mock fear, mugging ferociously for the cameras.

The water grew whiter, choppier, and the race was really on. The river was narrower and faster here, and the towering walls of the northern mountains rose up around them in jagged iron-gray sheets.

Elliot coaxed his engine to sharper life. With a sure hand La Donna wove them through the rocks. Every dip, every eddy was breathtakingly real, three times larger than life.

The water splashed up and licked at them, and Cadmann wiped at his face reflexively. Elliot's boat shot a short falls, landed flat-bellied, with a crash and a whoop from the hall.

The image switched back to Carlos, who was looking back over his shoulder at the approaching boat.

Cadmann's palms were sweaty and shaking. It was almost impossible to resist the urge to roll up his sleeves and grab a pole: there was a rock spur! Ah, good. Bobbi, with movements as quick and light as the flicker of a whip, nudged their boat away from it.

Everyone was cheering now, and it grew riotous as the image switched from one perspective to the other; the gap between the boats narrowed, and the race finally became nose to nose. The river narrowed as it sluiced through a gap between two towering slabs of rock, and Carlos narrowly held his lead, Elliot coming up fast.

Then, as they came out of it, and the way widened again, Elliot rammed Carlos from the rear. La Donna squealed as their boat hit a rock and lurched in a drunken circle. Elliot cursed fluidly as Carlos's craft shot past.

Elliot's boat spun twice, dipped and swung perilously and then finally stabilized.

The hologram switched to Carlos's craft and a triumphant Bobbi shaking her fist at Elliot as they widened the distance.

Carlos gunned the motor fully, and their boat rose in the water and shot north toward the ocean. Far behind them now, Elliot opened his throttle and skimmed along the surface, churning the water into white as he roared in pursuit.

Rock walls flashed by. Cadmann's heart thundered as he remembered the sheer speed of the boats, their near-hydrofoil design that kept a minimum of prow in the water, minimizing drag.

Fast!

But then . . .

"Switch back!" someone yelled, and suddenly they were with Carlos's boat, and it was in trouble. Something was terribly wrong, and the boat was spinning—

Another rock? But Carlos's face was distorted, and he was grabbing for Bobbi, screaming something unintelligible. The boat seemed to be collapsing, the holoimage buckling and blurring. The last image that they had was of rocks and water and churning foam, and a brief glimpse of Bobbi tumbling through the foam toward the rocks, thrashing her hands frantically as she disappeared beneath the surface of the water.

CHAPTER 16

ON THE CLIFF

All men think all men mortal, save themselves.

EDMUND YOUNG, *Night Thoughts*

FIRST THERE WAS a humming. Mama was a good distance from the water, and her mouth was full of blood and feathers. She looked for insects swarming. If she found the nest she would eat it whole. . . .

But the swarm sound was louder now, and too uniform, and there were no dark clouds that could be insects. Something strange, in unfamiliar terrain. Mama made for the water, not yet *fast* but already wary.

The humming was louder as she reached the water.

It came around a bend upstream. She couldn't see the intruder's shape; it was too distant yet. But it moved *on* the water, not through it. Moved *fast.*

Finally. Mama's eyes were above the water. The snorkel between her eyes drew air; her lungs heaved. There was rage in her, and something else: sphincter muscles relaxed back of her neck, *speed* began dripping into her blood, and her entire body began to fizz. The vulnerable snorkel withdrew into her head. She watched the intruder come—not quite toward her, she hadn't been seen yet—then why was the intruder already *fast?*

But Mama was *fast* now, and she moved.

This was her territory now. She knew it that well, she had been here that long. *Mine.* She too was almost above the water as she reached the intruder. She struck from the side. For a bare instant she knew that she had won.

Skin with a thin taste, a taste like metal but not as strong, ruptured on impact and tore in her jaws. No meaty texture, no taste of blood. Not won: lost! Tricked! And where was her enemy?

The metallic skin filled with water and began to sink. Confusing tastes drifted in its wake. Things thrashed the water in slow motion, beasts caught between fighters. She ignored them. Where was her rival?

Still *fast*, Mama streaked for her cave before she could be blind-sided. At the underwater mouth she turned. She couldn't be attacked now except from the front.

Now there was time. Mama lifted her eyes above the water and watched two beasts thrashing. If meat were suddenly snatched beneath the surface, she would know that her enemy was below. But the prey were swept downstream, thrashing, trying to reach the river's edge. They reached shore unmolested, and scrambled from the water unmolested.

Mama had been tricked. She had bitten something, but it wasn't meat, and where was her enemy?

There! Just like the other, it skimmed across the water, almost to-ward her. It swerved away as Mama streaked toward it. The intruder was fully on *speed*, and young, Mama thought. She herself had never moved so fast . . . but its turn was too slow. She was on it, and her teeth closed with terrible strength—

On thin, tough, tasteless skin, and flesh that ruptured and bone that broke—fragile bone, prey blood, prey meat, with no taste of *speed*. Not at all the flesh of her own kind, and she'd been tricked again!

She had barely slowed. She kept moving, fleeing the site of her kill, curving toward safety, sliding across the bucking surface of the water. *Where is my enemy? Where?*

Behind her, meat thrashed in the water, then subsided. More prey was climbing the cliff, unmolested, and that was hardly surprising. In the middle of a duel one does not pause to dine.

How may I lure my enemy?

My enemy's territory, my enemy's prey. Challenge!

* * * ·

CARLOS MARTINEZ was shaking: with cold, with shock and pain from the fractured cheekbone and the flap of scalp torn away when he wrapped himself around Bobbi's unconscious body to shield her from the rocks.

She lay curled on her side, flat stomach spasming, river water still trickling in a brown stream from her mouth, eyes glazed, but open and wandering blindly. (Alive, *vivo!* flashed insanely into his mind, alive, *vivo!*, scrambling his thoughts.) She was in shock, and probably concussed, but all that really mattered for the moment was that she was alive.

He gripped his head tightly, fighting the ringing and the pain. In a few moments they quieted, and he massaged Bobbi's rib cage firmly as he looked about him.

Later in the year, when the snow from the northern mountains melted, the spot he stood on and another thirty meters of tumbled rock would be submerged. In another ninety days there might not have been a place for them to crawl onto. He and Bobbi might have been dashed against steeply sloping walls of naked rock. A few hundred meters north or south the water dashed against sheer cliff. As bad and barren as this shelf was, it still represented something very near a miracle.

He would have to fight rapids or climb to get off the beach. He managed a quick prayer of thanks that he wouldn't have to try. Rescue would come soon. Thank goodness for the holo links! The camp would have seen exactly what happened.

His head throbbed. He kept up the steady, gentle massage on Bobbi's ribcage.

Her eyes fluttered open weakly. "Carlos . . . what happened?"

"We hit a rock." That had to be it. That was all that it could be. So why was there a wet red flag on part of the memory? Something trying to hide from him and warn him at the same instant?

Carlos ripped his shirt off and wiped her face with it. She seemed flushed. He bundled the shirt and tucked it under her head. Not long now. Elliot Falkland would be fighting upriver even now. He managed a smile to think of the rotund engineer piloting his way through the rapids. Bobbi would have treatment within the hour, and tomorrow they would be able to laugh about this.

The Colony would already be sending out Skeeters.

He thought that he could hear the hum of a distant engine. "I'll be right back, chiquita," he said, and kissed her softly. Her lips felt bruised and flushed.

She reached for him, gripped at the wet cloth of his shirt. "No. Don't leave me. Please."

There was help out in the river. It tore him, but he pried her fingers loose. "Shh. Shh. I love you. I'll be right back, I promise. O.K.?"

Shaking, unconvinced, she nodded her head.

Carlos scrambled over the rocks to the south, to a higher point where he could see the bend in the river. All he could see was the rush of the water, silver-white with dark patches as it exploded over rocks and took sudden dips and turns. To either side the mountain walls were steep, at least forty near-vertical meters of iron-gray, roughly weathered rock. The crusty gray was interrupted by bands of lighter color. High tides? Geological separations? His mind wasn't working properly yet.

From the new vantage point, he heard nothing, could see nothing, and that puzzled him. Where was Elliot? Then he saw.

He's been wrecked too! Dear God.

Elliot lay inert on a patch of rocks by the far shore. He must have been thrown clear. The second boat was no more than a few dark shreds of fabric which still fluttered, wedged into rocks. There was no sign of La Donna.

A dark, spreading stain grew from beneath Elliot's head and dripped down into the rushing water. Carlos's stomach went sour and tight. *I've got to help him—*

And then Carlos saw it. The thing ripped through the water like a black torpedo. That was what his subconscious had screamed to him. He had caught a bare glimpse of that dark juggernaut churning through the water, smashing through the side of the boat. . . .

The foam suddenly churned, and the black thing erupted from the water, flashing up into Elliot with the speed of a striking snake. Elliot's body jerked once, massively, and disappeared into the waves.

Something that felt like a cloak of cold slime swept over Carlos, numbing him. But in its wake his mind began to work. His first conclusion was inescapable: If he did not think very clearly, Bobbi was going to die.

What was there to do? The monster would find them. He'd be insane to assume anything else. They couldn't hope to outrun that creature under the best of circumstances. With Bobbi barely conscious, it would take a miracle to escape.

Do something. Odds don't matter. Act! In half an hour, no more, we'll be rescued. The camp is better prepared now. They were watching the race! They must already know what they're up against.

And Cadmann's back in camp.

Carlos scrambled back down to Bobbi. She wound her arms around his neck weakly, and her black hair streamed back over her shoulders like seaweed. "Carlos? What?"

"We've got to move."

"Why?" Her head lolled back as if her neck were fractured. She coughed wetly. "Why can't we stay here? I hurt. I'm so sleepy."

Lie, you bastard. "We need to be at a better vantage point for the Skeeters—if they're going to pick us up." He lifted her to her feet. She seemed a feather. "Come on, hon." He grunted as she found her feet. He bent, unknotted the pillow he had made of his shirt and slipped it over one arm.

He half pulled, half lifted Bobbi up over the first eastern row of boulders, then took the opportunity to reorient. They had to get away from the river—but another twenty-five meters up the rocks and they would be against the cliff. No hope there.

The mountain stretched above them, a splintered pale fortress carved from the primeval clay by ragged knife strokes. Above the ridge the clouds that had been fleecy and white an hour ago had darkened, were tinged with black as though heralding a sudden thundershower. The air had gone chill.

He might be able to climb that wall, but there was no way in hell that Bobbi could make it. And there was no place to make a stand here, nothing that would afford protection.

What it looked like, he thought grimly, was a damn good place to die.

There was an answer. Both of them could die, or one, or just maybe neither. But they had to separate.

Watching his footfalls carefully, he carried her along with him, pulling, coaxing, babying her along. Scraping arms and legs, protecting her as best he could, but aware that little scrapes didn't matter right now. *Have to get her to shelter. Have to get her to shelter . . .*

The going was steep now, and twice they almost fell. Once they did, sliding and skinning hands and knees. Bobbi was a little more alert now, and more help. She managed to thrust a leg out, halting a tumble. He laughed weakly and kissed her forehead, and then pushed her up another few meters.

Muscles tensing, tendons in his back stretching with the strain, afraid to stop for rest or to look back to see what was following them out of the water, Carlos helped Bobbi up the sharp incline. The pounding in his head grew worse. They slipped again, and this time her thigh caught on a sharp spur and made a nasty gash.

Damn! He whipped off his shirt and wrapped it around her leg quickly, before it could leak blood and destroy the tiny inspiration that had begun to flower. Above them and to their left was a shallow ledge, all but invisible from below. A single person might hide there. Maybe.

"Come on, just keep moving." She must have sensed or seen some of the dread in his manner, because she was glancing back down at the river now, at the churning white and pale rushing blue.

Carlos lowered her to the shelf. Perfect. There was even a slight overhang. If she crawled back into it, she would be safe.

If all went well . . .

He untied the hastily applied dressing and knotted the shirt into a tourniquet, applying it above the wound. Blood oozed in a sluggish stream. Good enough. One way or the other, it would do.

He looked back out at the river. Nothing yet. Now he could remember: the image of Elliot's body disappearing beneath the surface, fat arms and legs slapping the water once.

And another image: that of the first creature back at the Colony as it dashed through the searchlights in a nightmare of fanged and taloned rage.

He shivered.

"Now listen," he said, kneeling next to her. "I lied to you. We're not up here to make it easier for a Skeeter to pick us up. We're up here because there's another of those creatures in the water. I've got to go, to make a trail to lead him away from you."

Her eyes widened. Her fingernails tore at his arm. "But Carlos . . ."

"Listen to me," he whispered fiercely. "You've seen what those bastards can do. I don't want to give up what little chance we have."

Bobbi moved clumsily, trying to sit up. The blood trickling from the gash began to pulse more strongly.

"Your leg is bad. Don't make it worse." Carlos forced her back down. The leg! He had to do something, but there was no time at all, only hope.

"I have a chance," he said. "I don't think those things can climb as well as a human being. They're too heavy." He looked at the steepening wall. "I can climb that damn mountain and keep it busy until someone gets here. It can't be long. When I'm gone, climb as far back into the shadows as you can. Keep pressure on the tourniquet as long as you can."

"Carlos—"

His mind stuttered, trying to find the right words, something brave and reassuring, and couldn't. Finally he just held her, saying again, "I love you."

He left her. He climbed down again and examined her perch. Bobbi couldn't be seen from below. Not seen, but what about smell?

The first stop was the rock that had gashed her leg. It was blood-stained, and he searched until he found a fist-sized stone. He pounded at the spur until it shattered. He scooped up the fragments and flung them as far as he could.

There was no guarantee that his ploy would work, but one thing he knew for certain: he had to make a stronger scent trail for it to follow.

He did it the only way that he could, thankful that there was still fluid in his bladder, enough to leave a trail from beneath the blood-stained rock well to the right, away from Bobbi.

He began to climb.

He was quickly blowing for air. How long had it been since the crash? Twenty minutes? It seemed an eternity. But the Skeeter would be coming! *We lived longer than I thought we would.* He was up the grade above Bobbi now, and he saw that she had crawled farther between the rocks. Good girl.

Now he was high enough on the cliff to see down into the river. There was the blood slick where Elliot had met the rocks. Beyond were limp black fabric and boat fragments at the river turn. To the south, there was nothing but the rushing river. Where were the rescue Skeeters?

Where was—?

Oh, Jesus.

There was a movement in the water, and something moved up out of it, as steady and inexorable as a Titan, some god of the fishy depths. Carlos cried out reflexively.

It was the same as the first creature, only larger, half again as large, and fleshier. It paused as if getting its bearings, then stared right at him—

For one crazy, shameful instant he thought, *Let it have Bobbi. Let it have anything.*

Then it blurred, as if shot from the water by compressed air. It crossed the rocks, paused for an instant, then took off again, cutting an angular trail up toward the wall—paused and exploded into a series of zigzags that was like nothing so much as a crazy pinball game, then hit the wall and ran almost straight up at him.

Carlos tried to close his eyes, to wait in darkness for a swift and terrible death, but didn't have time. It was, it was—

It shot right past him and kept going until it perched on a rock shelf halfway between him and the top of the mesa.

The creature crouched above him. It ignored Carlos entirely as it scanned the river and rocks far below. Except for the rapidly turning head it stood entirely still, yet gave an illusion of motion, like an engine revving in neutral.

What was it looking for? More boats? Whatever it was doing, it wasn't watching Carlos.

It can move. Faster than anything I have ever seen. Faster than anything I have ever heard of. I can't outrun it. It must have seen me, but it doesn't act like it. Maybe—

The cliff was steep. A fall would kill him. *Better that than the monster,* he thought, but he couldn't make himself believe it enough to jump. He made his hands stop trembling, reached down, found a handhold, tested it. It was firm. He lowered himself a few inches, found a new hold, and—

The creature snarled: a high-pitched scream like a drill biting into metal. Carlos looked up into its vast dark disklike eyes. The message in them was unmistakable: *Where the fuck do you think you're going?*

"Ah, nowhere," he muttered under his breath. The creature watched him for another few seconds, then turned away.

Carlos pressed himself into the rock wall. Between terror and confusion, he couldn't guess what his next move might be. *But what does it think it's doing? Is it crazy?* A crazy thought, indeed. Carlos laughed, and it turned to look at him, and the laugh stuck jaggedly in his throat. It went back to scanning the river.

AT THE SHORE was injured prey, dying. Two more prey were climbing the cliff, characteristically clumsy. The enemy *must* regard these as hers. Mama planned her move, and then—

Challenge. Mama charged across the water, straight at the feebly moving prey. Her jaw clamped on its hind leg. She dived beneath the froth, released the meat at once and swam for her life. Three seconds later she surfaced far downstream, to watch her enemy come to reclaim stolen meat.

The corpse tumbled unmolested. Her enemy was too clever, far too clever for one so young.

Of the two other prey, one had disappeared. The last was halfway up the cliff.

Mama studied the cliff. It wasn't sheer, but the thought of being stranded there while something came at her was one she rejected at once . . . and retrieved, and toyed with.

She could see most of the cliff, and no danger showed there. Her enemy might be in the water or at the top of the cliffs. She never doubted it was watching.

There were footholds along the cliff. Take any path too fast and she might be stranded in midair, falling toward waiting jaws. Motionless in white froth, with only her eyes showing, Mama chose her path.

Then she moved. Across the seething water. Up along cracks in the rock, now quick, now slow, *dancing* her route, ready to face death with her footing firm. In seconds she was halfway up the cliff, poised on a ledge above live prey.

Challenge. Come and get what's yours!

CHAPTER 17

RESCUE

No man quite believes in any other man.

H. L. MENCKEN, *Prejudices*

"BUT WHAT could have happened?" Zack demanded.

Cadmann guided Skeeter One through the twisting canyon, barely noticing the naked rock walls rising to either side. "Don't know." The west side of the canyon was growing rapidly darker. The smaller sun cast shadows much sharper than he'd been used to on Earth. It made judging distances harder. Cadmann moved the Skeeter toward the brightly lit eastern wall. It was banded in orange and pale reds. "Don't know. Damn pretty country here."

"Yeah, sure—how can you be so calm?"

"I'm not, but what's the use of getting excited until there's something to do?"

"Yeah. You're right." Zack took a deep breath. "Those walls are pretty. Like the Australian outback. Ever go there?"

"No, the U.N. never needed soldiers out there."

"It was a rock. Cadmann, it had to be a rock."

"A rock that got two boats?"

"Why not? And we don't know that Elliot's boat is gone—"

"Like hell we don't." Cadmann's mouth was a grim line. "Look, Zack, you can kid yourself about interpretation, but not about what we heard, and the last thing we heard was La Donna screaming. And the last thing we saw?"

"*You* saw. I ran the tape and I didn't see what you saw."

"Oh, maybe I didn't see it either. There was something. Something dark in the water near Carlos's raft, something that I swear was moving across the current . . . well, no, I won't swear." Cadmann spoke into his comcard. "Skeeter Two."

"Here," Stu Ellington answered.

"We're coming up to the bend. You go right across the canyon, down to the rapids, and turn back. We'll start the search at the upstream end."

"Roger. Goddam, I'm glad you're with us."

"Me too," Zack said carefully. "I'm still hoping we don't find—"

"Nobody had to remind you to bring your rifle. And damned if that spare clip doesn't look loaded with incendiaries."

Zack grunted. "I'm not going to be stupid about it."

Skeeter Two rounded the bend ahead. Cadmann had just made the turn when Stu's voice came through the radio. "I've spotted wreckage downstream, but no sign of—holy shit! Nine o'clock."

Cadmann's eyes flashed to the left, and for a moment all he saw was the sheer rock face of the gorge. Then he focused, and he saw the creature, perched like a house cat on a bookshelf, only a dozen meters above a stranded Carlos.

"Straight in. Surprise. Shoot when you have a target," Cadmann ordered. *It's not moving. Just sitting there. A little closer*—"Zack, make the first shots count. Maybe it will forget about Carlos and head for the river. Stu!" He shouted into the radio. "You check the river! Look for other monsters."

"Look for Elliot and La Donna and Bobbi, too," Zack said.

Cadmann spun the Skeeter to hover twenty meters from the canyon wall. "Now!" he shouted.

Zack shouldered his rifle and squeezed off a burst. Spent shells whirred out of the rifle breech in a glittering arc.

The monster twisted, turned toward the Skeeter, then swiveled wildly, searching the river and the cliff above, finally looking back at the Skeeter.

Cadmann touched a button and spoke into the tiny microphone

attached to his helmet. "Carlos! Hang in there, *amigo*." His amplified voice echoed through the canyon.

Carlos was trapped, frozen except for one foot which slipped as he fought for a toehold. His hands and arms were stretched painfully taut. His head twisted back to look at them, then he pressed his cheek back into the cliff face again.

"What is it *doing* up there?" Zack demanded.

It was paying more attention to its sides than to Skeeter One. It licked at the bullet holes.

Zack fired again, a long burst. The creature recoiled against the rock. Its gaze rested on them for an instant, then its head twitched to the left and the right with the speed of a hummingbird's wings.

Then with no warning at all it dove off the cliff, ran down the side faster than a rock could fall, hit the ground and sped for the river. Cadmann couldn't pivot the Skeeter fast enough to see it dive between the rocks.

Skeeter Two was just whizzing back across the river when the creature disappeared with a splash.

Cadmann spoke through the amplifier. "Okay, *amigo*, you can come down now." He switched to radio. "Stu. Did you—?"

"I've got it, Cad. Not a clear view: there's too much disturbance in the water. But it looks like there's a cave mouth down there. I'd say we've got it penned."

Gotcha! Cadmann crowed silently. "Hover. If it shows up, blow it away."

"Roger—but Cad—we have the remains of *both* rafts. And Elliot's dead. We can't find La Donna or Bobbi."

The news hit home savagely, dulling the flash of pleasure.

"Stay over the cave. We'll look for the ladies."

"What about Carlos?"

"He's moving," Cadmann said. "When he gets to the ledge we'll see if he needs help. Nothing I can do from here right now." He turned back to Zack. "I could set you down where you can wait for Carlos. . . ."

"No." Zack squeezed out each word. "This isn't going to get any easier if we wait."

Cadmann pulled back on the stick, and the Skeeter peeled away from the wall and headed downriver, looking for what they really didn't want to find.

* * *

CADMANN stood, rifle butt braced against his thigh, watching the water boiling over the rocks. Somewhere beneath the foam was the monster who had killed Elliot and La Donna, and wounded Bobbi. "You're going to die down there," he whispered.

There was a sudden sound behind him, and Cadmann wheeled instinctively, rifle coming to bear without conscious thought.

Carlos gave a weak smile, shaking a cigarette out of a plastic pack. "Smoke?"

"No, thanks."

Several different emotions warred on Carlos's face, and he finally lowered the package. "Absurd, isn't it? I mean, to want to give you something. A cigarette . . . a handshake?"

Cadmann extended his hand.

"Thanks, Cadmann. I never understood what you went through until now." His dark face was relaxed, his voice very quiet.

"You've forgotten your accent."

Carlos gave a short bark of laughter. "Yeah. Wait around. Bullshit has a way of piling back up."

He exhaled a long stream of smoke. His hands were shaking badly. "Bobbi will be all right. Won't she? She won't wake up. Why am I asking you?"

His eyes lost focus, were gazing into the wall of rock on the far side of the gorge. Too well, Cadmann knew what they were seeing.

Skeeter Two was still hovering over the Miskatonic. "If there isn't another exit from the cave, then we've got the damn thing pinned, is that it?"

"That's it." Skeeter Six was humming in, loaded cargo hoist swinging pendulously. Cadmann looked at Carlos critically. "Are you fit?"

Carlos ground out the half-smoked cigarette. "I'm shaking. I'll be over it. And the best way is to kill that thing. What are your ideas?"

"You'll see."

The cargo hoist beneath the Skeeter was full, and the pilot lowered it. When it was down and released, the Skeeter touched down and Jerry dismounted, a rifle over his shoulder, a bulky square equipment case in his left hand. Skeeter Six took Two's place over the river.

Jerry clapped Carlos on the back, shook hands with Cadmann. "Camp is in an uproar, not a panic. We're moving."

They headed back to the temporary shelter, where Stu and Andy were unpacking equipment. Zack had flown Bobbi back to camp first.

There was very little said, and not much show of nerves. Just swift, purposeful action. With a grinding hum, another Skeeter bore in men and equipment.

Cadmann grunted satisfaction to himself. The Colony's response was swift and sensible. Maybe it took tragedy to bring out the survivor in them.

They walked over to join the man and woman dismounting from the newest Skeeter. Cadmann nodded in greeting. "We've got to move quickly. It's badly wounded now—"

"We may be able to capture it," Jerry interjected. "We need to capture it alive if at all possible, Cadmann."

"All right, Jerry, but don't expect me to take any chances with it. I'm laying the tightest trap I can. If everything goes perfectly, we may be able to take it alive. If one little thing fucks up, we kill it."

"And if more than a little thing goes wrong . . ." Carlos said grimly.

Together they walked to the edge of the rocks overlooking the swirling depths of the Miskatonic. They could see little. Cadmann touched his headphone. "Any sign of activity?"

"None yet. Flash on the tiniest movement."

"That's the way we want it."

The river bottom was dark, and cold, and somewhere down there was what Cadmann wanted. "You're mine," he whispered.

"What was that, *amigo?*"

"*Amigo.*" Cadmann looked at him in disgust. "I said I knew it was too good to last."

CHAPTER 18

DESCENT INTO HELL

> *One of the greatest blessings of virtue is the contempt of death. He who has learned how to die has unlearned how to serve. To be ready to die frees us from all bondage and thralldom.*
>
> MONTAIGNE, *Essays*

CADMANN WIPED AT his faceplate twice before he realized that the stain was on the inside. He waved to one of the waiting spearmen, got a nod and surfaced. Fresh air tasted good. He removed the faceplate and spat into it, rubbed out the fog and rinsed it. Better.

The Miskatonic churned around him. Even with weight belt and tether line, the current threw his balance off, increased irritability, drained his strength. The wet suit slowed his every motion. And well worth it! Many a man had survived a shark attack because of his wet suit. A wet suit didn't taste like blood; and if something tore into him anyway, it could hold him together like a body bandage until a doctor could reach him.

But he felt slow. He dared not hurry. Methodically he prepared himself for war, knowing that the enemy would interrupt him when it chose.

Anchoring the net had been nightmarish: two men hammering and screwing meter-long barbed steel stakes into the mud and rock around the cave, a third man hovering back, underwater lamp and spear gun at the ready. The net itself was stronger than steel cable and as thin as spider silk, a synthetic organic polymer that was predicted to last for hundreds of years of ordinary use. No lesser durability would have been approved for shipment aboard *Geographic*.

Ordinary use. Cadmann smiled thinly into his faceplate. This evening's exercise would hardly be considered *that.*

He reached back over his shoulder to adjust the re-breather apparatus. Very light, very compact, intended for underwater repairs on a docked Minerva. It was certified for an hour of swimming, half that of "vigorous activity." *It'll do. Half an hour fighting that thing and one or the other of us won't need oxygen any more. Okay, down we go—*

"Cadmann, this is Sylvia."

"Go." It was impossible to speak distinctly into the throat microphone.

"I've analyzed the photos. Cadmann, that thing has to be amphibious. It may spend more time underwater than on land."

"Uh-huh." *I already thought of that one. And they're hard enough to kill on land. . . .* "Thanks. More?"

"No—except, be careful."

"Uh-huh." He stretched and dove down to join the others at their work at the net. He felt the reassuring pressure of Zack's "monster killer" spear gun against his thigh.

Moscowitz had promised them a stopper. Joe Sikes's machine shop had delivered it. The device looked like a pistol with a webbed black plastic grip. Immediately in front of the handpiece was an ammunition clip that looked as if it were constructed for shotgun shells. This was almost true: special cartridges drove carbon-steel-tipped spears carrying enough high explosive to blow the engine out of a Skeeter.

This should stop them, and the net should hold them. Hah. The net had better stop them. This island is starting to look infested with the bastards.

He swam to the cave mouth and waved to the spear gunners watching the work. One waved back and went to join Carlos on the other side of the cave.

Carlos had opened his wet suit down the front. One of the spear guns was strapped to his leg. He worked methodically, carefully, but he never stopped. He'd done that all day, driving Cadmann on with his example, working through exhaustion, through fear . . . as if the devil was on his tail.

Welcome to hell, Carlos.

A silver trail of bubbles bobbled from the side of Carlos's mouth, and he gave Cadmann a "thumbs up." Cadmann wiggled the meter-long barbed-steel pinions holding down his corners of the net. No give to them at all. If the rock held, the net would.

A catfish and a samlon swam by almost in tandem, the samlon close behind, chasing playfully. Cadmann allowed himself a twinge of hunger. The fish were getting big and fat, especially the samlon. If he'd had time, he would have snatched that one from the water.

They began to ascend. Cadmann's aching muscles sighed relief.

Their heads broke the surface. Both scrambled out in almost comic haste, sucking air. The sun had dipped below the west wall and there were only a few minutes of light left.

Armed men and women surrounded the temporary camp. Packing and crating from boxes of hastily shipped equipment were piled randomly into a central area; no one had taken the time to collect or remove them, but they were out of the way, no shelter for monsters to hide behind. Two machine guns occupied the top of an empty crate.

A faint burning smell hung in the air. The low steady vibration of a flare drill tickled Cadmann's feet. An electric generator hummed near the shelter. A series of cables linked it to batteries of portable lights set up on every side, giving the entire area a bright greenish-yellow glow.

Cadmann and Carlos stripped off their mouthpieces and gloves. Cadmann opened the zipper on his wet suit.

Skeeters glided across the river. Their searchlights danced yellow ovals on the rushing water. Guards carrying explosive and incendiary rounds patrolled in tight shifts while the technicians erected their tents and tested their equipment. The canyon thrummed with the sound of a Skeeter bringing in a second generator.

Carlos pointed to the machine guns and patrols. "They take you seriously, *amigo.*"

Sure. Now. "Good."

A tent flap raised, and Jerry waved a thin arm at them. "Over here."

"Join you in *dos minutos*, Cad. Want to get a gel on my face cut."

Cad nodded, then crossed to the tent. He had to duck going in. A small gas heater burned in the corner, and the air was toasty. "What do we have, Jer?"

"Everything you wanted," Jerry answered. He held up a plastic pouch. Its contents seemed darkly purple in the artificial light. "This should do it."

"Great. How are the other preparations going? Andy?"

The big engineer spread out a sheet of color-coded graph sheeting on the table. "Deep radar shows a network of caves going back into the mountains for at least a kilometer. It would be death to go in there and take it on its own terms."

"There's no way in hell to kill it and be *sure* it's dead unless we go in. You know that."

"Swell. Shit, man. I don't like it at all."

"Have to burn the egg sac," Cadmann said.

Jerry grinned. "I've read *Red Planet* too." His look became serious. "All right, I grant you that. There may be young. Or eggs. And right now it's wounded. There isn't a better time, but I still don't like it."

"No more do I, but you just do the best you can up here. Do it right, and we won't have anything to do but collect a corpse."

"Corpses, if it has young. All right. Come on."

He led the way out and behind the tent where a tripod-mounted laser drill burned into the ground. The men working the drill were shielded and wore goggles against the glare and the fat sparks that popped and flew like flaming moths. Sizzling melted rock bubbled up out of the cavity, flowed a few inches, then turned sluggish and puddled.

Thirty meters away, a second drill was searing into the rock, and just beyond a rise Cadmann could see the sharp, flickering lights of yet another.

The laser shut down abruptly, and someone yelled, "We're through!"

"Lay the pipe through." Twelve meters of flexible metal piping was run through while the rock was still hot. The top end was fastened to a pump and a twenty-gallon drum.

"What have we got there?" Cadmann asked, curious now.

"Call it napalm, only nastier. Burns longer, hotter. Top layer will vaporize. When we touch it off there'll be a shock wave that should kill anything down there. Its waste products are toxic, it will burn up any oxygen down there."

"Just like Godzilla. Oxygen destroyer—"

Andy laughed. "Always wondered why they had that film aboard *Geographic*. This stuff isn't magic, but it's pretty nasty. Homemade, too."

"So was 'foo-foo gas.' "

"What the hell was that?"

"Gasoline and old-fashioned granular laundry detergent. Big factor in the 1995 Argentine revolution."

"*Viva la revolución.*" Andy grinned.

"Stealing my lines, *compadre?*" Carlos joined them. His facial scar was sealed tight under a waterproof astringent salve.

"You'll get your royalty payment." Andy breathed deeply. "You guys ready?" Cadmann and Carlos nodded. "Then let's do it."

CARLOS held the spear gun at the ready this time, while Cadmann worked the tip of his knife into the plastic unit of human blood Jerry had brought from the clinic.

The pouch was rubbery-firm for a moment, then, as its skin was pierced, it collapsed. Its contents spilled into the river upstream from the cave. The blood streamed through the lamplight in dark tendrils, then was sucked into the cave and vanished.

If it worked, the thing would come streaking out of the cave and into the net. And Cadmann didn't care if the effect was like pushing a pound of Cheddar through a cheese grater.

Carlos dimmed his light. Together they waited.

And waited, clinging to anchor spikes. Cadmann listened to the hiss of the river and the steady sigh of his own exhalations as he pushed them into the re-breather.

And waited.

Nothing.

After ten minutes, they surfaced. Cadmann spit out his mouthpiece as he climbed up, and swore savagely.

Zack helped Carlos past a slippery patch. "Let's go to plan two."

Andy was manning the pump, awaiting a hand signal from Zack before he sent the explosive liquid flowing into the ground.

"If it's in there," he said with obvious satisfaction, "this is going to make it *very* unhappy."

Cadmann nodded and found a comfortable place to sit. He was suddenly aware of fatigue and cramped muscles. Somewhere someone was cooking, and the fragrance of lamb stew with fresh vegetables was suddenly overwhelming.

Carlos appeared, holding two heaping bowls.

"They should give medals for this, Martinez."

"By the time the paperwork goes through, we'll both be dead and gone."

"Too true."

The stew was thickened with leftover Year Day rice, and utterly delicious. Cadmann leaned back against a rock, listening to the useful bustle around him, warmed by the food and the nearness of his friend.

The clouds shrouded the stars. The twin moons must have already risen, but another two or three hours would pass before they were visible this low in the gorge.

All there was now was the steady gurgle of the water and the human sounds around them. For some reason that he couldn't name, Cadmann felt a sudden, strong urge to see the stars, the moons.

Why?

Because you're going down there tonight.

"What are you thinking about, Cadmann?"

"Mary Ann." His teeth wrestled with an undercooked, mildly seasoned portion of lamb. It resisted for a moment, then his teeth found the grain. "I'm hoping she's not worried."

"*Sí.* I was thinking of Bobbi. I hope she's well, out of surgery, and not worrying about me. It is not good for *las palomitas* to worry."

"Especially when there's nothing to worry about."

"Precisely."

They turned to face each other, and Cadmann managed to hold his bland expression for about five seconds before both gave in to a wave of grim laughter.

"Clear the holes!" Andy shouted, and the hose was pulled from the ground, the pumps and barrels wheeled away toward the rock wall.

A wire was run down the pipes and its end clipped into a detonation switch. Andy came over to sit with Cadmann and Carlos, twenty meters from the hole.

"You ready for this?"

"If you're going to collapse this whole shore area, the least you can do is give us time to swim for it."

"Naw. We've got at least eight meters of rock under us. We've already identified enough outlets to release the pressure. Fireworks no. Earthquakes yes. Ready?"

"As we'll ever be."

He switched on his radio. "Two and three?"

"*Standing ready.*"

"Good news. On zero. Three, two, one—"

Cadmann squinted as Andy said "zero!" sharply, and twisted the detonator toggle. There was a dull thud that shook the rock beneath them, and a jet of flame-tinged smoke erupted from the hole.

There was a second, more violent tremor, and a tickle of panic shot up Cadmann's spine. Then silence except for a steady hissing sound and a jet of grayish smoke from the hole. Cadmann sneezed against a horrid chemical smell.

Andy got to his feet. "If it's down there, it should be very dead," he said.

*Should*s were going to get them all killed.

"How long before we can go down to check?"

"How quick can you get wet?"

"Got it. Zack?"

There was no reply, and he raised his voice. "Zack?"

The camp administrator's voice came in over the radio. "Is that Cadmann bellowing for me, or has one of our elephants gone into rut?"

"We haven't hatched any elephants yet."

"Then put Cadmann on."

The smoke streaming from the ground was taking on a darker color. *Got you . . . I hope.* "Zack, Cad here. I need those dozen men you promised me."

"You'll have them. You're sure you have to go in, Cad? It's probably dead." Zack hesitated. "No, dammit, 'probably' isn't going to help me sleep any better. We'll Skeeter in the last two from camp. Take about twenty minutes."

"Twenty minutes," Carlos mused. "Time for a short nap or a long prayer. Or another bowl of stew. Come on."

"Aren't you worried about cramps?"

"Nah. I've been through menopause."

Cadmann stood, shaking the stiffness from his knees. "You're a very sick man, Carlos. Probably your most endearing trait."

CHAPTER 19

GRENDEL'S MOTHER

Beowulf spoke:
"Let your sorrow end! It is better for us all to avenge our friends,
not mourn them forever. I promise you—she shall have no shelter, no
hole to hide, no towering tree, no deep bottom of a lake where her sins
may hide."

Beowulf

THE WATER WAS DARK and cool, shallow now and calmer than the rushing currents of the Miskatonic behind them. Cadmann's head broke the surface and he held his handlamp up. Its beam probed the blackness as he climbed out onto the limestone gallery.

Carlos surged out of the water, and their combined beams gave Cadmann a grasp of the dimensions of the chamber. The roof was only a meter above his head and was dappled with some kind of webbed moss. Something far to the left gave off a faintly purplish luminescence. Although there was no smoke in the air, it had to be rich with nerve poison. He didn't dare remove his mask.

The chamber was too small to hide anything much larger than a rat; the torchlight splashed bright and hard against the farthest wall. Shallow pools stood beneath embryonic stalactites. A slow, steady drip of water raised echoes everywhere.

The rest of the men were out of the water now, and Cadmann adjusted his throat mike.

"All right. Anyone see anything? Jerry?"

"Not a thing. I think it went deeper back."

"Agreed."

A slick, rounded hump of rock was the next barrier. Cadmann clambered to the top and played his torch down into the darkness.

"Andy!"

The engineer responded with a hand-held scanning unit. He clambered up to the top of the rock and perched there. Together they scanned the dark water.

"Nothing for at least twenty meters. Just rock and wet. Do we go for it?"

"You got anything better to do?"

"Not a thing."

Cadmann, Andy and Carlos hammered pitons into the rock, then attached cables and ropes and climbed cautiously down the side into a lower body of water.

The gloom was absolute, as if no ray of light had penetrated this deeply since the Miskatonic first cut this chamber from the rock.

Tiny blind things moved sluggishly aside as he swam through the murk. Some wriggled like eels, and others scuttled along the bottom of the pool like crabs. They groped through the dark, trying to avoid him, gliding through his torchlight as if totally unaware of it.

No sound but the faint re-breather hiss in his ears, no natural light at all now. Just eleven men and two sterile women swimming silently through the murk. *And we've all made our deposits in the sperm bank.*

The rock walls began to close in from the sides, and Cadmann bumped against first one and then the other as his finned feet flailed for balance before he found the right path.

"Andy," he croaked into his throat mike. He suddenly remembered the first time he had tried to use a mouthpiece and a throat mike at the same time: he had swallowed about two cups of Barrier Reef brine. "How far did you say these caves extend?"

"I didn't. All we can do is search for an hour, hope that we can find our target. 'Target.' Sounds like I expect it to be standing still, doesn't it? Anyway, then we make our way back out." Each of the thirteen members of the team carried two additional re-breather cartridges in their bulky backpacks.

That gave them a total of two hours—but Cadmann had no interest in letting things get down to the last few seconds. Fifty minutes in, fifty out. Twenty-minute margin for error.

If they couldn't find the corpse, they had to assume that the creature was still alive, and proceed from there. That meant traps, a doubled guard and a continuously activated mine field around the camp. *And constant worry until we know it's dead.*

The walls widened out again. Cadmann surfaced cautiously. He held the handlamp up to shine the beam around in the smoke-filled chamber.

There was another mild splash beside him, and Jerry surfaced, spear gun at the ready.

"Peaceful in here."

"But not silent. Hear that?"

Cadmann was about to ask, What?, then heard the distant gurgle.

The other twelve were up now. Their lamp beams pinked the darkness and smoke, running pale disks across bare cave walls.

"Let's go with the current for a while."

Their flippers barely moved as they let the current carry them toward the exit. Half the team watched underwater. The others stayed at the surface, with only their heads and lamps above the oily water. They swam in a V formation, each close enough to see two others. Sometimes the swirling smoke parted to show stalactites lancing down at them like yellowed fangs.

The current grew stronger. Cadmann surfaced. "Louder, I think."

"Rog," Andy answered.

"Stay together and head toward the shore!" Cadmann's arms and legs lashed powerfully at the water. Most of the others were right behind him. They were holding steady. He heard their regular breathing in his earphones.

Then a sudden anguished cry, and he saw someone disappear over the lip of a falls. Moments later Cadmann heard the splash.

"Who was that?"

A short pause, and then, "Kokubun, here. Wow! What a ride! Safe —only about a dozen meters. But it's lonely in here."

"Could you climb out, Mits?"

"No sweat. Come on down."

Cadmann considered for a moment. "All right. By twos."

His men swam toward the lip of the waterfall. A pair of snaggled, broken rocks divided the water flow, like the grinning mouth of a jack-o'-lantern as seen by the glare of the torches. The first two men tumbled down. There was silence for a moment, then laughter. "Piece of cake," one shouted.

Cadmann played his light behind him through the outer chamber. No disturbance, no movement. The yellowish smoke still swirled, but it was noticeably lighter even in the few minutes he had been there.

"Go by twos." Finally only Cadmann and Carlos were left, and together they swam for the lip. The pull of the current was strong, but not impossible to fight near the shoreline. When Cadmann let himself go there was a momentary sensation of weightlessness, then a ramp of water-polished stone to reach up from beneath them, and he slid the rest of the way into the water.

It took all of his discipline to restrain a whoop.

"Well." He shook his head, grinning under his mask. "That was refreshing. What have we here?"

The smoke was even deeper, and it looked sulphurous. The water was a little warmer than in the antechamber. Their lamp beams ate through the smoke to the blackened ceiling. Patches of steaming scum still floated on the water. It looked like something out of the *Inferno*.

"If it was in here," Andy said positively, "it's dead now."

"I'll go with that." A grainy column of light stabbed out. The chamber was smaller than Cadmann had thought, and it was empty. His flash showed three jaggedly framed black exits.

"Now what, Coach?" Jerry asked.

"It was your soup. What do you think?"

"I think there was more than enough."

"Yeah. We don't have any real choices, do we? Divide into three teams and look into each of those exits. How is everyone fixed? Anyone need to change yet?"

There was a quick chorus of negatives, and Cadmann checked his own supply. Still almost a third left on his first cartridge. Good enough.

Jerry headed one team, Carlos another, and Cadmann took the third. There was something about that middle tunnel. . . .

"If the tunnels split again, that's *it*. Wait at the junction and signal. Under *no* circumstances divide the team, do you understand? When you're ten minutes into the second cartridge, turn around and start making your way back. If the radios start giving out, turn around and head back to this chamber. We don't want any heroes. If you spot the corpse, call for the rest of us. All right. Be safe."

JERRY and Andy swam with slow, even strokes. The engineer was rather clumsy on the land, but in the water his extra girth was less of a liability.

A trail of tiny silvery bubbles escaping from Andy's re-breather reflected in Jerry's lamp beam.

Behind them, the other members of their team kept pace.

Something brushed Jerry, and he nervously followed it with the light. It was almost a meter long, and looked more like a snake than a fish.

"I'm surprised to see anything alive down here," Andy said.

"Water breather," Jerry answered. "It's probably blind. Even in the deepest caves on Earth, you can find blind salamanders and insects."

When this is over, I'm coming back with a net and a sample case, he promised himself.

"Think it's dead?"

"Sure. We still have to know."

"Gotcha. I'm checking topside."

Andy headed up toward the surface, and by Jerry's light it was as if the man disappeared above the shoulders. "We're through into another chamber. The air looks clear."

"Don't take off your mask. Not all of the fumes are going to be visible."

"No problem."

Jerry surfaced next to him, shone his light around in the cave. This chamber was a little larger than the last, but still not more than thirty meters long. He directed his light straight up, and Andy whistled.

Directly above, the ceiling opened in a circular orifice about three meters across. "Will you look at this pothole?"

"What's that?"

"A dry chimney, in spelunking terms. Vertical channels formed by water flow. Water dried up, so we don't call it a chimney anymore. Look over there." To the left were a series of rounded steps, as flat as fish scales, each a half-dozen meters across, like a badly skewed stack of silver dollars or a stage for a Vegas musical.

"Called 'gours.' Formed as carbonate is precipitated from turbulent water. Miskatonic must have been higher . . . more likely, it gets higher later in the year. Come on." Andy waved his light towards a widely arched opening. "I want to take a look back in the shadows. It might have crawled up there to die."

"Or get well."

"Come on, Jerry. No confidence in your soup? Hell, that stuff would have killed a dozen monsters."

Jerry followed Andy's lead. The side chamber was larger than the main cave they'd been in. Onyx and sparkling rocks glittered in the light of his flash. It was almost peaceful down here, and Jerry brought himself up short: that kind of thinking could easily get them both killed.

Another of the blind fish brushed past him. This one's eyes were pasty white, staring lifelessly in a broad face. Its mouth was crowded with needlelike teeth, and it nosed in for an experimental nip.

He knocked it away with the tip of his speargun.

"Looks like a dead end," Andy said. "I'll check out the far side." He kicked his bulky frame through the murk with surprising grace.

Andy went up, and up. He said, "Hey—"

And then his entire body just *levitated* from the water, whipped out as if vacuumed up with a suction pump.

What? Had he climbed out? Or pulled himself out?

"Andy?"

Andy's body smashed down into the water almost atop Jerry. Just his body: the head was gone. Black clouds jetted from the raggedly torn stump on his neck. They fogged the light. Hordes of blind fish streaked into the cloud, tussling and snapping at each other.

Jerry's chest froze, and he backpedaled frantically. There would come a lethal moment of water pressure, the single instant of warning before horror swooped out of the cloud of blood. In that instant he might have to trigger the spear gun into its grinning, gaping mouth. . . .

Then he was through, into the other chamber. He scrambled backward up over the gours, the grooved stone surface scraping at his hands and legs.

His voice was a squeak into the throat mike. "Danger. Mayday! This is Jerry. I . . . we found it. Andy is dead. Repeat, Andy is dead. Converge on left tunnel at *once*. Repeat. We have located animal. It is alive and deadly."

Arnie Donovan and Jill Ralston joined him at the water's edge. Together the three of them backed to the wall, spear guns at the ready.

Shit. He had seen those things kill before, but this . . . what in the world? Why had it killed Andy? And then thrown the body back almost disdainfully?

Whatever a man might hunt on Earth, there were other men to tell him how to do it. Thinking like the prey is an old game, hundreds of thousands of years old. The first shamans who propitiated the spirits of antelopes might have got it wrong, hundreds of thousands of years back, but the need was there. You cannot hunt what you cannot understand.

With this creature there was nobody to ask.

Carlos popped up in the water, and in a few moments Kokubun and two others joined them. Then Cadmann appeared, striding huge and implacable from the dark of the river, spear gun at the ready.

"What happened?"

Jerry slowed his trip-hammer breathing. His teeth chattered. "Andy and I went into th–the cave. He surfaced, and that was *it*. He went straight *up*. He didn't even have a chance to scream."

"Volunteers," Cadmann said. Carlos raised his hand immediately, and four of the others. "Fine. The rest of you—wait ten seconds and follow us in. Jerry?"

"I'm right behind you."

Cadmann nodded and slipped into the water.

Jerry was the last in. Suddenly the water felt *slimy* to him. Fear constricted his chest, and he couldn't breathe. The water surface was silver above him.

Andy had gone *up*, arms and legs thrashing, and back down without his head.

A flash of light ripped the darkness from the water. A moment later the shock wave hit, and the numbing, thunderous roar of sound.

Jerry surfaced.

"Dear God in heaven . . ."

The cave was smaller than the one he had just left, with a broad shelf of gours to the left. On it the creature was whirling, spinning like a top with something dark and hideously limp in its mouth. It took Jerry a moment to realize that it was a human leg, ripped from its owner's body like a twig from a sapling. Andy's leg; for Andy's headless corpse had been thrown clear across the cavity and was sliding down from near the ceiling.

The creature froze for an instant. Jerry had just time to make out its squat monitor shape, the spiked tail thrashing restlessly, the gaping mouth lined with daggers. Then with a blur it was among them, churning in a circle, frothing the water with blood.

Human and reptilian screams mingled. One of the spears exploded against the rock wall, one against the ceiling, another in the water with a blinding flash. The monster's tail whipped twice, then slammed down on a diver's head, driving it under.

There was horrific crunch, and a man flew from the water, smashing into a heap on the shore.

Cadmann tore out his mouthpiece and screamed at it, "Over here, you bastard! Here!" He whistled as loudly as he could, then put his mouthpiece back fast.

The water whirled as if whipped by a centrifuge. The creature righted itself and jetted straight for Cadmann, too quickly, too damned quickly. Jerry didn't have time to scream warning, or even blink: the creature had changed paths and was streaking—

Cadmann fired. The spear hit the monster precisely in the throat, and the explosion nearly decapitated it. Blood and bone and bits of flesh foamed from the water and showered on them. The water smoked as the shattered body rolled twice, then sank.

For a long moment there was silence. Jerry couldn't help shining his flashlight in Cadmann's face. There was an expression that frightened him there. Satisfaction, and vindication, and something else. Something primal, and terribly strong. Then it faded, and Cadmann was himself again.

He spoke slowly. "All right. All clear. We need a net in here, and medical care. Who's got a med kit?"

Mits raised a weary arm.

"Good. All right. Let's get it moving."

Cadmann pulled himself out of the water and sat on the shelf, feet dangling. His breath rasped in the throat mike. Cadmann slipped a re-breather cartridge from his backpack and clicked it into the front unit. He turned to look at Jerry, and his expression was indecipherable.

"Are you all right?" Jerry asked. *Why am I nervous?*

Cadmann smiled almost paternally. There was an edge to that smile, cold and sharp.

"Never better."

CHAPTER 20

AUTOPSY II

To stand still on the summit of reflection is difficult, and in the natural course of things, who cannot go forward steps back.

GAIUS VELLEIUS PATERCULUS (20 B.C. to 30 A.D.)

THE CORPSE STRETCHED almost fourteen feet from the tip of a rounded snout to the spiked ankylosaur tail. Its bulk filled two veterinary tables: its sour wet smell hung in the air like a curtain of flies. Its grayish-green hide was rent in a score of places. Ribs poked through in rows of stained ivory, denser and more roughly surfaced than human bone. Its webbed feet were torn and broken. The eyes, once golden, shone dull copper in the unwavering overhead light.

Sylvia noticed half a dozen gawking colonists still crowded in the door. *Triumph. They weren't there. They laughed at Cadmann. Now they gloat.* Unfair, and she knew it, but she savored the taste of malice. *You have your triumphs. I have mine.* She looked to the corner where Cadmann stood erect, not bothering to lean against the wall. *Cadmann has both. It was his radio message—*

Grendel is dead!

Grim humor that; grim but oddly appropriate even so minutely removed from the horror of Year Day. In death the creature ceased to menace their future, and thus assumed an oddly mythic quality. *Grendel is dead.*

It was funny. Even now, so soon after Bobbi's death, she knew it was funny. God, she wished she could laugh.

Carlos sat slumped in the corner, trying desperately to get drunk enough to cry.

"Grendel is dead," Sylvia said dully. "In the old legend they nailed Grendel's arm above the entrance to Heorot." She swept her hand to indicate the quarter ton of quiescent monster flesh. "We mutilate corpses too—"

Jerry paused in the act of of pulling on surgeon's gloves. "For answers, I hope."

"Damn right you'll get answers," Cadmann muttered.

There are so many questions.

Life?

Death?

Is the nightmare over? Or just beginning?

"Please," Jerry said. "I need room to work. Cadmann, Carlos, Zack —I'd appreciate it if you remained. Everyone else, *please.*"

The doorway cleared and the sheet-metal door closed. But Sylvia knew that their audience had not retreated far: their impatiently shuffling feet and choppy breathing hovered just beyond the threshold of perception.

Jerry inhaled deeply. The light from above shimmered around his stick-figure body like an aura. "Cassandra Program." The jury-rigged computer hummed. Gears chugged and ground. Everyone watched. Then slowly, in jerks, the camera moved to position itself above the table. Jerry nodded thanks toward Carlos. The cameras, like everything else, had been severely damaged during the initial assault. Everything had been designed for durability, but that was on Earth, in a design laboratory, damage simulated by computer, not inflicted by monsters. Now—with Omar Isfahan's help Jerry was redesigning the system, restoring lost capabilities. This was the first practical test of Cassandra's restoration. The computer hesitated another second, and then the gooseneck camera snaked down.

Carlos tore open a pouch of vodka, staring unblinkingly at the corpse. He guzzled half the pouch and coughed as it burned its way down. He handed the rest to Cadmann. There were no words.

All of Carlos's struggle had been for nothing. Bobbi had never come out of shock. Her heart had simply given up. Carlos had not cried; he had simply smashed his fist into the wall, damaging both plaster and knuckles. Without a word, he had gone to the camp liquor supply. No one had tried to refuse him.

Now he sat with Cadmann—camp comedian and the tall, hard warrior. Both seemed cut from the same dark, dangerous cloth.

Jerry moved the scalpel carefully along the creature's head, slitting and then peeling away the skin, exposing the skull's smooth, barely convex arch. "I don't see any fissures at all," he remarked for the record.

He switched to the band drill. It whined, etching its way through the tough layer of tissue. The stench of burning bone tickled Sylvia's nostrils through her gauze face mask.

"Thickheaded tart," Jerry muttered. "This one is definitely older an uglier than the first. Might even be its mama."

"Grendel and Grendel's mother," Sylvia said. "It fits." She winked at Cadmann. He pretended to ignore her. *You're the one who sent that message,* she thought.

Jerry lifted a section of skull to expose a pale layer of membrane protecting the brain. Slitting it exposed darkly pinkish jellied pulp.

"Cassandra. Watch this."

The camera moved in closer. Jerry dictated in a carefully controlled voice.

"This has to be olfactory brain tissue. It's well defined and coterminous with nasal passages. Well penetrated with air passages. This critter had one hell of a sense of smell.

"Behind and above that is more tissue that has some similarities, but it's also well defined, and doesn't appear to be part of the olfactory area. If there's any parallel with human evolution, this is the equivalent of cortex, although it sure doesn't look much like what we use for cortex. Lots of convolutions, though. Maybe that's a universal?

"From the size and shape, if I'm right about what this area is and does, the critter is at least as intelligent as a gorilla. Maybe more so. Better sense of smell than a dog or a cat."

The saw whirred again.

"Moving back, there's a whole series of enlarged ganglia complexes. Subsidiary brains, maybe? I know there are at least three more of these down in the lower spinal area. My guess is they really are subsidiary brains that control reflexes and locomotion. That's one reason the critter can move so fast. The central brain gives orders, but they get carried out by a whole batch of brains distributed along the systems."

Computer networks operate that way. Sylvia looked away from the monster and back to Cadmann. He was leaning forward, his teeth just showing.

Jerry continued to work. His hands moved deftly, guiding the instruments in precise motions, exposing without damaging. From time to time he called up ultrasound and X-ray images on the computer screen, consulted them, then went back to his grisly task. An hour passed.

Presently Jerry removed some tissue samples. "All right. Sylvia, we'll want microscopic examinations of this. Freeze and section and—"

"And the rest. Sure," she said. She kept her voice pleasant.

"Sorry—"

" 'S all right." Sylvia moved closer. "That oversized jaw. The first one was that way, too."

"Right. Species characteristic, I'd say."

"Yes. Jaw. Oversized feet. Webbed, but with claws, designed for fighting, but also for traction. No hands, though. It was never designed as a tool user."

"Right on that."

Carlos took another stiff drink, then slammed the canteen down. He stood, stepping out of the shadow and closer to the table.

"Traction? Want to see traction? Look at Cadmann's ribs. Damned scars haven't healed yet." She could see his eyes now. They were red-rimmed, bright with tears and loathing. "That bitch ran right up the cliff. It didn't climb, it *sprinted.* It just smashed into the boat, chewed it up like a grape skin. Bobbi never had a goddamned chance."

He was shaking, and seemed to calm only when Cadmann clasped his shoulder from behind. The tension drained out of Carlos and he retreated to the shadows.

"I saw that too," Cadmann said. "These things have two distinct gears, fast and superfast. I want some answers."

"You and everyone else, Cadzie. You've both done your parts. Leave the rest of it to us."

She felt a kick, a sensation of pulling, of her pelvic girdle stretching, accompanied by momentary faintness. She caught her balance and shut her mind to the fatigue.

"Sylvie? Are you all right?" Cadmann asked from the shadows.

He sees everything. "Fine."

"No, you're not—"

"Good enough. Look, I promise. As soon as we're finished with the preliminaries, I'll take a nap. I just can't miss being in on this one."

Saw and drills continued to sing and strip away the skin and the flesh from the thing that had haunted their nightmares, while ultrasound recorders watched and remembered. The dissection would later be computer-corrected to form an in-depth holographic template. Then the analysis could begin.

Zack spoke for the first time in hours. "I can almost feel sorry for it." He indicated Cassandra and the other complex instruments in the room. "It couldn't have known what it was up against."

Carlos growled deep in his throat and stood. Before he could move he was halted by Sylvia's laugh. She looked to Cadmann and grinned. "No. It couldn't."

Carlos sat on his stool as the saw began a new song.

They peeled away the ribs. At first Sylvia concentrated on the lungs: flatter than human lungs, less a pair of bags than a webwork with blood vessels running through them. Arteries and veins were thumb-thick, oversized, capable of pumping blood and oxygen to working muscles at a fantastic rate. She could only shake her head in wonder.

She probed into the gland sacks, flattened organs perching atop the lungs. "What in the world?" she whispered. "Cassandra. Close up." She sliced into them with the tip of her scalpel. The walls were elastic and wrinkled, shrunken to a third the size of the lungs. "Whatever this is, it can hold a lot more than it does right now." A brilliant carmine fluid jellied in the sacks, and she spooned out a sample. "I'm going to run an analysis on this."

Sylvia placed the sample in the spare biothermograph ferried down from *Geographic*. There was a faint humming sound as it pumped the air from the sample chamber.

Thank God that this apparatus, at least, had been duplicated. So much equipment had been lost; they would have a hell of a time working out this creature's gene patterns now. Its flesh might have to be preserved for years before such apparatus could be replaced.

When the BTG had finished evacuating, the dollop of red fluid was burned in a flash, and a quick band of color flashed across the viewer. Sylvia whistled softly.

"Eh?" Jerry prompted. He looked to the screen where the computer analysis of the chromatography would appear.

Sylvia's voice was pensive. "How can this stuff be biological? It looks like oxidizer for a rocket! Oxygen bonded with carbon, iron, magnesium, but mostly oxygen. I wouldn't have believed it. What's the structure of those sacks?"

"Honeycomb. They were filled with the fluid." He probed with the scalpel, frowned and cut again. "Hah. Muscle bands. Here—here—yep. Set up to constrict the sacs, which would inject this stuff into the blood streams. The duct leads directly into the heart chambers—"

"Super oxygenated blood supplement," Sylvia said. "Which means—"

"Right!" Jerry shouted. "That's it! Supercharger! Good lord, no wonder this thing is so damned dangerous."

"What?" Zack demanded. "What have you found?"

Jerry almost danced with excitement. "This is it, I'm sure of it."

"How can you be so damned happy about how powerful this thing is?" Carlos demanded.

"Don't you see?" Sylvia shouted.

"See what?"

Jerry brought calm back to his voice. "The monster depends on superoxygenation. That means it's vulnerable. We can kill it."

"Maybe I'm stupid," Zack said. "But I don't see—"

Jerry ignored him. "Cadmann. Was there, say, anything unusual about the amount of body heat from this thing? You've been closer than anyone."

Cadmann paused for a moment, then spoke. "Yes, dammit, there was. When the first one killed Ernst at the blind. It was stalking the calf, and everything was fine. But as soon as we took a shot at it, the temperature went through the roof."

"Enough to cause a flare in your infrared, as I recall."

"Right."

Jerry took a step back from the graying thing on the tables, the dead, cold hulk leaking blood and cloudy fluid drop by slow drop onto the stained tile floor. "And amphibian. We'll never find these things far from water. They need it to dump the heat! Listen. There can't be many of these things on the island—"

Carlos cursed vilely and smashed his pouch to the ground. "I swear to God. The next idiot who says that, I am going to break his face. Shit." He kicked at the plastic skin, squirting liquid out into a puddle. Cursing again, he scooped it off the floor and stormed out of the room.

"Before, it was a guess," Jerry said. He didn't sound worried. "Now we know."

"Know what?"

"There can't be many of them. By many I mean more than a dozen or so. Cadmann, there's not enough for them to eat! Look at the teeth. A couple of grinders. They can crunch of seeds and grass and bark in a pinch, but they're sure as hell not evolved for eating plants. They want meat, and lots of it, and there just isn't enough meat on this island."

"The pterodons," Sylvia said. "That's why they were so scared of the water! These things hide in the water. The poor pterodons! They have to fish, but they never know, when they dive for a samlon, but what one of these will be waiting for them—"

"Right." Jerry stepped back from the table and dropped his mask. "Look, we can wait for the computer analysis, but we don't really need it, do we? We had a brood of them. Heck, this one might well have been the mother. Picture her swimming over, or floating over on a piece of driftwood, or any other scenario you like. She's already pregnant, with a clutch of eggs ready to be laid. Land her ten or twenty years ago, perhaps, and they proceed to strip the island of animal protein."

"Everything except samlon," Sylvia said.

"Yeah." Jerry looked thoughtful. "And there is our next big mystery. There's no samlon in her stomach. What protects samlon? Maybe our monster only hunts on the land. And by the way—we need a name for this thing. We can't just keep calling it 'monster.' "

Sylvia forced a smile. "I think Cadmann already named it. 'Grendel.' "

"Name it be damned," Cadmann said. "You said it was vulnerable. How vulnerable?"

"In a minute," Jerry said. "Damn. It really is a puzzle. These things eat everything. Have eaten everything, they damned near stripped this island clean—Sylvia! It all fits! Dopey Joes in the hills, none near water. Pterodons, nothing else. Everything but the samlon. All right, what keeps the grendels from eating all the samlon?"

"Poisonous?" Sylvia asked. "Or—oh, damn."

"What?"

"Something—I have the feeling I'm forgetting something."

"Can't be important."

"Maybe. Anyway, could samlon be poison to grendels?"

"Doesn't seem reasonable. They ate cattle. We eat samlon."

"Yeah—"

"Or," Jerry said, "maybe Grendel only hunts warm-blooded creatures."

"Given its choice, sure," Cadmann said. "That bitch would eat her own children if she were hungry enough. Believe it."

"I don't know what to believe now. That's what we're—"

Jerry's voice faded out, and Sylvia groped for support as the room seemed to ripple and she lost her footing. Cadmann was under her in an instant, and the last thing that she felt before darkness overwhelmed her was the comforting strength of his arms, and his whispered words: "I'm here."

SYLVIA's eyes were open, but totally unfocused. Light and shadow mingled indeterminably. As her senses returned she heard the slow rumble of Terry's breathing, and finally realized that she was in her own bedroom.

Somewhere outside her window men were arguing. She recognized the voices: Stu Ellington and Carlos. Both sounded horribly drunk.

"—the hell, *marica?* You think you could have done better?"

"—don't have to think. You killed her, you left her and *ran*, you dickless wonder—"

She heard the sharp, sudden sound of bone meeting bone, and the side of her cabin shuddered as a body slammed into it.

Briefly the shadow of two struggling bodies fell across the window. She watched the dark, shifting shapes, overcome with an hallucinogenic sense of unreality. Another sharp crack. Gasps, a creak of tortured metal, the stifled sobs of pain and anger. A swift curse in Spanish, and a softer thud. Then Cadmann's voice: "Break it up. All right. You've both had enough. We have a bigger fight than this—"

There were a few more muttered words, then the voices faded. The shadows dissolved before the sweep of the searchlight, melded into the darkness, and once again the night was still.

Sylvia rolled over and hit the light. Terry reached for the trapeze bar above his head and pulled himself upright. "You're awake."

"Only when I heard the racket." Her head buzzed hollowly. *Somebody tranked me. . . .*

"Damn. Listen—you haven't had a full night's sleep for three days, and I want you to get one. You've been running on adrenaline."

His hand slipped from her chest to her belly, the warm, gentle swell there, and she suddenly realized the truth in his words. *Both* of her needed rest. And food. Now that the adrenaline rush had slowed, she could hear the dull roar of hunger and fatigue. The tension had masked it. The tension of waiting, of helplessly watching the search for Carlos and Bobbi. Of watching Cadmann and the others descend into the earth to do battle with the unknown. Of standing at Marnie's shoulder, waging a losing battle for Bobbi's life. Of waiting to convey the terrible news to Carlos . . . if Carlos survived.

There had been, could have been no rest.

But now . . .

Terry was right.

"Carlos and Stu just needed to get it out. They'll probably cover each other's backs tomorrow. There's nothing anyone can do for it." He ran his hands lovingly through her hair, scratching her scalp with the tips of his nails. "And anyway, I'm here to make sure that you don't go running off. Junior needs you to be reasonable."

For an instant she thought of arguing, then fatigue completed what tranquilizers and low blood sugar began, and she slipped back into a light and fitful sleep.

WHEN Sylvia finally emerged from the caverns of narcosis some ten hours later, the camp was on full alert. The mine fields beyond the perimeter fence were activated. Current pulsed through the wire. Sylvia's skin hummed if she approached it too closely.

She wrapped her sweater around her more tightly and headed through the thin morning fog toward the communal dining hall.

In the midst of total alert she felt a curious security: the Colony was not pitted against human enemies. *It's only an animal. Intelligent as a gorilla. Maybe as intelligent as a primitive human. Doesn't matter. It can't use tools! It's only an animal. We—Cadmann hunted it down, went into its den, and it wasn't a dragon at all. Only an animal, with a brain smaller than a man's, and no tools.*

A tiger in the dark room is a monster. Turn on the light, and it is just an animal. Cadmann turned on the lights for us.

Zack held the door for her as she entered the dining hall. She asked him, "How's Carlos?"

"Sleeping it off. Stu has a busted lip. Well earned, if you ask me."

Virtually every adult male, and half the women, were clustered in the hall. The walls and ceiling of the hall were illuminated with views of the Colony and points south. Cadmann stood in the front of the room. Near him, but separated, were ten colonists, his kill team.

He stands there—does he know just how arrogantly he's standing there? But the rest of them, they're taking it seriously. They accept it. I never saw him like this before. In his element. The bad time is over for Colonel Cadmann Weyland.

One of the wall videos wavered, and Cadmann's face loomed into focus. "We'll be using a portable holo system," he continued. "Rachel will carry it into the first assault—and I want her to stay *back*. The idea here is to perfect a system. If we make any mistakes, we want the camp to know it fast. If we do it right, we can be sure that the *National Geographic* people will be interested. This will head back to Earth along with the rest of the data on grendels. George, Jill, you'll bracket the pool here, and here—"

Sylvia looked at the maps. One was a digitalized thermal breakdown representing fresh water, hot springs and vegetation.

On the other wall was a contour map, and on a third a wildlife vector. Greatest concentrations of samlon had been detailed. Four of the water holes had been identified as likely hidey-holes. These had large populations of samlon, and no hot springs nearby. Grendels would want cold water to dump heat into. Distance from the other holes was an important factor. Any creature as voracious as a grendel had to be extremely territorial, requiring substantial hunting ground.

Sylvia found her eyes drawn time and again to the center maps. The Colony.

A small area, really. Terribly small when examined in contrast to the entire island. Barely two square kilometers.

The view from the *Geographic* made hollow their assertions of mastery. From that perspective, how very little change they had wrought.

So presumptuous had been the children of Earth. When all was said and done, might not this new world, this terribly old world, swallow them and their folly, leaving nothing behind but bones? Bones, and some films beamed back to an Earth that might or might not send others this way again. Earth was rich, and jaded.

She touched her belly, trying to sense the slumbering life within. It shifted, kicking, and suddenly she felt awesomely small and vulnerable. What was she doing here? What were any of them doing here? All she could think of was the image of that hideous beast twisting through the searchlights, sprinting forward like a windup toy with a broken spring. Bathed in flame, skin coated in jellied gasoline. By all sanity dead, but living still.

God in heaven.

Then there were the Knights of Avalon, men and women descending into the caves beneath the northern ravine. There, in the abysmal darkness, confronting a larger, more powerful version of the first beast. Armed with better weapons, more certain knowledge, and something else: the kind of foolhardy courage that had lured men beyond the edge of shadow since time immemorial.

Now forty grim determined men and women waited, armed and ready. Waited to follow the camp's only true warrior into hell if need be, to stand between Sylvia's unborn child and the hideous grasp of a grendel.

Suddenly her eyes blurred with tears, and an unbidden, heartfelt prayer echoed in her mind.

God be with you, Cadmann.

Because the Devil has already dealt himself in.

CHAPTER 21

KILLING GROUND

Chance favors the trained mind.

LOUIS PASTEUR

CARLOS WIPED his forehead with the back of a gritty hand and adjusted his throat mike. "Martinez here. In place."

The water hole was situated eighty miles north of the Colony, an hour's flight by Skeeter. Just a wet spot hidden by bushes, forty feet long by half that wide, one he would never have believed could be sixty feet deep. Some ancient seismic activity had torn the rocks apart and the Miskatonic had filled the hole. That was long ago. A monster lurked there now. *Probably,* Carlos reminded himself; but in his heart he knew.

You're there, and I have come to kill you.

The clearing was roughly horseshoe-shaped, narrowing into an eastern bottleneck where the stream trickled in from the main river. The overflow bubbled up over a western rise of crumbled stone and disappeared into a marsh.

Probability 78 percent. Those words had sounded encouraging back at the camp, but here at the killing ground, with twenty hunters surrounding the hole, that 22 percent uncertainty looked as big as Mucking Great Mountain.

In just a few minutes they would know. Carlos stared at the chill depths. *Grendel, Grendel, are you there? Grendel, we have come to kill you,* he thought; but all that Carlos had seen so far were samlon flashing like silver shadows.

Be here. Be here and die. Die slowly, die and taste death—

"You okay, *amigo?*" Hendrick Sills asked.

Carlos flashed a quick smile at his companion. *"Sí, compadre."* He let Bobbi's image fade, forgot the still, pale face and the memory of a last desperate kiss shared beneath a shelf of rock.

No mistakes this time. Twenty men and women surrounded this hole. *We have enough weapons to kill a tyrannosaurus rex. More than enough to take down one of these* bizcuernos.

The satchel team stood by. Three men: on signal they would run forward to throw eight kilograms of explosives into the hole, then run away as the charge sank until either the depth fuse or the timer detonated it. The hydrostatic shock would either kill or drive it out of the hole. Hendrick Sills, their chief engineer, had verified that there was no other exit.

And then? Well, Cadmann had worked that out well, using terms like "field of fire," "optimal egress" and "killing ground." Carlos had never heard the terms, but they resonated, sounded totally right, calmed him more than any prayer. *Cadmann knows these things.*

"Can you believe this?" Hendrick demanded. "Ten lightyears from home. When my grandparents took the solar system we didn't have anything like *this* to fight. Just physics, just our own ignorance. Another goddam *star* and we're standing here like a Stone Age tribe facing a tiger."

"They are strong, these grendels," Carlos agreed. "But—"

Hendrick grinned like a wolf. "But. Damn straight, 'but.' No brains."

Carlos felt unreasonable resentment. "They have brains. They—"

"Hey," Hendrick said. "It's okay, I'm on your side, remember?"

Carlos grinned. "I remember. My apologies. More, you are correct. The grendels must use instincts. What they know is in their genes. Not so with humans. Once we had conquered all the animals on Earth we began on each other. We have ten thousand years of war experience."

"And well enough," Hendrick said.

"And well enough. The objective is to kill them. And that we will do."

His comcard spoke. "Carlos, this is Cadmann. You ready?"

"As I'll ever be, *amigo.*"

"Let's do it, then. All units, general alert. Stand by."

The semicircle of armed men and women looked to their weapons, then waited.

"Alpha team, *go!*"

Three men ran forward, one of them George Merriot, still limping from his burn wounds. Ten feet from the sinkhole they paused. One stood with flame thrower ready as the other two swung the heavy satchel they held between them. "One, two, three, *go!*" The dark brown box arced out toward the swampy hole. "That's it!" the team leader called. "Run away!" They were laughing as they rejoined their comrades in the line facing the hole.

The bomb splashed into the dark water and vanished.

One. Two . . . Carlos counted half consciously . . . *ten, eleven* . . .

WHAM!

It came as a surprise, as it always did, no matter how hard Carlos tried to be ready for it. Water shot skyward, water and samlon and tiny crustaceans and mud.

Now wait . . .

For about four seconds.

The water exploded a second time as a quarter ton of scale and muscle burst from the surface of the water. The grendel came at an impossible speed over the lip of the sinkhole. It dashed over the flopping samlon that lay at the water's edge. Once it had a firm footing it paused, black bullet body glistening in the afternoon light. Its enormous saucer eyes glared at them—

Then fixed on Carlos. Directly upon him, and he froze in fear and impotent horror. *We can't do it. We can't kill this thing* . . .

"Shoot!" Cadmann ordered.

Someone fired automatically. Then someone else.

Carlos screamed wordlessly. He forced himself to center the grendel in the sights of his weapon.

It was out of the hole, out and charging, moving at speeds that no animal could possibly reach, moving so fast that although time had slowed for Carlos, the creature had become faster, so fast that everything happened at once—and he squeezed the trigger.

Carlos's bolt exploded in the bushes behind the creature. Three other hits. The grendel screamed, then screamed again as it tried to come forward but tripped over its own severed foreleg.

Even then it did not die. It pulled itself up onto the rocks and took off like a good racing car, away from the pain, away from the foaming, smoking water and lancing spears, running east through the shallow stream, toward the safety of the Miskatonic—

As Cadmann had said it would.

"Down!" Cadmann's voice was calm and reassuring in the earphones, and Carlos was *down*. One second later there was an awesome roar, and after that he was showered by dirt and falling rock. Two big mud drops struck his cheek.

"All clear." Cadmann sounded cheerful. "Chalk up one more."

One more.

"Like I said, no brains," Hendrick said. "They'll always go for the river. Plant some mines and wait—"

"Would you have thought of that?"

"Aw, I don't know."

"Nor would I," Carlos said. "Or, let us say it another way. You or I, perhaps we would have thought of the mines, and perhaps we might have thought of whatever it is that we will need when those no longer work. Would you be willing to bet that either of us will think of that before Cadmann does? Or *know* that it is right?"

Hendrick stood and shook off the dirt from his coveralls. "Lighten up. Let's go see what we got."

"Yes." Carlos stood. "Let us look at our grendel." His forefinger picked a speck of wet red flesh from his cheek. Not a raindrop.

There wasn't much. Craters in the dirt, splashes of bright crimson, torn alien flesh and bone, a flailing severed tail, ropy red strands splashed against the rocks. Carlos felt a grin pulling his face toward his ears.

Twenty hunters stood up from their positions around the clearing.

All twenty of them. They hadn't lost a single man, and the grendel was as dead as anything had ever been.

"Let's be sure," Cadmann ordered. "All units, stand by. Alpha team, move out."

Once again three men moved forward. One stood with flame thrower ready as the others tossed the satchel charge into the pothole.

WHAM!

Mud, water and samlon showered the area. Carlos stood tensely—

And nothing happened.

"All clear," Cadmann said at last. He left his command post and came over to Carlos. "And that's what I call ballin' the jack."

"Damn straight, *amigo.*" Carlos raised his weapon. "Damn straight!" The victory cry built deep inside him, rolling slowly up through his chest and out of his throat like the cry of a more primitive, more basic animal. The others joined in. Twenty hunters, screaming to the cloud-muddied sky, the glory and perfection of the moment connecting them with a simpler time.

They were alive, and the enemy was dead, its limbs and guts spread before them. Still the timeless scene seemed somehow incomplete. This was the time when the shamans, the ancient men and women of the village, should scramble out from behind the rocks, should examine lengths of twisted gut, stare into the scarred and lifeless eyes of a foe and speak of the signs within. Eat handfuls of jellied brain and sing of dark portents and bloody dreams.

Then again, he realized that he didn't need diviners to tell him the future.

Here, on Avalon, mankind was the future.

The howls from twenty throats rose to the sky . . .

JERRY sighed in disappointment as he examined the gutted corpse.

There was samlon meat in its belly. Jerry identified parts of three samlon, two nearly dissolved, one nearly fresh.

"Now we know. Nothing protects samlon," Jerry said. "No great secrets here at all."

"So why are they still around?" Sylvia wondered.

"They probably breed faster than hell, and there aren't enough grendels to wipe them out. That's good news. I guess. There *is* a limited number." Something attracted Jerry's attention, above the creature's staring eyes. He moved his tweezers under something, and lifted.

Half a meter of limp tubing rose from a cleft in the forehead.

"I'll be damned. Will you look at that? It's got a snorkel for breathing underwater. Here, you can see where the blood vessels fill to lift it. Just like a penis. Sorry."

Sylvia said, "We're out to kill them. You're starting to admire them."

"Know your enemy."

ONCE the technique was devised, the killings themselves became almost routine. The adrenaline was there, the sense of satisfaction, but experience had dampened the true danger, replacing it with caution and structure.

Because, after all was said and done, the grendels were mortal. Heirs to the same failings as any other creature of protoplasm. Vulnerable to the same techniques of killing that had worked on Earth, evolved through countless big-game hunts and wars since the beginning of recorded time.

Flush the beast.

Channel its retreat.

Bottleneck, and the killing ground.

The second killing team utilized an additional refinement. There was a chance, no matter how small, that a grendel might be hiding outside the water hole, or might find an auxiliary exit and attack them from the rear. Transverse observers were posted, one for every two hunters facing the killing ground. Two hovering Skeeters watched from above, scanning for grendels.

There were only twelve sites on the entire island with a probability above 30 percent.

Twelve holes. One a day, with the Colony kept under full battle alarm the entire time.

They would not lose another human being.

IT WAS good to have a system: Skeeter above, and a first pinning team moved into place while the engineering corps designed the mine field, worked with Cadmann to determine the field of fire that would best funnel the creature to its death.

Where natural walls of rock were insufficient, walls of flame were utilized, flame throwers backed by men and women with rifles and spear guns.

And always, always, a conspicuous bolt-hole. Someplace where a pain-maddened creature could run to safety, to freedom . . .

To certain death.

So died the fourth grendel, blown in half and then roasted by jellied flame, dead even as it crawled for the depths of the Miskatonic, pitifully torn claws outstretched, eyes open and fixed. Yearning, perhaps, for one last taste of the samlon flashing within.

And the fifth, dead before it ever reached the mine field, Carlos's explosive spear in its brain. He took limited pride: he had been aiming at the heart.

And always, always, there was Cadmann, driving them on and on, past exhaustion with his boundlessly murderous energy.

The spirit was infectious, and when they trudged back to their temporary camp at the end of the fourth day, no one wanted to be skeetered back to main base.

The temporary camp was a fifty-meter stretch of cleared brush, burned out and then chopped and plowed. Supplies were flown in from the Colony. The entire perimeter of the camp was mined, and a Skeeter flew in irregular patterns, scanning with infrared.

At first Carlos disliked the endless hum of the Skeeters overhead. Now, the cessation of the sound, or the occasional sound of two overhead rotors as Skeeters changed shifts, would awaken him instantly, sending a hand reaching out for the spear gun.

He was tired but happy. The muscles in his calves had seized up, and the tendons ached. He massaged them for a half hour before they stopped screaming.

Cadmann's tent was near the southern periphery of camp, and Carlos rapped on the foil, saying, "Knock knock."

Cadmann laughed. "Come on in."

The big man was sitting cross-legged on the ground. A light was suspended from the tent pole, shining onto a map.

"What do we have here, *compadre?*"

"Well, a peek at tomorrow's kill. We've identified the monster here —smaller than the others. It's the southernmost beast."

"Dumping blood, sheep intestines and chunks of monster into the other two water holes hasn't gotten us anything, but here we have one." He grinned, and turned to Carlos, teeth gleaming. "Do you know what that means?"

"It means that we're almost finished."

"By God, yes!" Cadmann slammed his fist down. "Cigar?"

Carlos shook his head at first, and then nodded. "I didn't even know you smoked."

"Only on verra special occasions, my man." He conjured two thin cheroots from a plastic pouch and clipped the tip off both. They lit and inhaled smoothly, enjoying the thick, sweet aroma. "About six months ago, I can remember being upset that we hadn't brought along a kodiak bear or a mountain lion."

"Well, your wish sure came true."

"Yeah—in spades. No offense, heh heh . . ." Cadmann leaned back against his bedroll and exhaled a long, fragrant stream. "No. I wondered if I was a little off my nut about that. Look around us. Know what I see?"

"What?"

"Survivors. We came, most of us, because life was too easy on Earth, but it was still a guided vacation. There were the colonists, and the crew. And me, Great White Hunter, professional killer. My God, most of them felt safe. That attitude would have been passed on to the children, and their children. And if something like this had happened in two generations instead of right now, our grandchildren might not have been able to handle it at all. So we've lost a few people, and they weren't dead weight, don't get me wrong—but the ones who are left are true pioneers, not tourists. Fighting for their wives and husbands and children, and their future."

Carlos nodded soberly. "I can see what you mean."

"I figured you would. And I couldn't sit here and tell you that I'm sorry it happened."

"Even with the death . . . ?"

"Everybody dies. The obstetrician slaps you on the ass with one hand and hands you a postdated death certificate with the other. What's important is that our children have a better chance. It's always been about the children. Always. Women have never loved being kept from education and treated as second-class citizens. Men have never enjoyed having their balls shot off in wars. Men and women didn't fall into their roles accidentally, and each side doesn't hate the other. It happened because for a thousand generations, that was the best way we knew to build a civilization, to build a better future for our children. The industrial revolution doomed slavery—racial, sexual, social. Civilization is worth fighting for."

Cadmann seemed more at peace than Carlos had ever seen him. And why not? Vindicated, loved, appreciated. Involved in the work he was born for. Regardless of what happened from this point forward, the work that Cadmann had done would earn him respect and honor for the rest of his life.

Cadmann was the Colony's only real warrior, but with luck, he could teach the rest of them to be soldiers.

"Here." Cadmann opened a flask and handed it to Carlos. It was strong, unwatered whiskey. Carlos sputtered, but didn't lose a drop. "You'd better not. Probably the most valuable thing in the known universe. Two-hundred-year-old Scotch."

"Salud." Carlos felt the sweet liquid fire flowing down his throat. "Jesus, that's good."

"Unfortunately, that's all there is."

"Yeah. Things could be a lot better." Sadness clouded his face as he drew deeply on his cigar, but he relaxed as he exhaled a misty wreath around the lamp. "But do you know something?"

"What?"

"Compadre, they have been a hell of a lot worse."

CHAPTER 22

THE LAST GRENDEL

The difference between a good man and a bad one is the choice of cause.

WILLIAM JAMES

NUMBER SIX was the last. All the other bolt-holes had been baited, all the other underground rivers mapped. If there was another grendel left on Avalon, it had no interest in blood, no fear of hydrostatic shock. It never turned on its supercharger at night, when *Geographic*'s thermal scan dissected every square meter of the island.

No, this one was the last, and here in the highlands, the farthest south on the island that any human had been, Cadmann felt a minute sense of loss.

He listened to the live tone in his ear from the radio link, and to his own breathing. He plucked a sprig of avalonia grass, chewed on it absently and spit out the faintly sweet fibers.

He was propped on his elbows at the edge of a bluff overlooking a marshy stream, just upriver from one of the largest hot springs. The thermal gradient had thrown the scans off for a little while, giving this last monster a temporary reprieve.

Skeeter Two had lured it out with grendel blood and fresh meat.

The monster had come sniffing out, growled weakly up at the Skeeter before it snatched the joint of raw beef. It looked and acted starved: much thinner than the others, and only two thirds the length.

The Skeeter's tape had been played back at the Colony. Cadmann vividly remembered the image of a gaunt, hollow-chested reptile tearing at the meat as if it hadn't eaten in a week.

Jerry had taken the podium and fought for the creature's life.

"We don't *know* we can find more of them on the mainland. Think about it—an animal which can produce a high-grade organic oxidizer. Imagine a herd of them. Hobble the legs or even amputate them. Breed them to get that oxygen-bonding stuff, that superhemoglobin, like cows give milk!"

Grendels, serving man? It might be. They would try it . . . once.

But Cadmann wondered to himself, wondered about the sadness that he felt. What if this was the last grendel in the universe? After all, there were earthly species restricted to just one subcontinent or group of islands.

On the mainland there were monsters. *Big* things, as large as anything that ever walked the Earth; creatures reminiscent of *Tyrannosaurus rex*, things that man would hunt only with robots and advanced weapons. They glowed in infrared. Easy to guess, now, that there were small, fast things too. Grendels or worse, blazing in infrared, then subsiding before a telescope could find the sources; mistaken for giants until now.

Cadmann tried to imagine Jerry's pet scenario: a single freshwater grendel, pregnant, clinging to a piece of driftwood after some natural disaster swept her out to sea, a clutch of eggs protected within her body or in an external case, to be deposited in safe territory.

These had to be freshwater creatures, didn't they? Nothing that could effectively compete with the grendels had been found in the oceans, and the oceans held plenty of food. The eggs, hatched downstream, would produce a brood of insanely competitive monsters who fought each other for the prime hunting grounds, driving their weaker siblings farther and farther south.

It didn't seem quite plausible, somehow. But if it had happened once, it could happen again.

The mainland was worth a look. Jerry was working on a possibility. Maybe a grendel could be *triggered* into releasing its superhemoglobin, by sonics or by the smell of an attacker. It would be forced to cook itself before it reached any vulnerable target.

When Jerry had something to test, then they would seek grendels on the mainland. Only for testing. The mainland belonged to another generation.

Today Avalon belonged to humankind.

A pregnant grendel on a piece of driftwood. A tricky, temporary current. *What's wrong with this picture?* Why was there a piece of the puzzle that seemed so distant, so lost? Hibernation Instability?

Damn, there it was—the possibility that he had kept from himself for so long. Certainly, anybody could suffer from Hibernation Instability. Anyone but Cadmann Weyland. And he could discount the mood swings, the inability to adapt to a changing social situation when adaptation meant survival, the need to move himself away from the Colony. Free men thought like that. Such symptoms could hardly be construed as symptoms of H.I.!

And he'd been scanned . . . but that could only diagnose gross structural damage. There were subtler problems, some of which only a battery of psychological tests would reveal.

He had taken no such tests. Cadmann didn't need them—no.

He brought his attention back to the bend in the river. As in the case of the second monster, the hole was difficult to see. It might have been no more than a fold in the shadow, but it was more. A quarter ton of death lurked there.

The last monster . . .

They would try to bring it back alive. And if a human being was put in the slightest danger, that would be *that.* They would return home with a leaking corpse. No woman would mourn her man, no child cry for its mother.

"Stage one," Cadmann whispered into his microphone.

Skeeters Two and Four rose up from behind the ridge, carrying the net between them. They lowered it into the water where its weighted edges settled quickly to the bottom. The two autogyros braced the hole, humming there like dragonflies hovering over a pond in summer. He smiled grimly at the lazy image. That image was about to explode.

Grendel-blood sacks were punctured and tossed into the water upstream from the hole. As the dark stain began to spread, Cadmann started a slow count. "One . . . two . . . three . . . fo—"

The water erupted. A clawed, toothed demon exploded from the depths. Both Skeeters juddered violently as it struck the nets, twisting and yowling.

Stu's radio voice screamed triumphantly from Skeeter Two: *"We've got it!"*

Engines whined with exertion. The Skeeters hoisted the creature free of the water. Cadmann watched carefully, ready to bark a command: if the grendel's struggle threatened the Skeeters, it would be released, dropped netted onto the land, and charred with flame throwers.

The Skeeters bobbed and twisted like paper airplanes for the first few hideous moments. Then Stu Ellington masterfully regained control of his craft, and the grendel was secured. The two autogyros maneuvered the creature over the far bank and set it down.

The net was a Tasmanian Devil of crazed motion, the creature's legs and head so entangled that it looked as if it was trying to break its own limbs. It wouldn't break the net. Of this they were certain. But *it* didn't know that, it couldn't know that, and when the Skeeters touched the net down, it burst into furious action and the grendel's roar of anger and . . . fear?

(Was that what it felt? *Could* it feel fear? He had never thought of them in those terms. Grendels were living death, and that was all. But something in its screams, its frantic, helpless contortions, flashed the sudden, dreadful image of a tortured child into Cadmann's mind. He squeezed his eyelids tight to make it disappear.)

Stakes had already been pounded into the ground to form a circle around the netted creature. Hooked cables ran in from each stake. From his position on the bluff, Cadmann saw his crew run up and connect each line into the net to stabilize it. Now the Skeeters were disconnected, and Stu flew back across the river, hovered over Cadmann and extended his hoist cable.

Cadmann wrapped the cable around his arm and hooked the bottom clip to his belt buckle. "You've got me. All right, Stu. Up." He had barely repositioned his rifle on his shoulder when Stu swooped up, yanking him into the air.

As he swung across the stream, the ring of colonists moved in to surround their captured grendel. Jerry rushed in with a tranquilizer pistol. His hand jerked up as he fired.

The creature twitched as the dart hit, then exploded back into movement.

Stu touched Cadmann down, and he unhooked himself. The grendel was in continuous motion, growing more frantic by the moment.

"What do you think?" Cadmann yelled.

Jerry's limp yellow hair whipped in the backwash from the autogyro. "All I can do is pump it full of tranquilizer. We sure can't move it like this."

"I—"

As if in response to Cadmann's question, the grendel lunged toward them. One of the stakes groaned and popped free from the ground. Faster than conscious thought, Cadmann unshouldered his rifle and thumbed off the safety.

But the other stakes held. The beast hissed and thrashed crazily, but couldn't come any closer. It began to convulse, its movements without direction or aim.

Jerry's eyes narrowed. "It's not slowing down—"

He loaded another tranquilizer dart, and then another. They lanced into the grendel's sides with dull *phutts*. It shrieked and twisted more frantically, clawing furrows in the rocky soil, snapping and glaring balefully through the tangled netting.

Jerry jumped back and shook his head. "Each of those carried enough somazine to knock over a rhino. I'm afraid I just don't understand how it's wired—" The thing snarled and lunged at them, sending fragments of rock spinning through the air. Another stake popped from the ground. Heat rose from its body in palpable waves, but it no longer seemed a threat to anyone but itself.

"It's dying," Jerry said softly.

Its labors were pitiful. It tried to head back toward the river, but the last six stakes held, and it just struggled at the end of the lines. And struggled. And struggled.

"Isn't there anything that we can do?" Cadmann said.

"We could let it go."

"No, thank you."

The large body movements were growing spastic now, replaced with a kind of overall tremble, a desperate, dying convulsion.

It exploded back into motion, moving so quickly that it scarcely seemed to be anything made of flesh, seemed more an engine with a shattered governor, a dark whirlwind. Its screech spiraled up and up and up the scale, clawing toward a terrifying crescendo. It bounced and thrashed at the end of the cables. The incredible effort went on and on, as if the creature were draining everything left in its body in one last all-out effort, nothing held back, nothing in reserve for the functioning of any organ, just the *now, now, now* of a creature with no way to tell its cortex that there is no threat.

Then it was still. Only its tail tremored. The hunting crew moved back in and re-anchored the loose cables. Jerry, his face glum, poked at the thing's tail with a long stick. It twitched reflexively.

"Asleep?"

"Dead." Jerry waved the Skeeters down.

The netting was refastened, the cable hoists reattached. Cadmann watched the Skeeters hoist the body, so hot it was almost sizzling, from the ground and into the air.

CADMANN was one of the last back to the camp. He supervised the final disarming and removal of all unexploded mines, and accounted for all weaponry. Then he commandeered a Skeeter and spun it up toward the eternally gray bed of clouds pillowing the sky. The campfires had been quenched, the tents packed and folded away. In days or weeks the underbrush would grow in to obscure the scars, to conceal the fact that this effort had ever taken place. That a group of determined, prepared human beings had journeyed together into the darkness, to meet and destroy the greatest natural predator the children of Earth had ever faced.

He breathed deeply as the Skeeter rose and headed north toward the mist-shrouded bulk of Mucking Great Mountain. The light of a setting Tau Ceti diffused redly through the clouds.

AT FIRST the landing pad was an indistinguishable part of the sprawling camp, then a postage stamp, and then cracker-sized, and finally the familiar square studded with radio beacons and lights.

Mary Ann stood there, looking a little rounder than when last he'd seen her. A little warmer, more vulnerable. She shielded her face from the wind and dust. The smile beneath her forearm shadow was wide and bright and welcoming.

She came to him, held him, and he buried his face in the warm notch between her neck and shoulder and felt her cool, moist teardrops against his skin.

They kissed in a roar of dying Skeeter engines. The whipping air began to still, and at last he could hear her whispered words.

"—you so much," she said, and kissed him again. She looked up to him, eyes shining with pride and relief. "You're done now," she said.

"Yes."

"Then let's go home."

He kissed her this time, marveling at the simple pleasure it gave him. He nodded. "Let's go home."

CHAPTER 23

MENDING WALLS

For one swallow does not make a summer, nor does one day; and so too one day, or a short time, or a great deed, does not make a man blessed or happy.

ARISTOTLE, *Nicomachaen Ethics*

TWEEDLEDUM BARKED energetically, wagged his tail and pranced to attract Cadmann's attention.

Cadmann chuckled indulgently and ignored him. He pointed down the hillside at the bare-chested workers who labored to widen his patio. "The house as planned now will be about twelve hundred square feet, with maybe another four thousand feet of greenhouse."

A warm wind from the south had blown away the usual mists. The view ran forever, from the tiny workmen across land and ocean to tiny mountains on the continent itself. It was as if he could see the whole planet.

They'll call it the new world. They always do, but it's as old as Earth, and we've taken it as we took the Earth.

Good day for this. Beside him, Carlos Martinez nodded solemnly: the role of video host suited him to the hilt. "I just can't believe how much progress you've made in the past five months."

"It's been a lot of work, but given enough time and manpower, almost anything is possible—"

"Hold it, Cad," Sylvia called from the hillside above them. "The field of focus is off."

"Can't have that. *Casa Weyland* is the star of the show."

Cadmann swallowed his irritation while Carlos climbed up to help Sylvia fiddle with her video pack.

Building a documentary had sounded great ten light years ago. It was fair enough. Building an interstellar starship had put the Geographic Society massively in debt. They were entitled to know the results. They would learn from the first expedition's mistakes. Sales to Sol system's twelve billion would help to finance a second expedition.

In practice the running documentary had become a pain in the ass. Cadmann might have given the whole thing a pass but for the chance to see his two friends.

He looked back down the hill, out over Cadmann's Bluff, down to where Mary Ann sat holding Sylvia's seven-week-old son. She waved one of Justin's chubby hands at them, and some of his irritation dissolved. Three months of pregnancy remained to her, and it warmed him to have a preview of his future family. Mary Ann's fringe of pale golden hair riffled in the mild salt breeze. She hugged their surrogate child while Tweedledee sat contentedly at her side. The sprawling silver ribbon of the Miskatonic split the valley behind and below her.

His crops were coming up in rows of green and yellow now, and the cages rustled with Joes. He was proud of what he had wrested from the soil, but his true joy was the spreading infrastructure of his homestead.

Hendrick Sills, Gregory Clifton and two former members of his kill team were immediately below him, deepening the boxlike foundation of his house. The original structure had been expanded east and west, but building farther back into the hill added the possibility of clerestories— staggered, louvered roofs that allowed greater view, greater access for light.

The effort would have exhausted a lone man. In the three and a half months since the death of the sixth grendel, the Colony had demonstrated its gratitude in the only way it knew how: by contributing time and labor. So the earth was broken, rocks moved and walls raised, floors and ceilings extended.

Cadmann's Bluff had become the showpiece of Tau Ceti Four.

Carlos clumped back down the mountainside. "All right. *Repitan, por favor.*"

"Hold it, Carlos, just hold it. This is getting old *real* quick."

"Don't be a spoilsport," Sylvia chided. "The view is beautiful. I've got the house, the bluff, the Colony, the northern mountains and the tips of the mainland peaks. Do you have any idea how rare it is for a hundred kilometers of mist to burn away?"

"That's a once-in-a-lifetime shot, *compadre*. Our sponsors expect it. *National Geographic* wants us to show Earth's landstarved masses the joys of homesteading in the stars—"

"There goes the local neighborhood."

"—and one of its joys is the chance to become a hero, like Avalon's greatest citizen, Cadmann Weyland, sometimes *yclept* Beowulf."

Sylvia whistled her approval.

Cadmann laughed disgustedly. "All right, all right. Get the rest of your damned footage and let's quit."

"Deal."

The camera ran. Carlos declaimed. They walked the perimeter of the cleared rectangle that would one day be the greenhouse. They skirted a new excavation to the northeast.

"And here," Carlos continued theatrically, "will one day reside the finest wine cellar on Camelot. Stored on board *Geographic* are frozen cuttings from some of California's finest vineyards. Someday, when the basic crops have stabilized, it may be time to start less . . . vital foodstuffs." He cleared his throat. "Purely for medicinal purposes, of course."

"Carlos, don't you know that grapes can be eaten straight?"

"No hablo Inglés."

They walked down the narrow path beside the house, past the massive boulder rigged as a deadfall, set to crush anything trying to force its way uphill. Cadmann winced as Carlos pretended to lean against it. Sylvia circled to get a better view. "This is probably an unnecessary precaution. The grendels are dead, slain by Colonel Cadmann Weyland. Even so, our Cadmann is a cautious fellow."

Cadmann raised his hand in protest. "Carlos. You've got to stop this. I don't like being painted as Beowulf. I just did what had to be done. I can't encourage this. I'm not interested in running for God."

"This isn't reality. This is theater."

"If it was only going to be seen throughout the solar system, fine. But you're going to show it down in the Colony, too. It's not good for them, it's not good for me."

Cadmann left them and followed Tweedledum downhill. He knew

that the colonists just wanted to thank him, and yet somehow it all seemed meaningless.

Sure, you saved the Colony. Right.

But Ernst is dead, and he was the only one you were really responsible for, dammit.

He stopped down by the Dopey Joe cages. Their flock had grown to twenty, and Carlos had created a modular cage design for Mary Ann, simple to build or expand, easy to clean. Cadmann was happy with the new model, and the sight of it eased his annoyance. He put on another smile for the cameras.

Just a few more minutes of this nonsense.

Mary Ann was suddenly beside him, holding Justin as if he were their own child. They'd love this image back on Earth. He leaned over and kissed her warmly. "Feeding time for our flock?"

"Just about. Justin is a nice baby," she whispered, "but ours is going to be much prettier."

"Hush." Cadmann grinned as Carlos and Sylvia caught up with them. He slipped a glove on, lifted a handful of green fodder into the slit at the top of Missy's cage.

He raised his voice as Sylvia focused. "And these little darlings are called 'Dopey Joes,' the only indigenous mammalians found on Camelot so far. They may hold the key to a treasure trove of—ow!"

Missy snapped her sharp little teeth into his glove, and Cadmann struggled to twist it free without breaking her furry neck.

"Bad girl." Sylvia laughed. "No dessert for you. You can't just eat the meat and ignore your vegetables—"

"Hah hah. Funny lady. That's it, I'm through." He pulled off his glove and threw it at Carlos, who caught it and thoughtfully examined the rip in the fingertip.

"Not exactly sheep, are they, Señora Weyland?"

"Baa baa." Mary Ann took Justin to Sylvia. "Unhook that camera and give it to Carlos. Will you take Justin? I want to talk to Cadmann."

There was a quick, clumsy exchange of burdens, and Mary Ann hooked her arm through Cadmann's.

"Carlos and Sylvie staying for dinner?" she asked. He heard her distantly, but gazed up at the expanded house, strong and solid in the warm Avalonian sunlight.

Up at the top of the hill, Gregory Clifton's bronzed, corded body arched, swinging a pick to break up resistant soil.

As with Carlos, the violent action and backbreaking labor of the pasts months had burned out Greg's hatred and healed his emotional wounds. Cadmann found it easy to respect that response, that need.

"Are Carlos and Sylvia staying?"

"Sure."

Mary Ann took his hand and led him to the edge of the bluff. They looked down over the valley. They had done so very much, and given time would do more. He didn't have to close his eyes to visualize the march of humanity across the valley, the slow spread of their cities. His grandchildren might live to see a city of a hundred thousand where once only jungle had sprawled.

But false heroes wouldn't help. Especially if they were used as a blind for guilt and uncertainty.

"I'm worried too," Mary Ann said quietly.

"I'm sorry. Am I upsetting you? It's nothing, really."

"You have your reasons, I have mine." He held her tummy and frowned. "I think you think I'm a little crazy."

"Pregnant women are supposed to be a little crazy. What's my excuse?"

"Don't need an excuse, you've got reasons, silly. I just know that something still bothers me about . . . Cad, I look around and the picture's wrong."

"It's an alien planet. Didn't anyone tell you? Two moons, bluer sunlight, critters and plants straight out of Oz—"

Sylvia moved up beside her, cradling Justin in her arms. His hair was pale straw, and he seemed to fit comfortably into a shoulder harness. He nursed contentedly at one discreetly covered nipple. "I know what you mean," she said. "We're still working on the corpses. I don't understand enough about grendels yet. I'd give anything to have one alive. If we'd known that they could burn themselves up like that, we might have cooled the last one off with water."

"It was that hot?"

Sylvia laughed. "It *cooked* itself."

"Heat. Fire," Mary Ann muttered.

"What?"

Mary Ann cuddled close to Cadmann. "I remember . . . I did a summer of study in the forests in Wyoming. And they told us about fires. It all seems like a million years ago." Cadmann hugged her comfortingly as she searched her memory, struggling to make the unlikely connection. "They told us about what happens in fall. Then, a forest fire that seems to be out can smolder under a mat of leaves. You can't see it. You can't smell it. But it's spreading underneath. It can surround you. And then suddenly break up to the surface, and *whoosh!*"

"Shh . . ."

"I'm so glad you're here," she whispered. "I'm so glad you're mine. Don't let anything happen to you, Cadmann. I'm not sure I'd know how to go on. I'm not sure I'd want to."

He was aware that Carlos and Sylvia were nearby, watching, and was also aware when they turned away to give the two of them privacy. For a moment Cadmann and Mary Ann were in their own secret world of warmth and familiar smells.

"Come on," he said soothingly. "Let's get dinner started for our crew."

THE EVENING'S meal was a simple affair, an open-air picnic around a roaring campfire. Decent-sized catfish and a huge samlon from the nets were the main course, cooked into a casserole with long-grain brown rice from the hydroponics garden down at the Colony. Carlos and Sylvia and Hendrick's four-man work team joined them.

Cadmann watched Mary Ann pick over her food. She had a strong appetite for rice and catfish, but couldn't bring herself to eat samlon. "More for the rest of us," he had teased her at first, but her glum smile told him that the joke had died.

Her eyes scanned from the edge of the bluff to the notebook at her side. From there to the Joe cages. Tonight the furry creatures chewed frantically at the wire and threw themselves against the wooden walls of their prisons.

Carlos watched them for a while. "The natives are restless. Do they think they're going to be dessert?" A branch popped on the campfire, and a cloud of sparks and oily smoke drifted up.

The night was a continuation of the phenomenally clear afternoon. A faint salt breeze from the ocean five miles west made the air clean and crisp. The twin moons were bright and unshrouded.

It should have been a night for laughter and song, but Cadmann felt another of his morose moods fall over him like a blanket. He couldn't seem to fight it.

Carlos tickled Justin, held the child for a few minutes, while Sylvia fed herself. The three of them seemed pretty damned comfortable together, and for a moment Cadmann indulged in pointless speculation.

Then Mary Ann took his hand and placed it over her swollen stomach, smiling wistfully as their unborn child thumped and bumped. "*Floop floop.*"

"Kid's doing a half gainer in there."

"He loves you already, you know."

There was more sadness than joy in that conversation, and he didn't know why, didn't know how to deal with it. *Crest of the Angeles Mountains. Los Angeles and San Fernando Valley spreading to opposite sides of a veranda. Carpets of light. Never again in my lifetime. Win something, lose something. . . .*

Hendrick Sills watched the four of them ruminatively. With his short, square-cut beard he looked every bit the Freudian analyst. "What's all the moping about?" he finally demanded. "We got a cracking good day's work under our belts."

"True enough," Greg said. His calm oval face was painted with the firelight. It was growing more difficult to remember him in that other time, on that other night, spewing jellied gasoline, the glow of madness in his eyes.

Carlos rose from the fireside. "I think that it's time for Sylvia and me to head back down."

"You could spend the—no, there's Justin."

Sylvia hugged Cadmann briefly. "Walk us to the Skeeter?"

"Sure. Mary Ann?"

"I'm a little tired. You go ahead."

He pushed himself up, helped Sylvia to her feet. As they moved away toward the eastern edge of the bluff, Hendrick's rough voice broke into song:

> Banish the use of the four-letter words
> Whose meanings are never obscure
> The Angles, the Saxons, those hardy old birds,
> Were vulgar, obscene, and impure.
> But cherish the use of the weaseling phrase
> That never quite says what you mean
> You'd better be known for your hypocrite ways
> Than as vulgar, impure and obscene. . . .

Another breeze stirred the foot-tall rows of corn as they walked. Cadmann found himself humming with the song, and he linked arms with his two friends.

"It's not so bad, is it, Cadzie?"

"It's like Carlos said a couple of months ago: 'It's been a whole lot worse.' " He dug at the ground with the toe of his boot, making a mental note to get some of the soil lichens started soon. "I just wanted to have this to get away from everything, and I seem to have brought a bit of the Colony up here with me."

"You can't get away from—" Sylvia started to say, but Carlos quieted her.

"*Amigo*, if you really don't want us up here, any of us, just say the word. We love you. We're grateful to you. We're still embarrassed about the . . . fiasco. Hendrick, Greg, the others, they're just responding to you the way men have responded to leaders since Alley Oop."

"I never wanted to be a leader."

"Some of us don't have choices. Just let them do a little more work —hell, you can use it, you know that's the truth—and then send them back. You'll be alone, and Greg will have had his therapy."

It was true, all true, but dammit, why was it so hard for a man to just be alone?

> *When Nature is calling, plain speaking is out*
> *When the ladies, God bless 'em, are milling about;*
> *You may wee-wee, make water or empty the glass*
> *You can powder your nose, even Johnny can pass.*
> *Shake the dew off the lily, see a man about a dog*
> *When everyone's drunk, it's condensing the fog.*
> *But please to remember if you would know bliss*
> *That only in Shakespeare do characters—*

"What the hell. Hendrick's right. It's been a good day. Listen, you two have a safe flight back. I'm going to go sing dirty ditties."

He shook Carlos's hand, kissed Justin and helped Sylvia buckle herself in.

Then Cadmann stood back, shielding his eyes as Carlos expertly lifted the Skeeter from the ground and spun it up into the sky. His friend flashed the landing lights in farewell and vanished over the lip of the plateau.

Feeling unseasonably warm, Cadmann walked back to the fireside, voice already rising in the next bawdy verse.

"I THINK he's going to make it," Carlos said.

"I never really doubted it." Sylvia looked at him. "How about you? I haven't really seen the old Carlos much lately."

"Has he been missed?"

"Muchly. Avalon's unmarried lovelies mourn almost nightly."

Carlos skimmed the Skeeter sideways, riding out a gust of wind. "What, in formal ceremonies? Perhaps it is time I began making my rounds again." He paused thoughtfully for a moment. "Only the unmarried ones?"

"Discretion, Carlos. Please."

"I'm nothing if not discreet." Carlos could have begun the descent then, but he kept the Skeeter hovering. "And what about you?" he asked soberly. "Terry's problem is hardly a secret. I know how you and Cadmann feel about each other . . ."

"I promised Terry. Anyone but Cadmann." She sighed. "I couldn't anyway. It would destroy Mary Ann. Cadzie and I just . . . had bad timing."

Slowly, Carlos began to dip toward the landing pad. He chose his next words carefully. "And where does that leave *Señora* Faulkner?"

Her answering voice was small. "Looking for a friend?"

Carlos reached out his hand, covering hers. Her fingers seemed so small, so warm. "Since Bobbi, I think that is what has stopped me. I haven't been looking for a relationship. Or just a *palomita*. I think I, too, need a friend. Perhaps . . ."

". . . we could both stop looking?" Sylvia squeezed Carlos's fingers, then pulled away and hugged Justin to her.

I hope so, Carlos said to himself, surprised by the intensity of his response. Warmth and cheerfully lecherous optimism spread through him like a brushfire.

Carlos hummed happily as he brought the Skeeter in for a landing.

CHAPTER 24

REMITTANCE MAN

> I strongly wish for what I faintly hope;
> Like the daydreams of melancholy men,
> I think and think in things impossible,
> Yet love to wander in that golden maze.
>
> JOHN DRYDEN, "Rival Ladies"

SYLVIA TOUCHED her lips to Justin's brow. She savored his baby smell of powder and clean linen. Her hands were cold, and she was careful not to touch him as she tucked the edges of the blanket around him. *Seven weeks old today. I should remind Terry.*

Justin had begun to lose the newborn's wrinkly look, to cease being a generic baby and take on a personality of his own. He could focus his eyes, reach and grab with coordination, make sounds that often seemed appropriate to the situation. Terry had read Kistakovsy's classic revisions of the Gesell studies and pronounced Justin well ahead of normal development.

Those things mattered, but there was a way that they didn't. Genius or idiot, she loved the tiny, helpless child as she had never loved anything in her life, as if he were still a part of her own body.

Plastic stars and pterodons dangled above his crib. They would circle at the slightest touch of a breeze. For now, they, like Justin, were still.

Terry was in the front room clearing away the debris of the evening meal.

Her hands shook. She couldn't let Terry see *that*. She forced herself to calm down, and thrust them beneath her arms until they started to feel warm.

Terry stacked the last dishes in the cabinet beneath the sink. One hand gripping the wheelchair arm, muscles in his arm and back standing prominent as he leaned far forward to reach. Done, and he smiled in satisfaction. His wheelchair purred as he glided it over to her. "Justin asleep?"

"For now," she said, honestly relieved. She waved at the sink area. "You're getting good at that. Making order out of chaos."

"Yeah. What I am, I'm good at. I *never* had arms this strong. Which reminds me—"

"The expedition."

"Yeah. Time to turn the plans over to Zack. It could be five or ten years before anyone actually goes to the mainland, but hell, our resources won't have changed much. The plans'll still be good. I'm afraid to tell Cadmann. He'd want to go now."

"Yeah . . . I've expressed enough milk to keep Justin happy if he wakes up. I'll only be gone a couple of hours." She stretched, forcing a mild yawn. "We have to get the tapes edited and off. We're overdue on our broadcast."

"You've been busy," Terry said.

His face, always slender, seemed unhealthily gaunt despite his smile. She knelt by the wheelchair. "You'll be all right?"

"Oh, I'm fine." His quick smile faded slightly, and he was looking past her. His gaze lingered on diplomas and plaques, a photo album, a pair of crystal goblets: the things they had brought from Earth.

"What are you thinking of, love?"

His smile saddened. "It's been a long time since you've called me that."

"I've thought of it every day."

"Have you?"

"Yes, of course—"

"You can't know how much I want to believe that. It's a trite old story, isn't it? Arranged marriage that results in love. Love on one side, anyway."

"Terry—"

"And then I found it was mutual. Marry, then fall in love. It really works. It wouldn't surprise our Hindu friends. They've known it all along. Go get your work done and ask Carlos to drop around once in a while. I don't see him enough."

She slipped on her shawl. It was a web of gold and umber yarn, every strand turned by the hand of her mother, over a century before. Its touch stimulated tactile memories: warmth, closeness, softness. It was one of her little pieces of home.

The click as the door latched behind her was uncomfortably loud.

After a few days of clear weather, the fog had descended upon Avalon with a vengeance, thicker and soupier than any night since the first grendel assault. It penetrated through the shawl as if she were naked, chilled right to the bone.

The searchlights atop the guard towers rotated tirelessly. Their beams stabbed out through the mist like silver fingers. The fog dampened sound as it did vision. After a few steps she looked back toward her house and her child and her husband. All were gone, vanished into the mist.

She drew the shawl tighter across her shoulders, and went on.

The electronics shack was in the rear of the camp, perched on the edge of the bluff. A single line of light burned through the shades. She paused a moment, listening to the muted rush of the Miskatonic, then rapped once and entered.

Carlos sat at the editing bench, absorbed in his work. She shut and latched the door.

"How is it going?"

"Just waiting for you, señora."

The shack seemed warmer than the house she had left behind. Terribly warm. Even with Carlos on the far side of the room, with the holo stage between them, he was stiflingly close.

"Coffee?"

"Maybe later."

"Let me know. We've got most of the video portion together. Just need you to look over your notes again. Take another look at the footage we did from the autopsy and the summation. Anything left to say? This is the last chance before we send it off."

Sylvia doffed her shawl and sat, enjoying her ease of movement. A month and a half before, she'd had to use her arms just to sit down. *There's the miracle fat cure. Lose twenty-six pounds in twenty-four hours. Have a baby.* Her joints no longer hurt, and her muscles were alive. She walked and moved like a new woman. Her body was ready for anything. Especially . . .

Oh, God . . . I hope I'm doing the right thing.

She focused on the holo, took a hand remote and fast-scanned. "This material on the increasing samlon size should be cross-referenced with their eating pattern. Joes and samlon are vegetarians, pterodons and grendels are carnivores. Good."

She flashed through the images and text, fighting to concentrate, almost overcome by the essential *maleness* of Carlos. She glanced over at him. He leaned back and sipped from his mug. She was dying to know what was on his mind. Why didn't he touch her? Or at least say something?

An image from the most recent Town Hall appeared. She remembered this vividly: the debate on whether to unfreeze the remaining embryos.

Zack, for the first time since Ernst's death, seemed rested and totally controlled. "The vote is close to even on this point, and I don't want to make a judgment until more of us agree. Final arguments?"

Terry appeared, and her heart leaped. In close-up it was easy to forget that he was crippled. "Cadmann isn't here to argue his own point," Terry began, "but I'll take the opposing view anyway."

There was scattered laughter. "I think that Cadmann is, as usual, being a conservative old maid. Avalon is safe at last. Let's put all of our eggs in one big basket. The odds are good; let's gamble with our children's lives. What the hell!" He paused; he was smiling, sort of. "The last time I said anything like this was the last time I ever stood up. And thirteen of us died."

Everyone laughed, sort of, but the vote that followed showed that Terry had made his point. Only a third of the remaining embryos would be thawed and revived.

She felt pride for Terry at that, pride that made some of her other thoughts dark and dirty. For a few seconds she considered simply telling Carlos that everything was fine, and leaving the shack while there was still time.

But this *did* have to be reviewed. She thumbed the scan into play. Images whizzed by, and through their transparency, she watched Carlos at his console. In one instant he seemed frighteningly strong and competent, and in the next like a little boy who needed comfort.

My body can't make up its mind!

She stopped the tape of her own image, part of a roundtable discussion of grendels that had been held three weeks before.

"—salt water isn't toxic to grendels," Marnie maintained. Sylvia had grown so used to Marnie's speech that she never noticed the lisp except in a tape. "Monsters can't drink salt water, but it won't kill them. I'd say that it irritates their nasal passages, and that is about all—"

Sylvia froze the picture. "I want a note here."

"Then slip it in. Tracks *siete* and *nueve* are free."

"Thanks. Subnote to preceding: Freshwater status of grendels established by evaluating salt content of tissues. Cross-reference autopsy."

Carlos nodded. "Everyone in the Colony has had a chance to add their own comments on Grendel."

"What was yours?"

"*I* think the bitch was smart enough to build a raft and float over from the mainland. I wouldn't put anything at all past them."

"That may be giving them too much credit."

"Better too much than too little."

Sylvia scanned through the rest of the tape, then signed off.

"I guess that's it," she said quietly.

Carlos nodded, and saved it. The computer silently sorted the notes and compressed the megabytes of data for transmission to *Geographic* in the morning. From there, it would be broadcast to Earth. Ten years later the data would arrive, for the edification and entertainment of the home worlds.

Once again the chill touched her, and she started to stand.

Carlos turned from the console and faced her. "I know, chiquita," he said. "Writing letters, sending messages, knowing that no one who ever knew me, ever touched me, will see them. No one to care. Strangers seeing pictures of strangers, and no one to care." Suddenly he was terribly close to her. His breath was warm, and smelled of coffee. "There used to be someone to care, you see? Someone who saw something beside the jokes, but I let her down."

Sylvia reached up to touch his face, to run her hand over the stubble on his chin. Her nerves jumped at the contact.

To love, honor, and obey. To cleave only unto . . .

"Anyone but Cadmann—"

Oh, God, it's been so long, so damned long.

"I care, Carlos."

He looked at her hard, with the beginning of something like tears in his eyes. Then his mouth became a fine line, and he said, "I don't know about this. Will you still respect me *mañana?*"

"You idiot. I don't respect you *now.*"

"Fair enough." He leaned forward that last few inches, and she backed away as his lips touched hers, then pressed against him, crushed her lips against him. Unfettered at last, all of the repressed feelings of the past months burned their way to the surface.

They stepped away from each other. Carlos squeezed her shoulders once, then turned off the equipment and the lights. He latched the door behind them, and together they set off through the fog for the warmth of his house. Within a few steps, the communications shack had joined the rest of the camp in the mist.

It seemed that there was nothing in the world but the two of them, doing the best they could do to find a path through the dark and the cold.

"I ALWAYS wondered what your bed was like." Sylvia giggled.

"You had but to ask," Carlos said gravely. "Move a bit, will you? Your lovely bosoms are squashing me."

Sylvia razzed him, and rolled off enough for Carlos to reach the bedstand. He felt among the empty beerskins for a full pouch, ah-hahed, and handed one to her.

The bed in question was a shell suspended like a hammock above the ground. Every attempt to extricate herself was a hazard, every movement during a delirious hour of lovemaking was enough to have both of them giggling like naughty children.

They swung there in a slight stupor induced by beer and afterglow.

She gave the pouch back to him and then snatched it away, dribbling foam over his chest and then kissing it off. He wrestled her to the bottom again, and she felt the heat flare in his body, triggering an immediate reply in her own. She wrapped her arms around him, then pulled the blankets over both their heads.

LATER, much later, it seemed, Sylvia and Carlos had exhausted the heat. They lay holding each other.

Is this what we really craved? Not the blaze, but the gentle warmth afterward, the peace you can only share with one who has walked the fire with you?

She played with the tight, dark curls of hair on his chest. "How did you end up at another star, Carlos? Not the stuff we all said back on Earth at the group-compatibility workshops."

"Great, weren't they? Jesucristo, the lies that were told that month."

"We all wanted to come pretty bad. Nobody was going to say anything to queer their chances."

"The truth." He sighed. With her face against his chest, she felt, more than heard, his heartbeat. It was strong, and slowing now. He had been as hungry for her as she had been for him. Or for someone.

God, this wasn't the time for thoughts like that. She shunted them back into her head and enjoyed the glow.

"How did I get here? Well, in therapy, you might remember when I said I'd been called back from Beijing where I was doing research on the T'ang Dynasty."

"You say that as if it isn't true."

"Oh, it's true all right. I had another reason for being in Asia for six years."

"Some almond-eyed lovely, I'd wager."

"You lose."

"Ooh. Guess what the stakes were. Claim your prize, you terrible man."

"Insatiable woman. Let me catch my breath. Where was I?" He ran his finger slowly down her back, then kissed her as softly and sincerely as she had ever been kissed in her life. "Oh, yes. Why was I in Beijing?" He laughed. "My family estate is in Patagonia, Argentina. We have fairly extensive holdings, actually. We raised shorthorn and Hereford, and Corriedale sheep. Very old family."

"Your whimsy certainly isn't high Spanish."

"Hell, half the time we spoke English. My mother was Canadian. I picked up colloquial Spanish in Mexico, in prep school and college. There was this little problem back home with a young lady. Her eyes, were, I recall, almond. The vegetable analogy unfortunately extended to her tummy, which was beginning to look like a casaba."

She felt a cold flash. "And you left—"

"No," he said quietly. "I didn't really love her, but I would have done the honorable thing. My father got there first, with checkbook in hand. She was poor, you see, and Papa wasn't having any of it. She went to visit untraceable cousins in Santiago del Estero, and I went north."

She relaxed again. "Where you stayed out of trouble, I hope."

"Hardly. I seem to have this talent."

"Mmmm. I've noticed."

"I was nothing but an embarrassment to my family. I can laugh about it now, but I really made a mess of things. I drank and gambled and wenched, and had the bad grace to stay in the top ten percent of my class. My father bought me out of one fix after another. Finally I got the royal invitation to get the hell off the continent. Live in Asia, drawing generous funds from the Bank of Hong Kong, or live penniless in the Americas. Being sensible, I opted for the mysterious East."

"A remittance man."

"Exactly. Want to know something?"

"What?"

"I'm half sure that my father bribed someone to get me my berth on *Geographic*. I don't think China was far enough away."

"Not a chance. You earned every mile. Your father must have been an interesting man."

"Aristocrat to the hilt. Used to retell Grandfather's war stories with relish. It was 'when the peons revolted' this, and 'in the fall of 1998' that, and firing squads and torched villages, and Indians dragged out of the jungle by their necks. He had holos of stacks of heads . . ."

He fell silent, and she didn't disturb his trance. At last he emerged. "To him it was all 'us' and 'them.' We had the land, they wanted it. As simple as that. I told him I hated that life, that I'd never be a part of it. And here I am. Watching the herds." Carlos chuckled darkly. "And fighting the natives, for that matter. Enough of that. How about some more of this?"

Sylvia looked to the clock on the wall. It was three in the morning. "No. I think that I had better go."

"When will . . . oh, nuts. *Chula mía*, it sounds ridiculous, I mean, it's hard to have someone here that I care about, and not know when I'll be able to be with her again."

"I don't know yet. I'm just glad we had tonight."

"As am I. Take care, *chiquita.*"

She kissed him again and then rolled carefully out of the hammock. She took a thorough shower, then slipped her clothes back on and left. Carlos was already asleep.

The fog had cleared some. Morning was still hours away, but she felt lighter, and warmer. Most importantly, she knew that she could face Terry with a clear conscience. What had happened between her and Carlos had nothing to do with her marriage, or her love for Terry.

But even if it had . . .

CHAPTER 25

LIFE CYCLE

> And now the matchless deed's achieved,
> Determined, dared, and done!
>
> CHRISTOPHER SMART, *"Song to David"*

MARY ANN pushed Cadmann away. "I can do it myself. I'm having a baby, not an operation." Clumsily, she pulled her legs up onto the delivery table.

Cadmann hovered nervously. "Are you sure you're all right?"

"Fine, darling. You look a little sick, though."

"I just hate leaving the important things to someone else."

"Trust me." She inhaled harshly, then released the breath as a contraction wracked her body. "Not much—uhhh—longer now."

Jerry patted her stomach comfortingly. "Just a few minutes, little soldier. We're almost ready for you."

"It's all right." She fought to stabilize her breathing, felt her pelvis stretch painfully, then release. She gasped for breath. "Ten lightyears from home and—" she labored for another breath—"we still don't have a better way to do this."

"Well, there's a Cesarean—"

"Invented in B.C. times for God's sa—ugh!" The pain stabbed

again, increasing in intensity and frequency. She gripped Cadmann's hand hard as Jerry seated her on the delivery table. She settled down into the saddle at the edge that would allow her to sit up and push, with gravity assisting her pelvic muscles.

"Now breathe."

All of Mary Ann's world contracted to a pinpoint centered on the ripple of pain that started deep inside her, then blossomed as her hips stretched to make room for the new life. The feeling intensified until it was neither agony or pleasure but merely sensation—

Dimly she heard Jerry say, "Cadmann, get the hell out of here."

"But—"

"But what? Get lost, Colonel. This is probably the only place on Avalon that you *aren't* needed."

"Mary Ann—"

"Go, stupid," she managed to say before another wave of pain hit her. Then another, and a third that broke like a receding wave, leaving her exhausted upon the shore.

"Breathe!" Marnie urged, and wiped Mary Ann's forehead. The pain was deep and vast, but not like a pain that would mean she was *hurt.* Her body was built for this. There was a burning, stretching sensation that receded and then strengthened, and she wanted to *scream*—

"Breathe!" With a start, she realized that she had literally forgotten to inhale. Everything vanished from her universe but the killing pressure in her abdomen, the sensation of a new life struggling through the darkness.

The light separated into coherent dots, floated away. Then they weren't dots at all.

They looked like tiny fish.

Samlon?

She almost laughed. What a time to think about—

"Breathe!"

This time the sensation was strong, almost like being pulled inside out, a long, shudderingly exquisite moment beyond time. The breaths and the minutes blurred, each a discrete entity, each forgotten as soon as it was gone. Consciousness fogged. How could she stretch so, without tearing? She would die. She would faint. The moment would never end, would go on and on—

A terrified Joe swam through the darkness, followed and swallowed by a larger something, just a shadowy glass fish shape, a samlon shape, swallowed in turn by something else, larger and more voracious. A grendel swallowed them both. It looked at her with blazing diamond eyes, challenging her. It fluxed like something out of an M.C. Escher painting, and was swallowed in turn by a mere samlon, but the legs of the grendel burst through its body, its teeth pierced through, so that as she watched, as she screamed, the samlon became—

"Breathe!"

"Push!"

The fragile hallucination vanished, wavered like steam above a hot spring and was gone, and there was only the reality of breathing. She held and pushed with the strong lower abdominal muscles.

There was a shared exclamation of relief in the room, and suddenly the stretching relaxed, the burning cooled. The pain was over. An unbelievably powerful wave of physical relief swept through her.

A sensation, cool, moist, rough terry cloth against her face.

A sound: a baby . . . her baby, crying.

Her vision was still blurry, but she saw Marnie cleanse a squiggling red-skinned thing that wailed like a siren, and Mary Ann's heart melted.

She closed her eyes again, and a moment later Jerry pressed a warm bundle into her arms. Its face was still daubed with blood and fluid, its eyes shut tightly against the strange and terrible world it had suddenly been thrust into. Its hands, just the size of walnuts, were fisted tightly.

And Marnie whispered, "It's a girl."

She tried to speak, to say, *Thank you for my daughter*, or anything at all. Nothing emerged but tears.

JUST NORTH of the Colony the Miskatonic had been dammed. The new lake rippled blue in the hazy light of Tau Ceti. A half mile across the lake the water spilled over a dam. When engineering completed the new construction, power would flow from a hydroelectric plant.

The dam. The solar cells. The fusion plant. Together they would make the colonists the wealthiest human beings in the history of mankind. They would have energy, and land, and the lessons of three hundred years of industrial Earth to guide them. A few more years, and wealth untold . . .

"I love it," Cadmann said, looking out over their artificial lake. "Hendrick has created a miracle. It's the only lake on the island fit to swim in."

Sylvia nodded. She shielded her eyes as she peered down the asphalt shoreline.

Two vehicles came toward them at high speed. On the straight flat road they moved faster than the designers had expected, or wanted. Mary Ann and Terry were racing motorized wheelchairs. Mary Ann was a meter ahead. Avalon's newest mother didn't *need* the chair, but it was fun to be babied.

Cadmann seemed more at peace with the Colony since Jessica's birth. His hair was a little grayer than it had been a year ago, but he stood taller, leaner, an animate extension of this hard and beautiful land. He gazed out over the lake, to where the iron peaks of the northern mountains rose up and tickled the clouds.

"Our work is never going to be finished," he said confidently. "Think of what we found lurking in our little corner of this planet."

"Terry's worked out plans for an expedition to the mainland."

"We should go as soon as we finish some of the other work. There's a lot to catch up on."

Her eyes searched the sky, "God, I feel so tied to this planet now. I wouldn't want to leave. I really wouldn't."

There was a shout from the edge of the lake. Mary Ann had pulled ahead of Terry.

"It's all right, isn't it?" Cadmann asked. "About us. About them."

"Absolutely."

"I look at Mary Ann. I think about Jessie, a bit of me that will go on after I'm gone. Everything just seems a lot righter. And she gave me that gift."

"I'm glad that we're friends."

"We couldn't be anything else, Sylvia."

She jumped: a shock wave as loud and sudden as a clap of thunder reverberated across the plain.

Mary Ann shrieked and pointed up into the sky. Cadmann whipped his binoculars up. "There she is. Don't you just love rocket ships? *Bring her down, Stu!*"

Sylvia spotted a thread of vapor trail as the Minerva began its descent. Now its shape could be seen: bastard birth of airplane and insurance building, the blunt bucket of a craft that had brought them down a precious few at a time, and delivered them to Avalon without an injury or mishap.

It hit the lake and skimmed across it like a drop of water on a white-hot plate. It had almost reached shore before its wings touched the glistening blue surface. Then clouds of steam rose up with a roar like a muted waterfall. It maneuvered the rest of the way in short bursts.

"This is your package, isn't it, Sylvie?"

"The very. *Nat Geo* gave me an early Christmas this year."

The Minerva thumped into the dock, rotated and locked in. After a moment the hatch opened, and Hendrick Sills climbed out. "Bumpy ride this time. We may have a storm coming in."

"Well, let's get the mail in."

Mary Ann and Terry pulled up to the dock.

"I win!!"

"She cheated."

Cadmann glared at them fiercely. "All right. What have you two been talking about?"

"Oh, about the same stuff as you and Sylvia."

"Then our relationship is doomed." Cadmann jumped up on the landing platform and helped Hendrick down. Stu emerged after. He carried a sealed metal box.

"We've got the goods here," Stu announced. "But hardier and more patient souls than I are going to have to download and sort them out."

"You don't look happy," Cadmann said.

"Maybe I'm not," Stu said.

"With good reason." Carolyn McAndrews came out of the hatch, followed by her sister Phyllis. Carolyn's face was tight with rage. "They proxmired the e-Eridani expedition."

"What?" Cadmann demanded.

"They canceled the e-Eridani ship," Phyllis said gently. "And all the others. There aren't any more interstellar flights."

"All true," Stu said. "Maybe our pictures weren't pretty enough—"

"That news is ten years old!" Mary Ann said. "Nothing we sent to Earth could have got there in time to make any difference!"

Carolyn glared angrily at Mary Ann. "We know." Her eyes softened. "He was joking, Mary Ann. Not a very good joke."

"We're all there is," Terry said. He looked down at his wheelchair. "Pretty heavy responsibility. I guess I'm glad we didn't know before we'd killed off the grendels. When too much depends on me, I always get stage fright."

Sylvia kept a greedy eye on the computer disk. "We're still here. And you're carrying a year's worth of news, and a complete encyclopedia update. With all of the data lost in the attack, this is what I've been looking for, and to hell with the proxmires."

"What is it? Just what are you looking for?"

"I don't know," she confessed. "I can feel things, patterns, trying to make connections in my head. Computers are good at that. We'll see what happens."

"Yeah. Well, you've got your mail." Hendrick lifted a box and carried it down to the pier's end.

Mary Ann stood up from her wheelchair. "Sylvia—do you need help? I mean, answering your questions. I get nightmares. I think I know what you're talking about. Something wants to come through. The samlon and the Joes and the grendels and—" She waved her hand. "They go together. It makes my head hurt."

"Sure." Sylvia smiled. "You're on the network. Whenever Jessica can spare you, get on. The conference name is GRENDEL—heck, that one's full of stuff. I'll start a new one. HEOROT."

Hendrick came back for another box. He was preternaturally silent. Cadmann caught his elbow and pitched his voice low. "Something else?"

"No."

"Come on." Cadmann eased him back from the others.

"You're the *last* man I'd . . . okay. I'm *tired* of this, Cadmann." His voice had been low-pitched, but it rose now and other voices stopped. "Ding dong, the monsters are dead. They're dead! And you'll never believe it, and that's good, because maybe it means *I* can take a break—"

"Hey, I haven't been pushing."

"No, but now everybody else has the bug. Okay. Go ahead and worry. There are going to be nightmares, sure, and we'll get over it sometime. Me, I'm finished," Hendrick said. "I finished my calibrations on *Geographic*'s antenna. I have some long-overdue fishing to get in, and I'm taking the weekend off."

"Sure. Alone?"

Phyllis sighed. "I've got a ton of work. Any volunteers?"

"None," Hendrick said, kissing her cheek. "So its just me and Boogie Boy. He never gets nightmares. Zack okayed it."

"Fine. Go. I went, and it patched me back together. If I knew a cure for nightmares I'd use it on Mary Ann. Take your break, man!"

Hendrick nodded. He hoisted his rucksack over his shoulder and walked away across the dock. He left an awkward silence.

Sylvia gazed at her husband suspiciously. "Ah-ha! So what was all the giggling about? Or can't you tell me?"

"Sure, I can tell you. I just can't tell the military arm."

"What is it?"

"Close your ears, Weyland. Mary Ann deliberately faked Cadmann out and had a girl. We're going to arrange a marriage for our hapless children. We figure our grandkids will have the best genes in the Colony and end up ruling the world. We can look forward to a comfortable, secure old age."

"Ah ha."

IT WAS late. Jessica was six days old and out of the camp's communal nursery with all tests completed. She lay sleeping in an elaborate hand-carved thornwood cradle in one corner of the biology lab. Mary Ann, Sylvia, Marnie and Zack's wife, Rachel, shared a pot of coffee.

"Cassandra!" Sylvia shouted. "Oh, damn."

"Problem?" Rachel asked.

"No more than usual. The computer's got holes in its head. *Cassandra: Background search. Reproduction cycles. Search all for match to terrestrial forms.*

"That gives her a hobby. Now. Speaking of reproduction," Sylvia said over her shoulder, "that leaves you and Marnie."

"Jerry and I are trying. . . ."

"I think I'm too old," Rachel said wistfully. "Thirty-seven now. Zack and I have just about given up on children."

"Need positive thinking," Mary Ann said. Her face suddenly lit. "Psychiatrist, heal thyself." She clapped her hands, delighted with the joke.

"Cassandra," Sylvia called. *"Find all on reproductive cycle emulations. Joes and pterodons."* She bit her lip nervously. "The way Cassie was bunged up I just don't know how much we can expect, but let's see."

A few seconds later, FILE NOT FOUND flashed in the air.

Sylvia sighed. "I'll find it. At least they're *in* there. Now all I have to do is figure out the file names."

Rachel frowned. "I thought Cassandra could find anything—"

"That was the general idea," Sylvia said. "But the first grendel trashed part of Cassie's memory, and the worst is we don't know *which* parts. She's got holes, the way—"

"Of course. I'm sure you'll find it. Is it really important?" Rachel asked.

Mary Ann took out a worn notebook and thumbed through its pages. "There was something I heard once. I keep trying to remember. I thought about it during *labor,* so you know how much it must have hammered at me."

"You'll think of it," Rachel said.

"What is it?" Marnie took the notebook browsed in it.

"I don't know, dammit. I just don't."

Sylvia said, "Nothing on this planet looks quite right. They're aliens, not Earth life forms. We found ducted glands in the samlon that hold stuff that swims around like active sperm, but they might be phagocytes of some kind. There's an embryonic set of what might be a uterus and an ovary. They're squashed flat across the intestinal wall, not much more than a pigment. And just when we were making progress, the grendel mushed up the labs! The only thing I can be sure of is that we're not sure of anything."

Mary Ann watched her with big, trusting eyes. How much had been lost from that brain? Like Cassandra, Sylvia thought. What might be triggered by the right words? "The grendels all appear to be female. They might be parthenogenic, but we don't have the equipment to be sure there isn't something like testes. The pterodons all seem to have both sets of sexual organs, but the Joes—"

"They mate like rabbits. Like we do sometimes." Mary Ann was wrestling with something, face wrinkled as if in agony, and Sylvia was only moments away from prescribing a sedative.

"Listen," Rachel said soothingly. "Stop trying so hard. Close your eyes for a moment. Stop being so serious."

"I can't help it."

"All right, what do you see with your eyes closed?"

"Joes and samlon and grendels chasing each other. I don't like it, Rachel."

"All right. Now pull back. See yourself watching that scene in a holo theater. Make the picture flatfilm. Black and white. Get some emotional distance."

Mary Ann's face calmed. "Better."

"Play circus music in the background."

Mary Ann laughed, clapping again. "That's it, it's perfect. Now they look like wooden animals on a merry-go-round. I hear a calliope in the background."

Sylvia sat back and grinned in admiration. She had never had a chance to watch Rachel work.

Rachel nodded. "Now. Open your eyes. Good. What did you have for breakfast this morning?"

"Juice and a chicken omelet. Cadmann made it. He's a good cook, good as me. I never knew."

"Good. Close your eyes again. What do you see?"

"Samlon and grendels and . . . frogs." Her eyes flew open. "That was really weird."

"Something Freudian, Rachel?" Marnie asked. "She might be telling you to jump in the lake."

"Maybe. Does that mean anything to you, Marnie? Any connection between Joes and frogs?"

"Behaviorally? Reproductively? Ecologically? It's probably some kind of pun."

"No, it's real," Mary Ann protested. "Something—diamonds?"

Marnie giggled.

"Oh, I just don't know." Mary Ann sat and stared at the wall. "Sylvie—"

Sylvia's eyes were unfocused. "Damn," she said softly. "You're right. It strikes a chord. Frogs. There was a special kind of frog. Something I read once. Cassandra," she said. "String search—frogs. Cross reference: Joes, samlon, grendels."

"Ladies—" Rachel yawned—"Zack has nightmares without me to hold his, uh, hand. Ahem. I'm calling it a night."

"Make it two," Marnie added. "Sylvia, Mary Ann, till morning. Are you going back tomorrow?"

"Yes," Mary Ann said uncertainly. Her eyes were still fixed on the whirring space above the holo stage. "Now I want to stay with Sylvia. Cadmann will be back for me."

There were hugs all around, and Rachel and Marnie left the lab.

Sylvia watched the fluxing holos, occasionally freezing the images.

There were visions of tree frogs and giant African frogs powerful enough to knock a man down. Pictures of frogs as they fed and mated and were spread out under the dissection knife.

Sylvia felt something cold and nasty in the pit of her stomach. A frog with nasty habits. She hadn't believed it the first time! But it did work, it did make sense. Oh, shit!

"Mary Ann," she said hoarsely, "I want to talk to Cadmann. Would you find him, please? Bring him here."

Mary Ann backed away from her, eyed wide and frightened. "Is something wrong?"

"I don't know yet. Maybe a chance in a hundred. I hope to God I'm wrong. Because if I'm right . . ."

With timing that was surreally precise, Jessica woke up, and began to scream.

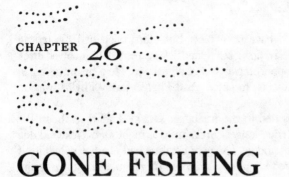

CHAPTER 26

GONE FISHING

"Why, Dr. Johnson, this is not so easy as you seem to think; for if you were to make little fishes talk, they would talk like whales."

BOSWELL, *Life of Johnson*

HENDRICK SILLS took Skeeter Four south toward Mucking Great Mountain. His back and shoulders and mind ached from three solid weeks of work, and he was more than ready for a rest.

Catfish had been sighted down south of Mucking Great. And plentiful samlon.

The monsters were all dead. *Ding dong!* The work was well and fully done, and it was time for a rest in the hinterlands. Only two days, there was work to do; but two days. Just him and a German shepherd and a fishing pole. Just a forty-eight-hour rest from troubleshooting the troubled Colony's many troubles. For a little while he didn't want to hear about flow rate and freshwater access, electricity, sewage and all the other little things. He didn't want to muck around doing brain surgery on Cassandra. He didn't want to oversee another team jury-rigging the veterinary clinic's ailing apparatus. "I'm tired of doing your job as well as mine, Carolyn McAndrews!" he shouted. The entire ordeal had been a drain, and now that the weeks and months of unrelieved tension were over, he was ready for some fun. *Ding dong!*

Company would have been nice. But Harry Siep had twisted an ankle. He wouldn't say how, but Hendrick suspected it involved back windows and the inopportune arrival of a husband. He'd be on his ass in the com shack for a week to come. And Phyllis, lovely Phyllis, was on duty.

Boogie Boy was tied to the passenger seat by a short leash. In the early days, they had tried longer cords, but one night an overexcited dog had leaped out at a pterodon. The poor creature had nearly lynched itself before the beleaguered chopper pilot could set the Skeeter down again. In the air, short leashes were s.o.p.

Hendrick peered out through the flowing, eternal mists. Cadmann's Bluff was down there somewhere. He couldn't see it. He dropped a little lower to get a better view.

The cultivated area of the plateau was beginning to bear fruit. From the air it now looked more like agricultural land than chicken scratches in the dirt.

And then there was the main house itself.

It had grown up the mountainside now. An underground house could be expanded far more readily than a traditional structure, and Cadmann had a dwelling that would do for a multigenerational homestead.

Deadfall boulders poised above the paths up either side. *Naturally.* Hendrick chuckled. And in a cleared strip at the bottom was the mine field that could be activated at the touch of a switch. "Can't blame him, maybe," Hendrick said aloud. Boogie Boy's tail thumped against the deck. "But damn it all, there's got to be a better way." The dog whined in sympathy.

Hendrick swerved up through the clouds and around the edge of Mucking Great Mountain. He headed south, picking up speed as he went. Two days. Then, perhaps, when he returned to camp, he would make a decision about Phyllis.

Baby fever! The contagion had infected the camp. Even Phyllis McAndrews, the eternal fiancée, had gotten gooey-eyed at the sight of Jessica Weyland. And last night, after an especially intense evening (God. Where *did* she get the energy? Or the flexibility?), Phyllis had hinted broadly of shooting the rapids. That the beautiful physicist might want a baby didn't surprise Hendrick: that she might want to be tied down to one tall, rawboned engineer did.

He laughed to himself. The tragedy that had befallen the Colony had an interesting side effect: ten surplus women in a community of fewer than two hundred. Hendrick was seriously tempted to remain a roving bachelor—yet he wondered if he could ever have claimed a prize like Phyllis back on Earth.

Decisions, decisions . . .

There was the strike camp. Overgrown now, but still clearer than the jungle that pressed in from all sides. Cadmann had singed the ground two months before, when the kill teams stalked the last grendels. The ground was flat, and a stream gurgled not thirty meters distant. Two months ago it had been choked with fat, flashing samlon.

The Skeeter settled with a bump. He unhooked Boogie Boy. The shepherd jumped down and sniffed the ground, bounded around in a circle and then set his paws back on the doorframe, begging Hendrick to come out and play.

Creepers and grass pushed back through the blackened earth and formed a thick cushion underfoot. He wished that the wind would clear away the mists, let him see the stars. There was nothing that Hendrick loved more than to lie on his back beneath a canopy of stars.

He'd done a lot of that when he was a boy in Michigan. Now Kalamazoo seemed just exactly as far away as it was. Impossibly far away, never to be seen again. Those had been good times, although the area was no longer as rural as it had been in his grandfather's day, when deer would come up to the back door.

Grandfather would have approved of Avalon.

Hendrick set up his lamp, then unrolled the air mattress and opened the valve. The mattress sucked air.

Boogie Boy bounded around him, then jumped onto the mattress, tail idling. When Hendrick said "Hey!" Boogie's tail whipped like a rotor. Hendrick shoved him away. The dog barked in frustration, then gave up and ran off toward the bushes.

Hendrick opened his fishing kit and examined the rod and reel. He checked his hooks and lures, and the play in his line, and was satisfied. Tomorrow was going to be a good fishing day. For now, there was little to do but sleep.

"Boogie?" The dog was gone, didn't answer, didn't bound back to the camp. Hendrick strolled down to the river and played his handlamp across the foam.

Beautiful. The light danced across the surface, and below its floating oval the water shifted with thick, dark shapes. Tomorrow would be a wonderful day for fishing.

The dog wasn't in sight, but Hendrick didn't worry. Boogie would be back.

He returned to camp. He peeled back the cover, slipped into the bag, and began to put himself to sleep.

SOMEONE pounded twice on their door, then yelled, "Goddammit, open up!"

Rachel rubbed Zack's nose firmly with hers. "That's what I get for sleeping with the boss."

"I can't believe this," Zack muttered resentfully. He rolled away and continued rolling until he was out of the bed. He pulled on his robe as he padded through the living room. He paused, gathering himself together before he swung the front door open.

Mary Ann looked frightened; Sylvia and wheelchair-bound Terry looked identically grim. Terry's hands fidgeted in his lap. "You're not going to like this," he said.

Zack pulled his robe tighter. "I'm sure you're right. I'd better let you in anyway."

They filed in like a jury prepared to deliver a death sentence. Each of the three looked to the others to speak first.

Rachel spoke from the bedroom. "What's going on?"

Her voice seemed to break Sylvia's mental dam. "What I remembered first was an African frog."

Mary Ann jumped. "Oh! Diamonds. Africa!"

"Diamonds and frogs and Escher drawings, Rachel. It was so simple that none of us could see it."

"See what?" Zack sat, trying to stay calm. "Slow down a little, will you?"

"Yes. Fine." Sylvia took a deep breath. "There's an African frog with nasty habits."

"Yes, yes, they eat—they eat their children!" Mary Ann shouted. "Yes, Sylvie, yes!"

"They eat the tadpoles," Sylvia said.

Zack waited. He heard Rachel move into the kitchen and start coffee. Coffee was for emergencies; Zack feared her instinct was right.

"It doesn't sound like a workable ecology, but it is," Sylvia said. "The simplest ecology you can imagine. Frogs and algae and nothing else. No insects, no fish. The frogs are carnivores. They can't eat algae. But the ecology's stable."

"Tadpoles eat algae," Mary Ann said triumphantly.

Zack said, "Ugh." He saw it already.

Sylvia nodded agreement. "The frogs lay eggs. The eggs hatch into little tadpoles. The tadpoles eat pond scum until they're big tadpoles. Then the adults eat big tadpoles. It's enough. And the big tadpoles that are agile enough or wary enough, they become adults—"

"You are talking about samlon, aren't you?"

"That's it, Zack. Samlon are tadpoles. Grendels are frogs. There's no way we could have known at the time, but we took the adults out of the picture, so there are a *lot* more samlon than there should be. And it's spring. And the samlon are getting big."

Zack felt numb. "What have we done? Sylvia? Do you know? Can there be any way to tell?"

"Not right now, but, Zack—" Sylvia spread her hands helplessly "—better late than never."

HENDRICK floated halfway up into consciousness. Something was pressing against his stomach: Boogie Boy, a warm, soft roll that gave a growl that was almost a purr. The German shepherd's tail thumped against the ground a few times, then it settled down to sleep.

"THIS ISN'T just guesswork," Sylvia said, finally winding down. "We *know* samlon are related to grendels. Remember when Cadmann came back with a piece of grendel and it tested out like samlon meat?"

"Jesus," Zack said. "And we didn't believe—"

"Yes," Mary Ann said. "You didn't believe him, and—"

"All right. It was my fault," Terry said flatly.

"And it took us this long to put it together," Sylvia finished.

"Yeah." Zack rubbed his eyes. "Thanks, darling." He took a refill of steaming coffee from Rachel and sipped. "Okay. Let's sort this out—"

Halfway to the kitchen, Rachel froze in midstep. "Zack?" She set the coffee tray down as if it were a soap bubble. "Hendrick."

"What about—?" It hit him too suddenly, and he almost dropped his cup. "Hendrick went fishing. We'd better get to the com shack. Sylvia, thanks for a lovely evening."

HENDRICK awoke suddenly, the fringes of a nightmare crumbling in his mind. Something was wrong. He reached out a hand for Boogie, and felt only the cool grass, pressed down where Boogie's body had been, and warmer there.

He heard the dog whine: a questioning, curious sound. As Hendrick sat up the whine rose into a pair of sharp yips, and then a growl.

What the hell?

Hendrick reached out for the explosive-tipped spear gun by his head. *Ding dong, the monsters are dead!* But mother hadn't raised any brain-damaged children, and Hendrick wasn't taking chances.

"Boogie?"

He pulled on his pants. Boogie suddenly appeared through the bushes and barked urgently at Hendrick, then disappeared again.

The barks abruptly became a ghastly shriek of pain, and Hendrick froze.

The moons were low and weak on the horizon. The mist wreathed the plants and twisted trees like clouds run aground. His handlamp barely pierced it.

Something was killing his dog. Following a response so basic it overrode his common sense, Hendrick took two nervous steps toward the brush. And then another . . .

The radio aboard Skeeter Four began to shriek.

Boogie . . .

Hendrick ran for the Skeeter. Leaves crackled behind him, and he glanced back as he ran.

Bits of the blackness *streaked* toward him. He batted blindly with the harpoon gun. The tip hit something resilient.

His leg flamed with sudden pain. He stomped back, heel crushing into something dog-sized. It hissed.

Hendrick was horribly aware that he was running for his life. He tore Skeeter Four's door open and dove in. His head banged against the instrument panel, but the door slammed shut behind him. He lay for a moment, then pushed the pain far down inside him. No locks on the Skeeter doors. *What's out there? What killed my dog?* He lay with his spear gun aimed at the door. Something scrabbled outside.

Hendrick looped one of the seat belts through the door handle, tied it shut. It would have to do. He forced himself to get off the deck and into the pilot seat. His leg was a bright sear of pain yammering for attention. It felt like a pit bull had taken a chunk out of it. Blood soaked through his tattered trousers and chamois shirt. He shut his eyes tightly and let his hand move gently downward. His fingers probed the wound: flaring pain, and a hole the size of a good-sized filet mignon.

The radio's squawk drilled through the pain. He struggled up and grabbed the handpiece, thumbed the transmit button and screamed, "God, my leg! Oh, *shit*. Something's out there killing my dog!"

The voice was Zack's. "Get out of there. Leave the dog."

"Damn straight!" Curiosity fought panic and pain. "What in hell is it?"

"Sylvia's trying to tell us that all the samlon are turning into grendels!"

Hendrick laughed hysterically. Something thumped against the door again and again, shaking the Skeeter. "She's damned right! Tell her her timing is for shit. Oh, Mother, it *hurts*."

"You're wounded? Can you fly? We'll send out a Skeeter—"

"No way I'm waiting. I can tourniquet my leg for the twenty minutes I'll need. Just have someone waiting to stitch me up."

Hendrick fumbled until he found the Skeeter's first-aid pack and pulled out the elastic tourniquet. The Skeeter juddered again, and the thin metal door bent inward.

He exhaled harshly and belted his calf tightly just above the wound. He flexed it once to test. "This will just have to do."

He started the motor turning, reached for the throttle, paused. Was he actually about to take off in the dark? Stupid. Muzzy thoughts. He turned on the lights.

Where he had piled the camp supplies, now dark shapes flashed in and out of a confetti storm of shredded plastic. Nothing was left whole. Half a dozen of the monsters must be batting at his door—he could hear them, feel the impact in his bones—but ten times that many were tearing into his supplies and each other. A knot of thrashing shapes suddenly separated, leaving shreds of Hendrick's self-inflating mattress.

The Skeeter shuddered once more before Hendrick got it into the air. Below him a circle of light expanded and dimmed. Somewhere out there, Boogie was being torn to pieces. "I'm sorry, boy," he whispered. "You probably saved my life."

The lights were only fogging his vision now. He turned them off. That wasn't so good either. It was dark down there. By compass he tilted the Skeeter north, toward the Colony. Some of the darkness was in his eyes.

Dark: the moons were down, the land was hidden. His thoughts wandered. Should he have taken off? *Could* he have stayed on the ground with unseen monsters batting at the thin metal hull?

Things batted at the hull; the Skeeter rang with the blows, and Hendrick screamed. There was texture in the dark. He'd fallen asleep, or fainted. Vertical spokes were tearing the rotor apart, smacking at the cabin walls.

CHAPTER 27

SALVAGE

It is much safer to obey than to rule.

THOMAS A KEMPIS

DÉJÀ VU:

The Avalon horsemane trees were tall and narrow and absolutely vertical: trunks white as paper, with a fringe of dark green running like a stallion's mane down the leeward side. Hendrick's Skeeter had smashed sideways into a grove of them. The wreck had fallen into what seemed to be shallow water. The rotor blades were nowhere to be seen, and the tail was bent at a right angle.

Cadmann's stomach soured, and something flipped in his mind, skewed dizzyingly. . . .

He was back in Zambia, southwest of the Zambezi River, on chopper recon over broken brushland. Below him were parched earth and brown, stunted vegetation. The year's drought had been harsh on the land, harsh on the people. This year, it was all too easy for the guerrillas to recruit starving tribesmen.

Thermal scan verified that the area was clear of enemy troups. The scans had greater range than the enemy's light antiaircraft projectiles, and a LAP had brought down Sergeant Mguvi's helicopter. Somewhere in the smoking mass of torn metal beneath him was one of the two finest men Colonel Weyland had ever had the honor to command. . . .

That image was strong now, too strong. The rage it engendered was not far behind.

Cadmann brought his Skeeter down close to the wreckage and played his searchlight beam over the trees and water.

Beside him, Carlos cursed in Spanish. His machine pistol spat crimson streams of tracers into the darkness. The streams chewed into the mass of minigrendels as they swarmed around the Skeeter, feuding for a scrap of Hendrick. Little knots of grendels were fighting and eating each other; Carlos fired spurts at those.

"There must be thousands of them," Carlos said hoarsely.

"Maybe a hundred, maybe two. Save your bullets. This is like spitting into the ocean."

Carlos's face twisted with loathing. "We can't leave Hendrick like this. We've got to bring him back."

Cadmann felt numb. "Dead or alive, we'll bring him in. We have to salvage the Skeeter. But I don't *see* any breaks in the cabin wall, and what are they fighting for if there's no more Hendrick? He *could* be safe."

"Why are they here if they don't smell meat? There's a breech. There must be."

"Colonel, we can't remain in the area. The intelligence people say there's a hostile force moving in from the northwest. We're not prepared to hold off an assault. . . ."

An ugly choice to make. The lives of six men were at stake. And it was already too late to do anything for the laconic, steadfast Mguvi.

So Colonel Weyland had left his friend in the singed brush, sealed in a crumpled tomb of steel and plastic. He had left a piece of himself there as well.

Not this time.

Cadmann swooped down once more, giving Carlos time to empty his clip. "Feel better? Then don't waste any more ammo," he said grimly. "Before this is over, we're going to need every last cartridge."

But if it really comes down to counting bullets, we're dead, all of us.

Carlos did seem calmer as he slipped in another clip. "What next?"

"Pick up the wreck and carry it home."

"Can we carry that much mass?"

"I'll sue the socks off somebody's descendants if we can't. It was in the design specs. We've got the power. There are lift rings built into the Skeeters. On top. The hooks have to engage."

"Ah. You mean, *amigo*—"

"I mean that one of us drops in a harness and clips the lift lines into the rings. Take over?"

"No. No, I do not fly and shoot at the same time, and if we must lose one of us, better it is me. No?"

Cadmann didn't answer.

"So. Give me a moment." Carlos got out of the copilot seat and scrambled aft. Cadmann heard him fumbling with the rescue harness.

"Done, *amigo*. Now tell me. Can these creatures leap to the top of a wrecked Skeeter?"

"Dam'fino. Carlos—Carlos, we could wait."

"But Hendrick cannot wait. *Mi coronel*, you must give me directions."

"Okay. We're supposed to have a harness operator. Isn't one aboard so you have to do it. Take that box there off the wall. Joystick in the center. Moving it up reels in line on your harness. Moving it down reels it out. Hang the machine pistol around your neck, then clip that box to your harness. Lose it and you're dead."

"Done."

"Test the lines. Try reeling in. And out."

There was a sharp whirr. "*Sí*. It works."

"Okay. I'll drop the tow lines as soon as you're on the way down. There's a lift ring just forward of the rotor base, and another about two thirds of the way aft. Clip the hooks into the rings and reel yourself up. Work *fast*."

"Fast. You know it. I'm ready. I am stepping out now."

A slight gust swayed the Skeeter. Cadmann compensated automatically. "Okay?" he called.

"*Sí*. I am lowering myself. There are—Cadmann, there are a lot of those things, but I believe you are right. I think they have not penetrated into the Skeeter. Hendrick may be alive in there."

"Toss a grenade. Well away from the ship."

"Okay. Here goes."

Five seconds later there was a sharp *whump!*

"It's working," Carlos called. "They are clustering there. Zip zip zip! Cadmann, some are on *speed* but most are not."

Cannibals. It figures. "Here come the towlines." Cadmann lifted the protective cover and threw the switches.

"Well done. Come to port. More. More. Stop. There. Hold it there."

Cadmann fought to hold the ship steady against the gusty wind off the stream. *Hurry up, hurry, you monarchistic son of a bitch—*

"The aft line is done. I am moving forward and—"

Weyland heard shots. One, two, then automatic fire.

"Carlos! Carlos, come in, Carlos—"

"Madre de Dios—" There were more shots.

Cadmann tugged a grenade from his harness and pulled the pin with his teeth. *Nobody does that. Well, I just did.* He held it in his left hand and tossed it out the window as far off to the left as he could.

Whump! "Carlos—"

"Done! I am reeling myself up. Go!"

"You know it, brother." Cadmann gunned the engines.

"I saw his face. He's not moving but . . . but none of it is missing, thank God."

"Good enough."

CADMANN, Jerry, Sylvia, and Marnie sat facing the assembled colonists. The room was silent as Zack spoke.

"We're not going to talk about this behind closed doors. We all need to make decisions. We've been caught with our pants down yet again. There's no way we could have known—"

Bullshit. Cadmann glanced at Sylvia. She shook her head slightly. Cadmann didn't respond. *I'm not the team of carefully selected geniuses who should have seen this. I'm only the guy who has to fix it. Too damn late, Sylvia!*

"How's Hendrick?" Gregory Clifton asked.

"Still in intensive care. He hasn't told us anything. He may lose the leg, the tourniquet was on a long time. Jerry promises a miracle. We'll see.

"This time we had more warning. Nobody's dead yet. Twenty-twenty hindsight is better than none." Zack hesitated and gripped the podium as if searching for strength that wasn't there. Then he straightened decisively. "You've all heard rumors. Samlon are baby grendels, and they're changing. We're in trouble. Sylvia and Jerry will try to tell us just how much trouble. Sylvia, take over."

Zack left the podium and came down to the front row. Cadmann indicated the seat next to him and half stood as Zack sat. Sylvia took the podium.

Jerry inserted a video cube into the viewer and the image of a samlon floated in the air in front of the dining hall. Sylvia said, "Samlon. Zero to two feet long. No teeth to speak of. Totally aquatic. Good eating."

She seemed to be speaking directly to her husband. Terry seemed calm and attentive. He was holding Justin. The child was asleep, his tiny pink fists balled, clutching at the fabric of his father's shirt.

A second image joined the floating samlon. "This was clinging to Hendrick's Skeeter. Sorry about the head. We clubbed it to death. It's still the best sample we've got. You can see it's over a meter long. Note that the dorsal fins have atrophied, and the ventral have thickened and begun changing into legs. The flexible beaklike jaws have differentiated into teeth. The *speed* sac behind the lungs is beginning to inflate. Their metabolic rate has to be off the scale. Only an unprecedented rate of calcium transport could explain the teeth and the thickened bones."

The third image was Cassandra's graphic representation of an adult grendel.

Sylvia cleared her throat. "There are equations in the literature. We ran them through Cassie and we got some graphs." The fourth image appeared: a three-dimensional graph chart that glowed like a range of neon mountains. "It's not a lot of help. We're missing some of the numbers, but what's happening is clear enough.

"Adult grendels are all female. Tadpoles are males. Most don't get much chance to demonstrate it because they get eaten. The grendels lay lots of eggs. The eggs turn into tiny samlon. The little samlon go away and eat the local scum until they turn into big samlon. The grendels eat big samlon.

"Now, evolution says there will be more grendels if grendels eat something other than their own children. The grendels will eat *anything* rather than samlon. They must have exterminated everything within reach of water long before we came. They were back to eating nothing but samlon. It's been a stable situation for hundreds of years, or thousands, or conceivably millions. The flyers have had time to adapt, and we should have noticed that too."

"Yes!" Mary Ann shouted. "The flyers. Of course! The way they fish—"

"We've—" Suddenly Sylvia laughed. The incoherent wave of sound that rolled across her audience was ugly. Nothing was funny now.

"Sorry," Sylvia said, and laughed again. "We've ruined the ecology, is what we've done! First we introduce new food sources. We won't be finding many catfish now. Then we killed all the adults. Mama hasn't been around to eat the samlon. Now it's spring, and all the samlon are growing up into grendels. The number of adolescent grendels is going to be far larger than the equilibrium population."

"Holy shit," Gregory Clifton whispered; but everybody heard. It had gone deathly quiet.

Mary Ann said, "Sylvie? Grendels eat all the time."

"What? Oh. Shit." Sylvia rubbed her temples. "Sorry. She's right, of course. They need a continuous food source, so they must lay eggs continually. This could have happened any time of year. We took out all the adults, so the samlon are all growing up."

Cadmann thought, *They still didn't have it right! I wonder what we're missing now.*

"How many grendels are we going to get?" Greg asked nervously.

"That is difficult to predict. We haven't tried to fold in the rate at which grendels kill each other. The one thing that we can be sure of is that in killing the grendels we have unleashed an even greater threat.

"We've got at least two things going for us. First, the grendels eat grendels. They'll fight for territory too. Clearly they'd rather eat someone else's children than their own. Evolution again. Second, we've been fishing. We've fished out the local environment. The majority of adolescent grendels haven't discovered us yet. They will. Before they do—" Sylvia shrugged. "It's Cadmann's problem now."

The hall murmured. Cadmann turned to Zack. "Sir?"

Zack took the stand again.

"We have considerable evidence that even after the metamorphosis is complete, the samlon and grendels need water. I propose the use of a biodegradable toxin. We rescue what catfish we can and use our present breeding pond as a water supply. We poison the Miskatonic at its headwaters—"

Jerry shook his head. "That's a wonderful idea, Zack. Unfortunately, we didn't come here to poison Avalon, and we're just not set up for it. The best we could do is pump some of the heavy-metal industrial wastes into the water. That won't kill them quickly, but would definitely kill us slowly. No go."

"What about the *Geographic?*" Carolyn McAndrew's voice was cracking. "Can't we evacuate up there?" Her face was tight, and Cadmann saw her blink hard, as if trying to keep the tears back. *One of the rifle troops. She saved my life that night.*

"We all saw what *one* of them did to us before," Carolyn shouted.

"Who are we kidding? There's no way in hell we can fight this. I say it's time to quit."

"Quit?" Phyllis asked softly. "Quit and do what?"

Carolyn stuttered for a moment. She scanned the room, looking like a lost little girl. "Go home. We can still go home. . . ."

Stu stood, and spoke regretfully. "We can't do that, Carolyn. *Geographic* has life support for about twenty colonists for about a week. Then the oxygen recyclers will go to shit. You forget—we've been disassembling the ship for almost two years. . . ."

"Cryogenics. We can freeze—" Her mouth worked wordlessly, then the realization hit her. "Oh, no. Hibernation Instability."

Phyllis reached up to Carolyn's shoulder. "Sit down, hon."

Carolyn shook the hand off. Her shoulders trembled.

Zack's face had something of the old strength in it, and even a grimly humorous curl to his lips. "This is it, Carolyn. No Fort Apache to reach. No bugle call. No way home. We fight and win, or we all die. And it's time to turn to the experts. Colonel Weyland?"

Carolyn collapsed into her seat. The room was swept by a flurry of whispers. The implications of putting Cadmann Weyland in charge of civilization were obvious.

Cadmann stood, and he felt that mantle of responsibility falling back across his shoulders. So be it. A job to be done, and at least the priorities seemed clear enough. "Sir."

"Please take the podium."

"Yes, sir." *Suck up that gut. Get your back straight.* Cadmann marched to the podium. *My job. And what in hell do we do? Doubtless something will suggest itself. First things first.* "Tomorrow morning we start running the Minervas in shuttle mode. Up and down at three-hour intervals. Pregnant women and children first. Then indispensable skills. Zack goes up, and Rachel with him. Next, if there is still space, the wounded. We need to make up a priority list: there isn't going to be much room.

"Meanwhile, all Colony defenses go into effect. All the other women will retreat to the Bluff with enough tools and equipment to improve fortifications there. Get to packing."

The room was silent for a long moment. "Without the crops here, we'll starve," Jerry said.

True, but you didn't have to say it. "There's food in *Geographic*. We found some things to eat in the highlands. The trick now is to get through the next few weeks." *After which there won't be as many mouths to feed.*

Sylvia raised her hand. "We need to capture a few grendels. Get them up to *Geographic,* where we can work on biological weapons."

"Sure you can handle a live grendel? Damn dangerous thing to do."

"We'll work on cages. Maybe we can catch samlon that are just changing. We need the information."

"Agreed if you can do it. Stu—handle that? Report to me before we try anything. Nobody risks a Minerva or the ship without direct approval from me. Nobody. Zack, you confirm that?"

"Uh—yes. Yes, he's right."

"What's the point?" Carolyn screamed shrilly. "Everything we do just makes it worse. What's the point in fighting? There's no safety—" Tears streamed hotly down her face.

Mary Ann stood, and scanned the room uncertainly. "No . . . no, that's not true."

She was taking it in with immense calm. She held Jessica tightly. The child's thin, short blond hair was as pale as spun glass.

"How can you know?" Carolyn shouted. "Mary Ann, you're like me! You can't depend on your thoughts. Or anything."

"I can sometimes," Mary Ann said. "Carolyn, *think.* We have Joes. They're alive."

"By God," Sylvia said. "She's right. It means—"

Mary Ann was triumphant. "That's what the Joes mean—it means that the grendels can only climb so high."

"They don't travel far from the water," Jerry added. "They'd cook themselves. We've seen how much heat their bodies give off when they're on *speed.* There's more than hope—as long as we don't panic."

We're a lot bigger than Joes. More meat.

"Now then," Zack said firmly, "it's time to make some decisions. If we're going to have any chance of surviving, we need total cooperation. We can do this, but only if we operate at peak efficiency. No holding back, no dissension. There's no time for that. First of all: Colonel Weyland will take charge of defense, and we're on a war footing. If you have any objections to that, make them now. Do I hear objections?"

"What do you mean, take charge?" Omar demanded.

"I mean, he says 'Frog,' you jump first and ask how high afterwards," Zack said. "If you want justification, look in the contracts we all signed. It isn't even fine print. It says that in the event of a threat to Earth or the Colony as a whole the normal rules are suspended and the

Administrator has plenary authority. Anyone still think we don't have a threat to the Colony?"

Someone smothered a lone giggle.

"So. You signed a contract that makes me God. I'm handing that to the archangel Cadmann. Objections? I hear none. So ordered. Colonel?"

"Thank you. People, this meeting is too large to get anything decided. Some things are obvious. We'll have to evacuate this place. As soon as you leave this meeting, go pack. Divide things: essential, important, frivolous, waste.

"Jerry, you're in charge of the technical stuff. Mary Ann, take him to the Bluff. Sylvia goes too. You'll work on defenses."

"Why your house?" someone demanded.

"It's the most defensible place on the island," Carlos said. *"Cabrón,"* he added softly so that only Cadmann and those in the front of the room could hear.

"Stu Ellington takes charge of the Minervas. They're the most important things we've got. Stu, we'll need to work schedules, evacuation versus power requirements for the Colony, but the most important thing is that we don't risk one Minerva and for God's sake we never risk both."

"Right," Ellington said.

"We'll want power as long as possible, but the first threat to a Minerva and that ship is *off,"* Cadmann continued. "Which means precautions about loading and unloading. Plan that as if the ship might go at any time. *Any* time. Even with people waiting to get aboard."

"Whew. Right," Stu said. "That's not the most pleasant thought you ever gave me."

"Donovan. We'll need a communications link between the Bluff, the town, and *Geographic.* Maintain constant input from *Geographic's* telescope and the Skeeters."

"Got it."

"In your spare time, keep the Skeeters charged up, and on patrol. Ferry the wrecked one off to the Bluff." Cadmann passed his hand through his hair. "I'll need a staff meeting as soon as this breaks up. All department heads. We've got a hell of a lot of details to plan. Questions?"

"Only one," Zack said. "I'll ask it for all of us. You're talking like we have to abandon the Colony. Are you sure of that?"

"Sure, no. But it's the way to bet it," Cadmann said. "Remember what one grendel could do? Now think about thousands of them. If there's a way to defend the Colony against that threat, I don't know it. Anyone have suggestions?"

There was silence. They knew more now, and Cadmann could smell the fear building. From the buzzing a voice rose. "Hydrogen. Liquid hydrogen. Burn them."

Interesting, Cadmann thought. "Jerry?"

"We don't have a lot, and the Minervas will need it. Containers. Transportation. I like the notion, but there are problems."

"Think about it," Cadmann said. "I won't have time. Next?"

"Come on, citizens, they're only *animals,*" Terry said. His hands were clenched, white-knuckled, on the wheelchair arms. He wants to be standing up, Cadmann thought. "We came across ten lightyears, and we came as conquerers! It's . . . it's funny, is what it is. Star travelers chased off by animals."

Carolyn cried, "You can say that? You?"

"I'm not the first man in history to be mauled by an animal. We're still king of the beasts."

Good for Terry. Cadmann looked soberly around the room. How many of these people were going to be alive in a week? It was up to them, it was up to him.

Jessica looked so terribly fragile. For an instant he recognized the very real possibility that nothing they did would be enough. That their defenses would crumble before an onslaught of grendels.

"As long as they don't chase us off the planet." Zack came back to the podium. "Cadmann, I expect you'll want to prepare for your staff meeting. Look, people, I know it's a shock—"

"Shock!" Jerry exploded in laughter. "Zack, how many shocks do we get?"

"Fortunately, this was the last," Zack assured them.

"Heard about Zacky's Comet?" Harry Siep called. "Boils the oceans every four hundred years. Oops, three ninety . . ."

Cadmann grinned. "Yeah."

"That's better," Zack said. "We'll make it. Look, we all know this won't be cut and dried. So what? Before we left Earth we didn't know what we'd face. Now we know the worst, and it's not as bad as some of us thought it would be! They *are* just animals."

Carolyn giggled hysterically. Everyone could remember: Carolyn and four others standing outside the corrugated-metal building, four generic warriors firing into a single demon.

"We just have to trust each other. We're each proficient in at least two vital skills. Some of us can handle three or four. I expect you to keep a running assessment of your emotional and physical reserves. Pitch in and help anyone beginning to fade. When you're fading yourself, first find a replacement, *then* go somewhere and have hysterics."

"But get permission from Cadmann first," Carlos said. "Hysteria without permission is strictly forbidden."

"Enough, then," Zack said. "Staff meeting in half an hour. The rest of you go pack."

CHAPTER 28

MARABUNTA

> There's a price for too much arrogance, a price for
> too much greed,
> And in complacent ignorance we've sown the whirlwind seed!
>
> DON SIMPSON, "Serpents Reach" (song)

CHANGES CAME with disorienting speed. Everything about the swimmer's new world was stimulation and strangeness.

There was a heat within its body. Its mouth ached. Its balance had changed, become awkward. Swimming was clumsier now.

There was nothing to eat. The green strands it had eaten all its life no longer smelled like food. In all of the swimmer's life it had thought of eating nothing else. The question had never even arisen. Now, confusingly, the flavor had gone flat.

The water itself had gone flat. Something was missing. Some feeling —powerful, dominant, a discomfort growing to panic and pain—was driving it out of the water.

It found itself trying to swim across mud.

The mud flat swarmed with its siblings.

It writhed in place. New muscles flexed and compressed, released, and fire flowed into its new lungs. The panic receded.

The fins which had grown clumsy now revealed new purpose. With great effort, what had been a swimmer thrust against the ground and rose up on unsteady legs, balancing. Its sides heaved, pulling air in and out. It looked at the world above the water.

This place was totally foreign to a swimmer's world of suspension, of placidity and constant pressure. Smells were different, weaker, stranger. Its tear ducts ran with oily fluid, keeping its eyes moist. It found the *squeeze* that would change its vision, and infinity jumped into its sight.

It felt the pressure of its own weight for the first time in its life. How could it feel weaker and more powerful at the same time?

Something even stranger happened. It turned, humping its body sideways in sudden alarm. One of its siblings was coming, dull black eyes fixed hungrily. It smelled wrong . . . smelled right. There was no image, no feeling to match this smell, but something within the swimmer began to flare. It felt suddenly weightless, no longer clumsy. . . .

Its sibling lunged forward.

All thought was overwhelmed by its instinctive response. The swimmer flopped to the side, and the strike of its sibling caught only air. The swimmer's head whipped around and it sank new teeth into its attacker's flank.

Never before had it fought one of its own. The only memory of survival stress was the struggle to evade the Big One, the One who ate swimmers. Many times the Big One had come, and the swimmer had moved swiftly. More swiftly than many of its siblings, because this swimmer had survived.

Once, the Big One had hung quiescent in the water, exuding a different smell. The swimmer had drawn closer, closer, unable to retreat. So close that the Big One could have caught it easily if it wished.

There followed a moment of such intensity that the swimmer could not clearly remember what had happened.

This moment held similar intensity: fear and rage and the taste flaring in its mouth and brain.

The sibling tried to retreat now, but the swimmer was suddenly ravenous. It had tasted something more delicious than all of the green muck in the world. It struck again and again. Around it, other siblings were joining in. They ripped and tore. The smell of blood filled its senses. The death agonies of its hapless sibling quieted, until at last there was nothing but the feast. . . .

* * *

TAU CETI wavered in the mist, stared out at Cadmann like a bloodshot eye. Vanished behind a strand of horsemane trees. Back, then gone again as the Skeeter skimmed the stream.

The swamp below him swarmed with grendels. He couldn't see individuals yet, but he saw darting streaks everywhere. Trees and brush and shrubbery shook, churned and chewed by the horde.

Carlos touched his shoulder. *"Amigo. Cómo está?"*

"Bien. Y usted?"

"Jitters. Cramps." Carlos gripped at his stomach. "The stress is not sweet. But I think I will make fewer mistakes."

"That's the picture. And from here on out, we can't afford any mistakes at all." Cadmann brought the Skeeter down closer to the river. Now he could make out individual grendels. They crowded the water like catfish in the breeding pond, writhing and biting at each other. Two chased a third up a horsemane tree. The leader was too slow, too clumsy. It lost its grip and fell; the others snapped at it as it passed, and the three fell in a writhing cluster.

"Carlos, you're more the mathematician than I am. What is the minimum survival population for our colony?"

"We worked that out. I read a paper on it once. Minimum genetic diversity, minimum skill spread. We *took* the minimum in adults, with three times that many in fetuses. But if one has faith in the Good Book, one man and one woman could repopulate a planet."

"Times like this, faith isn't a terrible idea." Cadmann grinned bleakly. He directed the Skeeter's camera to the knot of writhing grendels beneath them.

"Feeding frenzy. They trigger on their own. Let's see what Jerry's idea does." Carlos clipped the wire fastened just inside the door. One of the weighted sacks hanging from the side of the Skeeter dropped. Calf blood spilled into the water.

The grendels went crazy. They bit at nothing, drunken with blood lust. The water churned black.

"Damn, they're stupid."

"Yeah, but they're infants. The ones who survive will be smarter— and we don't have an unlimited supply of calf blood. The reflex is there, though. That's encouraging. We have a pretty creative group. Someone will come up with something even better."

They died by the hundreds. Chewed corpses floated belly up, choking the surface. Others moved in to feed.

"They are no longer fighting," Carlos said.

"No. Enough to eat? Something. Still, we got a lot of them." Cadmann's smile was grim. "Come on. We have work to do."

As THEY pulled up over the Colony, Minerva Two rose from the dam on a column of foam and mist. Cadmann hovered there, as thousands of gallons of water cascaded back into the lake with a thunderous roar. Waves crashed out in concentric rings, pounding at the dock.

The two friends watched the craft climb. It had vanished into the mist before the sound changed from one kind of thunder to another as the nuclear ramjet lit.

"I don't think I want to be behind a Minerva when it takes off," Carlos said.

"Nor I. How can we entice grendels to cluster there?"

"That's what I was thinking—"

"When you think of a way, be sure it's safe. Without the Minervas we're *dead.*"

They circled the camp. Its fortifications lay spread out below like a tabletop model.

The electric fence had a new, larger twin within the moat of mines. The outer fields had been harvested, the grain shipped up to the Bluff. Tractors under remote control chugged slowly in the barren fields. Cadmann could distinguish the flame-thrower nozzles welded to the fronts of the cultivators and irrigators.

The welding lasers, the torches, the plasma drills were all arrayed as weapons now. Virtually every tool from engineering had been modified to the defense of the Colony.

He could see the gunmen too, but he knew where they were beforehand: stationed at the corners of the fence, ready to fire along its length. Skeeters moved about, swooping to fire at grendels. There were not so many grendels yet, but they all had to be stopped before they reached the fences.

"I still say it's chancy," Cadmann murmured.

"Eh?"

"Both Minervas in flight. No power for the fences while they're both up. Lose both and we're dead."

"So why did you let them both go up?"

"Schedule. Sometimes you just have to take chances. It doesn't mean I like it."

They circled over stacks of thornwood faggots stacked at intervals, wired for ignition at command. "I hope it works," Cadmann said.

Carlos shrugged. "Jerry and Marnie swore by this. Do you trust them?"

"I trust the logic. Add heat to an already overheated grendel and watch it cook. I trust them. I'm just not sure I *believe* it."

The cattle and horse pens were empty. Cadmann could see the occupants moving uphill, horsemen and horsewomen on the outskirts of the herds: old movies played through his mind. *We've got rustlers like you never dreamed of, Duke.*

Cadmann settled the Skeeter lightly to the pad. As he unbuckled his safety belt, Zack opened the door.

"I thought you'd be aboard *Geographic* by now." Cadmann pulled the tape cartridge from the camera.

Zack said, "Nope. Not yet. I don't really want to go, you know."

"Yeah, and I don't really want to stay. People like you and me don't get a whole lot of choice in life. How is everything going?"

"Rachel says that the work shifts were implemented just fast enough. Everyone's so tired that the shock hasn't had a chance to sink in yet. When it does . . ."

"By the time that it does, this will be over, one way or the other."

A loud, miserable bray from the center of camp caught Cadmann's attention. "Damn!"

"Huh?"

"The horses. Let them go. The grendels aren't fully mature. The horses may be able to outrun them. A few may survive."

"Bloody unlikely."

"Yeah, but as the man said—the grendels are running for their lunch—"

"The horses are running for their lives. Got it. Besides," Carlos said soberly, "I'm sure they would rather die on the run than trapped in a pen." He looked thoughtful for a moment. "They would have a better chance if someone went with them. To guide them. Take them as high as possible."

Cadmann said, "Too right. But who? Someone not much use in a fight—Carolyn. She rides. Let her take the horses."

"She tends to panic," Zack said. "Oh—"

"Exactly. No room for her in *Geographic!* She's not a lot of use in a fight. But she can run. Send her."

"I will tell her," Carlos said.

"Why you? Oh. Well, okay. How's the big surprise coming, Zack?"

"We have a thousand liters of liquid hydrogen in each of the four storage tanks. It isn't enough, but it's all we can spare. We'll have to wait and see."

"What's the situation on the grendels?"

"Up to ten an hour. Best guess is that will double every couple of hours until the wave hits. When Minerva Two comes down, she stays down. We should power the fences soon. The main wave hasn't found us yet, but one grendel got through the north fence half an hour ago."

"Being fixed?"

"Already done. Now, you hook up Minerva Two for power, but you load the cargo too. Those fences can't hold up forever—"

"Soon as the fences go, the Minerva goes too. We've been through this. You'd better get over to the dam." Cadmann shook Zack's hand hard, then glanced up as a hypersonic shriek split the sky: Minerva One, returning for another load.

Zack sighed. "You know, Cadmann, there's just been no time. No time at all. I . . . you could have taken the Colony away from me, and we both know it."

"That's bullshit."

Zack seemed to be searching for something else to say. He gave up and turned, leaving Cadmann and Carlos.

"Virtues of the warrior," Carlos murmured.

"What are you babbling about?"

"The virtues of the warrior, since ancient times: Protection of the Innocent, Courage in Battle. The greatest of them was Loyalty to the King."

"The king." Zack's dejected figure reached the dining hall and disappeared inside. "I guess he's the only king we have, at that." Cadmann laughed. "Come on. We've got a lot more to do, before we're through today."

THE COMMUNICATIONS shack was busy. Marnie and Jerry were monitoring communications, coordinating thermal graphs from *Geographic*. Wedges of color showed the forward progress of the grendels.

There was no "wave." There was a growing density of heat sources along all the streams on Avalon, ruby red along the Miskatonic, with a gap around the Colony. The gap was filling in as grendels moved into open territory.

"How long now?" Carlos asked soberly.

Marnie switched her throat mike off to answer. "Twenty hours tops."

Jerry nodded optimistically. "It's going to get right down to the wire, but I think we can hold that long."

Gunfire sounded: several guns at once. Carlos watched one of the video screens. Baby grendels danced in the corn stubble—three, four.

We won't have bullets forever.

Carlos looked sour. "They're getting larger."

"They would be," Jerry said. "Ye gods, the growth rate—I worked it out myself and didn't believe it."

"They've got a hell of an incentive to grow."

Cadmann broke in on the chatter. "Get the Bluff for me, would you?"

"No problem." The holo stage cleared, and Jerry answered the line.

Cadmann clicked on his throat mike. "Is Mary Ann there?"

"One minute."

The stage was blank for about thirty seconds, and then Mary Ann was on. "Cadmann. She looked tired, but not depressed, not frightened.

"Mary Ann. This may be the last opportunity. Tell me again you won't go back to *Geographic?*"

"No one knows the Bluff like I do. I'll have to show everybody where things are. If Sylvia takes care of Jessica, I'll be happy."

"Yeah." He paused. "I'd feel better if you got out of there."

"No. No. They need me here to show them where things are. If the grendels kill everybody here, there won't be anything to come back to. I'd rather be here."

"All right. I just had to ask."

"I just had to answer." She chuckled. Cadmann clicked the line off.

Outside the communication shack, the smell of fear and smoke and baby grendels roasted by flame throwers mingled. The stench hung in the air like a shroud.

He and Carlos walked over to the fence above the Miskatonic. Carlos pointed at a black form wiggling up from the water below them.

It twisted its head slowly, questing, as if it could smell them. It tried to climb the rise, but slid back down into the rushing waters.

Over to the south, fire lashed from a Skeeter. A meteor raced at ground level toward the river, lost direction and finally stopped.

"Cadmann? Carlos?"

Sylvia. The wind stirred her hair ever so gently, and it ruffled in a halo around her face. She seemed so incredibly young, so beautiful. She turned, exposing the papooseka backpack that held Jessica.

Terry glided along beside her, carrying Justin in his lap.

She stepped back, framing the four of them with her hands as if taking a holo.

Cadmann closed his eyes and felt the old hunger race through him. The very real possibility that he might never see her again made it almost unbearably intense.

She hugged Cadmann, then reached up and kissed him gently. "For luck," she whispered.

Carlos stood quietly, his hands at his sides. Sylvia had to take his arms and put them around her. She whispered something to him that Cadmann couldn't hear, and then kissed him hard.

Cadmann turned away, embarrassed. Terry studiedly held Justin. Their eyes locked, and Terry raised his eyebrows.

When she had finished, she took Justin from Terry and stepped back again. "My three favorite men in all the world," she said soberly. "God bless and keep you. Keep each other."

She knelt by Terry and kissed him. At first it was a peck, then it became desperately hungry. Justin began to cry.

Sylvia pressed the child to her chest. Tears streamed freely down her cheeks. Without another word, she turned and ran to the Skeeter pad.

Cadmann hesitated, then said, "I'd like to ferry her over myself. Do you mind?"

"Not at all." Terry's voice shook. He stared at the ground and wiped at his face with an unsteady hand.

Stu was running the Skeeter shuttle. Cadmann grabbed his arm and swung him to the side. "Stu—why don't you do us both a favor and grab a cup of coffee?"

"S'all right, Cad. I can keep going for a while—" He glanced at Sylvia, and then back again. "Oh. Right."

Cadmann held the door for her, then hurried around to the pilot's side. He performed all the checks and instrument adjustments automatically. She made no sound until they lifted off, then sighed audibly.

"I might have known that it would be Carlos," he said.

"You understand, don't you?"

"How could I not? I just wish . . ."

"Don't say it, Cad. We've been through all of it already."

They could see Camelot clearly from their perspective. The angles and swirls, the rectangles of the home lots, the rolling parks. The schematics of their dream. A dream that had become a nightmare.

"Cadmann. Are we going to make it? I mean, *any* of us?"

"The answer is yes. We've made mistakes, bad ones. Not surprising —no one has ever dealt with an alien ecology before."

"But Cad—"

"No buts this time." He set the Skeeter down on the asphalt surrounding the dam. Minerva One waited there for them, her sides scarred with exhaust heat, the water still steaming around her. Cadmann twisted in his seat. "I swear to you—Justin and Jessica are going to live. They're going to have a place to grow up. They will inherit this planet. My solemn oath."

Sylvia melted against his chest, her face only inches from his. He bent to kiss her, felt his senses swim with her taste and touch and smell.

"You're our only hope, Cadmann. Please."

He bussed Jessica and then Justin, as if both were his own children. *And if there were any justice in the world, they would be.*

Sylvia climbed down out of the Skeeter, and closed the door behind her.

He watched, motionless, as she climbed onto the Minerva. With a final wave, she disappeared into the airlock.

That was that. It was almost all done. There was nothing left but to face the grendels.

CHAPTER 29

HOLDING

And O, ye Fountains, Meadows, Hills, and Groves,
Forebode not any severing of our loves!

WILLIAM WORDSWORTH, *"Intimations of Immortality"*

Geographic hadn't changed. Sylvia had seen it like this through a tiny window when the next-to-last shuttle brought her to board humankind's first interstellar spacecraft. Minervas had ridden the hull like limpets; they were gone now. The hull was scarred by decades of cosmic rays and micrometeorites. Skin tension had pulled the empty fuel tank to half its size. Yet this was still *Geographic*.

What was missing was inside. Electronics. Hydroponics, life support, computers, everything that could be used below had been sent down to Avalon. *Geographic* was no longer an interstellar spacecraft.

The air processors can't support more than thirty people for even seventy-two hours. We'll be breathing soup after fifty. "She's dead," Sylvia said.

"Not dead. Sleeping," Rachel said.

"Bloody right." Zack was grim. "We'll all live to take her to the planets—"

"Yeah, sure—"

"You are damned right, 'Yeah, sure!' " Rachel said. "What is this? Giving up already?"

"No," Sylvia said. "Little tired."

"We're still *Homo interstellar*. The one and only, now. If we fail here, what lesson will we teach in Sol system? There won't be another ship for a thousand years. Maybe never. We came as conquerors. Some of us died as prey, but we ate the samlon too. When we get through this, we'll eat every samlon in the Avalon rivers while our crops are growing. Jesus, I wish I'd recorded that!"

Zack crowed, "Me, too! Rachel, with a speech like that I could get elected to anything!"

Stu fired the retros, and the Minerva began to pivot. The restful azure curve of Avalon passed the window. Tau Ceti crested the horizon, rose like a flaming gemstone. Talons of searing white light raked at the shadows.

Avalon was neutral. The children of Earth might die, they might thrive. Avalon would embrace their bones or their progeny with equal warmth.

MIST SWIRLED below. Rain coming? Mary Ann stood at the edge of Cadmann's Bluff and strained to see through the swirl. The Colony was a geometric blur. After a while the breeze came up again, and the mists parted for a moment.

Tweedledum's cold nose thrust into her hand. "Good dog," she said absently.

The mist began to close again. For the moment everything was tranquil. The rapidly flowing Miskatonic, the neat lines of the Colony, the rows of unharvested crops. Off to the left, a Skeeter moved in curves. There was no trace of grendels. A picture-postcard day, for Avalon.

The wind rose again, a clean, brisk east wind. She treasured the feel of it, the way it wound around her, through her, dried and cooled the perspiration on her skin.

"Cadmann—" she whispered.

But he was down below her, with his own concerns. For now she was on her own.

Suddenly large hands were on her shoulders, massaging deeply. Waves of heat flooded away the fatigue and her knees sagged. She looked up over her shoulder.

"That's wonderful, Jerry. I'm yours."

"Dump Weyland and it's you and me, babe. Are you all right?"

"My body wants Jessica." She touched her breasts, the moist patches where she had leaked through the bra shields. "I think that she's crying for me. But we have six women up there who can make milk for her. She'll be all right."

"How about you?"

She grinned, nodded assurance, and they linked arms. Together they headed back toward the house.

Even from below, the changes were apparent. The house had expanded. Thirteen of Hendrick's crew had deepened and widened the foundations and reinforced the roof and walls with quarter-inch metal sheeting. That had been a cheerful time, when they reshaped Cadmann's Bluff just to keep Madman Weyland happy.

Jerry and Mary Ann passed among the same men now. They were harvesting, digging, driving tractors loaded with now useless machinery, machinery that could not become weapons. Their mood was greatly changed.

When the main camp was overwhelmed, Cadmann's Bluff would remain the most defensible area on the island.

The Bluff's cultivated rows of corn and hybrid melon cactus would never survive the onslaught. What was ready to be harvested was being gathered for storage. Perhaps when this was all over, they could begin again.

The Joes were restless in the cages. Twenty of them squealed and chattered, pressing their noses against the wire. They exuded sour, pungent fear musk. Something was coming from the south, a horror that had sent their ancestors fleeing into the mountains . . . but the Joes didn't know. It was the massive influx of strangers that had upset them.

Mary Ann took folded papers from her pocket. Cadmann's broad, strong handwriting and diagrams filled them.

She examined his drawings, matched them to the plateau that was now below them. The ground was turned and broken into dark moist chunks, save for a pathway ten feet across. That path zigzagged through the field. "Mines—all though this crescent." She pointed. "Except for the path marked with stakes. The mines are live now."

Jerry took the sketches. "Too bad we don't have the fuel for a moat. That might have worked. These asterisks . . . right, that's the last line of defense, what Cadmann called 'an array.' Said that it worked at Rorke's Drift, wherever that was."

"Africa," Mary Ann said. "A handful of British soldiers stood against the entire Zulu nation."

"Then it should work here," Jerry said. There was more hope than certainty in his voice. "The Zulus could think. Grendels react in fixed-circuits. Their attack patterns are genetically predetermined."

"Or mostly are." Mary Ann frowned. What were the words? "Dis . . . dis something." She stopped, embarrassed.

"Dispersion," Jerry said gently. "Random action. Evolution works better if there's random elements. *Most* of the grendels will be wired up to do what's been successful in the past. Not all. We'll have to be careful of that." He continued studying the sketches. "Mine field blows them apart. Smell of blood gets them into that feeding-frenzy state. They'll attack each other as quickly as us. Only—"

"What, Jerry?"

"They're not supposed to reach the mines. They'd be ten kilometers uphill from their water source. The internal heat should kill them if they go on *speed*."

"They fooled us before."

"Yeah. Yeah. If they get here at all, they've fooled us again. Then what'll they do? Sniff out the mines? Learn to fly?" His bemused eyes suddenly focused on hers. "Oh, Mary Ann, pay no attention to this. It's just my way of keeping my brain working. I shouldn't do it out loud."

Mary Ann nodded jerkily, not believing him.

She flinched as Minerva One plunged from the sky to rock the valley with its scream. She turned and watched as the shuttle dipped beneath the lip of the plateau and disappeared. "How long?"

"For which? For the Colony? Maybe eight hours until the first fence goes. Then Cadmann will turn on the mine field, and the fireworks begin. We'll hear that, if we don't see it. The second fence may never go at all."

"Pray to God. But it will, won't it?"

"I don't know. Honestly! We'll know if it does, because they won't need Minerva Two any more, and we'll see it take off."

She nodded.

"Mary Ann?"

"Yes?"

"Just in case . . . I just wanted you to know that Cadmann couldn't have made a better choice. Not in a hundred years."

Liar. She smiled. "Come on, flatterbox. There's work to do, and not much time to do it in."

Together, they headed up the zigzag path to the stronghold, the last hope of human life on Avalon.

* * *

THEY MOVED north along the streams. Where they clustered too closely, there were fights. The weaker or warier among the grendels stayed far from water, diving downslope where they saw no others of their kind, to immerse themselves and retreat uphill before they could be seen. A few had already discovered that if they moved slowly, calmly, they could reach the heights where flyers laid their eggs.

The largest of the grendels grew larger yet, up to a meter and a half long, and still they grew, for they were better fed. There was attrition among these. They had to stay closer to water. Some of their smaller siblings had learned to attack where they saw others attack. Larger grendels were torn to ribbons by grendels who attacked in concert, snatched mouthfuls of meat and vanished underwater before their chancy allies could choose another target.

They looked nothing at all like an army. They were refugees. Famine and war and overpopulation moved them anywhere their tiny minds might seek food or safety. But they moved north along the rivers, following the vacuum of the fished-out Miskatonic, until wind and water brought them a wild variety of scents from what had been pastureland.

Then each savagely independent grendel turned in the same direction.

What reached the farmlands was more enraged and starving carnivores than had ever been alive in Avalon's history, and they moved very much like an army.

THE RIVER and its shores swarmed with dark shapes moving upstream. Carlos made a final inspection of the door gun. "Okay. I'm starting now," he said into the intercom. He fired carefully, in short bursts, aiming at widely separated groups.

The water below exploded into frenzied life. Grendel shapes leaped from the water. Others pursued them. Frothy red tinged with orange spread across the water.

"It's working," Carlos said. "Die!" He fired again. One of his tracers speared into a larger grendel's back, with spectacular results. The *speed* sacs made a terrific oxidizer. The grendel streaked for the river with its back burning like thermite, and burned even after it was in the water. Carlos whooped.

Greg wheeled the Skeeter back around for another pass. "By God, it is working! Drive them crazy! Use that damned supercharger against them! Bless Sylvia's knotty little head, she said it would work."

The Skeeter dove down between the trees. "Die, defenseless, primitive natives!" Short bursts, he told himself. Short and careful. Conserve ammunition, we will need it. The river churned with blood, foamed with the dead and dying.

But all we're really doing is feeding the others, Carlos admitted to himself; and pushed the thought away in savage enjoyment of the opportunity to kill before dying.

"Running low on power," Greg said. "I can get us back to camp. By now they must be hooking up Minerva Two. We can recharge."

"Do it."

Carlos got on the radio. "I am returning to camp—"

He couldn't tell who answered: a masculine voice edged with panic. "Pick up Jill Ralston on the way. She's hurt. She's on a ridge, eight kilometers west and a little north of the northwest corner of the outer fence."

THEY SHOULD have had an hour of daylight still; but the western range cut the day short, and clouds were banking in from the sea. It was already dark enough that Carlos could see the dying fire spilling downslope from the ridge. He pointed, and Stu took the Skeeter down.

She lay at the high point of the ridge. A meter below her was a grendel. It didn't move when they came close, but Carlos fired a short burst into it anyway.

Jill was lying on her side a short distance from the fire. She watched them land but didn't wave. As Carlos ran from the Skeeter she was trying to stand up.

"Lie down, dammit." Her left arm looked awful. Cooked. He unsealed an anesthetic ampoule and slid the needle into her shoulder.

He got around to her right side and half carried her to the copter. He strapped her in before he asked, "Is there equipment we should recover?"

She shook her head and swallowed hard. "The flame thrower's dead," she whispered. "It's in the fire."

He squeezed in behind her. She stank. Her arm was cooked from shoulder to fingertips. She lay back against the seat and every now and again she sat up and looked around as if she couldn't believe she was safe. Carlos had always found her attractive, to no tangible purpose. "What happened?" he asked.

"They were coming up the defile. Ida van Don dropped me on the ridge with the Skeeter. She flew around shooting grendels, and I flamed them when they got close enough. Sandra ran out of power and had to take the Skeeter back for a recharge. Me, I kept shooting. A flame thrower works just fine on a grendel. It scares them. They go into *speed* and burn themselves up inside."

"Sure. Are you all right?"

"I am *now.* They kept coming. The flame thrower over-heated—"

"You're not supposed—"

"I could feel my hands burning. Then the torch nozzle clogged and spit jellied gasoline on my arm. I ran and rolled and kept rolling, and behind me the damn thing exploded. I've been waiting to see what would get here first, you or the grendels."

Which is why we have to be careful with these egregious excuses for makeshift weapons. "Well, we're here. It's all over now." Down below Carlos could see grendels on both sides of the ridge. They'd gone around the other side of the fire. *And it is lucky for you we came when we did. Five minutes more—* She couldn't see him as he shook his head. *Such a waste.*

"They kept coming. I shot one with my automatic. Little one, under a meter. I hit it four times, I think. It could have taken me, but it never went on *speed.* Too hot already. It—" She shuddered. "It fell over. By itself. You saw it. They can die. They can."

"HEAR THIS. HEAR THIS." Cadmann's voice boomed from loudspeakers placed around the perimeter of the camp. "FENCE POWER GOES ON IN TEN MINUTES. TEN MINUTES TO FENCE POWER."

Carlos glanced at his watch. Naturally Cadmann would wait until the last minute of light to power the fences. They needed power to recharge the Skeeters, for the vehicles, to make hydrogen. There was just enough light to see—but they should have had an hour till sunset.

There were thick black clouds across the west.

"Hey, buddy," Greg called. "Running out of steam?"

"No." Wearily Carlos went back to loading Hendrick's wrecked Skeeter. Small boxes. Lightweight items. Blankets, sleeping bags. Before an item went into the wreck it was placed on the scales outside. The Skeeter itself would be needed uphill, for parts. Might as well use it to carry other gear.

Shooting grendels had been easier work.

Cassandra displayed the cumulative total mass they'd put aboard. "Some to go yet," Greg said.

"Yes." Wearily Carlos flexed his arms and bent over to stretch his back. "A pity."

"Cheer up. You could be laying bricks."

"Not me. I am a warrior."

"You're also a carpenter," Greg said. "But I won't remind them." He jerked his head to indicate the power room, where half a dozen men worked frantically to seal the blockhouse with bricks and mortar and welded bars. Others filled the blockhouse with equipment too heavy to send up to *Geographic* or ferry to the Bluff.

If the blockhouse held intact it would save months in rebuilding civilization. If it didn't— "It will be terribly inconvenient," Carlos said to himself. "But not deadly." He went back to the commons kitchen for another load. All food would be sent to the Bluff.

Minerva Two must almost have finished recharging the two Skeeters. The third was well uphill, beyond reach of the grendels. George Merriot had spent too much time shooting grendels—until it was too late to return to the Colony. He had taken the Skeeter as high as he could before the fuel cells went dead. Cadmann had been furious. Now there were only two Skeeters in operation, and work enough for ten. *But we'll take George up to the Bluff anyway.* Carlos felt like telling the idiot to fend for himself.

What could be moved to *Geographic* was aboard Minerva Two. Lightweight stuff, and all the food, was going into Hendrick's Skeeter; they would carry it to the Bluff. Equipment too heavy to be moved was going into the blockhouse. The grendels would never get through all that brick.

You *had* to believe that there were things grendels couldn't do.

Then there was the computer shack. It had been emptied of equipment. Cassandra stood outside, and the shack now held nostalgia items, never more than ten kilograms from any colonist save one. Carlos still only half believed that they had let him put his bed in there.

And they'd brick it up to preserve Avalon's memories of civilization, but only if the grendels gave them time. Carlos set his load inside the wrecked Skeeter and staggered out. They'd almost finished bricking up the power house. Next, the computer shack; and Carlos wanted to help.

THE WOODEN tower stood next to the main entry door to the main power room. Brilliant blue flame danced below as the welders completed their work on the power blockhouse door.

"Hear this. Fence power in thirty seconds. Get away from the fences. Hear and believe. Fence power in thirty seconds." Cadmann put down the microphone and used his binoculars to scan the perimeter area. No flares. No rockets. He lifted the mike again. "Okay, power on."

He had held off on this even after Minerva Two was hooked up. While gunmen could protect the fence, he could repower the Skeeters with all of the Minerva's power. But it was getting too dark to find the monsters and protect the fences. Now the fences would protect them.

Green lights turned to red on the console in front of him. "That ought to hold them," Joe Sikes said. "Fry the little bastards."

"And some of the big ones," Cadmann said. "But not for long."

"How long do you think?" Sikes asked.

"Through tomorrow if we're lucky, but I'll be satisfied to have tonight. Okay, make the last run to Minerva. What are you carrying?"

"Cassandra, mostly."

"Right." Cassandra might as well live aboard *Geographic*. She didn't use oxygen, and it would be damned hard to rebuild without her.

Landing lights flashed as Skeeter One rose. The dark shape of Skeeter Four, Hendrick's wrecked machine, dangled below it. As the Skeeter crossed the fence perimeter its searchlight stabbed downward, circled, then flowed across the cornfields.

The fields were alive. Stalks fell, disappeared beneath large shapes. "Holy shit," Joe Sikes said. "We won't be eating that for a while—"

The Skeeter hovered for a second longer. Cadmann reached for his microphone, but before he could lift it the Skeeter wheeled and headed off in the general direction of the Bluff.

Cadmann unslung his rifle. "Play the tower spot out there in the center of the field, will you?"

"Sure thing."

He sighted where the dark seemed to move and squeezed off a round. For a moment, nothing: then a feral scream from the field. More screams, and the area exploded with grendels. Cadmann smiled in grim satisfaction. "As long as they clump up like that. Find me another clump, will you?"

"Shouldn't be difficult."

A gust of wind blew mist across his face. Cadmann grimaced. "Joe, shine the spot *up* for me."

"For what?" But Joe Sikes was already doing it. The beam swung up and blazed against thickening cloud cover.

"We won't like it if it rains," Cadmann said.

CHAPTER 30

CHALLENGE

As to moral courage, I have seldom met with the two o'clock in the morning courage: I mean unprepared courage.

NAPOLEON BONAPARTE, Memoirs

"HERE THEY COME!"

Darkness flowed across brown earth. There was too little sound: a hissing like ocean waves across sand, rustling of a thousand feet on loose dirt. They came in a wave, too much like an army.

Blue arcs flashed. Smoking meat suddenly flavored the humid air. Grendels seared by electricity smelled too much like a samlon just ready to come off the barbecue. It was distracting: it spoke to the wrong part of the brain.

"Here!" someone screamed. Blue arcs, closer, much too close. The tower searchlight swung over. Impossibly, a grendel had torn through the outer fence, past the mine field, and had fallen against the inner fence. The grendel was dead, but the two who chased it were both on *speed*.

Cadmann leveled his rifle and waited. The fence arced. One grendel leaped back. The second leaped after it. Cadmann smiled grimly. "Save ammunition," he called to the others. *Let the fences kill them. We won't have fences for long.* . . .

The searchlight danced farther out, to the outer perimeter fifty meters away. Dark shapes were piled there. A dozen or more grendels had flung themselves onto the still-charged fence. Electricity sizzled deep within the pile, but other grendels climbed over the stack of corpses. Still more used their tails to drag dead siblings away from the fence.

"A scene from the *Inferno, amigo.*"

Cadmann didn't turn. "I expected the outer fence to hold longer than *that.*" He took out his comcard. "Com shack. Exec one here. Patch me to the loudspeaker."

A moment later his voice boomed from the speakers on the colony buildings. "HEAR THIS. OPEN FIRE. TRY TO KILL SOME OF THEM OUT IN THE SPACE BETWEEN THE FENCES. OUT."

Carlos nodded, unslung his rifle and knelt beside Cadmann. He squeezed off rounds in slow and deliberate fire. Elsewhere mad volleys sounded. Cadmann winced. "I'm going up in the tower. Hang on here."

"*Sí, compadre.*"

Carlos's rhythmic gunfire was comforting. *They've got to keep their heads.* "SLOW FIRE. THAT AMMO HAS TO LAST." If only there had been time and ammunition for a full combat-rifle course.

Near him someone cursed viciously. Omar Isfahan wrenched at his rifle. "Jammed, dammit, it's—"

"Slow down," Cadmann said brusquely. He took the rifle from Omar's hand and worked the bolt. "It's not jammed, it's *empty.* Now just relax and get yourself together, mister."

Omar took two deep breaths. Tension seemed to flow out of him in waves. "I'm . . . sorry. All right now."

"Sure. And be careful with that ammo." He handed the rifle back. "We'll win this if we don't panic."

The engineer grimaced. "Sure." He went back to his place at the fence.

At least he's stopped shooting at shadows. Cadmann hurried toward the tower. *Break in the fence. They'll pour in. How long have we got?* There were sounds everywhere. Gunshots from across the compound. Half a mile away. What could they be shooting at?

He slung his rifle and climbed rapidly.

"H'lo." Greg sounded calm enough. Cadmann nodded and took over the searchlight. He swung it to the fence break—

Nothing. Grendels came over the pile of bodies, but as individuals. They weren't pouring through as any decent army would.

"Like I thought," Cadmann said.

"Yes?" Greg tried to keep his voice calm.

"Kill enough of them, most will stop to gorge. They don't keep coming. They're *not* an army."

"No. Thank God."

Rachel would be convinced it's God's doing. Maybe so. "I'm lying, of course."

"Uh?"

"I didn't think it at all. If I'd been commanding the grendels I'd have poured everything I had through that fence break." He clipped his comcard to the collar of his jacket. "Skeeter One. Are you fully charged?"

"Full charge, Cad." Stu sounded sleepy.

I'll wake you up. "Okay. Take up the load of kerosene. Dump between fences and all around the break in the outer fence. I'm going to try to drive them out so we can go repair that break."

"Repair that break. Jesus. Who'd do that? Okay, I'm off."

Dismembered grendels screamed in the mine field. More hissed as they fought and died. As in all battles, there was mostly confusion, but now he could see the entire perimeter. Grendels continued to come in through the break in the outer fence, but not in a wave; they came in ones and twos, and they separated to vanish in the darkness between the fences.

The fields beyond the outer fence were a shambles, torn by knots of struggling monsters, the very earth grooved by their *speed*-augmented frenzy. *They've plowed it for our next planting.* Cadmann chuckled grimly.

"Something?" Stu's voice spoke from his collar.

"No. Forgot the mike was on. Random thought."

More explosions in the mine fields. *We'll be running low on mines. I should have had someone counting, so we'd know how many are left. Doesn't matter. Nothing to trigger mines but grendels, and there are plenty of them!*

Too many grendels. "How the fuck can they grow so fast?" Cadmann demanded.

"You want the long answer or the short one?" Greg asked.

"Neither. I've heard both."

"Cadmann! Minerva calling Cadmann!"

Cadmann frowned. "Cadmann here."

"I've got to take off!"

"What?"

"I hear them! They're out there, in the lake—"

Who was that? Marty hadn't been hit by Hibernation Instability, had he? But how could you really tell? "Of course they're out in the lake, Marty. They're samlon—"

"No, no, I mean right here, I hear them pounding on the hull! Cadmann, they'll get in the air intakes! We'll lose the Minerva! I'm going to take off—"

Cadmann took a deep breath. "No. You're not going to take off. If you take off now, we lose all our power. Our fences go. We can't recharge the Skeeters. Everyone here in this camp will die. You stay there until you're told to leave."

"We have to have the Minervas! What happens to the people up in Geographic? *I've got to get out of here!"*

"Stay tight," Cadmann said. Skeeter One rose from the center of the Colony compound. "Look, we've got a situation here. I'll get back to you as soon as I can. Stay tight."

The Skeeter reached the area between the fences. Cadmann played the tower light around the outer fence break. Other lights moved in the area between fences. Grendels tried to attack the light.

The Skeeter whirled past in tight circles. Two men and a woman leaned out of the doorway to dump kerosene. The rotor blades scattered the oily liquid. The stench merged with burning flesh and the heavy Avalon mist.

"Three more cans and we're done," Stu reported.

"Right."

The Skeeter was forty feet off the ground. A grendel standing atop the piled corpses at the fence break leaped upward. The tower light caught it in mid flight. Its upward arc stopped just short of the Skeeter. Then a smaller dark object followed it down.

"Jesus!" Cadmann shouted. "Get up higher! I swear, Stu—"

"I know. Ida saw it. She says it damn near got its jaws on the skid! Cad, they're not even *grown* yet!"

"How's the kerosene?"

"She dropped the can on top of that one. We're done."

"Get upwind." Cadmann flipped switches. His voice boomed from the loudspeaker. "FLARES. CARLOS. ISFAHAN. USE THE FLARES. BE CAREFUL."

"Cadmann! Damn it, they're out there!"

"Marty, for God's sake!" Cadmann snapped. "We've just used up part of Skeeter One's power. We have to recharge, and we have to have the fences, and I have to think! Shut up and sit tight, damn it!"

"I hear them. They're coming up the tailpipe!"

"There's nothing there to eat. Marty, I don't have time for this. Out."

Cadmann watched Greg load a makeshift crossbow with a flare tied to an arrow. The bolt left a smoky trail toward the outer fence break.

Flames leaped upward.

"What about the Minerva?" Greg asked. "Isn't he right? The longer you wait, the better the chance a grendel will crawl up the tailpipes. What will that do to the ramjet?"

"I don't know."

"You don't *know?* Damn all—"

"I know this," Cadmann said carefully. "If all of us here are killed without even a fight, the Bluff goes. Then what?"

Greg stared at him for a moment, then went back to the search-light.

A THICK PALL of smoky death smells lay over the Colony. A few small fires still burned in the area between fences, but mostly it was dark there. The tower searchlight played through the area.

Cadmann spoke softly into the comcard clipped to his collar. "Okay, *amigo,* have the volunteers assemble by Mary Ann's old place." He continued to play the spotlight through the area between fences.

"If there's anything alive in there I can't see it," Greg said. "Cadmann—is this smart?"

"I think so. We want dead grendels here. Lots of dead grendels. The more we kill here—"

"Yeah." Greg's new wife was pregnant and up in *Geographic.* "Yeah, I can see that. Too bad I have to stay and run the searchlight—"

"I can do that." Jill's head appeared at the platform level. She climbed carefully, using her right arm. The left was bound in gauze and immobilized.

"You ought to be—"

"I ought to be in the Mayo Clinic," she said. "But that's not here. It hurts too much to sleep, and—and I don't want to be near fires. I can run the spotlight."

"Okay. Greg—"

"I didn't hear myself volunteer." He looked at Jill's arm, then led the way down the ladder.

Jill's voice followed them. "Don't take chances."

It wasn't funny, and she couldn't hear him, but Cadmann laughed.

The house had been Mary Ann's: large, with a garage for a tractor, next to the farm-implement gate in the inner fence. When Cadmann got there Carlos was waiting. Six men and two women stood with him. They bristled with tools and weapons.

"All right. Nobody gets killed," Cadmann said. "Flame throwers. Look to the flanks. And *keep looking*. Don't get distracted. Greg, you're watching out behind us. Keep looking that way. Unless somebody actually tells you to turn around, *watch our backs*. I don't expect any trouble; if there are any grendels between the fences, they're laying pretty low. They'll be overheated and hoping to cool off; so if we leave them alone, they should leave us alone."

"If they do not, we will reason with them," Carlos said. He held a spear gun poised and ready.

"Let's go, then." Cadmann spoke into his comcard. "Kill the juice." He waited. "Right. Follow me."

The others came through gingerly. Cadmann grinned to himself. The fence was damned dangerous. It made him nervous too.

Ten meters out was half a grendel. Entrails had been pulled out of it to stretch along for another two meters.

It tried to move. Attached by bloody cords, the tail thrummed. Cadmann's flash showed that it had only half of one hind leg. The other was missing. Blood welled from the socket. Cadmann led the way around it, still giving it plenty of distance.

"Damn. They die hard," Phyllis McAndrews said.

"That they do," Cadmann said. "Watch our flanks."

There was little sound. In the distance, a grendel's scream ran the scale and clipped off. Out beyond the external fence grendels clustered in shadow, feasted. There was a slow, constant motion of grendels dragging meat toward the river.

"Here's the tricky part," Cadmann said. His light played out beyond the outer fence, but it wasn't needed. Fires still burned there and cast flickering yellow light out into the misty darkness. No eyes peered back.

"They do not like fire," Carlos said.

"That they don't. Gives us a chance." Cadmann triggered his comcard again. "Power back on in the inner fence. Power off on the outer fence. Repeat that." He listened. "Good. Okay, here's the drill. Greg, watch our backs. Carlos, you're watching to the front. We'll never clear out those bodies, so we won't try. Wire around them. Splice in on either side. At least it won't short out the rest of the fence. And work fast—"

"Cadmann!" Carlos shouted. He fired his spear gun into the darkness. It exploded into snarling jaws. Carlos was getting good at that.

"Jesus," someone shouted.

"Skeeter One. We'll need a little fire support," Cadmann said.

"Coming now." The Skeeter flashed overhead. Its lights played out beyond the fence perimeter.

"Cadmann." Stu's voice was urgent. "There must be a thousand of them out there. Not a hundred meters from you. Get *out* of there."

"Shit. Not until we get that fence fixed. Are they coming toward us?"

"Not yet—"

"Let us know. Harry, get that damn fence taken care of. Move!"

"Slave driver—"

There were things out there, humping through the darkness.

A flash of movement near the fence. A tongue of flame licked out, caught the grendel in mid-charge. Coated with jellied gasoline, it bolted off into the ravaged fields, chased its tail in diminishing circles. Finally it lay on its side, jaws mindlessly snapping at its own smoldering limbs. Its hungry siblings ringed it, crawled closer, waiting patiently for the fire to die.

Harry fussed with continuity meters. "Weld there," he said. Mits Kokubun's torch flared briefly. "And there."

"You might get on with it," Greg said.

"God damn it, I'm doing all I can—"

"Sorry, Mits, didn't mean you to hear—"

"Shut up." Cadmann tried to see everything at once. Harry with his meters. Mits and his minitorch. Greg watching behind. Carlos and—

"They're moving in," Stu said. "Cadmann—"

"Got it," Harry whispered. "Done!"

"Then let's get the hell out of here. Move away from the fence. Everybody clear?" He touched the comcard. "Activate outer fence."

"What about the inner fence?"

"Leave it on. Gimme the speakers. HEAR THIS, BOTH FENCES ARE ACTIVATED. TOUCH 'EM AND DIE.

"Okay, now *move.* Greg, you're point man. Watch to the front. Carlos, you're watching our backs. Stay alert. Avalon needs all the lerts it can get. Mits, don't look at *me,* look off to the right! Now move."

* * *

CADMANN stared at his watch. *Midnight?* Dawn was hours away. It seemed a week since they'd repaired the fence break, but in fact no more than an hour had passed.

Greg's rifle spat once beside him. "Another one. Got him."

"Her," Cadmann said absently. The outer fence still held. Grendels must learn from other grendels: there hadn't been another mass assault on the fence. They still came by ones and twos over the pile of dead at the original fence break, but almost none got through alive: two lights and half a dozen rifles guarded that break.

It couldn't last. *Half an hour. Give me that. Half an hour.*

He got twenty minutes.

CADMANN was asleep standing up. A flurry of gunfire brought him awake.

"Thousands of them!" Greg was shouting. The searchlight jittered wildly. Black shapes darted over the bodies piled at the break. The light swung. Twenty meters to the left was another pile of still smoking bodies. Grendels came over that.

"South side. Fence is broken on south side."

"Break on the west side."

"The outer fence is shorted. No power left in the outer fence. All the circuit breakers have popped."

The searchlights swung through no-man's-land between the fences. Grendels swarmed there. Mines detonated. Pillars of fire rose from cans of buried kerosene. Rifles fired wildly into the melee.

No pattern. They come. They avoid each other, they'll attack the same target, but they don't cooperate. No strategy—

If you're outnumbered bad enough, strategy doesn't matter. Who said that? My tac officer at the Point, or some ancient Trojan?

There were arcs from the inner fences. Not as many. Off to his left, Carlos was directing flame throwers through the fence. Someone else raced across camp to another fence break.

"Stu. Time to do your stuff," Cadmann said.

"Okay, but this is it for kerosene. And I'm at three-quarter charge."

"Charge you'll get. The outer fence isn't drawing power any more. Now GO before we all do. Outer fence is gone. Protect the inner one."

"Roger."

The Skeeter rose into view. Stu must have lifted the instant he heard Cadmann speak.

Once again the Skeeter whipped around the inner periphery as the crew dumped kerosene and other inflammables.

"FLARES," Cadmann ordered.

The fires leaped up. Grendels tore at each other, ran from the flame, leaped at the fence; the ground worked with grendels. And gradually the arcing at the fence stopped.

"*Cadmann. I hear them, Cadmann. They're out there. We'll lose Minerva, and it's all your fault, you stubborn bastard—*"

"*Marty.*" It was a different voice. It took Cadmann a moment to realize: *Geographic* had come over the horizon, and Rachel was speaking. "*Marty, just take it easy. Cadmann knows what he's doing.*"

They said more to each other, as if Cadmann couldn't hear. He turned off the speaker.

Cadmann knows what he's doing.

"Stu."

"Yeah?" Stu sounded sleepy again.

"Better start shuttling people out. Women and wounded first. Get 'em up to the Bluff."

"*Cad—you sure? You've held this long—*"

"I've held this long, and Marty isn't about to sleep or relax or anything else. I want that Minerva out of here. It's one less damn thing to worry about."

"*Okay, buddy. Can't even say I'm sorry.*"

"*He will be,*" Jill said.

"Uh?" Cadmann frowned.

"*No picnic at the Bluff. We can't hold them here, with the fences and mine fields and power for the Skeeters. No picnic at the Bluff.*"

"Yeah. You don't need to tell everybody."

"*I won't.*" She went back to the searchlight.

The Skeeter took off five minutes later.

JILL RALSTON bit her lip, fighting through the pain. Her eyes were huge and frightened as Cadmann belted her into the Skeeter. She was the last female defender of the camp. Her burned left arm was wrapped in gauze; it looked like a big white pillow. Her thin face showed determination and an edge of pain. Her short mane of coarse black hair stirred in the Skeeter's turbulence.

Cadmann tested her belt, grunted in satisfaction. Jill flinched as he brushed her bandaged arm.

"What's my assignment once I get to the Bluff?"

"Have Jerry take care of that arm. Get some rest if you can. You're going to need it. By that time I'll be up there too."

"Don't be long," she said, settling back into the Skeeter seat, voice already becoming drowsy.

Cadmann slammed the Skeeter door closed. "Take it, Stu."

"Roger."

The autogyro's rotors whipped dust around him. It rose and peeled away.

"Precious cargo, *amigo*," Carlos said from behind him.

"One day you're going to sneak up on me and I'll shoot you. Precious. Should she have been on *Geographic?*"

"No, no, she is not pregnant yet—"

"I see."

"But I did rescue her from the ridge."

"And heroes get their rewards." *When her arm heals. If it heals. And if it doesn't, old Carlos may be the best medicine she'll ever find.*

"Quiet."

"Too quiet. But I like it."

"Enough meat for all, I think," Carlos said. "They fight and they feed, but they prefer not to feed on each other."

"Son of a bitch. I think you've got it," Cadmann said. "But can they cooperate?"

"I do not know. Sometimes it seems they do. But Cadmann, they do not talk—"

"Not as we think of talking."

"Hah. *Amigo,* if you are willing to believe them telepathic—"

"No, not telepathic. But—hell, Carlos, I don't know what I mean. Let's walk around the perimeter."

"You put me in charge here. Recall?"

"Oh. All right, I'll go alone."

The view was much the same everywhere. The outer fence was gone, but the inner held; and the outer fence had lasted long enough to kill hundreds, perhaps a thousand grendels. The mine field had stopped more. Out beyond the inner electrified fence a mountain of grendel dead fed the living. They clumped by the hundreds: twisted, blackened, torn carcasses. Many were stripped to white bone. Tiny insects buzzed fiercely. By daylight the camp would be utterly infested. In days, the stench of rotting meat might poison the valley.

Greg was doing stretches, transferring his gun from one hand to the other for weight. "Quiet," he said without taking his eyes from the grendel-infested wilderness. "Maybe they don't make deals with each other, but they do stir each other up."

"Reading grendel minds is a full-time hobby," Cadmann answered. "What are they going to do next?"

Greg shrugged. Cadmann kept walking.

For now, the grendels had little incentive to try to break through the inner fence. They looked up curiously as lights shone on them. If someone fired—it still happened but not often—the wounded grendel ran amuck until it aroused others to sufficient fury to attack it.

His tour of the fence completed, Cadmann took the opportunity to sit down. He was exhausted. Adrenaline could certainly carry him further, but it was good to snatch the rest while he could. He pulled a barrel up to the fence and sat heavily.

A groggy, full-bellied grendel walked up to the wire. The tower searchlight slid across the mine field and touched them, joined human and grendel in its bright yellow oval.

The monster stared at Cadmann with the detached interest of a man selecting tomorrow's lobster.

Cadmann's teeth showed in a tired grin. "I'm not finished with you yet. Just wait." He slapped his pockets, looking for a nonexistent cigarette. "Just wait."

The grendel waddled closer and brushed against the fence. It shied back, whipped its spiked tail at Cadmann. The fence sparked again. The grendel disappeared over the twisted outer wire and into the darkness. There was a scramble of claws and teeth.

Then silence once again. Another searchlight slid over Cadmann, and he shielded his eyes with a grimy hand. He held it out in front of his face, looking for a tremor. It was there, all right, and his craving for nicotine grew stronger. There were no longer cigarettes on Avalon.

Cadmann's earphone buzzed. Jerry's voice came on line. *"Cadmann . . . rerouting a message from Sylvia. Hold on."*

"Cad?"

"Right here, lady. Your signal's a little weak."

"How are you holding up?"

"So far, so good. Evacuating the main camp. A few injuries, no casualties."

"None? You're wonderful."

"Lucky at any rate."

Grendels wandered around outside the fences, gorged on meat, their bellies heavy. They watched one another suspiciously. Something happened—Cadmann, watching with professional interest, still couldn't tell what sparked it, but two grendels blurred into *speed*, passed each other, curved back in a mist of pink blood, attacked like a pair of enraged buzz saws.

Sylvia said, *"Get out of there fast. You're going to be up to your hips in rain. It's a major storm. You can't electrify the fences in the rain, can you?"*

"No. How long have we got?"

"An hour. Then it'll last for days."

"Rain! You won't need me!" Marty's voice broke in.

"Right. We won't need you," Cadmann said wearily. "But we do need to get the Skeeters up to full charge. And the spare fuel cells. Marty, if the fences go, you can get out of here. We can't."

"Marty—" Sylvia's voice was horror held under rigid control.

"Hey, look," he said. *"Dammit, I'll do my duty! But bloody hell, Cadmann, I don't even know if I've still got motors, and you can't hold on in rain!"*

"I know, and it's hardly a surprise. We're already sending people out. You want anything else?"

"No."

"Then shut the fuck up for a while. Sylvia, you have any *good* news?"

"Actually, yes." Even through the static, her excitement was plain. *"Cad, this 'superhemoglobin' in the sacs above their lungs is what gives them their speed. The speed is attack mode—for hunting and for defense against other grendels."*

"Right."

"Jerry seconds my assumption. We know that they trigger on the smell of blood. In the water they undoubtedly trigger on the smell of superhemoglobin metabolites as well. Almost certainly it's an involuntary response."

Her voice dissolved into static for a moment, and Cadmann tapped his earpiece. "Wait a minute. Jerry? I need some enhancement here. Filters . . . something. Thanks."

The static died down.

"Can you hear me now?"

"Better. Go ahead."

"Collect grendel corpses. Cut out the sacs, liquefy in water and feed it through one of the Skeeter crop-spraying attachments. Spray it over a mass of grendels. It should drive them berserk."

Despite his fatigue, Cadmann grinned. "Thanks, hon. That just might work."

"My pleasure. Cadmann . . . how is Terry holding out?"

"He's all right. Already up at the Bluff."

The floodlights flickered, dimmed, then strengthened again. "That's all the talk, Sylvie. We're losing the lights."

"How many of you are left?"

Cadmann made a quick assessment. Skeeter Two was just humming back in. "Seventeen. Another three loads. We should be all right for that long. These grendels are feeling lazy. I'll talk to you later. Jerry? Are you there?"

"Nowhere else."

"Good. Get someone digging through the miscellaneous equipment up there. We need a blender, food processor, something like that. And the crop-spraying attachment for the Skeeters. Have both ready in an hour."

"Got it."

Skeeter Two was fully charged. In an orderly fashion, the men retired from their positions and retreated to the makeshift landing pad. Two climbed up into the cabin. Three crammed into the cargo hoist beneath.

Skeeter Two swooped back out. Skeeter One was coming in. He'd want to put a full charge on it for what he had in mind. Cadmann counted rapidly. There were only six men left, quickly and quietly dismantling the machine guns. The grendels displayed only token interest.

"Rick," Cadmann called softly. The little machinist left his post and scurried over.

Cadmann was examining a section of fence that bulged inward with dead grendels. "They killed each other here, drove each other across the mine field and into the fence. They pushed from behind while the ones in front burned." His voice held a savage satisfaction. "I want to cut a piece away here. Can we get a bypass on the current, cut a hole in the fence and drag some of these bastards through?"

"Can do. What do you have in mind?"

"Butchery. I need one man to stand guard with a flame thrower. Someone to cut the fence and monitor the current. A man to drag them through. I'll do the rest. That's four of us. Two more at the north and south corners of the camp to give warning. Right now, I don't think we have much to worry about. You choose the crew, and make it fast."

Rick scrambled from man to man, whispering to them. One at a time they left their posts, and joined Cadmann. As if by magic, tools appeared, and wire, and a voltmeter.

The fog drifted in quickly as the air lost heat. Its mist cloaked them as they worked.

Rick whispered, "Now," and shut down the power. The camp lights brightened as the overworked batteries were unburdened. Two men, working quietly and swiftly, ran a cable from one fence post to the next, severed the electric leads, and spliced. They nodded, and Rick threw the switch. The camp lights dimmed and then strengthened.

They tested the fence section: not a flicker from the voltmeter.

Cadmann grabbed a pair of clippers and locked their jaws into the fence links. He gritted his teeth, scissoring the handles. One at a time the links broke, and he moved on to the next until they had cut a semicircle two feet in diameter.

A grendel head popped through the hole, inverted, looking up at them with fixed, milky, dead eyes. Cadmann sank a baling hook into its neck and dragged it through the opening.

Rick said quietly, "You wouldn't want to do that to a live and curious grendel. Whack the tail with a stick first and see if it wiggles."

"Hell, Ricky, there isn't any back end to this one." Cadmann went for another, but he picked up a stick first.

The mass of grendels outside the fence were only vaguely interested in the butchery. One at a time, corpses were pulled through and hacked apart with a machete. Cadmann chopped the glands out, tossed them into a bucket. He slashed the corpses until his arms ran with blood.

There was no way to get used to the stink. Putrescence wasn't far advanced, but it was flavored with puffs of weird chemical reek from the *speed* glands.

"That's it," he finally whispered. "My arm is numb."

Skeeter One floated back in over the camp. They disconnected the last batteries and hooked them to the Skeeter's cargo hoist. Two men piled into the cabin, and the Skeeter rose up and disappeared into the fog.

Cadmann, Ricky and two other men stood in the center of a deserted camp. Beyond the fence the grendels growled and snored, utterly sated.

Cadmann used the comcard. "Greg! Come and get your ride."

"Yo." Far down the line of the inner fence, a shadow detached itself and jogged toward the lights.

"Damn, they're quiet now," Ricky said. He depressed the trigger of the flame thrower, testing. Fire squirted out and puddled on the ground.

"Not for long. They're gorged now. Come tomorrow their bellies will be empty again. Corpses will begin to putrefy. Maybe they're scavengers, and maybe not. Between the survivors here and the ones still coming north, we're going to have our hands full, believe it."

"Still . . . it's just too damned quiet."

Skeeter Two came in for them.

"Find me an empty barrel," he said to Rick. "Half fill it with water."

The little man tested two, then found one. "This'll do." He ran a hose in. Water thrummed against the side of the barrel.

Cadmann shook his arms. Drops of orange blood and superhemoglobin spattered against the ground. The wind shifted slightly, and grendels stirred, alarmed by the scent.

He dumped a quarter of the bucket into the barrel and sloshed the brew around with a stick. God, it stank.

"All right, you two squeeze into the cabin. Ricky, with me in the hoist."

Carlos leaned out of the Skeeter. "What's the plan, *amigo?*"

"Just take us up gently. Hover over the fence: I have an unpleasant present for our friends."

"Bueno. Send them my very best regards."

Cadmann touched his throat mike. "Jerry. Is everyone accounted for?"

"The whole camp. We haven't lost anyone. Just get out of there, will you?"

We made it! No one dead. Christians 2,000; Lions zip. "Marty."

"Yo."

"We're getting out of here. Give us five minutes and the Minerva's all yours. Five minutes, and you're gone when you want to be."

"Whoopee! Cad—look, I didn't mean to be a drag—"

"Fine. Out." He took one last look around. "All right, Carlos. Up! Wh—?"

Two shadows moved at surreal speed. The first grendel, the prey, hit the inner fence and died in a blue flare. The second smacked into the first in the same instant. The fence tore. The second, living grendel rolled, found its footing, swiveled its head. Its legs blurred and it . . . expanded . . .

It was coming straight at him. Cadmann tried to bring up his rifle.

Twenty meters away, the grendel jarred to a stop. It screamed at him: a challenge.

In that moment Greg fired from the side.

The grendel was outraged. It whipped around and was gone, charging into a second stream of bullets. It hit Greg and knocked him flying, turned, and was coming back at Cadmann when three streams of bullets chewed it to rags.

Rick sprinted toward the spot where Greg had fallen. Cadmann called, "Rick. Back. Now."

Rick stopped, looked, and found two grendels investigating the break in the inner fence. He ran.

Cadmann was set to lift the barrel. Rick, puffing, took the other side. They climbed into the cargo hoist and braced the barrel between them.

Cadmann's stomach lurched as the Skeeter swung up, lifting above the deserted camp. The lights were dimmed now, save for the beam from the belly of the Skeeter. The Colony looked asleep, almost peaceful.

"Any final words?" Rick asked bitterly.

The Skeeter flew over the fence. Its light revealed a dozen grendels burrowing their way into a heap of the dead. Three were at Greg, pulling him apart like a chicken.

"Yeah," Cadmann said flatly. "My challenge. Dump it!" They tipped the barrel over, and the gallons of bloody fluid rained down.

Suddenly there was a storm of activity. *Speed*-drunken grendels streaked from every direction, congregating beneath them in a hissing mass. He could hear their screams even above the whip of the rotors.

"Bastards."

Rick's eyes gleamed.

Cadmann hawked and spit down into the whirlpool of motion. "Carlos. Get me out of here. I have work to do."

Carlos spun them around and headed toward the swollen silhouettte of Mucking Great Mountain.

CHAPTER 31

GRENDELS IN THE MIST

> When a strong man armed keepeth his palace, his goods are in peace.
>
> But when a stronger than he shall come upon him, and overcome him, he taketh from him all his armor wherein he trusted, and divideth his spoils.
>
> *LUKE 11:21–22*

MARY ANN watched the sun rise behind a roiling mountain of storm. The dark had shown her nothing of what was happening down there. Neither did the light.

She heard slow thumping behind her.

Hendrick was on crutches. One leg was encased in a balloon cast while the ruined calf muscle regenerated. He was awkward on the crutches, and tired too. "I thought we sent you to bed," he said.

Mary Ann shook her head. "You sent me to rest."

"You resting?"

"Yes. How's Terry?"

"In place. We perched him on that big rock you call Snail Head. You can see him from here."

She looked. Yes, a shadow-man sat on a big white boulder, rifle in his lap, legs in a wide V. She turned back to the clouds.

The covered veranda had become the fire-control area. It had a wonderful field of view, but hers from below the veranda was almost as good. She could see along the winding silver ribbon of Amazon Creek as far as the edge of the bluff, and beyond to the sea of storm.

Half a dozen colonists were digging up mines, altering them and burying them again. The mines had been set to be harmless to a dog, death to an adult grendel. Now they must be reset, and the dogs penned up, kept out of the field.

The dogs didn't like that at all. She could hear their protests from inside the house. Tweedledee and Tweedledum were teaching their litter brothers and companions how to howl.

Another Skeeter was landing above the house. "I'll take it," Hendrick said. She heard him thumping away.

"I'll show them," she said, but he was already going, and she didn't insist. It was her house. Her house, but she was tired. She *should* be in bed.

Hendrick and Jerry and others were running the defenses, enlarging the privy, caring for the livestock. Other voices maintained communications with *Geographic*, the Minervas, the Skeeters. But when a Skeeter load came in, room had to be found for the refugees.

The livingroom floor, with the small stream running right down the middle, was the men's bedroom. No other room was that size, so women were bunking in smaller clumps. Newcomers had to be shown everything. "We have to ration. Talk to Cadmann if that's a problem for you. You don't raid the kitchen. Sorry. The privy is down through the mine field. Follow the marks. We made maps and copied them and they're on every wall. Wash up in the big tubs outside. The water comes in from upstream above the house. It's cold but it's safe.

"The only hot water is in the kitchen and the main bathroom, and there really isn't much of it because the heaters were designed for just two people. Sorry. We don't have energy to spare. Not for heat, not for lights. Sorry. There's soap, but there isn't much, and we're saving some for the medical people. Sorry."

Sorry. She was getting very tired of using that word.

It seemed that nobody but Mary Ann could find anything. Hendrick had found her in the kitchen finding utensils for the cooks. They had ordered her to bed, and seen her to her door before Terry went on duty.

Her bed was big. They'd moved it into a storage room; the bed nearly filled it. At least she was alone. Few of her guests could say as much. She had the bed to herself because Cadmann was down there in the mist surrounded by grendels, with the outer fence ruined and rain about to short out the inner. And she stood below the veranda, watching the clouds.

Damn you, Cadmann. You didn't have to be there.

Maybe he did. Maybe we had to try to defend the Colony, and if we lost the Colony, and he wasn't there, he'd blame himself forever. But damn him, he didn't have to be the last man out. Let someone else be a hero. For once.

The diverted stream ran into and through the house, across the veranda, down a series of small falls, and rejoined the Amazon lower down. It was no more than knee-deep anywhere. The Amazon might have been armpit deep in spots. Running a stream through the house sounded so good, she'd clapped her hands when Cadmann suggested it. He'd half remembered something, an American architect, and she'd told him! Frank Lloyd Wright. The house was called "Falling Water" and was his best work, and she'd remembered it, and Cadmann built it for her. They'd even planned to stock it with samlon.

The Minerva roared out of the clouds at a forty-five-degree angle. Mary Ann held her breath as she watched the craft accelerate. She'd heard the panic in Marty's voice. And Cadmann had seemed desperate when Marty wanted to take off during the long night. The Minerva rose higher. *If you crash, it serves you right.* There was a puff of fog as it went supersonic . . . a change in the wake as the nuclear scramjet came on . . . a belated roar.

No explosion. No grendels in the intakes after all. And the Minerva was gone.

No power now, no fences. He *had* to come out now. Should have left when the Minerva did. *Before* the Minerva. He should be here *now. Where are you, big guy—?*

The clouds stirred and she saw the Skeeter emerge.

She climbed up to the veranda. She asked the first person she saw, "Is he alive?"

It was Joe Sikes. "I've got Carlos. He says they lost Greg. Nobody else."

"Greg . . ." She shook her head. She couldn't say, Good. Greg. Lost how? His new wife was in Minerva. Who? All she could remember was Alicia. Alicia and the baby. So much death. The new name was gone. *Doesn't matter. She'll know soon enough.* "It's over then. Thank God." She went off to bed.

* * *

CAROLYN watched the sun rise below. Noon yesterday she had ridden out of the closing mist, moving southwest, uphill and toward the glacier, riding until nightfall. She'd led the horses all night. It was a mistake. While trudging uphill and trying to report her position she'd dropped the comcard and stepped on it. The horse she led stepped on it as well. Now it didn't work. No one knew where she was. Maybe they'd send a Skeeter to look for her. Maybe they wouldn't. She couldn't go back to the Colony—

Southwest and uphill. He's said southwest and uphill. They'd look for her there, and it was the safest place she could find.

Again the sun rose in blue brilliance, but today it rose over a sea of mist. Clouds had rolled in from the sea; they covered the Colony like a lid, with a great contoured thunderhead for a handle.

Carolyn and the horses were well to the north and west of Cadmann's feudal stronghold, and that, too, was hidden.

The land had flattened out like a tilted table. A line of horses trotted uphill with White Lightnin' at their head.

The horses were all yearlings or younger. Even White Lightnin' wasn't all that big; but Carolyn was small. The horse carried her easily.

She fumed as she rode. *They didn't want me with them! Cadmann Weyland is off fighting Ragnarok with his picked crew, and I'm not in it. They wanted Phyllis, perfect Phyllis, but not me. Not worth fighting with, not worth fighting for*— Yet she wasn't truly unhappy with Cadmann's decision. Where would she have wanted to be? At the Colony, waiting for the grendels to swarm? Aboard *Geographic* while the air grew stale and the Minervas failed to arrive? She had quite another reason for her anger.

Anger held back the fear.

Carolyn had never been on a horse until long after she reached Avalon. She'd tended the colts, and grown used to them, and learned that they were skittish, balky, untrustworthy. If Carolyn lost control of herself, if she screamed at a colt or swatted it, it remembered; it shied from her next time. She had learned to control herself around horses.

Around people . . . well, people were more complex, and they talked to each other. Word had spread.

Once she had known how to steer people where she wanted them. Once she had been Zack's second in command. Without Rachel behind him, Zack would have been working for Carolyn! Though he would still have been part of *Geographic*'s crew, the best of the best.

Hibernation Instability had merely touched Carolyn, but it had left Zack alone.

And of course, Phyllis. Nothing ever stuck to Phyllis. She had Hendrick, she could have had Cadmann, everybody knew it. Phyllis could fall into a mountain of horse manure and come out with roses in her hair.

I'm still smart. Smarter than she is! But I get scared. And that thought was frightening too. She took deep breaths and looked back—

The mist was coming after her in a cloud like a breaking wave, and there were grendels in the mist. She could see lightning flashes in the tops of the clouds. *Rain. The grendels love it. Maybe they won't come out.*

The Colony might have vanished already in a sea of ravening miniature grendels. For all Carolyn could tell, the only earthly life on Avalon was herself and twenty horses. She found herself hoping with savage fervor that that irresponsible butterfly Carlos had made her pregnant before Sylvia took him.

The Geographic Society sent no woman who didn't want babies, she thought. *I'm locked into that. Preprogrammed.* Hibernation Instability should have taken that too.

Thus far she had avoided water. She couldn't do that forever. Horses could go a long way without food, but not without water. It shouldn't be a problem. She was taking them toward the glacier that ran down the slope of Mucking Great Mountain. There would be streams and springs.

She looked down toward the edge of cloud. . . .

She knew what it was as she reached for the binocular case. She was almost relieved. At this distance it looked like a black tadpole. Through the binoculars there was not much more detail: a mini-grendel, plump and streamlined, moving on quick, stubby legs. A meter long, she thought; not one of the big ones. Eyes. Watching her. How well could it see? It looked at her—

Binoculars. They're lenses. The lenses in the dead grendels are strange. Distortable. Big. It could be seeing me as well as I see it.

"Charlie," she said, as if naming a thing were the same as understanding it, controlling it. Her lips twitched toward a snarl. She lifted the harpoon gun high in the air. "Charlie, is it too late to negotiate?" The grendel watched.

She decided (working against her own well-understood tendency to hysteria) that there was no point in urging the horses to greater speed.

Moving uphill, that trot was all they could manage. They hadn't smelled anything yet.

The grendel seemed in no hurry.

It was out of the rain, with no water immediately ahead. There was every chance that it would give up.

She had been given a harpoon gun and four explosive harpoons. There were boulders on the plain, some huge. Carolyn thought of climbing a rock, sending the horses ahead, waiting for the grendel to pass. Her mind worked well enough unless she was pushed. But . . . to wait and wait, while the grendel watched her and considered . . . she would crack. She knew it.

Keep the horses moving. See what happened.

MARY ANN *popped* awake, and sat upright in bed. Noise in the corridor. The glow of her comcard on the stand told her that more than an hour had passed.

She put on a robe and stepped into the corridor.

Cadmann and Hendrick were receding. Mary Ann shouted. "Cadmann!"

He turned as she hurried toward him. Blood all over his coveralls. Blood on his boots. Thin crescents of blood tracked on her floor.

He was still talking as she ran to him. "Not much power in the Skeeters. We need another way to shoot that juice. Catapults? Crossbows. A good steel-spring crossbow, designed for range—"

"Right," Hendrick said. "We can get Sikes on it. He did wizard's work on the spear guns."

There was fatigue in deep lines across his face, and a smell, an alien smell that stirred hair on the back of her neck even as she hugged him. She hugged him harder for that, to feel his ribs sag inward, to *know* that she had Cadmann despite what her senses told her: she held a ghost, an alien impostor. . . .

He hugged her back with too little strength. "That's it for your peignoir, love," he said. "It's not my blood, though. You're smelling *speed* sacs from umpty-dozen grendels."

"*Speed* sacs. Grendels?"

"I had to chop them up myself. Nobody else to do it," Cadmann told her.

"Oh."

Hendrick said, "I'll clean him and return him. He has to sleep. You hold him down. Go back in the room and pass me the robe out. Cad, I'll start a team grinding up grendel sacs—"

"Put 'em in gloves and coveralls—"

"I heard you the first time. All clothes go in a separate pile. Mary Ann, the robe goes too. If grendels get close enough to smell the *speed* extract, we want nobody in that robe."

She had trouble extracting information from that. *They aren't crazy. Am I that stupid?* She nodded. Went back in. Took off the robe. Passed it through the nearly closed door. Went back to bed, naked, pulled up the covers and was gone.

She woke when the bed shook. When she found the strength to rise up on an elbow, Cadmann seemed already asleep. His mouth was open, his beard was four days old, and he looked worse than he'd ever looked with a mere hangover. He was clean, though.

And alive, despite appearances, and safe.

She rolled off her elbow and let her eyes close. The thought of demanding her marital rights came from a long way away and receded at once. He needed sleep. She needed sleep. *I need sleep, he needs sleep, all God's—*

Some indeterminate time later, she must have changed her mind. Or he did. Or— "Watergate," she murmured as they lay in each other's arms, both half conscious and receding.

"You've got the damndest information-retrieval system," he said. "Why Watergate?"

"Can't remember. Oh. Old scandal. They taught us in history class. Who ordered the cover-up? One of the defendants said, 'Nobody ever suggested that there would *not* be a cover-up.' "

"So?"

"If neither of us says, 'Let's not make love—' "

"Gotcha. Go to sleep."

"CHARLIE" was among the oldest of grendels, and she was just turning female. What had been a double layer of cells along her abdominal wall now held tiny eggs ready to be fertilized. The sensation of internal change was minor compared to what she had experienced in the past two days.

Her siblings had been part of the environment, like the water. Now they were death and life. She had won two fights before the scent of something different lured her uphill, away from water.

There had been no fights since. Her chewed foreleg had nearly healed.

Water called her, but water would have siblings in and around it. She was content while the rain fell. There was growing hunger; but she followed the smell of meat in motion, a scent quite alien to that of grendel flesh. Sometimes there were thick stalks to chew. They were not satisfying. She needed meat. . . .

A grendel would eat almost anything rather than a samlon or another grendel. Grendels fought when they must—and when grendels were everywhere, they *must* fight—but what they wanted was more like —like . . .

There had been no image until she left the fog. Then: they were there. A score of alien creatures, far upslope, each bigger than anything her belly could hold. The most distant was misshapen, or carried a parasite. She found herself locking eyes with . . . with something like the creature that had spat fire at a dozen of her siblings and started a battle that she had only barely escaped.

Meat and danger: death and life. She put that one, the creature on the lead horse, in the same class as her siblings. But her hunger was growing.

MARY ANN awoke slowly. Eyes still closed, she reached out, snuggled back, tried to find Cadmann's warm body. Nothing was there. It was time, then. She sat up and blinked into the darkness, then rolled out of bed.

The silence was around her while she slipped on a clean robe. It was uncannily quiet. No dogs, no human voices. She didn't hear the thump of a hammer or the sound of a Skeeter rotor. If she listened hard she could hear the whisper of the wind. Nothing else.

Mary Ann padded the few feet down the hall to the living room. Four men were asleep on the floor. Two sat wrapped in blankets, half asleep as they sipped coffee. Stu hefted his cup and broke the spell. "G'morning."

From the light filtering in from the clerestories she judged it to be just past noon, perhaps one o'clock. "It's not morning."

"That's all you know. Until I've had coffee it's *always* morning."

Me too. She went to the kitchen and poured a cup. It was only lukewarm. She didn't bother to heat it. This wasn't to save energy. Gas might be short, but there was enough for that. Instead she took the lukewarm coffee to the shower room.

No time. No time. A clock in her head ticked on, driving her to a terrible, baseless sense of urgency.

She showered carefully. Thoughts tumbled through her mind in no order at all. Details of the shower system: water diverted from the stream, funneled through fifty meters of narrowing pipe to build pressure; through a maze of pipes exposed to the south for heat; into the house. Water cascading down the small branch of the stream, to run through the livingroom. Then back into the Amazon. Cad had the damndest sense of humor. Amazon: a creek barely deep enough to swim in in the swiftest pools. There was a place where the water ran fast, between two boulders, and you had to fight your way up to it, and there was a seat there in the water where you could sit and let cool water rush past you.

Why am I thinking this?

We were going to put samlon there. She shuddered, and not just with the cold, though the water was cold.

She relished the cold while she scrubbed. The last vestiges of fatigue washed away with the lathered water. Still she rubbed her skin until it burned, and rubbed between the toes, in and behind her ears, scrubbing away ectoplasmic filth. She wanted to be *clean,* and didn't know why.

She toweled and dressed. Only then did she go out to the veranda.

Hendrick and Jerry were half asleep in front of the communications console. Joe Sikes sat on the low wall at the veranda edge and stared downhill through binoculars. Tension and fear showed in the set of his shoulders.

Joe Sikes. He had been a quieter, deeper man since Evvie's death, but she still didn't like him. He'd been friendly, more than friendly. Before Cadmann, he was always a willing bed partner. Never more, but it was good to have someone you could just crook a finger at. She could lose herself in him and forget that she was no longer Professor Eisenhower, nothing more than a brain-damaged brood mare. Then one night she'd heard him talk about her.

Boo! She didn't dare say it. "Hello."

Sikes spasmed, then whirled around. "Oh. Hi."

She didn't laugh out loud.

Jerry sat up fully. "Hello."

"The quiet woke me," Mary Ann said. The sun was just about overhead. "What's going on?"

"Not much," Jerry said. "Beautiful day up here, but you can see that. *Geographic*'s trying to get us some information, but so far nothing you wouldn't expect. IR doesn't go through fog—uh—"

"I understand. They can't tell what's happening below that." She pointed to the mushroom lid that sat above the Colony site.

"I know this much. They're not coming out of it," Jerry said. He found an empty cup on the console table and stooped to rinse it in the stream that cut across the veranda. Then he filled it with coffee from a thermos and thrust it at her. He refilled his own. "Cadmann said you'd be up by now."

"Where is he?" The coffee was bitterly strong, and hot. She treasured each sip.

Jerry shrugged. "Moving fast. Looking for new things to worry about. What'd you expect?"

"I expect we'd all be dead without him."

"Me too," Jerry said cheerfully. "He's making the rounds."

The ground fell away sharply below the veranda. Below the veranda were two more levels, bedrooms and storage. Then the ground sloped away again. "We put the house on the military crest," Cadmann had said. The phrase meant nothing to her. She didn't think it ever would have.

The mine field began a hundred meters below. Off to her left ran the little ridge that separated the Amazon from the smaller branch that flowed through the house. Halfway down that ridge, between the house and the uphill edge of the mine field, was a tall boulder. *Snail Head. Terry's Rock.* Something colorful fluttered atop that rock.

She walked downhill. The sound of the stream pulled her, called to her, and she followed it. She slipped off her shoes and walked barefoot through the shallows.

Terry's silhouette still showed atop the glacier rock. She didn't see his chair. He must have left it at the base; Hendrick and Terry's own strong arms would have lifted him onto the peak.

She called. "Terry!"

"Hi. Sunrise was beautiful. I hope to God you slept through it."

"Oh, yeah. Anything?"

"Hendrick brought me breakfast. Biggest event of the day so far. Cadmann's down there somewhere along the Amazon."

Nowhere did she see Cadmann. She went back up toward the veranda, then stopped to look back.

Something lay beside the stream, about where the mine field ended.

Wasn't that clothing? She strained to see. A body? She ran up to the veranda, sloshing coffee, and found Jerry. "Is someone out there?"

He laughed softly. "Laundry. The stuff Ricky and Phyllis wore when they chopped up the gland sacks, and Cadmann's clothes, and your robe. They all stink of *speed*. I hope you took a damned good shower. If a grendel gets a whiff of you . . ."

That was why. She clapped her hands happily. "You don't have to worry." She closed her eyes and forced herself to remember. "The *speed* stuff. They've already made everything up?"

Jerry pointed up past the veranda, where Stu now lounged near the makeshift Skeeter pad. "We have two tanks of stuff that will drive any red-blooded grendel into hysterics. Bank on it."

She lost Jerry's next words as Cadmann scrambled up from below the wall. His fatigues were very clean, with sharp permacreases. He had shaved; there was new life in his step; he looked more rested than he could possibly be.

She came to him. He put an arm around her, gave her a formal peck of a kiss and said, "Come with me?"

They walked down and around the perimeter again.

"They won't come here," she said. "Why would they?"

"I don't know. But that's just it. We don't know much about grendels."

"The big ones are dead. How many did you kill down there?"

"Hundreds. A thousand? Maybe more. Certainly not all of them."

"They grow so fast. They'd have to eat a lot."

He nodded agreement. "But there's a lot to eat. Each other, of course. All our crops. Anything that moves. We'll be on rationing for a long time."

The way led back down, across the front of the house, then up to where the Snail Head ridge parted the Amazon. Cadmann helped Mary Ann up the rocks to the white boulder where Terry sat, his rifle still across his knees.

Terry grinned down at Cadmann. "What's the word?"

"Johannesburg. You've been up here all day, Terry."

Terry stretched. "I like it here, you know? Good view. I can see right down the Amazon."

"Terry," Cadmann said calmly, "if anything comes up the Amazon you'll be cut off. You can't move fast enough—"

Terry's eyes darted from Mary Ann to Cadmann. "Now, Cadmann. You know perfectly well nothing's going to get this far. Let the damn grendels kill each other off in the lowlands. In our copious free time we'll go down and kill off the last half dozen and reclaim our territory."

"Just how serious—"

"Then again, I could hide in the basement with the rest of the cripples and think about Justin and Sylvia and wonder what's going on outside. Cadmann, I lost my *legs* thinking we had it all figured out. They aren't coming. They *can't* come. And when they get here you'll want sentries." He wasn't smiling. "Leave me here. I'm *fine.*"

Cadmann's mouth opened and shut again. Finally he nodded. "First sign of trouble, sing out. We'll send somebody to get you."

Terry seemed infinitely relieved. "Right. Thanks."

Cadmann turned and started back down the rocks. "Cadmann!" Terry called.

"Yeah?"

"I just wanted you to know. You're a good man, Weyland. We couldn't have done any better." Terry's mouth thinned in a smile. Then it was as if they ceased to exist for him. He turned and peered down his rifle scope into the Amazon.

The cattle pens had been built in haste. Fifty head were crowded into them. They lowed and milled restlessly. Cadmann said, "We can protect them, somewhat. But there's someone we can't."

She didn't know what he meant until he led her to the Joe cages. Missy and her children and relatives stared at Mary Ann through the wire-mesh cage doors, their huge dark eyes identically terrified.

"I thought that you should have the honors," he said.

Mary Ann unlatched the cage doors one at a time. At first the Joes sat there motionless. Then Cadmann reached in and with great gentleness lifted Missy out (her paws held immobile in his fingers) and nuzzled her. "Goodbye, old girl. We'll miss you." He handed her to Mary Ann.

"Do we have to?"

Cadmann shrugged.

"Oh." She set Missy on the ground. Missy sniffed the air, then ran south, up into the mountain. One at a time, the other Joes followed.

"And now what?" she asked.

"We wait. Walk around and inspect the guard, I guess. Or look into the crossbow-making. Or—"

"We can just walk for a while." *You feel useful, and I have you to myself.*

They walked the zigzag through the mine field, up to the low perimeter wall. The plain was still thinly veiled with mist, but the northern mountains were visible as dark jagged peaks.

A pterodon swooped down from above them, its gauzy wings stretched as it arced through the sky. Cadmann looked after it as it disappeared into the clouds. His eyes were dark-ringed but alive with speculation.

He helped her down the rocks. She felt the tightness of his muscles, could smell the fatigue on his breath. He must have spent much of his life like this. This must be what most of war was like: preparations and fear. When Cadmann's comcard buzzed, she *knew*.

"*Chief,*" Joe's voice said, "*Jerry says we have some movement down on the plain.*"

"It's started. Are you sure?"

"*No, not really. Just—something's moving around the stream. Could have come down from the glacier, for all I know. What have you seen swimming through your living room?*"

Cadmann was receding, moving faster than she could. He said, "Not one damn thing, ever."

Jerry met Cadmann as they crossed the stream, handed him a pair of binoculars. "Take a look, Cad."

He walked carefully through the mine field and peered down. "Those are grendels. Two. Hard to tell, but I'd say they were pretty small." He shifted the lenses. "And a couple more coming out of the Miskatonic. . . ."

A curious expression touched his face. The binoculars traced and retraced a short arc.

"Shit," he said. "Get into the house. Don't let anyone bathe in the living room, or throw any kind of refuse into it. The Amazon feeds right down into the Miskatonic—"

Jerry's eyes widened. "People soup."

"Yeah. *Then* send someone for Terry—"

A shot, and then a volley. Cadmann swiveled toward the glacier. Terry waved at him as his comcard buzzed. "Cadmann, grendel coming up the Amazon. I got him, but it's bad news—"

"Terry, listen closely. *Where's the corpse?*"

"I hit it and it went on *speed*, ran in a big circle and back into the water. I can see it. It looks dead now, but it's half in and half out of the water. The tail is still . . . Cad, it's bleeding and it's still in the water!"

Jerry and Cadmann exchanged horrified glances. "That's it."

Cadmann screamed into the card as he ran toward the zigzag. "Omar, Rick—get that corpse out of the water *now*. Maybe it's not—"

Jerry, falling behind, yelled, "We should have diverted the stream—"

"Oh, great," Cadmann replied. "Tell me again, three weeks ago."

Mary Ann ran for the house, her heart thundering in her chest, the words *This is it. This is it* . . . yammering over and over in her mind.

CHAPTER 32

THE KEEP

I have paid my price to live with myself on terms that I will.

RUDYARD KIPLING, *Epitaphs: The Refined Man*

THERE WERE FIVE grendels below Carolyn. Four were just clear of the mist; to the naked eye they were mere specks, wide apart and still separating.

"Charlie, do you know you're being followed?" From left to right, she set names on the intruders: "Ayatollah, Khadafi, Jack, Son of Sam . . ." Too long. "Mareta." Mareta Lupoff was the only single human being ever to set off a hydrogen bomb within a city.

Charlie was much too close: two hundred meters away, plodding along at a speed somewhat greater than the horses could manage.

The horses were holding up well, moving a little slower because they were tired. They hadn't smelled anything yet. Carolyn kept them moving, but she kept watch too.

Twenty horses in a line, linked by rope. Should she free them from the rope? Let them fight their own war?

Grendels. Creatures of mystery and fear, and the more you learned, the more terrifying they were. Those four at the fog level . . . three? One must have turned back. Was it Jack?

They don't cooperate. That's not what Beowulf, excuse me, Weyland, would call a flanking action. It's just grendels trying to stay away from each other. But that near one—Charlie's almost close enough to shoot, and I bet I can guess what it wants.

Carolyn had listened, she wan't stupid, but it was hard to think of grendels as *she*. Picture Jack the Ripper or Muammar Khadafi as a woman: it was silly.

Those rock knobs had the look of boulders deposited by a glacier—intruders dropped on land scraped flat. That one a hundred meters ahead, twice her height: that would do.

When White Lightnin' was alongside the boulder (and the near grendel was a hundred and fifty meters downslope), she dismounted. She took all four harpoons and the harpoon gun from the saddlebags. She slapped Lightnin' to get her moving.

Lightnin' didn't move.

Patiently, with no overt sign of panic, Carolyn walked down to the end of the line (toward the grendel, toward Charlie). She shouted and slapped the trailing horse, Gorgeous George. The young stallion glared at her, but he moved. She slapped him again and, jogging ahead of him, repeated the slap on the next horse, who was already moving. The tail of the line moved; the wave moved forward; the grendel was a hundred meters distant and watching curiously. Carolyn reached the rock. The line of horses moved past her as she climbed. The grendel was seventy meters away.

Forty. Twenty. Jesus, it was on *speed*. The horses screamed. Carolyn smelled it herself, a whiff on the wind, bestial and chemical both. She was halfway up the rock, and the grendel had reached the horses.

She set her back solidly against the rock and lifted the gun while . . .

Gorgeous George reared back on his hind legs, forelegs pawing the air, prepared to stamp holes in an enemy. A torpedo shot under the forelegs and snapped at one of George's ankles without ever slowing. George was yanked backward hard enough to snap the line that bound him. The grendel was behind the rock before Carolyn could fire. George fell downhill, tumbling, screaming. His left hind leg was gone below the knee. *Where was the grendel?*

Coming up the rock be

Carolyn jumped. She landed without breaking an ankle. She ran away from the rock, trying to see the rock and the horse both—

The grendel was downhill, dragging Gorgeous George. George was very much alive, screaming, thrashing. Carolyn aimed carefully and fired.

She'd have hit it. She would! Charlie must have seen something coming; she saw it shy. The harpoon exploded against George's chest. It ripped the horse wide open. The grendel looked at her for the barest particle of an instant, then dodged behind the dying horse.

The other horses were on the run. Carolyn was reloading. Wait? Watch the grendel? But the horses couldn't be left alone. She ran after them. If she scared them they'd keep running: fine, she'd catch them eventually.

But death was behind her, and she kept looking back. Where was the grendel? As fast as it moved, it could be anywhere.

THE GRENDEL was in no hurry. She was overheated, yes, but not to the point of distress. She was small, and had been on *speed* for less than half a minute.

The horse was not much fun. The grendel fed, trying to avoid tearing vitals for the moment; but the beast had stopped moving almost immediately.

The taste was far better than grendel meat.

Three of her siblings were in sight. They came in a line. Vectors of attraction and repulsion held them in position: fear of each other, fear of the one above them, smell of *speed*, mist of horse's blood in the air. Hunger was winning.

Charlie tore into the horse. She ate with some haste now. When her belly was full to the point of pain, she ripped one of the horse's hind legs loose and moved uphill, dragging it with her tail. The other grendels closed in behind.

They would ⊥ and grow strong. Let them. Perhaps they would fight. But they would not catch up. Meanwhile nineteen animals moved upslope with their ali guard to tend them. Well and good.

TERRY sighted carefully a squeezed off another shot as a second grendel poked its head up over edge of the bluff. He caught it between the eyes: its head snapped violently and was gone. *Blood in the water. He wiped his forehead. When I hit it, it went on speed, mit, I did wait. It was on dry land. Of course.rse, and overheated, of course, and went back to the creek. Of course.*

Omar and Rick arrived first. They looked, crazily, like some vintage comedy team: Omar the tallest man on the planet, Rick the shortest. There was nothing comical about them as they poked at the dead grendel, then clubbed its head with an ax when the tail jittered. They hauled it out of the water. Its corpse leaked blood.

Something blurred near the lip of the drop-off, and Omar spun, swinging his ax.

By luck, surely by blind luck, the ax struck the grendel in its open mouth. Its death spasm ripped the tool out of Omar's hand as it flipped back down the hill.

They ran uphill. A dark shape burst from the water behind them. Terry sighted over the top of the scope, firing by instinct. Once. Twice. The grendel leaped, turned, looked directly at Terry. It knew. It moved at blinding speed toward Snail Head. Terry fired again. The grendel continued—and ran directly into the rock. It fell and twitched. Omar and Rick were halfway to the house now, and running hard. Omar's legs were almost twice the length of Rick's, but Rick was winning the race.

Alarms went off all over the stronghold. Up at the house the dogs snarled and bayed. Cadmann's horses whinnied in terror. Down below grendels screamed challenge.

Terry felt great. Adrenaline flowed. *A year of calm, two years, and we'd have rebuilt all the hospital stuff. I'd have new legs. And a working prick.*

Downstream the water parted in strange places, new ripples and eddies where there weren't any before.

His comcard buzzed.

"Terry. Stay still. Maybe they won't notice you." Joe Sikes was trying to talk like Cadmann, but he couldn't manage that unholy calm. "Just sit still."

"Not if I can shoot something."

They weren't just eddies in the Amazon now. They were dark shapes, dark shapes coming upstream. *I called them. General Weyland, sir, we've lured the enemy within range.*

"Terry!"

There were shapes on both sides of him now. "I'm cut off. Watch out for the little stream! They'll be in your living room!"

"Terry, hold on, we'll get someone down there."

Someone. There's only one someone who'd come here, now. "Don't. You're about to be up to your neck in grendels, you idiot!" Terry turned and faced up the small stream. His spine was barely that flexible above his immobile legs. He fired toward the house. Something exploded from the water. Another shape shot forward and grabbed it. There was gunfire from the veranda.

He turned back to the Amazon. "There's a lot of them. In the Amazon, and up on both sides of it. You are infested!"

"Any on *speed*?"

Cadmann's voice: "I see half a dozen."

"I see shadows," Terry reported. "The ones you can't see, they're not on *speed*. Fifty, and that's just near the house."

"We're sending up the Skeeter. Look, Terry—"

"I've figured it out, Cadmann. Without you nobody lives. See you in hell, hotshot. Tell Sylvia—" He grimaced to himself. *Tell her I don't release her from her promise.* "Tell her any damn thing you like. Out." He set the card on the rock and took aim. Half a dozen grendels clustered in the water, twenty meters away: he couldn't miss. The solid kick of the rifle felt just right.

The grendel jumped at the impact. It was instantly on *speed*, charging from the water. The rest charged after it, tore it apart, and, shying from each other, towed pieces of their sibling back into the stream. The water foamed red. Terry snarled to himself, at himself. Then he took out the card again. "About forty left the water. Some are fighting, some are coming your way. Do you hear?"

"*I hear,*" Joe Sikes said.

"Good." Quite deliberately, he bent his comcard in half, destroying it. *Never liked the damn things. Whatever happened to solitude?*

Gunfire from above. Off to the side more grendels, grendels on *speed*, grendels blurring over the lip of the bluff. More shadows in the water, lying low, avoiding each other. And two grendels in line coming upriver toward him. One looked up. Its eyes met his. Then it *moved.*

A gray-brown dust plume whizzed over the rocks, headed directly for him. Terry squeezed off one shot, a second, with no effect. He threw the change lever over to full automatic and held the trigger down. Shots rippled out. The barrel heated. The grendel leaped straight into the air, blood streaming from its back and shoulders. Two others snapped at it, then began rushing in frantic circles. Others came up the stream.

Terry aimed and pulled the trigger. Nothing happened. He checked the breech. Empty.

Quite calmly, he searched his pockets. There were no more clips, but it was always best to be sure.

More grendels below him now. They fought. *Fighting to see who gets me.* He wished there were some way to disappoint them. He wished he'd asked them to patch him through to *Geographic*, to Sylvia, before it was too late. But they'd said everything there was to say.

He wished he could see Justin again, but at least the child was safe. One of the grendels had won the battle below.

It moved up the rock. Terry didn't want to look at it. He turned to look toward the house. Skeeter One was rising from behind the house.

THE SKEETER floated downslope. Stu kept it low enough to gain some advantage from the ground effect. He had only a quarter charge, and when that was gone they'd be down there with the grendels.

Mits was behind him, sitting on one of the tanks of *speed* soup. He said, "When you give the word."

"Hold off."

"Lots of grendels below."

Stu could see that. Thirty or forty grendels on *speed* were streaking out of the water, snapping at the corpses of grendels already dead, snapping at each other, circling back to the stream. Several clustered around a white rock: Terry must be dead already. A few slow ones crawled upslope at their leisure, following the scent of men and cattle.

He said, "Keep your head, Mits. We don't *want* grendels going on *speed* near the house. We want them on *speed* down there, where they'll burn themselves out."

"Yeah. Sorry. The goddamned stream is *seething* with them. I would have bet anything it was too small for that."

"Really? Anything?"

". . . No. O-o-oh, Lord."

Stu looked back. Grendels were into the mine field now. He could see the explosions—and a line of grendels tracing the zigzag that marked the safe path. Following the markers. Following the smell left by men's shoes.

The house receded. The water was growing denser with grendels. A few must have followed the taste of human garbage in the water, but the rest had followed garbage and grendel blood too: the taste of territory to be taken.

They were almost halfway to the drop-off. "Now," said Stu.

He didn't have to look. The stink told him: Mits had the stopcock open and was spraying along the river. The Skeeter blades scattered the stuff; it must be falling over a path a hundred meters wide.

And every *speed* sac they'd put through the blender had been quite flat. Grendels used up their *speed* when they were dying. That mist must be as thin as hope.

Grendels surged from the water. It worked beautifully! Half the grendels were murdering the other half! No, not quite. But the flying was easy, and Stu freed one hand to touch his comcard.

"Anyone there?"

"We're kind of busy," said Joe Sikes. "They're coming through the fucking mine field."

"I'm halfway down to the bluff. We're spraying. The grendels are all on *speed*. This stuff is magic. I'd say only about half of them are reacting to it, but they set the others off. We're going to lose about two thirds of them in an orgy of murder."

"Good news."

"Bad news is, about a third of them are just running away from each other. Say, just guessing now, four hundred are now fighting and two hundred just scattering, the cowards, and of the two hundred, a hundred and fifty are going up. Toward you."

"I read you. A hundred and fifty coming."

"We're getting close to the drop-off and . . . the batteries read dead. I think—"

Mits called from aft. "I've got the other tank in place. It's running."

"Sure is. Joe, we'll stay up as long as we can and then try to get away from the stream."

"I copy. You think the Skeeter cabin will hold?"

"Sure."

"That's a relief." Trace of sarcasm there? "Stu, Mits . . . ah . . . on behalf of all of us and world civilization, I want to express our thanks."

"Don't be pompous, Joe. Save it for the victory speeches."

Joe shouted something incoherent. Then there was only the popcorn sound of gunfire, and not enough of that, and it was dwindling.

Grendels seethed in an orgy of murder. Some of the warier grendels had sprinted away from the water *before* the spray reached them. At a good, safe distance from the battle, far from the stream, they watched the Skeeter. More and more of them, left and right of the river, watched Stu in the Skeeter cockpit.

The batteries had to be on their last gasp. Stu veered left, away from the stream, and angled uphill too. Grendels that had been watching were suddenly in the spray pattern. Stu grinned: half of them were streaking away, escaping, but they did it by going on speed.

Then the power was gone. Stu called, "Dump it!"

The tank tumbled out.

The ground came up hard.

"Button us up." He'd done the best he could. The tank was spraying its remaining *speed* juice into one square meter of ground, and that was between the Amazon and the Skeeter. Grendels would go crazy before they got here. It might be enough.

CADMANN slammed a rifle into Mary Ann's hands and spun her toward the steps. "Get in the goddamned house!"

By the time she scrambled past the deadfall to the house, the rifle fire was a steady crackle.

In the living room, a dozen of the weak and wounded were sequestered. They huddled in clumps, eyes huge. They stared out the clerestory slits. Outside, the actions of other men and women decided their fates. "Everyone away from the spring!" she screamed. "Against the far wall!"

They pushed into the far corner. Mary Ann's mind fought the panic. Somehow, in a hurricane of terror, she found an eye of calm.

The house shuddered as mines exploded to the west: the grendels were coming over the wall! Dirt and shattered rock rained on the roof above her. A grendel leg slid through the clerestory and thudded to the ground in front of them. It twitched.

Next to her, Jill screamed and screamed. Mary Ann savagely backhanded her. Jill reeled back, stunned.

Mary Ann flexed her hand. It hurt. Then she hunkered down, tucked the rifle butt into her shoulder, and waited.

CHAPTER 33

THE LAST STAND

Thou hast covered my head in the day of battle.

THE BOOK OF COMMON PRAYER

THE HORSES were thinking about letting her catch up. Carolyn cursed the stupid animals in her mind; she didn't have breath for more. Thirst was a fire in her throat. Her burning legs were ready to collapse, and her ride receded coyly before her.

The horses stumbled from time to time. She'd have to get those ropes off them if they were to have any chance to live.

They wheeled to the left. She followed.

The stream was a sudden surprise. It was small and pretty and it ran in graceful curves. She hadn't seen it lower down. It might curve south and join the Amazon; it might seep into the water table and disappear. She could hear it bubbling now, and the thirst rose up in her like a grendel.

The horses lined up to drink. They didn't flinch as she joined them. She had swallowed two cupped handfuls before she noticed how dirty the water was. She was downstream, and the horses had fouled the water.

She spat out the grit. Thirst was still there, but she took the time to free the horses from the line of ropes. *Do everything slowly and carefully. Fool yourself into being calm.* She patted their necks, she called them by name, she walked around and among them and knelt to drink clean water upstream. And saved her life thereby.

When her belly was a cold fullness, she stood and looked back.

Far down toward the edge of storm, a cloud of spray rose from the stream.

Something dark came out of it. Came fast. Charlie had gone for water first, but now he was on *speed* and coming for the horses. Carolyn stepped back behind a rock that was only hip high. Knelt. She concentrated on arming the harpoon gun. She didn't lift her head until she was armed.

Just her eyes peeped over the rock.

The horses were scattering, all but Shank's Mare. Shank's Mare had gone thirty meters before the thing tore into her. Now she thrashed with blood spraying from her ravaged hind leg—Charlie had developed a habit—and the black streak circled back to bite away half of the horse's head. Shank's Mare convulsed, then collapsed like a bag of old laundry. The grendel hooked her with its tail and dragged her back into the stream.

Carolyn stood up and walked forward. There was no running from a grendel. Charlie was occupied and the time was *now*.

The horses had hidden her, and then the rock, but now . . . Charlie must have seen her at once. The grendel came straight at her, pulling the mass of the horse and a mass of water too, moving no faster than a jogger. It realized its problem and stopped to shake the horse free. Carolyn shot it from six meters away.

The harpoon exploded against Charlie's wide face.

The grendel came for Carolyn. It was free of the horse, and it accelerated like the best of motorcycles. Carolyn wouldn't have had time to move even if she'd had the nerve and another weapon. The thing went past her in a wind that twisted her around, and she saw it smash into the hip-high boulder, bounce over it, land tumbling, look about—

Look with what? The blast had torn its face entirely away, leaving cracked red-and-white bone. No eyes, no nose, most of the mouth blown away. A grendel's ears were nearly invisible, but she couldn't believe those weren't gone too.

There was blood in Carolyn's mouth. She had bitten deeply into her lower lip. Blood soaked into her trousers, and a line of pain crossed her leg above the knee: the tail of the thing must have brushed her. She lowered the harpoon gun and felt the pain in her cramped hands. "Stupid," she whispered. "Stupid, Charlie. Pulling a horse! I hope your sisters are that stupid."

Charlie's tail was a blur like the blades on a Skeeter. She charged in a straight line, with no clear target. Only by accident did she intersect the stream. She stopped then, sank underwater, then lifted again. To breathe. The snorkle was gone too.

Carolyn became aware that she was grinning like a grendel.

The rest. Where were they? She couldn't see them; the ground curved strongly, but they must be at least several hundred meters downslope. Three grendels—and two harpoons left. She remembered a line from Dickens and told herself, "I have every confidence that something will turn up."

She knelt to drink again, then set off to join the horses.

THE MIST was thin now. The sun had burned it away, giving them a warm afternoon.

Thank God. Grendels on *speed* would move through that heat.

The grendels struggled in knots. Screams of challenge crowded the air. Chilled the blood. There was war where Mits had dropped the spurting tank of *speed* soup. A mere seven grendels had rounded that distraction to reach the Skeeter.

They must have been the bright ones. They screamed challenge at each other, circled each other, they took turns butting the cabin walls and the door; but not one had died.

Mits sat in the cargo hold fingering an ax. He watched dents appear in the steel. "I have to admit it's getting to me," he said.

"It's the only entertainment we've got," Stu said. He cracked a window and set his comcard in it with its solid-state memory set to *record.* "And this is for the National Geographic Society."

"You're nuts," said Mits.

Maybe. But today would see the end of one species. Grendel or man. This, these final sounds of struggle, would be preserved for posterity.

Someone's posterity.

TOO MANY. Cadmmann knelt at the western edge of the veranda. He fired carefully, making each round count. There wouldn't be nearly enough ammunition. Not rifles, not spear guns.

"Wound up," Jerry said beside him.

"In place," Joe Sikes said. "Let her fly." The crossbow bolt flew out, over the lip of the bluff, to shatter a jar of *speed* extract. Something screamed defiance down there. Jerry grinned like a thief. "Winding," he said.

"Watch it!" Carlos shouted. He fired his spear gun: the grendel had come over the low wall of the veranda. The explosive bolt caught it at the withers and crippled its left side. It began to drag itself toward them. Harry Siep ran up and smashed its head with an ax. The tail lashed out and knocked Harry against the wall.

"Siep?" Joe Sikes yelled.

"Kicking. Stupid but kicking."

For the moment there were no more grendels. "Hang on here a minute," Cadmann said. Carlos nodded. Cadmann sprinted across the veranda to the eastern corner where Omar and Rick had set up a machine gun. Five riflemen stood with them.

"Omar. Take the gun over to Carlos and set up there."

"Uh—"

"Over there. By Carlos. Set up there," Cadmann said.

"All right." Rick reached out to lift the gun.

"Not by the barrel," Cadmann said.

"Oh." The barrel wasn't glowing, but it was hot enough to boil water.

Cadmann stood on the wall and used his binoculars to scan the area downstream. *Seems strange to do this in a battle. Never to worry about them shooting back.*

Grendels all along Amazon Creek. Too many of them. But for every grendel in the water, six more faced them on land. In twos and threes they toppled from the internal heat; in twos and threes they attacked the defenders of the stream, and died or won—and if they won, they became the new defenders. Grendels on *speed*, grendels cooking themselves from inside, couldn't reach the water because other grendels kept them from it. And none of those presently threatened the house.

But there were attackers enough.

If they could be stopped far enough away— But they couldn't be. Cadmann touched numbers on his comcard. "Ida. What's your status?"

The dentist's voice was strained. *"Maybe five minutes of power in the Skeeter. No more than that."*

Five minutes. They'd spread the solar panels, but the sun hadn't come out in time. "Not enough time. Unload the *superspeed*. Load up the kerosene."

"Kerosene. You want me to fly around with kerosene with five minutes' flying time?"

"That I do."

"And then what?"

"Ida, the next wave may get through. If they do, you and that kerosene will be critical. Spray around the house, just below the veranda. Then throw flares into the soup. Then go uphill and land."

"And pray I'm far enough from the fire."

"Something like that. Will you do it?" If she wouldn't, who would? Fifteen minutes to put another pilot in place. Carlos? Me?

"Yeah, I guess so—"

Explosions rocked the plateau. The cattle, penned to the east, lowed and stomped.

And attracted grendels.

Some sped across the perimeter. Cadmann saw several of them actually collapse before they could reach the cattle. *Ran out of speed. They're burning up.*

Wiser, stronger siblings hooked the twitching dead and dragged them away.

Everywhere grendels were dying, but the line of corpses moved closer and closer to the house. Grendels fought each other, dragged each other away, climbed over their own dead in a mindless fever to reach the house.

A cluster of grendels broke through the mob, racing for the livestock. Omar Isfahan clambered out onto the hill. He lifted a spear gun, sighted with unsteady hands.

He missed. The grendels became suddenly, horribly aware of his presence, and streaked for him. Before Cadmann had time to yell warning, Isfahan was down, three grendels at him. He screamed once, and then there was nothing left to scream with.

"Jerry! Inside," Cadmann ordered.

The doctor hesitated for a brief second. "Right. Going."

The cattle had gone mad. They broke free of the pens and stampeded. Grendels brought them down one by one. Grendels died of heat prostration trying to drag butchered cows to safety, or they ran out of *speed* and were crushed beneath the hoofs of the herd.

The cattle raced to the low wall, over, down the mountainside. Grendels followed.

It was as if a signal had been given. The grendels surged forward, up the hill. Grendels exploded in the mine field, but others were weaving along the safe path. Bullets found some of them; other grendels stopped, considering, looking for an enemy. Too many came on.

Gunfire erupted from within the house. And grendels fell. Flame throwers coughed their last bit of jellied fuel, and scorched monsters reeled away, streaking for the stream.

Monsters crowded up the hill.

"Ida? Now."

"Need a couple more minutes," she answered. *"Getting that damned water tank out—"*

"Right. But get going as soon as you can." Cadmann raced across the veranda. "Deadfall," he shouted.

"Sí." Carlos followed. They left the veranda and raced down the hill.

The deadfall: an enormous boulder, held in place by large chocks. Above it were dozens of smaller boulders ready to plunge down, along the cleared path through the mine field.

Chocks held the deadfall boulder in place. A dying grendel crouched against the chocks.

"Son of a bitch!" Cadmann shouted.

Carlos grinned and fired. The explosive shell struck the grendel in the chest. It leaped upward—and struck its head on the boulder above, and fell in a heap, still blocking the chocks.

"Aw, shit," Carlos said.

"You said it. Here." Cadmann handed him the rifle. "Hold 'em off while I pull."

"You'll need help—

"Bullshit I need help! You watch for grendels."

"All right."

The corpse might have weighed eighty kilos. They were getting big, and this one must have fed well. Not too much to drag, but awkward. Cadmann reached for the tail. It lashed. Spikes caught his thigh. He fell heavily against the boulder.

"Amigo—"

"Look out ahead!" Cadmann shouted.

More grendels coming. Cadmann desperately reached the lines holding the chocks in place. "I got it. Be out of the way!"

"For sure."

He heaved against the lines. The chock moved slightly. He pulled again. It was hard to brace his good leg against the rocks and still have purchase on the line. He pulled again. The corpse moved; crimson foam ran from its back, frothed down against the wooden chocks. This time when he pulled, the chocks moved—

Carlos was firing rapidly now.

One final heave. The chocks came loose. The massive boulder seemed poised in space. Then it began to roll. Down, followed by a mass of others.

Carlos joined in his shout of triumph.

A grendel came *over* the large boulder, sprang between the smaller boulders, tried to dance among them. It didn't quite succeed. A rock the size of a footstool hit it in the side. Carlos shot it twice more. Still it thrashed forward, toward Cadmann, who lay with his legs toward it, legs spread, monster crawling up, up, *between* his legs. Cadmann writhed, twisted. The grendel fell onto his uninjured leg. Something snapped. Pain surged.

Carlos stood staring wildly. Grendels below them. He couldn't shoot and carry Cadmann at the same time. He looked the question.

"How the fuck do I know?" Cadmann said. He was surprised at how soft his voice was. The grendel hadn't moved. Sixty kilos of dead meat. Both legs screamed their agony in his brain; he couldn't think past that. *I've used up all my adrenaline. Like a goddam grendel uses up its speed. No adrenaline, and I don't even care what happens.*

Carlos fired twice. Cadmann couldn't see what he was shooting at.

THE GRENDELS leaped like fleas among the bounding boulders. The dead-fall was taking its toll: he could see smashed grendels, he could hear the weakened challenge-screams of grendels facing death. *How do you see death,* amigos? *A mature grendel the size of a mountain?*

But a grendel in the air had no control of its path. They leaped, and Carlos took them at apogee, rapid-fire practice with pop-up targets, shoot and forget.

It was over. The slide continued, a horde of rocks among the horde of grendels, crossing the brook and onward. How long had it taken? A minute? Less.

And he had leisure to help his friend.

Cadmann was no more than half conscious. One leg was crushed; the other looked broken. Carlos worked his way under him and heaved. Cadmann was lifted from the ground, a big man in high gravity, and Carlos walked. Weaponless. Both hands occupied.

The stench of *speed* was a shroud. It hung in the air thick as fog; it clouded his mind. There was nothing to think about anyway. Pick up Cadmann and walk until you're in the house. Depend on hysterical strength. Any passing grendel is on his own.

A larger grendel climbed one of the bigger boulders left by the deadfall. It perched there, looking them over. Carlos paid little attention; he had to watch his feet; he was on uncertain footing, with a mass of ninety-five kilograms sagging from his shoulder. The grendel climbed down at leisure, hooked the ravaged corpse of a heifer and went away. The door was closer.

Cadmann stirred, tried to say something, gave up.

Joe Sikes was in front of him, then up against him. When Cadmann's weight eased off, Carlos almost fainted in relief. Then they were through the door, and Harry Siep closing it behind them, and Mary Ann swearing as they eased Cadmann to the floor.

MARY ANN saw Phyllis McAndrews die. It didn't have to be. She could have come in earlier, but she'd stayed at the communications console a moment too long. What could she have been hearing from *Geographic?* Whatever it was—

By the time she turned to run to the door a grendel had got behind her. It was heat-exhausted. Its sides heaved, and it was no longer running as a blur. It was still faster than a man, and stronger. It charged, struck Phyllis, and she fell.

For a moment Mary Ann hoped that Phyllis could throw the weakened creature off. Then its teeth closed. Blood spurted hotly over its muzzle as it tore her face away.

From behind her Joe Sikes fired three times. Twice at the grendel. Once lower . . .

Mary Ann turned and threw up.

Carlos dragged Cadmann into the room. Someone had let the dogs out: Tweedledum met them at the door, barking and trying to lick the blood off Cadmann's leg. Carlos brushed him aside.

Mary Ann handed her rifle to a now sober Jill and went to Cadmann. He wasn't quite unconscious. He stared up at her, through her, with pain-dilated pupils. He tried to say something. It made no sense.

"Ida," he said.

"Ah." Carlos took out his comcard. "Ida. Cadmann says go now." Nothing answered.

"I'll go look," Joe Sikes said.

"Get her moving—"

"Sure." Sikes went out through the back of the house.

"We've done what we can," Carlos said.

Cadmann stared at him for a moment, then nodded. All the strength seemed to drain out of him at once.

Mary Ann bent over.

Carlos helped her slit his trouser legs. There was blood, and a sliver of bone knifed out of the left leg. "Spiral fracture," he said. She was amazed at how calm she could be. *I'll collapse later.* For now she had work to do.

Blood flowed freely from the right thigh. "Venous blood," Carlos said. "It flows, not spurts. Jill—give us a hand here, please."

Cadmann's mouth worked as he fought to speak. No words came out, but he coughed and a bubble of blood formed at his lips.

"Bruises. Perhaps a punctured lung. The thing fell hard against him," Carlos said.

"You're in charge," Cadmann muttered. "Get out of here."

Carlos looked down helplessly. "I'll find Jerry—"

"He's in the back room," Mary Ann said. "I don't know what you're supposed to do, but it's your job now. We'll find Jerry."

Tweedledum barked in rage at the clerestory.

Something crawled up through the stream. Three of the dogs met it there, crowded to get at it. The grendel, weakened, managed to get its teeth into Tweedledee's neck before the other dogs tore it apart.

Tweedledum turned from the corpse, licked at his sister's wounds. She whined softly and died.

Stu rushed in, rifle in hand. "The Skeeter's up! They're burning out there! Burning and running away—"

There was a sudden burst of gunfire from outside, and twin screams, human and grendel.

The roof sagged, bulged inward. Two grendels fought to push in through the clerestory.

Jill grabbed a spear, shrieked, and stabbed one in the throat. It writhed, whipped its tail, and she backed off. The spear remained in the wound.

It fell into the livingroom. It pawed weakly at the spear, eyes ablaze with hatred and pain. It tried to go on *speed*, but had nothing left. They clubbed at it, everyone striking at it, dogs darting in.

The roof collapsed, and two more grendels fell through. One landed nearly atop Jill, and had its jaws in her leg before anyone could move.

Mary Ann shot it, shot again, then turned, hearing a splash. More grendels. More. Coming in up the stream bed, up the stream that ran through the living room.

She fired at full automatic. The gun stopped almost immediately. Out of ammunition. The grendels were still coming. She looked back toward Cadmann—

A river of fire flowed down. It flowed from the bedroom into the living room, under the earthen walls of the house. Flames danced from the water, and Mary Ann thought she had lost her mind.

"Sikes!" Carlos shouted. "He's poured the kerosene in the river!"

Joe Sikes. I owe you. I guess I already paid.

The fire flowed down to engulf the grendels. They turned downstream, fleeing in terror.

And then there was quiet, save for coughing from the smoke. There were no live grendels in the house.

Another volley of shots.

Somewhere a grendel screamed.

The surviving colonists pulled smoldering furniture and cloth against one of the earthen walls, then smothered the heap with a blanket.

Cadmann stirred and looked at Carlos. He tried to say something. *"Madre de Dios,"* Carlos said. "Shut up for a moment!"

It was very quiet in the room.

THE VERANDA was covered with blood. Four men, one woman, three grendels; all dead.

Below the veranda and as far downhill as Carlos could see, the plateau was littered with corpses. Men and dogs and cattle; but mostly grendels. Hundreds and hundreds of grendels.

Some lay still. Some crawled, torn nearly in half, trailing entrails from shattered bodies. The air hung heavy with the stench of kerosene and burnt meat. Patches of fire burned twenty meters from the veranda. Ida had brought the fires very close indeed.

The stream no longer burned. It was also no longer choked with grendels. They had retreated in front of a river of fire. Grendels seeking cold had fled from the river and died in the hills.

Other people came out of the house and down from the roof. Gunshots from up above the house: one, two, three, then silence. Rick Erin held a bloody spear. He held it high and shook it in defiance.

The command console had been knocked off its table. Hendrick limped over to pick it up and set aright. He touched the switches, and lights glowed.

Tau Ceti was low on the horizon. Carlos limped out to the edge of the plateau and looked out. The mist had dissipated. He looked for grendels on *speed*, and found none. Here and there a grendel dragged the corpse of a grendel or a cow toward the water. He saw them met by emerging grendels, and torn apart.

Something had happened. Something had changed, and Carlos knew it. The grendels knew it!

Human beings were no longer prey. Man was the ultimate killer on Avalon. Grendels were smart enough to learn. The survivors now stalked each other instead of the aliens from the stars, the creatures who had brought death to thousands of Avalon's former masters.

"*Geographic—*"

"We're here. Are you all right?"

Hendrick looked toward Carlos. His face was grimy and haggard, his eyes bright. "What do I tell them?"

"Tell them we've won."

CHAPTER 34

HUNTING PARTY

Leviathan, that great dragon in the sea . . . .

Come not between the dragon and his wrath.

King Lear, Act I, Scene 1.

Thou shalt tread upon the lion and adder: the young lion and the dragon shalt thou trample under feet.

PSALM 91:13

IT WAS A SMALL POND up a stream that fed the Miskatonic—a stream not much larger than Cadmann's Amazon. The pond was the nearest possible thing to an oxbow lake, still connected to the stream but without the rushing waters. There were boulders piled at its lower end. Mits Kokubun wondered about those boulders. Could grendels have put them there? Beavers were smart enough to build dams. Why not grendels?

Correction: *grendel*, singular. They were too damned competitive to cooperate, ever.

A nest of boulders overlooked the pond. It was a good place, high enough and steep enough that the resident grendel would have problems getting there. Mits searched the pond area with his binoculars. "Still nothing."

"Still nothing," Joe Sikes said. "Half the morning gone. Christ, what does it take to get the mother out of there?"

"Some of them just won't come out and fight." Mits tapped his comcard. "Stu. Still nothing."

"*Well, it's* there. *Samlon in the pool and* Geographic *photographed the shadow. Those things should have more respect for our explosives shortage. I'll try* speed *soup again.*"

"Well, okay, but I don't think it'll do any good."

"*So? We've got more* speed *than explosives. Stand by.*"

They waited. After a moment Skeeter One skimmed across, twenty meters above the pond. Its cabin had a pebbled, battered look, but it flew well. A thick pinkish mist cascaded down and was blown into the pond scum and into the rocks around its bank.

They waited. Nothing happened.

"That was your Skeeter," Sikes said.

"Yeah."

"What was it like?" Sikes asked. "I mean—"

"I know what you mean. What do you want me to say? Stu and I sat there in the Skeeter while the mothers backed dents in the hull. It was fun. Just as it was starting to get dull, a big one bashed its head right through. Damn near got my foot. I chopped it with the ax. It tried to pull its head out, but it was caught on the torn hull metal where it poked through, and then the others outside started eating it. They ate it alive."

"I'd have liked to watch that," Sikes said.

Mits looked at him. Sikes didn't seem to be kidding.

The comcard squawked. "*Nothing, huh?*"

"Not a damn thing," Mits answered. "Let's get a move on. I want sashimi tonight."

"*Okay, okay. I'll use a bomb. Have to call that in. Stand by.*"

"Our luck, everybody will be busy," Sikes said.

"Nah. They're too hungry to be busy. Fresh samlon."

"I guess I'm getting sick of fresh samlon."

"It's better'n nothing. It's way better'n grendel." Mits swept his binoculars around the edges of the pond. Nothing. Not even bushes. Grendels would eat anything in preference to samlon. Then they ate samlon.

"*Got it approved,*" Stu's voice said from the comcard. "*You ready?*"

"Ready here. Set it for max depth. The damn thing's hiding on the bottom, trust me."

"*Stand by.*"

The whish of rotors grew louder. The craft came over the low lip of the rock basin surrounding the pond. It hovered at the center of the pond, and a dark barrel fell from the doorway. "*Bomb away. And me too,*" Stu said. The Skeeter darted off west.

The pond exploded in a geyser. Mits waited, counting seconds to himself.

A half-grown grendel burst from the water. It scrambled onto the beach and ran in drunken curves. Blood poured from its mouth. It rolled and found its feet again, ran, rolled, stopped to take its bearings.

"*Sayonara*, sucker," Mits hissed. He held the sights on the area just behind the head, down five centimeters from the back ridge, the central ganglion complex that corresponded more or less to the human medulla oblongata. He squeezed off the round. The grendel darted ahead one step and died.

Mits thumbed the comcard. "Tell 'em. Meat!"

The samlon were starting to float to the surface.

THEY CAME in tractors and jeeps and on foot. A team set up nets across the river downstream from the pond. Others inflated boats and set out on the pond. They spread nets. The pond would be seined again and again.

Dead samlon floated belly-up. They weren't very big—from half a meter down—but there must have been fifty in sight, and the team downstream would take more yet.

Skeeter Three came in carrying a prefabricated smokehouse. Colonists trickled in from uphill, bearing firewood. Hendrick Sills moved among the various groups. "Load the Skeeters as fast as it comes in. Some of us'll have to walk home to leave room. When the Skeeters are full we can start filling the smokehouse. Ida, what are you doing?"

"Sushi." She'd sliced up a foot-long samlon and started on another, nibbling as she worked. "Have some."

"The rest of the Colony gets to eat too. Them's the rules."

She sighed. The nightmare was still graven in her face, still caused her to wake at night, moaning for Jon. But they were helping each other heal. This wasn't a perfect world, but together they could make it a good one.

"Hendrick, dear, half the Colony is *here*. Are they supposed to look at all this and salivate? Look, Skeeter One's already off, and they're piling fish in Skeeter Three as fast as it comes in. We're saving none of it for the damn pterodons."

Hendrick thumbed his comcard. "Skeeter One, air conditioning?"

"It's on. We're freezing. Don't be such a nitpicker, Hendrick!"

The Skeeters would have their air conditioning on max to keep the samlon fresh: a nice example of Avalon's mix of high technology, low, and none. Hendrick tapped again. "Joe. You set up downstream?"

"Sure am. Somebody bring me lunch?"

"We'll think about it."

"Do more than think, or else if I see a grendel I'll cheer her on!"

"Okay, okay, Ida's made you some sushi."

Not that there was much chance of a grendel. The pools downstream had all been cleaned out. One hundred days had passed since the battles. Grendels had established territories and fought to keep them. Like Siamese fighting fish: one grendel to a pool. But unlike the fish who fought only until one retreated, if one grendel intruded on another's territory the result was one dead grendel and one well fed.

This one must have been well fed. There was plenty of samlon here. A good find. No fear that all the meat would be eaten here—as long as the pterodons could be kept under control.

The air stank of *speed* soup, and recorders on the boats were playing the recording Stu had made during the final attack. Screams of grendel-challenge and grendel-death ravaged the air. The flying appetites hovered, shrieking their anger, afraid to come down.

It was good that they didn't have to use bullets on the pterodons. Too few bullets now. When humans were finished here the pterodons could have the grendel's corpse. Hendrick himself had tried to eat grendel meat—starvation was much to be preferred.

Skeeter Three lifted away, carrying tonight's feast.

SYLVIA used an optical pen to underline one of the passages in the old report Terry had written. It felt a little odd to play back Cassandra's old files. Old notes on the expedition to the mainland, back when all the grendels were gone from Avalon and everything was wonderful. *Good stuff. We can do it almost the way Terry outlined it*—and then a brief, sad flash: *Terry . . .*

"It isn't fair," Carolyn said.

Mary Ann looked up from changing diapers. "What isn't fair?"

"You've got men. You monopolize them."

"Foo," Marnie said. "You can't blame *me* if Jerry prefers my bod to yours."

"Plus the fact that you'll give him pure holy hell for weeks," Mary Ann said. Her voice was strained through diaper pins.

"And if I seduce Cadmann?" Carolyn asked.

"I'll kill you." Mary Ann finished her diaper job. "Now, if you want to *marry* him—"

"What?" Carolyn was jolted.

"I could use a junior wife," Mary Ann said. Her eyes took on a dreamy look. Then the smile vanished. "Sylvia—"

"It's all right," Sylvia said. *Terry, you bastard, you could have relieved me of that promise. You could have.* "What's the matter, Carolyn? Don't want to join the commune?"

"Meow," Mary Ann said.

"Sorry. But not very. Look, we have five monogamous marriages plus chaos. There's no point in being delicate about it. Especially among ourselves." *Five monogamous marriages, except I could make that four plus another bigamy, and Mary Ann wouldn't mind, and Terry, Terry, you could have said something noble! You muffed your line—*

"We're getting off the subject," Marnie said. "Carolyn, this next broadcast is probably our last chance to change anything back in Sol system. By the time they get this message, it will have been twenty years since their interstellar program was proxmired. They're probably bored to tears, ready to hang on our every word. Did we survive the grendels? The suspense must be killing them.

"This isn't just for the Geographic Society. The whole solar system will be listening! Billions of people who watched while they didn't build the interstellar ships will be still alive. A little nostalgic. Getting older, wondering where the excitement went. So we want to make all our points while we've got them hooked! Sylvia, what have you got on-screen?"

"Terry's mainland expedition. We'll send them that, of course. Adventure calls, even on Avalon! We're short one Skeeter now, and the mission has changed a little because we're hungry. We'll want to anchor a Minerva in a bay, then take the Skeeters halfway up some mountain, above where the grendels can reach. Collect some Joes, if nothing else, and reseed the island."

"Any way we can put visuals in that lecture?"

"Visuals of what? They've seen the equipment. We've improved the orbital maps. I guess we can put in Joes. . . ."

"Summon up those notes for the broadcast."

"Yeah." Sylvia tapped. She read off the list:

"*Full details on grendel attack. Bored on Earth? Come to romantic Avalon and find adventure. Emphasize that we won. We control the grendels. Nail it down by showing us hunting out a grendel pond.* I sent Sikes down with a camera; he'll get that today.

"*De-emphasize hunger. De-emphasize fatalities.* But we can talk about the taste of local life, Joes and samlon. We can't show another harvest because nothing's come up yet—"

"They've seen a harvest," Marnie said.

"Joes are cute," Mary Ann said. "Don't say we eat them. . . ."

"I suppose. Anyway—*set 'em up for the foray to the mainland.* I'll bet my ass we find something weird and interesting *there*. What eats grendels?"

"Shudder," Carolyn said; and she *did* shudder. Sylvia chose not to notice. For a moment Carolyn was somewhere else. For a few seconds she wasn't Carolyn, she was Phyllis, dying under the claws of a grendel.

Rachel had worked especially hard with Carolyn. They had all worked to pull her back into the community, caring for her as they never had when her twin was alive. She needed them now, probably more than any of them could understand.

"We can't avoid it," Sylvia said, deliberately raising her voice to cut into Carolyn's train of thought. "We have to tell Earth how many of us died, but we can just send a bald list. And we'll give 'em a list of what we need. It's short. Ruined equipment. They're bound to have fancier computers than Cassandra. We lost some life forms too. I want just enough of a list to let them know visitors would be welcome.

"But we have to hammer hard on how we *beat* the grendels. We took on one and two and six and then ten thousand, and we're mopping them up in detail. Carolyn, you have to tell your story for the broadcast back to Earth!"

"That's what Carlos says," Carolyn admitted. "But damn all, I don't want to."

"Why not?" Marnie asked.

Carolyn looked down at her hands.

She was sliding away again, and Mary Ann caught it. "We care. Earth will care." She lowered her voice. "And Phyllis would be so proud of you. I bet she is, anyway."

Carolyn's smile was weak. "It was such a *little* story compared to the last stand at Cadmann's Bluff."

Sylvia shook her head violently. "Jeez, here Marnie and I are all jealous of you—"

"Jealous?"

"Sure. We were up there in *Geographic,* all safe, and you were out slaying grendels!"

"You don't mean that. You're just being—"

"I was never more serious."

"But Mary Ann—"

"You saved the horses," Marnie said. "Which is a very lot more than I did. Tell them a story, Carolyn! It's not little, it's compact! Tell—tell *us.* Now. Then it'll be easier when you tell it for Earth."

"Yes, yes, tell us," Mary Ann said.

Carolyn looked at them, realized that they meant it and that they understood. "All right," she began tentatively. "Did I tell you I gave them names?"

"Yeah," Marnie said. "Cassandra record."

"No!" Carolyn protested.

"Cassandra. Record. File as dry run." Marnie grinned. "Surely you don't think of Cassie as an eavesdropper? She's your friend too."

"Yeah. Yes, I guess so." Carolyn straightened in her chair. "I named them all. I named the first one after Charlie Manson." Suddenly Carolyn was grinning like a grendel. She had presence. She'd been on camera before. "Charlie must have been suffering from Hibernation Instability. He came at me through water, dragging half a horse! I just stood up from behind a rock and shot him.

"That left me with three grendels after me and two harpoons to my name. I started being careful, but I was in a hurry too. I got the horses as far as the base of the glacier. By then I could see that the grendels had reached Charlie and what was left of Shank's Mare. One of them was too chicken to get close. That was Mareta—"

Sylvia shuddered. *Teheran. The whole city. Omar lost cousins. Well, Mareta Lupoff certainly got the world's attention—*

"—but Mareta stayed behind and ate the leavings when the other two went on. I kept going up the glacier, leaving the horses behind.

"I was fifty meters up when Khadafi went on *speed* and came for me. She hit ice. It surprised her, but she kept coming, legs churning, ice flying, getting slower and slower as the ice got steeper. She was running in place when I shot her.

"I thought I was in a good place, then, so I stayed. Nothing to eat, but plenty of water. Mareta and the Ayatollah stared at me for a while, but neither of them wanted to try it. I was almost hoping one would. But not both.

"After a while Joe Sikes found me. We managed to take ten of the horses down. The rest are still up there with two grendels. There's not much point in going after Mareta and the Ayatollah."

"Yes, that's right," Sylvia said. "There have to be lots of grendels in the hills, but they'll never lay fertile eggs. The samlon are the males. They have to come down for that."

"So. That's what happened," Carolyn said. "It was scary enough, but . . . it felt so damned good to sh—shoot those things I was so scared of."

"Cassandra end file," Marnie said.

"I think it's wonderful," Mary Ann said. "A really good story."

"You? You killed a dozen with your bare hands—"

Mary Ann laughed. "I don't know who you listen to."

"And anyway, they won't give me my job back."

"No, they won't," Sylvia said. "Would you put Mary Ann in charge of anything?"

Carolyn gulped and was silent.

"I wouldn't," Mary Ann said. "I know I'm still smart, but there are things I don't know that I'm supposed to. I don't trust me."

"Cadmann does," Carolyn said.

"He trusts my instincts." Mary Ann kissed Jessica's ear.

"Besides, he's in love," Sylvia said. "Now. Let's solve Carolyn's problem."

"Look, it's a simple situation," Marnie said. "You want a baby. We all do. We *have* to. Genetic programming, Colony in danger, instinct and heredity and common sense all say we get pregnant and have babies." She patted her six-month bulge. "Babies need fathers. Some of us have husbands, but there are more women than men."

"Which makes Carlos happy enough," Carolyn said. "Only—"

"He's responsible enough," Mary Ann said complacently.

Marnie giggled. "Godfather to half the unborn kids here. Well, maybe not half. Look, Carolyn, you're not in love with anyone. Right? Right. You want a man of your own, but you're not going to get one. There aren't enough to go around."

And even if there were, you'd last about a year, Sylvia thought. She knew that wasn't fair: Carolyn had been married for nine years to a hydraulics engineer who hadn't survived frozen sleep. *But she's such a bitch, and maybe that's Hibernation Instability, and maybe she just had a bloody saint for a husband.*

"So," Marnie continued, "you have some choices. You can try to seduce one of the seriously married men and hope that either his wife doesn't find out or that she won't kill you if she does." When Carolyn tried to say something, Marnie held up her hand. "There's celibacy. Doesn't appeal to you? Don't blame you. Choice three. Get in on one of the orgies, and have group sponsorship of your kid. Maybe you don't like that much, either. Choice four. Choose a father, have him provide you with a sperm sample. It's easy: he produces a rubber balloon, he and his wife make whoopie. You take your teaspoon of baby syrup and do-it-yourself.

"Or. Final choice. Sleep with anyone you want to, but get pregnant from the sperm banks. Anonymous father. Nobody to be jealous, in case romance blooms later."

The father doesn't have to be anonymous. Sylvia felt herself blush. *They don't know. Cadmann doesn't even know. Terry, Terry, I kept the goddamn promise, Terry. I didn't sleep with him. . . .*

MARY ANN sat on the low wall, looking downhill.

She needed no binoculars to see that the new Colony was a fortress. Curved concrete walls surrounded the living areas. Fences and mine fields enclosed the croplands. Inside the compound were naked scars, remains of the grendel attacks, but most of those were being built upon or plowed over. In a year there would be no traces.

Mits and Stu had found a grendel. Hah! Now that Cadmann and Zack and Rachel understood them, grendels were less a danger than a resource. With grendels came samlon, and feasting.

It wasn't always easy to remember. Grendels laid eggs, which hatched into samlon. But samlon were male grendels. They ate pond slime. Adult samlon were female grendels, and they ate everything, but if there wasn't anything else they ate samlon. If they could force grendels to eat all the samlon, there just wouldn't be any more grendels. So there had to be nothing else to eat in the streams and rivers.

And when she asked why they couldn't plant more catfish in the streams, that's what they told her.

I'm sure it all makes sense. But I used to like catfish.

The mist was light enough today for her to make out the rows of crops, the animal pens where the horses and young cattle grazed. The Colony was to be rebuilt, and that was fine; but Cadmann would never live there. *This is his home. Our home. Cadmann's Bluff.* She patted Jessica. *Our home, and yours. We live in the high places.*

She turned as the rhythmic thump of Cadmann's jog-stride became louder. He was stripped to the waist, and his muscular body gleamed with sweat. He no longer winced when his left leg hit the ground.

The artificial limb was sound enough, strong enough for him to take his laps around the plateau. Tweedledum ran with him, gently urging him with tail-wagging enthusiasm.

One day. Someday he'll trust them enough to go to the new hospital and let them grow him a new leg. Someday.

A thought came up unbidden. *When he's whole again, he won't need me. But he's never needed me, not really. Maybe all I have is promises. His promises have to be enough.*

She heard the burr of the Skeeter before it rose into view.

It juddered up over the western lip of the plateau, spun once and touched down on the concrete landing pad Hendrick had installed a week before. Cadmann jogged in place for a minute, then wiped his face and walked over.

Sylvia climbed out of the cabin, then lifted Justin out and set him on the ground. The toddler wobbled, then caught his balance and ran to them.

Mary Ann saw in Cadmann's eyes a flash of sadness, immediately masked. He hugged Justin fiercely.

"*Amigo,*" Carlos said, and embraced Cadmann. "The leg is working well?"

"Oh, for a widget. I'll get it regrown when they get the hospital running. We'll have that expedition yet. But tonight—you came to give us a ride?"

"But of course!"

Sylvia held Justin's hand. Her slender figure was slightly swollen with yet more life. Carlos's child? Sylvia had never said, but Mary Ann thought so.

Cadmann's eye found the swelling, and he smiled. "You better take good care of that, now."

She rubbed her tummy affectionately. "Boy or girl, I'm naming it Terry."

Carlos nodded approval.

Sylvia looked to Cadmann and waited.

"Terry. Right."

"Right," she said. She smiled and suddenly reached up to pull the combs from her hair. It tumbled down, much longer than it had ever been before.

Would look great spread out on a pillow. Mary Ann smiled softly.

That would turn Cadmann on, and— Her thoughts were a jumble. *I love Cadmann and I love Sylvia, and Cadmann loves Sylvia only Sylvia won't sleep with Cadmann, and I'm glad she won't but I wish she would so he can stop wanting to and this is silly.*

There were new lines on Sylvia's face. *She's still beautiful. Cadmann will never get over her. And so what? He's mine. Not hers. Mine.*

"You've done a lot of work here," Sylvia said. She swept her hand in a broad arc to indicate the new walls, Joe cages, cattle pens, fortifications, even a new deadfall: he'd found a building-sized rock, higher up, and dug under it, and laid a new mine field below it. She put her hand on Mary Ann's shoulder and smiled wryly. "Well, lady, you won the grand prize."

Mary Ann tried to smile but couldn't. "Sylvia—Oh dammit, what can I say? I'd never be jealous of you!"

"I think I believe you. Doesn't matter. Mary Ann, don't you understand? The man adores you! Oh, sure, get him drunk enough and he'll probably try to seduce a grendel—but he won't make them any promises."

"Hey," Cadmann said.

"Keep out of this," Sylvia said. "We're discussing you, not inviting contributions."

"Always after my bod, never my mind."

"Something like that. Can I change the subject?"

"Please!"

The four of them faced each other, and suddenly, as if with a single sigh, they came together in a group hug.

"I still can't quite believe we're safe."

"Maybe that's good," Cadmann said seriously. "Maybe we're only safe as long as we're a little afraid."

"Beowulf killed Grendel after all." Carlos laughed, trying to lighten the mood. "Of course, the dragon got Beowulf in the end. . . ."

Sylvia glared at him. "You have no sense of timing."

"That's not what you said—" She hit him with her elbow. "Ouch. Anyway, that story's already been written. This one we create as we go. Come on. Let's go down to dinner. Hey, *amigo*—I think that leg *might* be enough of a handicap. Race?"

Cadmann bent into a sprinter's crouch. "Loser cleans samlon. With his teeth." Cadmann took advantage of Carlos's burst of laughter to dash off.

"Hey—"

Sylvia and Mary Ann watched the two friends sprinting through the deactivated mine field, shoulder to shoulder as they hit the hill.

"They look so strong," Sylvia said softly. "Sometimes it's hard to believe how fragile life is. How precious."

Who knows what we'll find on the mainland . . . ?

Beowulf killed Grendel after all.

"Beowulf was killed by the dragon," Mary Ann murmured.

"What?"

A moment's chill went through her, and she wanted to cry out, to call him back, to end his thoughts of a new quest, a new frontier. "Why can't he stay here? Haven't we paid enough?"

Through her tears she watched him. Tall and strong, the gray more pronounced in his hair now. Her heart nearly broke.

She felt Sylvia's touch on her arm. "Love, what will be will be. We all came to die here. What matters is how we live."

Mary Ann picked Jessica up and held her in the air, kissed her soundly. Together she and Sylvia followed the men they loved up to the house.

It was too late for any of them to change.

And perhaps, just perhaps, there was no dragon after all.

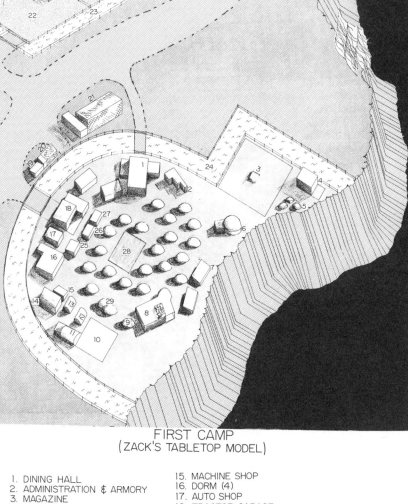

FIRST CAMP
(ZACK'S TABLETOP MODEL)

1. DINING HALL
2. ADMINISTRATION & ARMORY
3. MAGAZINE
4. SEWAGE TREATMENT
5. HYDROPONIC GARDEN
6. POWER PLANT
7. ELECTRONICS/CLEAN LAB
8. DORM (6)
9. SICK BAY
10. SKEETER PAD
11. HANGAR
12. RADIO SHACK
13. ASSAY LAB
14. POWER TOOL SHED

15. MACHINE SHOP
16. DORM (4)
17. AUTO SHOP
18. TRACTOR GARAGE
19. AUXILIARY MACHINE SHOP
20. CHICKENS
21. DOGS
22. CORRAL (CALVES & HORSES)
23.& 24. MINE FIELDS
25. FARM TOOL SHED
26. WOOD SHOP
27. SHOP
28. QUAD
29. BIO LAB & VET